Proudly Published by Snowbooks in 2012

Snowbooks Ltd.
email: info@snowbooks.com
www.snowbooks.com

British Library Cataloguing in Publication Data
A catalogue record for this book is available from the British Library.

Paperback ISBN 978-1907777-69-1
Hardback ISBN 978-1907777-76-9
ebook ISBN 978-1907777-77-6

Time discovers truth.
—Seneca

Dedicated to

Rebeca Camara

Acknowledgements

When I began writing these tales of Burton & Swinburne, I couldn't help but worry that I might be insulting the memory of men and women who, by virtue of their hard work and astonishing talents, had made their mark on history.

My concerns were assuaged when enthusiastic readers told me that, while reading my novels, they repeatedly consulted Wikipedia and other sources to learn more about the real lives of the people I had "hijacked."

This delights me. It means, for example, that PC53 William Trounce might now be recognised by a few more as the hero who stepped up to the mark when John Francis tried to assassinate Queen Victoria in 1842 (and yes, I meddled with that historical fact). It means a greater awareness of Richard Spruce, who despite being treated as a villain in these works, was in truth a quiet and unassuming man possessed of sheer genius in the subject of botany. It means more people turning to Swinburne's astonishing poetry, more people marveling at Lord Palmerston's political astuteness, more people wondering whether Samuel Gooch really existed, then finding out that he did, and that he was amazing.

This, I hope, will be considered by any descendants of the characters herein who might feel offended by my treatment of them. Please note that these novels are *very obviously* flights of utter fancy and very definitely *not* biography. My alternative histories are places where individuals have encountered different challenges and opportunities to those met in real life, and have thus developed into very, very different people. They should not be in any way regarded as accurate depictions of those who actually lived.

In this volume, my account of Africa circa 1863 follows closely the descriptions left to us by Sir Richard Francis Burton himself. His *The Lake Regions of Central Africa* (1860) is, in my opinion, by far the most fascinating journal of any of the Victorian explorers. Burton tended to adopt his own spelling for villages, towns and regions, and throughout the African chapters I've retained his version of place names.

Finally, my thanks and deepest appreciation to Lou Anders, Emma Barnes, and Jon Sullivan.

THE FIRST PART

The Voyage to Africa

One of the gladdest moments in human life, methinks, is the departure upon a distant journey to unknown lands. Shaking off with one mighty effort the fetters of Habit, the leaden weight of Routine, the cloak of many Cares and the Slavery of Home, man feels once more happy. The blood flows with the fast circulation of childhood ... afresh dawns the morn of life ...

—Sir Richard Francis Burton's journal, 2nd December, 1856.

CHAPTER 1

Murder at Fryston

The future influences the present just as much as the past.
—Friedrich Nietzsche

Sir Richard Francis Burton wriggled beneath a bush at the edge of a thicket in the top western corner of Green Park, London, and cursed himself for a fool. He should have realised that he'd lose consciousness. He should have arrived earlier to compensate. Now the whole mission was in jeopardy.

He lay flat for a moment, until the pain in his side abated, then hefted his rifle and propped himself up on his elbows, aiming the weapon at the crowd below. He glanced at the inscription on its stock. It read: *Lee-Enfield Mk III. Manufactured in Tabora, Africa, 1919.*

Squinting through the telescopic sight, he examined the faces of the people gathering around the path at the bottom of the slope.

Where was his target?

His eyes blurred. He shook his head slightly, trying to dispel an odd sense of dislocation; the horrible feeling that he was divided into two separate identities. He'd first experienced this illusion during fevered bouts of malaria in Africa back in '57, then again four years later, when he was made the king's agent. He thought he'd conquered it. Perhaps he had. After all, this time there really were two of him.

It was the afternoon of the 10th of June, 1840, and a much younger Richard Burton was currently travelling from Italy through Europe, on his way to enrol at Trinity College, Oxford.

Recalling that wayward, opinionated, and ill-disciplined youngster, he whispered: "Time changed me, thank goodness. The question is, can I return the favour?"

He aimed from face to face, seeking the man he'd come to shoot.

It was a mild day. The gentlemen sported light coats, top hats, and carried canes. The ladies were adorned in bonnets and dainty gloves and held parasols. They were all waiting to see Queen Victoria ride past in her carriage.

He levelled the crosshairs at one person after another. Young Edward Oxford was somewhere among the crowd; an insane 18-year-old with two flintlock pistols under his frock coat and murder on his mind. But Burton was not here to gun down the queen's would-be assassin.

"Damnation!" His hands were shaking. Lying stretched out like this would have been uncomfortable for any man his age—he was forty-eight years old—but it was made far worse by the two ribs the prime minister's man, Gregory Hare, had broken. They felt like a knife in his side.

He shifted cautiously, trying not to disturb the bush. It was vital that he remain concealed.

A face caught his attention. It was round, decorated with a large moustache, and possessed a palpable air of arrogance. Burton had never seen the individual before—at least not with this appearance—but he knew him: Henry de La Poer Beresford, 3rd Marquess of Waterford, called by many the "Mad Marquess." The man was the founder of the Libertines; a politically influential movement that preached freedom from social shackles and which passionately opposed technological progress. Three years from now, Beresford was going to lead a breakaway group of radicals, the Rakes, whose anarchic philosophy would challenge social propriety. The Marquess believed that the human species was restricting its own evolution; that each individual had the potential to become a *trans-natural man*, a being entirely free of restraint, with no conscience or self-doubt; a thing that did whatever it wanted, whenever it wanted. It was a dangerous idea—the Great War had proved that to Burton—but not one that concerned him at this particular moment.

"I'll be dealing with you twenty-one years from now," he murmured.

A distant cheer echoed across the park. The gates of Buckingham Palace had opened and the royal carriage was steering out onto the path.

"Come on!" Burton whispered. "Where are you?"

Where was the man he'd come to kill?

Where was Spring Heeled Jack?

$\mathcal{S}$

He peered through the 'scope. The scene he saw through its lens was incomprehensible. Shapes, movement, shadows, deep colours; they refused to coalesce into anything of substance. The world had shattered, and he was splintered and scattered among its debris.

Dead. Obviously, he was dead.

No. Stop it. This won't do. Don't submit to it. Not again.

He closed his eyes, dug his fingernails into his palms, and pulled his lips back over his teeth. By sheer force of will, he located the disparate pieces of himself and drew them together, until:

Frank Baker. My name is Frank Baker.

Good. That felt familiar.

He smelled cordite. Noise assaulted his ears. The air was hot.

Frank Baker. Yes. The name had slipped from his mouth in response to a medic's query.

"And what are you, Mr. Baker?"

A strange question.

"An observer."

An equally strange answer. Like the name, it had come out of nowhere, but the overworked medics were perfectly satisfied with it.

Spells of nothingness had followed. Fevers. Hallucinations. Then recovery. They'd assumed he was with the civilian Observer Corp, and placed him under the charge of the short squeaky-voiced individual currently standing at his side.

What else? What else? What were those things I was looking at?

He opened his eyes. There wasn't much light.

He became aware of something crushed in his fist, opened his hand, looked down at it, and found that he was holding a red poppy. It felt important. He didn't know why. He slipped it into his pocket.

Pushing the brim of his tin helmet back, he wiped sweat from his forehead, then lifted the top of his periscope over the lip of the trench and peered through its viewfinder again. To his left, the crest of a bloated sun was melting into a horizon that quivered in the heat, and, ahead, in the gathering gloom, seven towering, long-legged arachnids were picking their way through the red weed that clogged No Man's Land. Steam was billowing from their exhaust funnels, pluming stark white against the darkening purple sky.

Harvestmen, he thought. *Those things are harvestmen spiders bred to a phenomenal size by the Technologists' Eugenicist faction. No, wait, not Eugenicists—they're the enemy—our lot are called Geneticists. The insects are grown and killed and gutted and engineers fit out their carapaces with steam machinery.*

He examined the contraptions more closely and noted details that struck him as different—but different to what? There were, for instance, Gatling guns slung beneath their small bodies, where Baker expected to see cargo nets. They swivelled and glinted and flashed as they sent a hail of bullets into the German trenches, and their metallic clattering almost drowned out the chug of the vehicles' engines. The harvestmen were armour plated, too, and each driver, rather than sitting on a seat fitted inside the hollowed out body, was mounted on a sort of saddle on top of it, which suggested that the space inside the carapace was filled with bigger, more powerful machinery than—than—

What am I comparing them to?

"Quite a sight, isn't it?" came a high-pitched voice.

Baker cleared his throat. He wasn't ready to communicate, despite a vague suspicion that he'd already done so—that he and the small man beside him had made small talk not too many minutes ago.

He opened his mouth to speak, but his companion went on:

"If I were a poet, I might do it justice, but it's too much of a challenge for a mere journalist. How the devil am I to describe such an unearthly scene? Anyone who hasn't actually witnessed it would think I'm writing a scientific romance. Perhaps they'll call me the new Jules Verne."

Think! Come on! String together the man's words. Break the back of the language. Glean meaning from it.

He sucked in a breath as a memory flowered. He was on a bed in the field hospital. There was a newspaper in his hands. He was reading a report, and it had been written by this short, plump little fellow.

Yes, that's it. Now speak, Baker. Open your mouth and speak!

"You'll manage," he said. "I read one of your articles the other day. You have a rare talent. Who's Jules Verne?"

He saw the little man narrow his eyes and examine him through the twilight, trying to make out his features.

"A French novelist. He was killed during the fall of Paris. You haven't heard of him?"

"I may have," Baker answered, "but, I must confess, I remember so little about anything that I'm barely functional."

"Ah, of course. It's not an uncommon symptom of shell shock, or of fever, for that matter, and you suffered both severely by all accounts. Do you know why you were in the Lake Regions?"

The Lake Regions? They are in—they are in Africa! This is Africa!

"I haven't the foggiest notion. My first recollection is of being borne along on a litter. The next thing I knew, I was here, being poked at by the medical staff."

The journalist grunted and said: "I did some asking around. The men from the Survey Corps found you near the western shore of the Ukerewe lake, on the outskirts of the Blood Jungle. A dangerous place to be—always swarming with Germans. You were unarmed; that odd glittering hieroglyph appeared to have been freshly tattooed into your head; and you were ranting like a madman."

Hieroglyph?

Baker reached up, pushed his hand beneath his helmet, and ran his fingers through his short hair. There were hard ridges in his scalp.

"I don't remember any of that."

I don't remember. I don't remember. I don't remember.

"The surveyors wanted to take you to Tabora but the route south was crawling with lurchers, so they legged it east until they hooked up with the battalions gathering here. You were in and out of consciousness throughout the hike but never lucid enough to explain yourself."

The correspondent was suddenly interrupted by the loud "Ulla! Ulla!" of a siren. It was a harvestmen spider signalling its distress. He turned his attention back to his periscope and Baker followed suit.

One of the gigantic vehicles had become entangled. Scarlet tendrils were coiling around its stilt-like legs, snaking up toward the driver, who sat high above the ground. The man was desperately yanking at the control levers in an attempt to shake the writhing plant from his machine. He failed. The harvestman leaned farther and farther to its left, then toppled over, dragged down by the carnivorous weed. The siren gurgled and died. The driver rolled from his saddle, tried to stand, fell, and started to thrash about. He screeched as plant pods burst beneath his weight and sprayed him with acidic sap. His uniform erupted into flames and the flesh bubbled and fizzled from his bones. It took less than a minute for the weed to reduce him to a naked skeleton.

"Poor sod," the little man muttered. He lowered his surveillance instrument and shook dust from his right hand. "Did you see the weed arrive yesterday? I missed it. I was sleeping."

"No."

"Apparently a thin ribbon of cloud, like a snake, blew in from the sea and rained the seeds. The plant sprouted overnight and it's been growing ever since. It seems quite impassable. I tell you, Baker, those blasted Hun sorcerers know their stuff when it comes to weather and plants. It's how they still drum hundreds of thousands more Africans into the military than we do. The tribes are so superstitious, they'll do anything you say if they believe you can summon or prevent rain and grow them a good crop. Colonel Crowley is having a tough time opposing them—the sorcerers, I mean."

Baker struggled to process all this. Sorcerers? Plants? Weather control?

"Crowley?" he asked.

The shorter man raised his eyebrows. "Good lord! Your brain really is shot through! Colonel Aleister Crowley. Our chief medium. The wizard of wizards!"

Baker said nothing.

The correspondent shrugged in bafflement, pressed up against the side of the trench as a line of troops pushed past, chuckled as a sergeant said, with a grin and a wink, "Keep your heads down, gents, I don't want holes in those expensive helmets," then turned back to his 'scope. Baker watched this and struggled to overcome his sense of detachment.

I don't belong here. I don't understand any of it.

He wiped his sleeve across his mouth—the atmosphere was thick with humidity and he was sweating profusely—then put his eye to his periscope's lens.

Two more of the harvestmen were being pulled down into the wriggling flora. He said: "How many men must die before someone orders the blasted vehicles to pull back?"

"We won't retreat," came the answer. "This is our last chance. If we can capture German resources in Africa, we might be able to launch some sort of counter attack in Europe. If not, we're done for. So we'll do whatever it takes, even if it means forlorn hopes. Look! Another one has gone down!"

The three remaining harvestmen set their sirens screaming: "Ulla! Ulla! Ulla! Ulla!"

The journalist continued: "Terrible racket. One could almost believe the damned spiders are alive and terrified."

Baker shook his head slightly. "Strictly speaking, they're not spiders. Spiders are of the order *Aranaea*, whereas harvestmen are *Opiliones*."

How do I know that?

The war correspondent snorted. "They're not of any order now—not since our Technologists scraped 'em out!"

All along the British trenches, men started to blow on whistles.

"Damn! Here comes our daily dose of spores. Get your mask on."

Baker moved without thinking about it. His hands went to his belt, opened a canvas container, pulled out a thick rubber mask, and slid it over his face. He and his companion looked at each other through circular glass eyepieces.

"I hate the smell of these things," the smaller man said, his voice muffled. "And they make me claustrophobic. Far too stifling an item to wear in this infernal climate. What say we go back to the dugout for a brew? It's getting too dark for us to see much more here anyway. Time for a cuppa! Come on!"

Baker took a last glance through his periscope. His mask's eyepieces blurred the scene, and Africa's fast descending night obscured it even further, but he could just make out that on the far side of the weed a thick yellow cloud was advancing, appearing luminescent against the inky sky. He shivered, turned, and followed the other along the front-line trench, into a communications ditch, and back to one of the dugouts. They passed masked soldiers—mostly Askari, African recruits, many of them barely out of childhood— who sat despondently, waiting to go over the top.

The two men arrived at a doorway, pushed a heavy curtain aside, and entered. They removed their helmets and face gear.

"Make sure the curtain is hooked back into place, it'll keep the spores out. I'll get us some light," the journalist said.

Moments later, a hurricane lamp illuminated the small underground bunker. It was sparsely furnished with two wooden beds, two tables, three chairs, and a couple of storage chests.

"Ugh!" Baker grunted. "Rats!"

"Nothing we can do about 'em. The little blighters are everywhere. They're the least of your problems. In a couple of days, that nice clean uniform of yours will be infested with lice and you'll feel like you're being eaten alive. Where's the bloody kettle? Ah, here!"

The little man got to work with a portable stove. In the light, his eyes were revealed to be a startling blue.

Baker stepped to the smaller of the two tables, which stood against the wall. There was a washbasin on it and a square mirror hanging on a nail just above. He sought his reflection but for some reason couldn't focus on it. Either his eyes wouldn't let him see himself, or he wasn't really there.

He moved to the other table, in the middle of the dugout, and sat down.

"The spores," he said. "What are they? Where do they come from?"

"They're more properly called *A-Spores*. The Hun propagate giant mushrooms, a eugenically altered version of the variety commonly known as the Destroying Angel, or *amanita bisporigera*, if you prefer your botany, like your entomology, in Latin. It's deadly, and so are its spores. Breathe them in and within seconds you'll experience vomiting, cramps, delirium, convulsions, and diarrhoea. You'll be dead in less then ten minutes."

"Botanical weapons? The weed and now the mushroom spores. How horribly ingenious!"

The other man looked back at Baker with an expression of puzzlement.

"It's common knowledge that the Germans use mostly plant-based armaments, surely? And occasional animal adaptations."

"Is it? I'm sorry. As I said, my amnesia is near total. You mentioned something called *lurchers*?"

"Ah. Hum. Yes. Carnivorous plants. They were one of the first weapons the Germans developed. Originally they were battle vehicles, used throughout Africa. Then one day they spontaneously mutated and consumed their drivers, which somehow resulted in them gaining a rudimentary intelligence. After that they spread rapidly and are now a danger to both sides. If you see one, and there isn't a flamethrower handy, run for your life. They're particularly prevalent in the Lake Regions, where you were found." The journalist paused, then added: "I didn't realise your memory was quite so defective. What about physically? How are you feeling?"

"Weak, but improving, and the ophthalmia has cleared up. I was half blind when I regained consciousness in the hospital. That confounded ailment has plagued me on and off ever since India."

"You were in India?"

Baker frowned and rubbed his chin. "I don't know. That just popped into my head. Yes, I feel I may have been."

"India, by crikey! You should have stayed there. It might turn out to be the last bastion of civilisation on the whole bloody planet! Is that where you joined the Corp?"

"I suppose so."

There came a distant boom, then another, and another. The ground shook. The journalist glanced at the ceiling.

"Artillery. Peashooters. Firing from the outskirts of Dar es Salaam."

Baker muttered to himself, "Derived from *bandar es-salaam*, I should think. Ironic. It means *harbour of peace*." He said aloud: "The landscape and climate feel familiar to me. Are we south of Zanzibar? Is there a village in the area called Mzizima?"

"Hah! Mzizima and Dar es Salaam are one and the same, Baker! Incredible, isn't it, that the death of the British Empire had its origins in such an insignificant little place, and now we're back here."

"What do you mean?"

"It's generally believed that this is where the Great War began. Have you forgotten even that?"

"Yes, I fear I have. It began in Mzizima? How is that possible? As you say, it's an insignificant little place!"

"So you recall what Dar es Salaam used to be, at least?"

"I remember that it was once nothing more than a huddle of beehive huts."

"Quite so. But that huddle paid host to a group of German surveyors who landed here a little over fifty years ago. No one knows why they came, or what occurred, but, for some reason, fighting broke out between them and Al-Manat."

"The pre-Islamic goddess of fate?"

"Is she, by gum! Not the same one, old chap. Al-Manat was the leader of a band of female guerrilla fighters. It's rumoured she was British but her true identity is shrouded in mystery. She's one of history's great enigmas. Anyway, the fighting escalated, Britain and Germany both sent more troops here, and Mzizima became the German East Africa Company's stronghold. The *Schutztruppe*—the Protection Force—formed there some forty years ago and rapidly expanded the settlement. It was renamed Dar es Salaam and the place has been thriving ever since. A situation our lads will reverse this weekend."

"What do you mean?"

"I mean, my friend, that on Saturday, HMA *Pegasus* and HMA *Astraea* are going to bomb the city to smithereens."

More explosions thumped outside. They were increasing in frequency. Everything shook. Baker glanced around nervously.

"Green peas," his companion noted.

"You can tell just from the noise?"

"Yes. Straightforward impact strikes, like big cannonballs. The yellow variety explode when they hit and send poisonous shrapnel flying everywhere. They annihilated millions of our lads in Europe, but, fortunately, the plants don't thrive in Africa."

Baker's fingers were gripping the edge of the table. The other man noticed them, and reassured him: "We'll be all right. They take an age to get the range. Plus, of course, we're non-combatants, which means we're permitted to shelter in here, unlike the enlisted men. We'll be safe unless one of the blighters lands right on top of us, and the chances of that happening are very slim indeed."

He got the kettle going and they sat wordlessly, listening to the barrage until the water boiled, then he spooned tealeaves into a metal pot, and grumbled, "Rations are low."

Baker noticed that his companion kept glancing back at him. He felt an inexplicable urge to duck out of the light, but there was no refuge from it. He looked on helplessly as the other man's face suddenly displayed a range of emotions in sequence: curiosity, perplexity, realisation, incredulity, shock.

The smaller man remained silent until the tea had brewed, then filled two tin mugs, added milk and sugar, handed one to Baker, sat down, blew the steam from his drink, and, raising his voice above the sound of pounding shells, asked: "I say, old chap, when did you last shave?"

Baker sighed. He murmured "I wish I had a cigar," put a hand into his pocket, and pulled out the poppy. He stared at it, and said, absently: "What?"

"Your most recent shave. When was it?"

"I don't know. Maybe three days ago? Why do you ask?"

"Because, my dear fellow, that stubble entirely ruins your disguise. Once bearded or moustachioed, your features become instantly recognisable. They are every bit as forceful as reported, every bit as ruthless and masterful! By golly, those sullen eyes! That iron jaw! The savage scar on your cheek!"

Baker snapped: "What the devil are you blathering about?"

"I'm talking of the completely impossible and utterly incredible—but also of the perfectly obvious and indisputable!"

The journalist grinned. He had to shout now; the barrage was battering violently at their ears. "Come come! I'll brook no denial, sir! I'm no fool. It's out of the question that you could be anyone else, even though it makes no sense at all that you are who you are."

Baker glowered at him.

The other shouted: "Perhaps you'd care to explain? I assure you, I'm unusually open-minded, and I can keep a secret, if you want to impose that as a condition. My editor would never believe me, anyway."

There was a detonation just outside. The room jerked. The tea slopped. Baker started, recovered himself, and said loudly, "I really don't know what you're talking about."

"Then allow me to make it clear. Frank Baker is most assuredly not your name."

"Isn't it?"

"Ha ha! So you admit that you may not be who you say you are?"

"The name occurred to me when I was asked, but I'm by no means certain that it's correct."

Baker flinched as another impact rocked the room.

"Fair enough," the journalist shouted. "Well then, let us make proper introductions. I was presented to you as Mr. Wells. Drop it. No need for such formality. My name is Herbert. Herbert George. War Correspondent for *The Tabora Times*. Most people call me Bertie, so please feel free to do the same. And, believe me, I am both astonished and very happy to meet you." He held out his hand and it was duly clasped and shaken. "Really, don't worry about the shelling, we are much safer in here than it feels. The Hun artillery is trying for the support trenches rather than the front line. They'll gain more by destroying our supplies than by knocking off a few of the Askaris."

Baker gave a curt nod. His mouth worked silently for a moment. He kept glancing at the poppy in his hand, then he cleared his throat and said: "You know me, then? My actual name?"

"Yes, I know you," Wells replied. "I've read the biographies. I've seen the photographs. I know all about you. You are Sir Richard Francis Burton, the famous explorer and scholar. I cannot be mistaken." He took a sip of his tea. "It makes no sense, though."

"Why not?"

"Because, my dear fellow, you appear to be in your early forties, this is 1914, and I happen to know that you died of old age in 1890!"

Baker—Burton—shook his head. "Then I can't be who you think I am," he said, "for I'm neither old nor dead."

At which point, with a terrible blast, the world came to an end.

§

The world came to an end for Thomas Bendyshe on New Year's Day, 1863. He was dressed as the Grim Reaper when he died. A committed and outspoken atheist, his final words were: "Oh God! Oh, sweet Jesus! Please, Mary mother of God, save me!"

His fellow members of the Cannibal Club later blamed this uncharacteristic outburst on the fact that strychnine poisoning is an extremely painful way to go.

They were gathered at Fryston—Richard Monckton Milnes's Yorkshire manor house—for a combined New Year and farewell fancy dress party. The farewell wasn't intended for Bendyshe—his demise was utterly unforeseen—but for Sir Richard Francis Burton and his expedition, which was leaving en route for Africa later in the week.

Fryston, which dated from the Elizabethan Age, lacked a ballroom but behind its stone mullioned windows there were many spacious oak panelled chambers, warmed by inglenook fireplaces, and these were filled with costumed guests. They included the Pre-Raphaelite artists, leading Technologists, authors and poets and actors, government ministers, Scotland

Yard officials, and members of the Royal Geographical Society. A number of high-ranking officers from His Majesty's Airship *Orpheus* were in attendance, and among the female notables were Miss Isabella Mayson, Sister Sadhvi Raghavendra, Mrs. Iris Angell, and the famous Eugenicist—now Geneticist— Nurse Florence Nightingale, making for a very well attended soiree, such as Monckton Milnes was famous for.

In the smoking room, Bendyshe, in a black hooded cloak and a skull mask, spent the minutes leading up to his death happily pranking the Greek god, Apollo. The diminutive flame-haired Olympian, actually the poet Algernon Charles Swinburne, dressed in a toga, with a laurel wreath upon his head and the gold-tipped arrow of Eros pushed through his waistband, was standing near a bay window with the Persian King Shahryār, Oliver Cromwell, Harlequin, and a cavalier; otherwise Sir Richard Francis Burton, the secretary for war Sir George Cornewall Lewis, Monckton Milnes, and the Technologist Captain of the *Orpheus*, Nathaniel Lawless.

Swinburne had just received a full glass of brandy from a passing waiter, who, like all the staff, was dressed in a Venetian *Medico Della Peste* costume, complete with its long-beaked bird mask. The poet took a gulp, placed the glass on an occasional table at his side, and turned back to Captain Lawless, saying: "But isn't it rather a large crew? I was under the impression that rotorships are flown by seven or eight, not—how many?"

"Counting myself," the captain replied, "there are twenty-six, and that's not even a full complement."

"My hat! How on earth do you keep yourselves occupied?"

Lawless laughed, his pale grey eyes twinkling, his straight teeth whiter even than his snowy, tightly clipped beard.

"I don't think you've quite grasped the size of the *Orpheus*," he said. "She's Mr. Brunel's biggest flying machine. A veritable titan. When you see her tomorrow, I'll wager she'll take your breath away."

The Technologist Daniel Gooch joined the group. As always, he was wearing a harness from which two extra mechanical arms extended. Swinburne had already expressed the opinion that the engineer should have outfitted himself as a giant insect. As a matter of fact, though, Gooch was dressed as a Russian Cossack. He said: "She's magnificent, Mr. Swinburne. Luxurious, too. Designed for passenger cruises. She'll carry the expedition, the supplies, and both your vehicles, with plenty of room to spare."

Bendyshe, standing just behind the poet, with his back to him, and conversing with Charles Bradlaugh—who was done up as Dick Turpin—surreptitiously took the brandy glass from the table. He slipped it beneath his mask, drained it in a single gulp, put it back, and winked at Bradlaugh through his mask's right eye socket.

"Are all the crew positions filled, Captain?" Burton asked. "I hear you had some problems."

Lawless nodded. "The two funnel scrubbers supplied to us by the League of Chimney Sweeps proved rather too young and undisciplined for the job. They were playing silly beggars in the ventilation pipes and caused some considerable damage.

I dismissed them at once." He addressed Gooch, who was serving as Chief Engineer aboard the vessel: "I understand the replacements will join us at Battersea?"

"Yes, sir, and they'll bring with them a new length of pipe from the League." One of his mechanical hands dipped into his jacket pocket and withdrew a notebook. He consulted it, and said: "Their names are William Cornish and Tobias Threadneedle."

"Nippers?"

"Cornish is a youngster, sir. Apparently Mr. Threadneedle is considerably older, though I expect he'll prove childishly small in stature, like all his kind."

Unable to stop himself, Gooch glanced down at Swinburne, who poked out his tongue in response.

"A Master Sweep, no doubt," Burton offered. "I believe The Beetle is attempting to incorporate their brotherhood into the League." He paused, then said: "Where have I heard the name William Cornish before?"

"From me," Swinburne answered, in his high, piping voice. "I know him. And a fine young scamp he is, too, though rather too eager to spend his evenings setting traps in graveyards in the hope of catching a resurrectionist or two!" He reached for his glass, raised it to his lips, started, looked at it ruefully, and muttered: "Blast!" He signalled to a waiter.

"Resurrectionists? The Beetle? Pipes? What in heaven's name are we talking about?" Cornewall Lewis exclaimed.

Burton answered: "The Beetle is the rather mysterious head of the sweeps' organisation. A boy. Very intelligent and well read. He lives in a factory chimney."

"Good Lord!"

Swinburne took another glass of brandy from the waiter, sipped it, and placed it on the table.

"I never met the Beetle," he said, "but I worked with Willy Cornish when I served under a Master Sweep named Vincent Sneed during Richard's investigation of the Spring Heeled Jack affair. Sneed was a vicious big-nosed lout whom I had the misfortune to bump into again during last summer's riots. I knocked the wind out of the swine."

"You fell on top of him," Burton corrected.

Unseen, Bendyshe took the poet's glass, swallowed almost all of its contents, and slid it back into position. Bradlaugh whispered to him: "Are you sure that's wise, old man? You'll end up sloshed if you're not careful!"

"Nonshence," Bendyshe slurred. "I'm jober as a sudge."

Monckton Milnes turned to Lawless. "What exactly does a funnel scrubber do?"

"Normally, he'll be based at a landing field," the aeronaut answered, "and is responsible for keeping a ship's smoke and steam outlets clean and free of obstruction. However, in the bigger vessels, which fly at a higher altitude, extensive internal pipe systems circulate warm air to ensure that every cabin is maintained at a comfortable temperature. The pipes are wide enough for a nipper to crawl through, and it's a funnel scrubber's job to do just that, cleaning out the dust and moisture that accrues."

"That sounds like dashed hot and uncomfortable work!"

"Indeed. But not compared to cleaning chimneys." Lawless addressed Swinburne: "As you obviously know from personal experience, sweeps lead a dreadful existence. Those that get work as funnel scrubbers are considered the fortunate few."

"I hardly think that such a promotion completely justifies the word fortunate," put in Burton. "Funnel scrubbers are still emotionally and physically scarred by their years of poverty and brutality. The Beetle does what he can to protect his lads but he can't change the social order. To improve the life of sweeps, we'd need to instigate a fundamental shift in the way wealth is distributed. We'd have to raise the masses out of the sucking quagmire of poverty into which the Empire's foundations are sunk."

He looked at Cornewall Lewis, who shrugged and stated: "I'm the secretary for war, Sir Richard. My job is to protect the Empire, not right its wrongs."

"Protect it, or expand it, along with its iniquities, sir?"

Monckton Milnes cleared his throat. "Now, now, Richard," he said, softly. "This isn't really the occasion, is it?"

Burton bit his lip and nodded. "My apologies, Sir George; I spoke out of turn. I've been rather sensitive to such matters since the Tichborne riots."

Cornewall Lewis opened his mouth to speak but was interrupted by Swinburne, who suddenly screeched: "What? What? Has the world gone giddy? How can I possibly be guzzling my drinks at this rate? I swear I've barely tasted a drop!"

Burton frowned down at his assistant. "Algy, please remember that you are Apollo, not Dionysus," he advised. "Try to regulate your imbibing."

"Regulate? Regulate? What in blue blazes are you jabbering about, Richard? Nobody drinks more regularly than me!"

The poet gazed at his empty glass with an expression of bemusement. He signalled to another waiter. Behind him, Bendyshe and Bradlaugh smothered their chuckles.

"Anyway," said Gooch. "When the nippers arrive, the crew will be complete." He produced a slip of paper from between the pages of his notebook. "I have the complete roster here, sir."

Lawless took the note, read it through, and nodded his approval.

"May I see that, Captain?" Burton asked.

"Certainly."

The king's agent took the list and scrutinised it. He read:

Commanding Officer: Captain Nathaniel Lawless

First Officer: William Samuel Henson

Second Officer: Wordsworth Pryce

Helmsman: Francis H. Wenham

Assistant Helmsman: Walter D'Aubigny

Navigator: Cedric Playfair

Meteorologist: Arthur Bingham

Chief Engineer: Daniel Gooch

Engineer: Harold Bloodmann

Engineer: Charles Henderson

Engineer: Cyril Goodenough

Engineer: James Bolling

Chief Rigger: Gordon Champion

Rigger: Alexander Priestley

Rigger: Winford Doe

Fireman: Walter Gerrard

Fireman: Peter Etheridge

Stoker: Thomas Beadle

Stoker: Gwyn Reece-Jones

Funnel Scrubber: ~~Ronald Welbergen~~ William Cornish

Funnel Scrubber: ~~Michael Drake~~ Tobias Threadneedle

Steward/Surgeon: Doctor Barnaby Quaint

Assistant Steward/Surgeon: Sister Sadhvi Raghavendra

Quartermaster: Frederick Butler

Assistant Quartermaster: Isabella Mayson

Cabin Boy: Oscar Wilde

"I trust Quips is living up to my recommendation?" Burton asked the captain.

"Quips?"

"Young Master Wilde."

"Ah. An appropriate nickname—he's a very witty young man. How old is he? Twelve-ish?"

"He celebrated his ninth birthday a couple of months ago."

"Good Lord! That young? And an orphan?"

"Yes. He lost his entire family to the Irish famine. He stowed away aboard a ship to Liverpool, made his way to London, and has been working there as a paperboy ever since."

"Well, I must say, I'm impressed by his industry. There's an unpleasant amount of bureaucracy associated with the captaincy of a rotorship and the youngster picked up the paperwork in a flash and keeps it better organised and up to date than I could ever hope to. Furthermore, I find that whenever I say 'hop to it,' he's already hopped. I wouldn't be at all surprised if Oscar Wilde captains his own ship one day." Lawless ran his fingers over his beard. "Sir Richard, what about these young ladies? Having women serving as crew isn't entirely without precedent, but are you sure it's wise to take the Sister with you on your expedition? Africa is harsh enough on a man, isn't it? And what about all that dashed cannibalism? Won't she be considered too dainty a morsel to resist?"

"It is indeed a cruel environment, as I know to my cost," Burton answered. "However, Sister Raghavendra is from India and possesses a natural immunity to many of the ills that assail a European in Africa. Furthermore, her medical skills are exceptional. I wish she'd been with me on my previous excursions. I assure you she'll be well looked after all the way to Kazeh, where she'll remain with our Arabian hosts while the rest of us hike north to the supposed position of the Mountains of the Moon."

"And the cannibals?"

The corners of Burton's mouth twitched slightly. "Those few tribes that feast on human flesh do so in a ritualistic fashion to mark their victory in battle. It's not as common a phenomenon as the storybooks would have you believe. For a daily meal of arm or leg, you'll have to go to the other side of the world, to Koluwai, a small island to the south east of Papau New Guinea. There, they will very happily have European visitors for dinner—and I don't mean as guests. Apparently, we taste like pork."

"Oof! I'm rather more in favour of lamb chops!" Lawless responded.

Cornewall Lewis interrupted: "You'll leave her with Arabians? Can they be trusted with a white woman?"

Burton clicked his tongue impatiently. "Sir, if you choose to believe the lies propagated by your own government, that is up to you, but despite the calumnies that are circulated in the corridors of parliament, I have never found the Arabian race to be anything less than extraordinarily benevolent, courteous, and entirely honourable."

"I meant only to suggest that there might be a risk in leaving an Englishwoman in non-Christian hands, Sir Richard."

"Christian? Do you then stand in opposition to Darwin's findings? Do you also believe that your God favours some races over others?"

"I use the word merely out of habit, as a synonym for civilised," Cornewall Lewis protested.

"Then I'm to take it you don't consider the Arabians civilised, despite that they invented modern mathematics, surgical instruments, soap and perfume, the windmill, the crankshaft, and a great many other things; despite that they realised the Earth was a sphere that circles the sun five hundred years before Galileo was tortured by your Christian church for supporting the same notion?"

The secretary for war pursed his lips uneasily.

"That reminds me," said Monckton Milnes. "Richard, I have the manuscript we discussed; the Persian treatise."

"The what?"

"The translation you were looking for." He stepped forward and hooked his arm through Burton's. "It's in the library. Come, I'll show you. Excuse us please, gentlemen; we shan't be long."

Before Burton could object he was pulled from the group and propelled through the guests towards the door.

"What blessed treatise?" he spluttered.

"A necessary fiction to remove you from the battlefield," Monckton Milnes hissed. "What the blazes has got into you? Why are you snapping like a rabid dog at Cornewall Lewis?"

They left the room, steered across a parlour, past a small gathering in the reception hall, entered a corridor, and stopped at a carved oak door. Monckton Milnes drew a key from a pocket in his costume, turned it in the lock, and, after they had entered through it, secured the door behind them.

They were in his famous and somewhat notorious library.

He pointed to big studded leather armchairs near the fireplace and snapped: "Go. Sit."

Burton obeyed.

Monckton Milnes went to a cabinet, retrieved a bottle and glasses from it, and poured two drinks. He joined Burton and handed one to him.

"Vintage *Touriga Nacional*, 1822, one of the finest ports ever produced," he murmured. "It cost me a bloody fortune. Don't gulp it down. Savour it."

Burton put the glass to his nose and inhaled the aroma. He took a taste, smacked his lips, then leaned back in his chair and considered his friend.

"My apologies, dear fellow."

"Spare me. I don't want 'em. I want an explanation. By God, Richard, I've seen you angry, I've seen you defeated, I've seen you wild with enthusiasm, and I've seen you drunk as a fiddler's bitch, but I've never before seen you jittery. What's the matter?"

Burton gazed into his drink and remained silent for a moment, then looked up and met his friend's eyes.

"They are making a puppet of me."

"Who are? How?"

"The bloody politicians. Sending me to Africa."

Monckton Milnes's face registered his surprise. "But it's what you've wanted!"

"Not under these circumstances."

"What circumstances? Stone me, man, if you haven't been handed a rare opportunity! The Royal Geographical Society was dead set against you going, but Palmerston—the prime minister himself!—forced their hand. You have another chance at the Nile, and no expedition has ever been so well funded and supported, not even Henry Stanley's! Why do you grumble so and flash those moody eyes of yours? Explain!"

Burton looked away, glanced around at the book-lined walls, and at the erotic statuettes that stood on plinths in various niches, pulled at his jacket and brushed lint from his sleeve, took another sip from his glass, and, reluctantly, returned his attention to Monckton Milnes.

"It's true, I have long wanted to return to Africa to finish what I began back in '57," he said. "To locate, once and for all, the source of the River Nile. Instead, I'm being dispatched to find and bring back a damned weapon!"

"A weapon?"

"A black diamond. An Eye of Nāga."

"What is that? How is a diamond a weapon? I don't understand."

Burton suddenly leaned forward and gripped his friend's wrist. A flame lit in his dark eyes.

"You and I have known each other for a long time," he said, a slight hoarseness creeping into his voice. "I can trust you to keep a confidence, yes?"

"Of course you can. You have my word."

Burton sat back. "Do you remember once recommending to me the cheiromantist Countess Sabina?"

Monckton Milnes grunted an affirmation.

"These past weeks, she's been employing her talent as a seer for Palmerston. Her abilities are prodigious. She's able to catch astoundingly clear glimpses of the future—but not our future."

His friend frowned, took a swallow from his glass then laid it aside and rubbed a hand across his cheek, accidentally smudging the red harlequin makeup that surrounded his left eye.

"Whose, then?"

"No, you misunderstand. I mean, not the future you and I and everyone else in the world will experience."

"What other future is there?" Monckton Milnes asked in bewilderment.

Burton held his gaze, then said quietly: "This world, this time we live in, it is not as it should be."

"Not as—you're speaking in blessed riddles, Richard!"

"Do you recall all the hysteria eighteen months or so ago when people started to see Spring Heeled Jack left right and centre?"

"Yes, of course."

"It wasn't newspaper sensationalism. He was real."

"A prankster?"

"Far from it. He was a man from the future. He travelled back from the year 2202 to 1840 to prevent his ancestor, with whom he shared the name of Edward Oxford, from shooting at Queen Victoria. His mission went terribly wrong. What should have been a botched assassination succeeded thanks to his interference. It altered everything his history had recorded and, what's more, it wiped him out of his own time."

Monckton Milnes sat motionless, his eyes widening.

"While he was trying to escape from the scene of the assassination," Burton continued, "Oxford's strange costume, which contained the machinery that enabled him to move through time, was damaged by a young constable with whom we are both acquainted. In fact, he's here tonight."

"Wh—who?"

"William Trounce. He was just eighteen years old. His intercession caused Oxford to be thrown back to the year 1837, where he was taken in and looked after by Henry de La Poer Beresford."

"The Mad Marquess?"

"Yes. While in his care, Oxford dropped vague hints about the shape and nature of the future. Those hints led directly to the establishment of the Technologist and Libertine castes and their offshoots, and sent us down a road entirely divorced from that which we were meant to tread. History altered dramatically, and so did people, for they were now offered opportunities and challenges they would not have otherwise encountered."

Monckton Milnes shook his head wonderingly. "Are—are—are you spinning one of your Arabian Night yarns?" he asked. "You're not in earnest, surely?"

"Entirely. What I am telling you is the absolute truth."

"Very well. I shall—I shall attempt to suspend my incredulity and hear you out. Pray continue."

"Trapped in what, for him, was the distant past, Oxford began to lose his mind. He and the marquess, who himself was a near lunatic, cooked up a scheme by which Oxford might be able to re-establish his future existence by restoring his family lineage. This involved making short hops into the future to locate one of his ancestors, which he managed to do despite that his suit's mechanism was rapidly failing. One of those hops brought him to 1861. Beresford had, by this time, formed an alliance with Charles Darwin and Francis Galton. They intended to trap Oxford, steal his suit, and use it to create separate histories, moulding each one as they saw fit, manipulating us all. I had to kill them, and Oxford, to protect the world from their insane plans."

Monckton Milnes stared at Burton in shock. His mouth worked silently, then he managed to splutter: "This—this is beyond the realms of fantasy, Richard. Everyone knows that Darwin was murdered by religious extremists!"

"False information issued by the government. You'd better take another swallow of this fine port. There's a great deal more to the tale."

Monckton Milnes, forgetting his earlier directive to Burton, downed his drink in a single swig. He looked at the empty glass, stood up, paced over to the cabinet, and returned with the bottle.

"Go on," he said, pouring refills.

"Countess Sabina can see far more clearly into the other history—the original one—than she can into ours, perhaps because none of the decisions we make here can have an effect there. The histories are quite different, but there is one thing common to both. There is a war coming. A terrible war that will encompass the world and decimate a complete generation of men. That is why the prime minister wants the African diamond."

"War? My God. So what is it, this diamond? Why is it so important? What's it got to do with Spring Heeled Jack?"

"Are you familiar with the fabled Nāga?" Burton asked.

Monckton Milnes furrowed his brow.

"I—yes—I believe—I believe I've come across references to them in various occult texts. Weren't they some sort of pre-human race?"

"Yes. There are carvings of them at Angkor Wat. They are portrayed as seven- or five-headed reptiles."

"So?"

"When this planet was young, an aerolite—a huge black diamond—broke into three pieces in its atmosphere. One piece fell to earth in what became South America, another in Africa, and the last in the Far East. The Nāga built civilisations around the impact sites. They discovered that the diamonds possessed a very special property: they could store and maintain even the most subtle of electrical fields, such as those generated by a living brain. The Nāga used them to fuse their minds, to form a sort of unified intelligence."

"If any of that is true, how can you possibly know it?"

"That will become apparent," Burton responded. He went on speaking in a low and urgent tone: "The human race waged war on the Nāga, and the reptiles became extinct. The diamonds were lost until, in 1796, Sir Henry Tichborne discovered one—the South American stone."

"Tichborne!"

"Indeed. He brought it home and hid it beneath his estate. In the history that was meant to be, it remained there until the future Edward Oxford's time, when it was discovered after Tichborne House was demolished. Oxford cut small shards from it and used them in the machinery of his time suit. When he arrived in the past, those shards suddenly existed in two places at once. They were in his suit and they were also still a part of the diamond under the estate. This paradox caused a strange resonance between them, which extended even to the two as yet undiscovered Nāga diamonds. It caused them all to emit a low, almost inaudible musical drone. This led to the recovery of the Far Eastern stone, in Cambodia, which had been shattered into seven pieces when the humans conquered the Nāga many millennia ago."

"My head is spinning," Monckton Milnes murmured.

"Not just yours," Burton said. "The resonance also awoke a hitherto dormant part of the human mind. It made mediumistic abilities possible. Thus Countess Sabina, and thus a Russian named Helena Blavatsky."

"The woman they say destroyed the Rakes last year?"

"Quite so. She stole two of the Cambodian stones and used them to peer into the future."

"Which future, ours or the other one?"

"Ours. And in that future, in the year 1914, another Russian, a clairvoyant named Grigori Rasputin, was gazing back at us."

"Why?"

"Because he foresaw that the Great War, which was in his time raging, would lead to his assassination and the decimation of his beloved Russia. He came looking for the events that sparked off the conflict, and he found them here, in the 1860s."

Monckton Milnes regarded his friend through slitted eyes. "Are you referring to our role in the American hostilities?"

"No. The world war will pitch us against united German states, so I'm of the opinion that the recent Eugenicist exodus to Prussia, which was led by the botanist Richard Spruce and my former partner John Speke, might be the spark that lights the flame."

"So this Rasputin fellow observed the defectors at work? To what end?"

"He did much more than that. He possessed Blavatsky and used her to steal the rest of the Cambodian stones and recover the South American diamond from the Tichborne estate, thus changing history again. He then employed them to magnify and transmit his mesmeric influence, causing the working classes to riot. He intended nothing less than the wholesale destruction of the British Empire, so that United Germany might win the war against us without Russian assistance. Once that heinous outcome was achieved, Russia would swoop upon a weakened Germany and defeat her."

"Bloody hell!"

"Blavatsky didn't survive and the plot failed," Burton said. "I caused Rasputin to die in 1914, two years before his assassination, meaning that history has diverged yet again, although that particular bifurcation won't occur for another fifty-one years."

Monckton Milnes flexed his jaw. He clenched his fists. He blew out a breath, reached for his glass, emptied it, and refilled it again. He was trembling. "By thunder!" he muttered. "I actually believe all this! Where are the Cambodian and South American diamonds now?"

"The South American stone was broken into seven fragments when I defeated Rasputin. They are in Palmerston's possession. The Cambodian stones are embedded in a babbage probability calculator."

"They are? For what purpose?"

"During the Tichborne riots I was assisted by a philosopher named Herbert Spencer. He died with the stones in his pocket and his mind was imprinted onto them. Charles Babbage had designed a device to process just such an imprint. We fitted the diamonds into it and placed the mechanism in my clockwork valet. Herbert Spencer thus lives on, albeit in the form of a mechanical contraption. That is how I know the history of the Nāga, for the reptile intelligence remains in the stones, and Herbert can sense it. Actually, so can I, in a vague way. The Nāga came to me in a dream and left me with the phrase 'Only equivalence can lead to destruction or a final transcendence.' It was that which guided me in the final ruination of Rasputin."

Monckton Milnes again rubbed his face and again smudged his Harlequin make up.

"So only the African diamond remains undiscovered and Palmerston is sending you to find it?"

"Precisely. As the last remaining unbroken stone, it will be more powerful than its splintered counterparts. He means to use the Eyes to wage a clandestine war on Prussia through clairvoyance, prophecy, and mediumistic assassinations. He intends that Bismarck will never unite the Germanic states. Do you see now why I'm wishing this expedition had never been commissioned?"

He received a weak nod of understanding.

"Yes," came the whispered response. "You can't possibly allow Palmerston that kind of power. By God, he could manipulate the whole world!"

"Just as Darwin and Galton and their cronies would have done."

Monckton Milnes gazed at his friend a moment. "By James, I wouldn't be in your shoes for anything, Richard. What are you going to do?"

Burton shrugged. "I have to retrieve the stone if only to prevent it from falling into Prussian hands. I feel certain that my erstwhile partner is going after it, with Bismarck's sponsorship. As to what I'll do with it once I have it—I don't know. There's a further complication: it was the African Eye that Rasputin employed in 1914 to probe into the past. So I already know I'm fated to find it and, after I do, it will somehow find its way to Russia."

They sat in silence for a few minutes, then Burton muttered: "I feel like a bloody pawn in a game of chess."

Monckton Milnes roused himself from the reverie he'd fallen into. "I have every faith in you, Richard," he said. "Go to Africa. Do whatever you must. You'll find an answer, of that I'm certain."

Burton sighed and gave a slight jerk of his head. He became conscious of the buzz of conversation and merriment that filled Fryston. He looked down at himself, then at his friend, and suddenly chuckled. "Bismillah! King Shahryār of *A Thousand Nights and a Night* discussing fantastic notions with Harlequin! What a confounded joke!"

Monckton Milnes smiled. "Go back to the party. Relax. Enjoy yourself. I'll join you in a few minutes. I want to sit here a little longer."

Burton rose and crossed to the door. He looked back and said, "If Palmerston learns that we had this conversation, I'll be thrown into the Tower."

"Bedlam, more like," Monckton Milnes murmured.

"No. The government keeps secret rooms, including prison cells, beneath the Tower of London."

His friend held up his hands as if to ward off the king's agent. "Have mercy! No more, I beg of you!" he cried. "My capacity for revelations is all used up!"

Burton unlocked the door and left the room. He made his way back across the entrance hall, through the parlour, and into the smoking room.

"I say, Captain," Humpty Dumpty called, as he entered. "Where's that wonderful housekeeper of yours?"

Burton turned to the rotund fairy-tale figure.

"Is that you in there, Trounce?"

"Yes, and I feel an absolute ass, but it was Mrs. Trounce's idea and I thought it wise not to kick up a fuss, seeing as I'm abandoning her for the next few months. It's blasted awkward, I can tell you. I'm having dashed difficulty in steering food and wine lipwards, so to speak."

"I shouldn't complain. It's looks like you could stand to lose a pound or two."

"That's quite enough of that, if you don't mind! You know full well that my current circumference is all padding!"

"If you say so. Who has the esteemed Mrs. Trounce come as?"

"Old Mother Hubbard, which, admittedly, didn't require much by way of dressing up. She's eager for a gossip with Mrs. Angell but what with all these fancy getups she can't locate the dear lady. So where is she and who, or what, has she come as?"

"She's a rather too matronly Queen Bodecea, and is off doing your wife's job, I think."

"What do you mean?"

"She's gone to give a dog a bone."

"Eh?"

"She's down in the kitchen procuring a morsel for Fidget, though I suspect she's actually seeking refuge from all these lords and ladies. She feels a little out of place, but I insisted upon her attendance. She deserves a taste of the high life after all I've put her through recently."

"You brought your confounded basset hound as well?"

"She made him a part of her costume—harnessed him to a toy war chariot and had him trotting along beside her. He was most indignant about it."

A loud high-pitched howl rose above the general hubbub.

"Would you excuse me?" Burton said. "It sounds like Algy needs to be reined in."

He moved back towards the bay window. As he reached the group gathered there, a waiter pushed a glass of port into his hand. Absently, Burton placed it on the table, his attention on Swinburne, who was hopping up and down, waving his arms like a madman.

"I'm not in the slightest bit tipsy!" the poet was protesting vociferously. "What an utter disaster! I've become immune to alcohol!"

"Through over familiarity, perhaps?" Cornewall Lewis offered.

"Nonsense! We meet frequently, I'll admit, but we're nought but nodding acquaintances!"

Doctor James Hunt, a Cannibal Club member, joined the group just in time to hear this. He roared with laughter and declared: "Hah! I rather think there's a great deal more intimacy than that, Algy! You and alcohol are practically wedded!"

"Tosh and piffle!" Swinburne objected. "Claptrap, balderdash, cobblers and bunkum!"

Someone spoke quietly at Burton's side: "I should have you arrested."

The explorer turned and found himself facing Sir Richard Mayne, the lean-faced Chief Commissioner of Scotland Yard.

"Something to do with me whisking four of your men off to Africa?" he asked, with a raised eyebrow.

"Yes," Mayne answered, glancing disapprovingly at Swinburne's histrionics. "Trounce and Honesty are among my best detectives, Krishnamurthy commands my Flying Squad, and Constable Bhatti is in line for promotion. I can hardly afford to have them all gallivanting around the Dark Continent for a year. I can only conclude that you're in league with London's criminal underclasses. Am I right, Sir Richard? Are you getting my men out of the way prior to some villainous coup? Perhaps plotting to have them consumed by lions and tigers so you can break into the Tower of London and steal the crown jewels?"

Burton smiled. "Funny, I was just talking about the Tower. But no, and there are no tigers in Africa, sir. Did Lord Palmerston explain the situation?"

"He delivered to me some vague waffle about it being a matter of national security."

"It is."

"And he ordered me in no uncertain terms to provide you with whatever you want. I shall do so, of course."

"Thank you. I ask only that the men receive extended leave and that their families are looked after."

"Have no worries on that account." The commissioner took a sip of his wine. He sighed. "Keep them safe, won't you?"

"I'll do my best."

They shook hands. Mayne wandered away. Burton reached for his drink and was surprised to find that his glass had mysteriously emptied itself. He pursed his lips and looked at his assistant, who was still stamping his feet and protesting his sobriety. He concluded that Swinburne was either in the midst of one of his infamous drinking sprees or he was the victim of mischief. Then he noticed the Grim Reaper hovering behind the little poet and, though he quickly recognised Thomas Bendyshe—which explained everything, for the anthropologist and atheist was Swinburne's most dedicated tormenter—he nevertheless felt a momentary chill needling at his spine.

"Richard!" Swinburne screeched. "You've seen me in my cups more than most. Do I seem inebriated to you?"

"Of all people, Algy, you are the one in whom it's hardest to tell the difference," Burton answered.

The poet gave a shriek of despair. He yelled for a waiter.

Time passed, the party continued, and the king's agent moved from group to group, chatting with some, debating with others, joking with a few.

At a quarter past eleven, Monckton Milnes reappeared, with make-up restored, and herded his guests into the music room, where Florence Nightingale surprised Burton by demonstrating an unexpected proficiency on the piano as she accompanied Sister Raghavendra, whose singing voice proved equally impressive. They entertained the gathering until close on midnight, at which point everyone fell silent and listened to the chimes of the grandfather clock. As the final note clanged, they hooked their arms, Nightingale started playing, and the Sister sang:

"Should old acquaintance be forgot,
and never brought to mind?
Should old acquaintance be forgot,
and old lang syne?"

The guests happily launched into the chorus:

"For auld lang syne, my dear,
for auld lang syne,
we'll take a cup of kindness yet,
for auld lang syne!"

"And surely you'll buy your pint cup," the young singer trilled. "And surely I'll buy mine—"

"Oh God!" someone yelled.

"And we'll take a cup o' kindness yet, for auld lang syne."

"Oh, sweet Jesus!" came the agonised voice.

Burton peered around the room as the crowd launched into the chorus again.

"For auld lang syne, my dear,
for auld lang syne,
we'll take a cup of—"

The song tailed off and the music stopped as someone screamed: "Please, Mary mother of God, save me!"

The explorer unhooked his arms from his neighbours, pushed people aside, and hurried towards a commotion near the fireplace. Men were kneeling beside a prone figure. It was Bendyshe. His skull mask had been removed and his face was contorted into a ghastly expression, eyes wide and glassy, mouth stretched into a hideous rictus grin. His whole body was convulsing with such ferocity that it required four men to hold him down. He writhed and jerked, his backbone arching, his heels drumming on the floor.

Detective Inspector Honesty—a slight, wiry man, with a flamboyantly wide moustache that curled upward at the ends, who normally sported lacquered flat hair, parted in the middle, and displayed a fussy dress sense, but who was currently outfitted as one of the Three Musketeers—appeared at Burton's side and muttered: "Fit. Overdoing it. Excessive indulgence."

"No," Burton said. "This is something else." He pushed forward until he reached Monckton Milnes's side, and hissed: "Get the crowd out of here."

The host of the party looked at him and said: "Gad, what am I thinking? Of course."

Monckton Milnes turned and, in a loud voice, announced: "Ladies and gentleman, unfortunately one of our fellows has been taken ill. Would you mind moving into the other rooms please? We should give the poor chap space to breathe."

With utterances of sympathy, people started to wander away.

A hand gripped Burton by the elbow. It belonged to Doctor James Hunt.

"Come here," he whispered, and dragged the king's agent over to the window, away from everyone else.

"What is it, Jim? Is Bendyshe going to be all right?"

"No. Quite the opposite." Hunt caught his lower lip between his teeth. There was a sheen of sweat on his brow.

"I'd recognise the symptoms anywhere," he hissed. "Bloody strychnine. The poor devil's been poisoned!"

Burton momentarily fought for balance as his knees buckled. "*What?*"

"Poisoned. Purposely. A man doesn't get strychnine in his system by accident."

"Can you save him?"

"Not a chance. He'll be dead within the hour."

"No! Please, Jim, work with Nurse Nightingale and Sister Raghavendra. Do whatever you can for him."

Hunt gave Burton's arm a squeeze and returned to the dying man. The king's agent saw Trounce standing by the doorway and moved over to him.

"Get out of that ridiculous costume. There's trouble."

"What's happened?"

"Murder, Trounce. Someone has poisoned Tom Bendyshe."

"Great heavens! I—um—I'll round up the troops at once. Damn this bloody padding! Help me out of it, would you?"

Some minutes later, Trounce, Sir Richard Mayne, and Detective Inspector Honesty ushered the guests and staff up the stairs, while Commander Krishnamurthy and Constable Bhatti guarded Fryston's front and back doors to ensure no one slipped out.

Bendyshe was now frothing at the mouth and thrashing even more wildly.

Charles Bradlaugh, sitting on his friend's legs and being bucked about as they spasmed beneath him, looked at Burton as the explorer squatted beside the dying man. "I can't believe it," he croaked, his eyes filling with tears. "Hunt says it's poison. Who would do this to poor Tom? He never hurt a soul!"

"I don't know, Charles. What was he up to before he was taken ill?"

"Singing along with the rest of us. He was rather sloshed. He's been stealing Algy's drinks all night."

Burton turned to James Hunt. "Could strychnine have been in one of the glasses?"

"Yes," the doctor nodded. "It's an incredibly bitter poison but if he was blotto enough he might have swallowed it without noticing the taste."

"He was half cut, to be sure," Bradlaugh put in.

Burton reached past Nurse Nightingale, who was mopping Bendyshe's brow, and placed a hand on the man's chest. He could feel the muscles jumping beneath his palm.

"Tom," he whispered.

He cleared his throat, stood, and gestured for Hunt to follow him. The two men left the music room and went into the smoking room, crossing to the table near the bay window.

"The poison was probably in one of these glasses," Burton said, indicating the various empty vessels.

"If so, it won't be difficult to find out which one," the doctor answered. He picked up a glass, sniffed it, muttered "brandy," then dipped his index finger into the dregs at the bottom. He touched the finger to his tongue. "Not that one."

"You won't poison yourself?"

"Strychnine is occasionally used in small amounts as medical treatment. The merest dab won't harm me."

Hunt tested another glass, then a third and fourth. The fifth made him screw up his face.

"Bitter. The port would have gone some way to disguising it, but the taste is strong, nevertheless."

"The drink is port?"

"Yes."

Burton went through the other glasses one by one. As their shapes suggested, they had all contained either brandy or wine.

"Damnation," he muttered. "Get back to Tom. I'll talk to you later."

He strode off and made his way to the entrance hall where he found Richard Monckton Milnes, Algernon Swinburne and Commissioner Mayne in quiet conversation at the bottom of the staircase. Mayne's expression was grim. "Are you certain it's attempted murder?" he said as Burton joined them.

"Not attempted. Successful. There's no antidote."

"But why kill Tom?" Swinburne asked, miserably.

"It was a mistake," Burton answered. "He wasn't the intended victim. I was."

CHAPTER 2

Underworld and the Orpheus

GOVERNMENT NOTICE

IT IS ILLEGAL TO INTERFERE WITH STREET CRABS

THOSE WHO SEEK TO BLOCK A STREET CRAB'S PATH, ENTANGLE ITS LEGS, EXTINGUISH ITS FURNACE, DIVERT IT INTO HARM'S WAY WITH A PURPOSELY LAID TRAIL OF LITTER, OR IN ANY OTHER MANNER PREVENT IT FROM FULFILLING ITS FUNCTION, WILL BE FINED A MINIMUM OF £25.

STREET CRABS KEEP YOUR STREETS CLEAN!

"You?"

Richard Monckton Milnes, Algernon Swinburne and Sir Richard Mayne had all spoken at once.

Burton nodded. "The poison was in a glass of port. It was pushed into my hand by one of the waiters. Tom drank it by mistake." He addressed Monckton Milnes. "Would you order your waiting staff and household manager into the parlour, please? We'll question them there."

This was duly done, and it was quickly made apparent by Mr. Applebaum, the manager, that a man was missing.

"Two of the waiters are permanent here at Fryston," he told Burton. "The other four we hired from an agency, just for this party. These are the temporaries—" He indicated three of the men, "—and their colleague, sir, is the one that's done a bunk."

"Where is the agency?" Burton asked.

"In Thorpe Willoughby, a village about four miles east of here. Howell's by name. It has offices over the high street bakery."

Burton turned to one of the hired hands, a small man whose fingers moved nervously. "What's your name?"

"Colin Parkes, sir."

"And the missing man?"

"Peter Pimlico, but he ain't one of us. It was meant to be Gordon Bailey workin' tonight, but he was taken poorly, like, with a bad tummy, so he sent this Pimlico fellow, what is a friend of his, along in his stead. Leastways, that's how Pimlico explained it."

"Do you know where he lives?"

"Pimlico? He said in Leeds, sir. He came with us in a carriage from Thorpe Willoughby. He's been renting a room there for the past few days. There are only two hostels and one inn in the village, so I reckon he's in one of them."

"What does he look like?"

"Blonde. Big side-whiskers. Blue eyes. A bit soft around the middle. I should say he eats more'n he serves."

"Thank you, Mr. Parkes."

Sir Richard Mayne sent the staff back upstairs and said: "I'm going to order my men to search the house."

Forty minutes later, the police commissioner reported back to Burton: "Commander Krishnamurthy found the missing man's fancy dress costume dumped in a back room near the kitchen. The window was open. Doubtless that was his means of escape. I'll send Bhatti to the local railway station."

"Pointless," Burton said, curtly. "There's no service at this time of night."

"Then where do you think he—?"

The commissioner was interrupted by Swinburne and Hunt, who joined them, their faces drawn.

"Tom Bendyshe is dead," the doctor said, tonelessly. "Mercifully quick for strychnine. His heart gave out."

Burton turned back to Mayne. "I'd like to borrow Detective Inspector Trounce. I have my basset hound here. He's an excellent tracking dog. We'll give him a sniff of that *Medico Della Peste* outfit and see where he leads us."

"Very well."

Burton—after quickly changing into rather more suitable evening attire—found Fidget happily gnawing on a bone in the kitchen downstairs.

"Sorry, old thing," he said, lifting the dog's lead from a hook behind the door. "You're going to have to save that for later."

Fidget growled and complained as the explorer removed the bone and clipped the lead onto his collar. He whined and dragged at the tether until Burton got him out of the kitchen, then settled down and padded along beside his master up the stairs and out of the back door.

A cold breeze was blowing outside. Burton's breath clouded and streamed away. Stars shone in a clear night sky and a three-quarters moon caste its silver light over Fryston's grounds.

Swinburne—now in his normal day clothes but with the laurel wreath still entwined in his hair—and Trounce were waiting by an open window. The Scotland Yard man was squatting on his haunches, holding a lantern over the ground. "Footprints in the flower bed," he said, as the king's agent joined them.

Swinburne stepped back. Fidget had an unfortunate fondness for his ankles and had nipped at them throughout the train journey from London to Yorkshire. The poet held out a bundle of clothing and said, "Here's the waiter's costume, Richard."

Burton took the clothes and applied them to Fidget's nose. "Seek, boy!" he urged. "Seek!"

The basset hound lowered his head to the ground and began to snuffle about, zig-zagging back and forth. He quickly caught the trail and dragged Burton away from the window and across the lawn. Swinburne and Trounce followed. The frozen grass crunched beneath their feet.

"Pimlico must be almost two hours ahead of us by now," Trounce panted, as he hurried along.

"We're heading east," Burton noted. "I suspect he's gone back to Thorpe Willoughby. If he had a vehicle waiting there, he'll have made off and we'll lose the trail, but if he intends to travel back to Leeds by railway, he has no choice but to wait until the morning, and we'll nab him."

Fidget pulled them to the edge of the estate, along the bordering wall, and over a stile. They proceeded down a country lane edged by hedgerows until they reached a junction. The basset hound veered right onto a better-travelled road, and, as they followed, the men saw a sign that read: *Thorpe Willoughby 3½ Miles.*

"Confound it!" Swinburne muttered, as they pushed on. "Tom was one of my best friends, even if he was a giant pain in the rear end. Why did this Pimlico chap try to kill you, Richard? I don't recall his name. He's not someone we've had dealings with, is he?"

"What? You?" Trounce exclaimed, not having been privy to the revelation earlier.

"I was meant to be the victim," Burton confirmed, "and I've no idea why. As far as I know, Pimlico has no connection with any of our past cases. His motivation remains a mystery."

The road led them to the brow of a hill and down the other side. They saw the outlying houses of the village some little distance ahead, lying beyond patchwork fields and dark clumps of forest. From the centre of the settlement, an irregular line of steam curved up into the night air, slowly dissipating in the breeze. It was instantly recognisable as the trail of a rotorchair.

"Hell's bells!" Trounce growled. "It looks like our bird has flown!"

Fidget, making little yip-yip noises as he followed the scent, led them into the village.

The exertion kept the men warm, despite the low temperature, and by the time they reached the houses, Trounce was puffing and had to wipe at his brow with a handkerchief.

They passed cottages and small terraced houses, kept going straight past the inn, and eventually arrived outside a square and rather dilapidated-looking residence. The ribbon of steam was slowly drifting away above it. A notice in one of the lower windows read: *Robin Hood's Rest. Bed & Breakfast. No Foreigners.* Fidget stopped at its front door and pawed at it, whining with frustration.

Trounce reached out, grasped the knocker, and hammered.

They waited.

He hammered again.

A muffled voice came from within: "Keep yer bleedin' hair on!"

The portal opened, and a fat man in an off-grey dressing gown blinked at them.

"What the bloomin' heck are you wantin' at this time o' night?" he demanded, his jowls wobbling indignantly.

"Police," Trounce snapped. "Do you have a Peter Pimlico here?"

"More bloody visitors? I told him, none after ten o'clock, them's the rules o' the house, and what happens? I get nothin' but bleedin' visitors! You ain't foreigners, too, are yer?"

"We're English. Answer the question, man! Is Pimlico here?"

"Yus. He's in his room. I suppose you'll be wantin' to go up? You're police, you say? In trouble, is he?"

"It's distinctly possible," Trounce answered, pushing his way past the man and into the narrow hallway beyond. "Which room?"

"Up the stairs an' first on yer left."

Trounce started for the stairs but stopped when Burton asked the landlord: "You say there was a previous visitor for Mr. Pimlico? A foreigner?"

"Yus. A fat bloke with a big walrus moustache."

"Nationality?"

"How the bleedin' heck should I know? They're all the same to me!"

"And when was he here?"

"'Bout half an hour ago. Woke me up landing his bloody contraption right outside, then thumped on the door. Pimlico came down the stairs like a bloomin' avalanche to answer it, they both stamped up to his room, then a little bit later the foreigner came clod-hopping back down an' slammed the door behind him afore setting the windows a-rattling again with his blasted flying machine. I tell yer, it's been like trying to sleep in the middle of a bleedin' earthquake, and you ain't helpin'. Am I to get any kip at all tonight?"

"We'll not disturb you for long, Mr.—?"

"Emery. Norman Emery."

"Mr. Emery. Remain here, please."

Burton tied Fidget's lead to the bottom of the bannister, muttered: "Stay, boy," then, with Swinburne, followed Trounce up the stairs. The policeman knocked on the first door on the left. It swung open slightly under his knuckles. He looked at Burton and raised his eyebrows.

"Mr. Pimlico?" he called.

There was no reply.

The Yard man pushed the door open and peered into the room. He let out a grunt and turned to Swinburne. "Get Emery up here, would you?"

The poet, noting a grim aspect to the detective's face, obeyed without question.

"Look at this," Trounce said as he entered the room.

Burton stepped in after him and saw a man stretched out on the floor. His face was a blotchy purple, his tongue was sticking out between his teeth, and his eyes were bulging and glazed.

"Strangled to death," Trounce observed. "By Jove, look at the state of his neck! Whoever did this must be strong as an ox!"

"And a practiced hand," Burton added, bending over the corpse. "See the bruising? Our murderer knew exactly where to place his fingers and thumbs to kill in the quickest and most efficient manner. Hmm, look at these perforations in the skin. It's almost as if the killer possessed claws instead of fingernails!"

Trounce began to search through the pockets of the dead man.

Swinburne reappeared with the landlord, who, upon looking through the doorway and seeing the body, cried out: "Cripes! And he ain't even paid his rent!"

"Is this Peter Pimlico?" Burton asked.

"Yus."

Trounce uttered an exclamation and held up a small phial.

Burton took it, opened it, sniffed it, then tipped it until a drop of liquid spilled onto his finger. He put it to his tongue and screwed up his nose.

"Strychnine. No doubt about it."

"It was in his pocket," Trounce said. He addressed the landlord: "Does the village have a constable?"

"Yes, sir," Emery replied. "Timothy Flanagan. He lives at number twelve."

"Go and get him."

"He'll be asleep."

"Of course he'll be asleep! Bang on his door! Throw stones at his window! I don't care what you do—just wake him up and get him here, on the double!"

Emery nodded and disappeared down the stairs.

The detective turned back to the corpse, running his eyes over it, taking in every detail. He suddenly uttered an exclamation and bent close to Pimlico's swollen face.

"What is it?" Burton asked.

Trounce didn't answer. Instead, he pushed his fingers between the dead man's lips, groped to one side of the tongue, and pulled something out.

It was a small withered leaf, a dry brown colour, with spitefully thorny edges, and it was attached to a tendril that, though Trounce gently tugged at it, refused to come out of Pimlico's mouth.

"Captain," he said. "Would you prise the jaw open, please?"

Burton squatted, placed his hands around the lower half of the corpse's face, and pulled the mouth wide while Trounce pushed his fingers deeper inside.

"What in the blazes?" the Yard man hissed as he drew out a second leaf and the vine to which it was attached tightened. "Look at this!"

He leaned back so Burton could peer into the mouth. The king's agent emitted a gasp of surprise, for the little plant was growing straight out of Pimlico's upper palette.

"I've never seen anything like it!" Trounce said. "How can it be possible?"

Burton shrugged distractedly and started to examine the dead man's head in minute detail. He quickly discovered other oddities. There were tiny green shoots in the hair, growing from the scalp, and a tangle of withered white roots issuing from the flesh behind both ears.

"I don't know what to make of it," he said, rising to his feet. "But whatever this plant growing out of him is, it's as dead as Pimlico. What else did he have in his pockets?"

Trounce went through the items. "Keys, a few shillings, a box of lucifers, a pipe and pouch of shag tobacco, a pencil, and a 'bus ticket."

"From where?"

"Leeds. Let's search the room."

Swinburne looked on from the landing as the two men went over the chamber inch by inch. They discovered a small suitcase under the bed but it contained only clothes. No other possessions were found.

"Nothing to tell us who the foreigner might be," Trounce ruminated. "And no clue as to where Pimlico lived in Leeds."

"There's this," Burton said. He held out the tobacco pouch—the brand was Ogden's Flake—with the flap open. On the inside, an address was printed in blue ink: *Tattleworth Tobacconist, 26 Meanwood Road, Leeds.*

"If this is his local supplier, perhaps the proprietor will know him."

"Humph!" Trounce grunted. "Well, that's something, anyway. Let's wait for the constable, then we'll leg it back to Fryston. There are plenty of rotorchairs there—I'll commandeer one. It'll be close on dawn by the time I get to Leeds. No sleep for me tonight!"

"Nor for me," Burton said. "I'm coming with you."

"And so am I," Swinburne added.

Some minutes later, footsteps sounded on the stairs and a young policeman appeared, looking somewhat dishevelled and unshaven. Mr. Emery lurked behind him.

"There hasn't really been murder done, has there?" the constable blurted. He saw Pimlico's body. "Blimey! In Thorpe Willoughby! And who are you gentlemen, if you'll pardon my asking?"

"I'm Detective Inspector Trounce of Scotland Yard. This is His Majesty's agent, Sir Richard Francis Burton, and his assistant, Mr. Algernon Swinburne. To whom do you report, lad?"

"To Commissioner Sheridan in Leeds."

Trounce spoke rapidly: "Very well. I want you to wake up your local postmaster and get a message to the commissioner. Inform him that this chap—his name was Peter Pimlico—was strangled to death by an as yet unidentified foreigner. Then get the county coroner to call first at Fryston, then here to take care of business. I'll report to Commissioner Sheridan myself, later this morning."

"Yes, sir. Fryston, sir? Why so?"

"Because this scoundrel—" Trounce gave Pimlico's corpse a disdainful glance, "—poisoned to death a guest there."

Constable Flanagan gaped, swallowed, then saluted.

"What about me?" Emery grumbled. "Can I get back to me bleedin' bed?"

Trounce snorted. "If you think you can sleep with a corpse in the house, by all means. First tell me; when did Pimlico start renting this room?"

"Five days ago."

"Did he receive any visitors before tonight?"

"Nope."

"What did he do while he was here."

"Got drunk in the local boozer, mostly."

"Did he cause you any trouble?"

"Not so much as he's bleedin' well caused since he kicked the bucket! He just thumped up an' down the stairs when he was comin' an' goin', that's all."

"Were there any letters delivered for him?"

"Nope."

"Do you know anything about him?"

"Nope, 'cept he said he was here to get work with Howell's agency."

"Nothing else?"

"Nothin'."

A few minutes later, Trounce, Burton, Swinburne and Fidget were retracing their steps back to Monckton Milnes's place. Glancing back at Thorpe Willoughby, Swinburne noted that the trail of steam had almost vanished.

"Which direction to Leeds?" he asked.

"West," Trounce answered.

"Our strangler flew south. I wonder why he killed Pimlico?"

"Perhaps to stop him talking," Burton said. "I'm certain I've never encountered him before, so I doubt he had any personal motive for doing away with me. I rather think he was hired to do it by our mysterious foreigner. He probably expected to be paid and assisted in escaping from the area tonight. Instead, he was killed."

"Ruthless," Swinburne muttered. "But I can't say he didn't deserve his fate, the bounder! But what of the strange growth?"

"That," Burton said, "is a much bigger mystery. It seems unlikely that it was in his mouth earlier this evening, while he was playing waiter at Fryston. Such a rapidly growing monstrosity smells to me of the Eugenicists and the botanist Richard Spruce."

They reached Fryston and found that a great many of the guests had already departed, despite the hour.

"I've sealed off the music room," Monckton Milnes reported. "Poor Bendyshe will have to stay there until someone comes for him."

"The coroner is on his way," Burton reported. "May I ask a couple of favours of you?"

"Of course, anything I can do."

"We need to borrow three rotorchairs. We have to fly to Leeds immediately."

"Take mine, Jim Hunt's and Charlie Bradlaugh's. They're on the front lawn. I'll walk you to them."

"Thank you. I presume Mrs. Angell has gone to bed?"

"Yes. I gave her one of my best guest rooms."

"Would you ask Captain Lawless to accompany her and Fidget to the airfield in the morning? Trounce, Algy and I will have to fly there directly from Leeds. We'll see to it that the rotorchairs are delivered back to you later in the day."

"I'll take her myself, Richard. I want to see you off."

Monckton Milnes escorted his friends back out of the house and to a group of flying machines parked in the grounds. As they walked, he pulled Burton back a little from Swinburne and Trounce and whispered: "Has this any connection with your mission to Africa?"

Burton gave a shrug. "I don't know. It's certainly possible, maybe even probable."

They reached the rotorchairs and Monckton Milnes watched as the three men placed their hats in the storage boxes, put goggles over their eyes, and buckled themselves into the big leather seats.

"See you later, chaps," he said. "And best of luck!"

They started their engines, which belched out clouds of steam. Above their heads, blade-like wings unfolded from vertical shafts and began to spin, rotating faster and faster until they became invisible to the eye.

Burton gave his friend a wave, then pulled back on a lever. The runners of his machine lifted from the grass, and it rose rapidly on a cone of vapour. Swinburne and Trounce followed, and the three rotorchairs arced away and vanished into the night sky, leaving silvery white trails behind them.

§

An orange glow lit the eastern sky as three flying machines descended onto the cobbles of Black Brewery Road. Two of them touched the ground gently; the third hit it with a thump and skewed sideways for five feet amidst a shower of sparks before coming to rest.

"Ridiculous bloody contraptions!" Trounce cursed. He turned off the engine, waited for the wings to fold, then disembarked and joined Burton and Swinburne.

It was their third landing in Leeds. The first had been to ask a constable on his night beat for directions. The second had been outside the Tattleworth Tobacconist on Meanwood Road.

Mr. Tattleworth, swearing volubly at his rude awakening, had eventually confirmed that he knew Peter Pimlico.

"A bloody thief," he'd said. "What you might call a denizen of the underworld. But a regular customer. Lives a couple o' streets away. Number 17 Black Brewery Road."

They could have walked, but, preferring to keep their vehicles in sight, they took off and almost immediately landed again.

"It's this one," Swinburne said, pointing at a terrace. "Let's see how many profanities our next customer can spit at us!" He reached for the door knocker and banged it with gusto.

After a couple of minutes and a second attack on the door, a gruff and muffled voice came from behind it.

"Oo's thah?"

"Police," Trounce barked.

"Prove tis!"

"I have credentials," Trounce said, impatiently. "Open up and I'll show you."

"Ah durn't believe thee. Tis a trick. Thou b'ain't no trapper. A tallyman, more like!"

Swinburne squealed: "Ha ha! Tallyman Trounce!"

"Oo were thah?" came the voice.

"Algernon Swinburne!" Swinburne called. "The poet!"

There was a moment of silence, then the voice said: "Ah durn't need owt pottery fro' thee! Be off an' durn't come bah!"

"Sir!" Trounce bellowed. "Open the blasted door this very moment or I'll kick the damned thing in!"

The rattle of a chain sounded and a key turned in the lock. The door opened a crack and a rheumy eye peered out.

"Wah durst thou want? Ah aren't dressed. Am havin' us mornin' pipe."

"Does Peter Pimlico live here?" Trounce demanded.

"Aye. In t' flat upstairs. Ee durn't be in. Not fur'n week."

"I know. He's dead."

"Huh?"

"He was murdered earlier tonight."

"Good. Ee were a dirty oik an nowt else. So?"

"So we're here to search his rooms. Let us in."

The eye took in Trounce from his bowler hat to his police issue boots, then flicked to Burton and examined his swarthy and scarred face and broad shoulders, then down to Swinburne, who stood with laurel leaves tangled in his long bright red hair, which was sticking out wildly after the flight from Fryston.

"A poet wit' trappers?"

"Police pottery," Swinburne said. "Ceramics Squad. Stand aside, please!"

Trounce put his shoulder to the door and pushed, sending the man behind it reeling backwards. "What's your name?" he demanded, stepping into the house.

The man, who would have been tall were it not for his rickets-twisted legs, stood shivering in his striped nightshirt. He was wearing a nightcap over his straggly brown hair and bed socks on his large feet. There was a hole in the left one and his big toe was poking out. A smoking corncob pipe was clutched in his gnarled hand.

"Ah be Matthew Keller. Thou can't barge int' us 'ouse like this!"

"Yes, I can. It's your premises? You're the owner?"

"Aye. Get thee out o' it!"

"Not yet. So you rent the upstairs to Pimlico, is that right?"

"Uh huh, an' ah be glad t' be rid o' 'im, t' good fer nowt bastard."

"Trouble, was he?"

"Aye! Alweez drunk n' thievin'."

"Any visits from foreign gentlemen?"

"T' week past. Fat, ee were."

"Name?"

"Durn't knah."

"Nationality?"

"Durn't knah."

"Walrus moustache?"

"Aye. Now then, ah 'ave t' get dressed fr' work."

"You'll do nothing without my leave. We're going up to Pimlico's rooms."

"They be locked."

"Do you have a master key?"

"Aye."

"So get it!"

Keller sighed impatiently.

"Jump to it, man!" Trounce exploded.

The householder flinched, then moved to the rear of the small hallway, opened a door beneath the staircase, and took a key from a hook. He returned and passed it to the detective.

Trounce started up the stairs and Swinburne followed. As he passed Burton, who stepped up after him, the king's agent noticed that his assistant's grin had quickly faded.

By nature, Swinburne's emotions were as fiery and wild as his hair, always changing rapidly, never consistent, and often entirely inappropriate. The poet was subject to a physiological condition that caused him to feel pain as pleasure, and, it seemed to Burton, this might be the origin of his quirky, unpredictable character. Emotional hurt, such as that caused by Bendyshe's demise, became internalised and concealed behind wayward behaviour, which, unfortunately, frequently involved the consumption of copious amounts of alcohol. Swinburne's inability to judge what might harm him made him one of the bravest men Burton had ever met, but also one of the most dangerously self destructive.

"Follow us, Mr. Keller," Trounce called. "I want to keep my eye on you."

Keller protested, "Us an't gonna t' do nowt," but mounted the stairs behind his unwelcome visitors and struggled up, groaning at the effort. "Legs," he complained. "Bad all us life."

Pimlico's flat consisted of a bed-sitting room and a kitchen. It stank of rancid lard and bacon and hadn't been cleaned in a long time. Threadbare clothes were scattered over the floor. A porcelain washbasin, containing dirty water and with a thick line of grime around its inner edge, stood on a dressing table in front of a cracked mirror. There was a cutthroat razor and a soiled bar of soap beside it. The sagging bed was unmade, a chair was piled with betting slips from the local dog track, and issues of *The Leeds Enquirer* were stacked beneath the window.

Swinburne and Keller hung back while Burton and Trounce went over the rooms.

"Note book!" the Scotland Yard man exclaimed, lifting a small bound volume from the bed. He flicked through it, page by page. "Nothing but odds on dogs. He was a gambler, this Pimlico fellow."

"Ee were a loser," Keller said. "Lost every bleedin' penny ee earned. Nearly alweez late wit' rent."

"How was he employed?" Burton asked.

"At t' Pride-Manushi factory, packagin' velocipede parts what they send to sales rooms o'er in Coventry. But ee was laid off a fortnight since, after ee got nabbed fr' thievin'."

Burton's eyebrows arched. "What happened?"

"Ee climbed through t' window at Cat n' Fiddle, skanked a couple o' bottles o' whisky, an' jumped straight out int' arms o' trappers. Spent a night in clink."

Trounce frowned. "Just one night? After breaking into a public house?"

"Aye."

"Where was he held?"

"Farrow Lane Police Station."

Some minutes later, the Detective Inspector called to Burton, who was searching the kitchen: "Captain, your opinion, please."

Trounce pointed down at the bare floorboards near the window. Burton stepped over, looked, and saw a small glob of something blackish and fibrous. He squatted, took a pencil from his pocket, scraped its end in the dried up substance, then raised it to his nose.

He winced in disgust. "Stinks of tooth decay—and something else. Mr. Keller, did Pimlico use chewing tobacco?"

"Nah. Ee smurked Ogden's Flake, same as what ah does."

Burton stood and addressed Trounce. "I've made a study of tobacco odours. I'm certain this is Kautabak, a Prussian brand. Not widely available in England."

"And you think it was left by the foreigner? Our murderer is Germanic?"

"I suspect exactly that, yes."

They spent another twenty minutes searching but found nothing of any further use.

"Well then," Trounce said, "we'll take our leave of you, Mr. Keller."

"Aye, an' ah'll not be sad t' see thee go," the householder muttered.

As they descended the stairs, he added: "Ee were expectin' t' come int' brass, ee were."

Trounce stopped. "What?"

"Pimlico. Ee were expectin' brass—were goin' t' pay me what ee owed in rent, or so ee said."

"Money? From where?"

"Durn't knah."

Outside the house, the Yard man looked up at the sky, which was now a pale overcast grey.

"As from today I'm officially on extended leave," he said. "But I'll be damned if I'll leave this alone." He turned to Burton and Swinburne. "Next stop, Farrow Lane. I want to know why Pimlico was released."

They climbed back into their vehicles and took to the air. Once again, they had to search for a constable to give them directions. Fifteen minutes later, they landed outside the police station and Burton and Swinburne waited in their vehicles while Trounce entered to make his enquiries. He was gone for twenty minutes, during which time the poet discussed his latest project, *Atlanta in Calydon*, with his friend.

"I'm moved to heighten the atheist sentiment by way of a tribute to old Bendyshe," he said. "He was determined to drive the last nails into the coffin that Darwin built for God."

"Tom would have appreciated that," Burton responded. "For all his larking around, he never had anything but praise for you, Algy, and he adored your poetry. He was one of your most dedicated advocates."

An uncharacteristic hardness came to the poet's eyes. "Do you remember me once telling you about how, in my youth, I wanted to be a cavalry officer?"

"Yes. Your father wouldn't allow it, so you climbed Culver Cliff on the Isle of Wight to prove to yourself that you possess courage."

"That's right, Richard. And, at one point, I hung from that rock face by my fingertips, and I wasn't afraid. Since that occasion, I have never once shirked a challenge, no matter how dangerous. I don't baulk at the idea of warfare; of engaging with the enemy; of fighting for a principle. As a poet, my roots are deeply embedded in conflict."

"What's your point, Algy?"

"My point is this: as of now, I'm on a mission of vengeance."

§

The Royal Naval Air Service Station was situated some twenty miles east of Fryston. It had originally been established for the building of dirigibles, an endeavour the Technologists had abandoned after a sequence of disastrous crashes and explosions. Those failures had led to the development of rotating wing flight mechanics, and a breathtaking example of that particular form of engineering ingenuity currently dominated the largest of the station's landing fields.

HMR *Orpheus* was the most colossal rotorship Sir Richard Francis Burton had ever seen. Side-on, she appeared long and flat, two decks high, with a humped up cargo hold slightly to the rear of centre, a conning tower at the front, and a glass enclosed observation deck occupying her pointed prow. Eight flight pylons extended from either side of her—a total of sixteen, which made her the most powerful rotorship ever constructed.

Most of the crew and passengers were already aboard, ready for the short trip to London. Burton, Swinburne—sans laurel wreath—Captain Lawless, and Detective Inspector Trounce stood at the base of the boarding ramp, bidding farewell to Monckton Milnes and Sir Richard Mayne. The latter, nervous of flying, had opted to ride the atmospheric railway to the capital later in the week.

"So the fat Prussian bailed Pimlico out," Trounce told the police commissioner. "He gave his name as Otto Steinrück, and an Essex address."

Swinburne added: "Probably false."

"No," Trounce said. "The address had to be verified before his bail could be accepted. It exists and it's registered in his name."

"You're off duty now, Detective Inspector," Mayne said. "But if you want to pursue this in an official capacity during what little time you have left before your departure, then you have my permission."

"I would, and thank you, sir."

Mayne nodded, then looked up at the ship. "What a monster!" he exclaimed.

"The first of a new breed," Lawless told him. "Mr. Brunel surpassed himself with this one!"

"And she'll take you all the way along the Nile?"

"Unfortunately, no."

Burton said: "Mechanical devices refuse to function in the Lake Regions, Chief Commissioner. Some sort of emanation prevents it. Henry Morton Stanley's rotorchairs were found there, and their engines were as dead as a doornail. We fear that if the *Orpheus* flew too close she'd drop like a stone, and since we have no clear idea of where the zone begins, we have little choice but to go in on foot."

"Besides which," Lawless added, "this ship sacrifices economy for speed, so she'll need to stop for fuel, which can't be done in central Africa."

"So what's your route?" Monckton Milnes asked.

"Our first leg is London to Cairo," Lawless replied. "The second Cairo to Aden, then we'll fly to our final stop, Zanzibar, where the collier ship *Blackburn* awaits us with a hold full of coal. The expedition will disembark, we'll refuel, offload the vehicles and supplies on the mainland, and head home."

Burton added: "A hundred and fifty Wanyamwezi porters have been hired in Zanzibar and are already making their way inland with supplies purchased on the island. They'll deliver the goods to a village in the Dut'humi hills and will await our arrival. When we get there, they'll be paid and fresh porters from the nearby Mgota tribes will be hired. We'll then push on and, hopefully, will reach Kazeh before we have to abandon the vehicles. From there, we'll hike north to the Lake Regions and the Mountains of the Moon."

Lawless said: "Well, chaps, we'll never achieve any that if we don't get under way, so I'd better check that my ship is flight ready. We'll be off in ten minutes. I'll leave you to say your goodbyes." He gave a nod to Mayne and Monckton Milnes, touched a finger to the peak of his cap, and walked up the ramp and into the *Orpheus*.

Sir Richard Mayne drew Trounce aside and engaged him in a quiet conversation.

Monckton Milnes grasped Swinburne's hand and gave it a hearty shake. "Good luck, young 'un," he said. "You stay safe, do you hear me?"

"Perfectly well, old horse," Swinburne replied. "Don't you fret about me. I'll be fine. I'm too slight a morsel for a lion or crocodile to bother with, and I plan to keep myself soaked in gin to fend off the mosquitoes."

"Good lad! I look forward to some inspired poetry upon your return."

Swinburne caught Mayne's eye, gave him a salute, and boarded the ship.

"Are you sure he's up to it, Richard?" Monckton Milnes asked Burton. "As much as I admire him, he's the very last person I'd expect to be trekking through central Africa."

Burton gave a wry smile. "You know as well as I do that he's far from the delicate flower he seems. He's a tough little blighter and I need his insight into the Nāga business. Anyway, he'd never forgive me if I left him behind."

"And you? What of your health? Last time you tried for the Nile you were blinded and crippled for months on end."

"True, but mostly because John Speke was pouring huge doses of Saltzmann's Tincture into me. But that aside, we have Sister Raghavendra with us. That should make a considerable difference to our wellbeing."

Monckton Milnes nodded thoughtfully. "The Sisterhood of Noble Benevolence is a confoundedly strange organisation. I've never understood how they move around the East End without coming to harm. You know there's a rumour they possess some sort of supernatural grace that protects them?"

"I've heard as much, yes. It may be that their ability to heal and soothe is, indeed, supernatural. Perhaps it's another effect of the resonance from the Nāga diamonds. Whatever the explanation, I'm sure she'll prove a most valuable member of the expedition." Burton looked up at the grey sky. "Africa again," he muttered. "Maybe this time—"

"You aren't obliged to put yourself through it, Richard," Monckton Milnes interrupted. "Palmerston can find other pawns for his chess game."

"For certain. But it's not just the diamond business. I want the Nile. Every day, I ask myself 'Why?' and the only echo is 'Damned fool! The Devil drives!' That bloody continent has been shaping my life for nigh on a decade and I feel, instinctively, that it hasn't finished with me yet."

"Then go," said Monckton Milnes. "But Richard—"

"Yes?"

"Come back."

"I'll do my level best. Listen, old chap, on the subject of Palmerston, there's something you might do for me while I'm away."

"Anything."

"I'd like you to keep an eye on him. Follow, especially, his foreign policies with regard to Prussia, the other Germanic states, and Africa. You are one of the most politically astute men I know, and you have a plethora of friends in high places. Use them. When I return, I'll need you to give me an idea of which way the wind is blowing where our international relations are concerned."

"You think he's up to something?"

"Always."

Monckton Milnes promised to do everything he could.

They shook hands and bid each other farewell.

Detective Inspector Trounce returned and joined Burton on the gangplank.

With a final wave to their colleagues, the two men entered the rotorship.

$\mathcal{S}$

The great swathe of the world's territory that Britain had once controlled was still referred to, in its final days, as the Empire, even though there'd been no British monarch since the death of Albert in 1900. "The King's African Rifles" was a misnomer for the same reason. Traditions die hard for the British, especially in the Army.

Two thousand of the KAR, led by sixty-two English officers, had set up camp at Ponde, a village about six miles to the south of Dar es Salaam and four miles behind the trenches that stretched around the city from the coast in the north west to the coast in the south east. Ponde's original beehive huts were buried somewhere deep in a sea of khaki tents, and their Uzaramo inhabitants—there were less than a hundred and fifty of them—had been recruited against their will as servants and porters. Mostly, they dealt with the ignominy by staying as drunk as possible, by running away when they could, or, in a few cases, by committing suicide.

Perhaps the only if not happy then at least satisfied villager was the man who brewed *pombe*—African beer—who'd set up a shack beneath a thicket of mangrove trees from which to sell the warm but surprisingly pleasant beverage. The shady area had been supplied with tables and chairs, and thus was born a mosquito-infested tavern of sorts. *No Askaris permitted! Officers and civilians only!*

It was eleven in the morning, and the individual who now thought of himself as Sir Richard Francis Burton was sitting at one of the tables. It was an oppressively humid day and the temperature was rising. The sky was a tear-inducing white. The air was thick with flies.

He'd refused *pombe*—it was far too early—and had been provided with a mug of tea instead, which sat steaming in front of him. His left forearm was bandaged. Beneath the dressing there was a deep laceration, held together by seven stitches. His face, now more fully bearded, was cut and bruised. A deep gash, scabbed and puckered, split his right eyebrow.

He dropped four cubes of sugar into his drink and stirred it, gazing fixedly at the swirling liquid.

His hands were shaking.

"There you are!" came a high-pitched exclamation. "Drink up. We have to get going."

He raised his eyes and found Bertie Wells standing beside him. The war correspondent, who seemed much shorter and stouter in broad daylight, was leaning on crutches and his right calf was encased in a splint.

"Hello, old thing," Burton said. "Take the weight off. How is it?"

Wells remained standing. "As broken as it was yesterday and the day before. Do you know, I snapped the same bally leg when I was seven years old? You were still alive back then."

"I'm still alive now. Get going to where?"

"Up onto the ridge so we can watch the bombing. The ships should be here within the hour."

"Can you manage it? The walk?"

Wells flicked a mosquito from his neck. "I'm becoming a proficient hobbler. Would you do me a favour, Sir Richard? Next time I pontificate about the unlikelihood of a direct hit, will you strike me violently about the head and drag me clear of the area?"

"I'll be more than happy to. Even retrospectively."

"I must say, though, I thoroughly enjoyed the irony of it."

"Irony?"

"Yes. You affirm that you are quite impossibly in the land of the living, and seconds later, you almost aren't!"

"Ah, yes. Henceforth, I shall choose my words with a little more care. I did not at all enjoy being bombed and buried alive. And please drop the 'Sir.' Plain old 'Richard' is sufficient." He took a gulp of tea and stood up. "Shall we go and watch the fireworks, then?"

They left the makeshift tavern and began to move slowly through the tents, passing empty-eyed and slack-faced soldiers, and heading toward the northern border of the encampment.

The air smelled of sweat—and worse.

"Look at them," Wells said. "Have you ever seen such a heterogeneous throng of fighting men? They've been recruited from what's left of the British South Africans, from Australia and India, from the rag tag remains of our European forces, and from all the diverse tribes of East and Central Africa."

"They don't look at all happy about it."

"This isn't an easy country, as you know better than most. Dysentery, malaria, tsetse flies, mosquitos, jigger fleas—the majority of the white men are as sick as dogs. As for the Africans, they're all serial deserters. There should be double the number of soldiers you see here."

They passed alongside a pen of oxen. One of the animals was lying dead; it's carcass stinking and beginning to swell.

"Do you have a thing about poppies?" Wells asked. "You pulled one from your pocket just before we got bombed, and now I see you have a fresh one pinned to your lapel."

"I think—I have a feeling—that is to say—the flower seems as if it should mean something."

"I believe it symbolises sleep—or death," Wells responded.

"No, not that," Burton said. "Something else, but I can't put my finger on it."

"So you're still having trouble with your memory, then? I was hoping it'd returned. As you might imagine, I've been beside myself with curiosity these past few days. I have so many questions to ask."

"Odd scraps of it are back," Burton replied. "It's a peculiar sensation. I feel thoroughly unassembled. I'll submit to your interrogation, but if you manage to get anything out of me, you must keep it to yourself."

"I have little choice. If I publicised the fact that you're alive, my editor would laugh me right out of the news office and straight into the European Resistance, from which I'd never be seen again." Wells jerked his head, coughed, and spat. "These bloody flies! They're all over me! The moment I open my mouth, there's always one eager to buzz into it!" He saluted a passing officer, then said: "So what happened? Did some quirk of nature render you immortal, Richard? Did you fake your own death in 1890?"

"No. I have the impression that I came here directly from the year 1863."

"What? You stepped straight from three years before I was born into the here and now? By what means?"

"I don't know."

"Then, why?"

"I don't know that, either. I'm not even sure which future this is."

"Which future? What on earth does that mean?"

"Again, I don't know—but I feel sure there are alternatives."

Wells shook his head. "My goodness. The impossibilities are accumulating. Yet here you are."

"Here I am," Burton agreed.

"An anachronic man," Wells muttered. He stopped to adjust his crutches.

Moans emerged from a nearby tent, its inhabitant obviously wracked by fever. The sound of his misery was drowned out as a group of Askaris filed past, singing a mournful song. Burton listened, fascinated by their deep voices, and was able to identify the language as Kichagga, a dialect of Kiswahili, which suggested the men were from the Chagga tribes that originated in the north, from the lands below the Kilima Njaro mountain.

They were far from home.

So was he.

"I once discussed the possibility of journeying through time with young Huxley," Wells said, as the two of them got moving again. "It was his assertion that no method would ever be invented for, if it were, then surely we'd have been overrun by visitors from the future. It didn't occur to either of us that they'd actually come from the past. You say you don't know how it was achieved? But was it through mechanical means or a—I don't know—a mental technique?"

"I have no idea. Who's Huxley?"

"A boy I was acquainted with. He had a prodigious intellect, though he was almost entirely blind and hardly out of short trousers. He was killed when the Hun destroyed London. I don't understand, Richard—how could movement through time have been possible in the 1860s yet remain a secret today?"

"My guess is that—that—that—wait—who is—was—is Palmerston?"

"Pah! That villain! In your day, he was prime minister."

"Yes!" Burton cried. "Yes! I remember now! He had a face like a waxwork!"

"What about him?"

"I think he might have suppressed the fact that the boundaries of time can be breached."

"The devil you say! I should have known! That wily old goat! Does he know you're here?"

"Not to my knowledge."

"Maybe my editor would help you to contact him."

"I have no means of sending a communiqué into the past."

"I mean now, here in 1914."

Burton exclaimed: "Surely you don't mean to suggest that he's still alive?"

"Ah. You didn't know. Yes, he's with us. Famously so. Or perhaps 'notoriously so' would be a more accurate assessment. He's a hundred and thirty years old!"

"Bismillah!" Burton gasped. "Palmerston! Alive! Is he still prime minister?"

"No, of course not. There's been no such thing since the Germans overran Europe. And let me tell you: few men who ever lived have had as much blood on their hands as Palmerston. He called us to war. We were making the future, he said, and hardly any of us troubled to think what future we were making." Wells waved his hand at the tents that surrounded them. "Behold!"

Burton looked puzzled. "But there's more than this, surely? What of the Empire?"

Wells stopped in his tracks. "Richard," he said quietly. "You have to understand. This is it."

"It?"

"All that remains. The men commanding these two battalions of Askaris, plus perhaps three thousand in the British Indian Expeditionary Force, scattered groups of soldiers around the Lake Regions, maybe twenty thousand civilians and Technologists in our stronghold at Tabora, and whatever's left of the British European Resistance—there's nothing else."

Burton looked shocked. "This is the Empire? What in heaven's name happened?"

"As I told you before, it all began here. By the 1870s, despite the efforts of Al-Manat, the German presence in Africa was growing. Palmerston was convinced that Bismarck intended a full-scale invasion. He believed that Germany was seeking to establish an empire as big as ours, so he posted a couple of battalions over here to prevent that from happening. The Hun responded by arming the natives, setting them against us. The conflict escalated. Palmerston sent more and more soldiers. Then, in 1900, Germany suddenly mobilised all its forces, including its Eugenicist weapons—but not here. It turns out that Bismarck never wanted Africa. He wanted Europe. France fell, then Belgium, then Denmark, then Austria-Hungary, then Serbia. The devastation was horrific. Britain fought wildly for five years, but our Army was divided. Almost a third of it was here, and when they tried to get home, Germany blockaded all the African ports. My God, what a consummate tactician Bismarck was! We didn't stand a chance. Then he gained Russia as an ally, and we were conquered. India, Australia, South Africa, and the West Indies all quickly declared their independence, British North America fell to a native and slave uprising, and the Empire disintegrated."

Burton sent a breath whistling through his teeth. "And Palmerston was to blame?"

"Completely. His foreign policy was misjudged in the extreme. No one really understands why he was so obsessed with Africa. A great many Britishers have called for him to be tried and executed. After all, it's not reasonable that those who gamble with men's lives should not pay with their own, and he was the greatest gambler of them all. But Crowley insists that he should be kept alive—that, somehow, the survival of Tabora—the last British city—depends on him."

They reached an area where the tents thinned out and row after row of Mark II Scorpion Tanks were parked, hunkered down on their legs, claws tucked in, tails curled up.

Burton noted that, though the war machines' design was new to him, the technology seemed to have advanced little since his own age.

"Let's rest again for a moment," Wells said. "This bloody leg is giving me gyp."

"All right."

Burton leaned against one of the arachnids and batted a fly from his face.

Memories were stirring. He was trying to recall the last time he'd met Lord Palmerston.

Shut the hell up, Burton! Am I to endure your insolence every time we meet? I'll not tolerate it! You have your orders! Do your bloody job, Captain!

The prime minister's voice echoed in a remote chamber of his mind but he was unable to associate it with any specific occasion.

"So he's at Tabora?" he asked.

"Palmerston? Yes. He's kept under house arrest there. I find it incredible that he still has supporters, but he does—my editor for one—so it's unlikely he'll go before the firing squad, as he deserves. You know he buggered up the constitution, too?"

"How so?"

"When he manipulated the Regency Act back in 1840 to ensure that Albert took the throne instead of Ernest Augustus of Hanover, he left no provision for what might happen afterwards—no clear rules of succession for when Albert died. Ha! In 1900, I, like a great many others, was a staunch republican, so, when the king finally kicked the bucket, I was happy to hear calls for the monarchy to be dismantled. Of course, equally vociferous voices were raised against the idea. Things got rather heated, and I, being a journalist, got rather too involved. There was public disorder, and I'm afraid I might have egged it on a little. When a man gets caught up in history, Richard, he loses sight of himself. Anyway, Palmerston was distracted, and that's when Bismarck pounced. I feel a fool now. In times of war, figureheads become necessary for morale. I should have realised that, but I was an idealist back then. I even believed the human race capable of building Utopia. Ha! Idiot!"

They slouched against the machines for a couple more minutes, the humidity weighing down on them, then resumed their trek, moving away from the tanks and up a gentle slope toward the ridge. The ground was dry, cracked and dusty, with tufts of elephant grass standing in isolated clumps. There were also large stretches of blackened earth, "Where carnivorous plants have been burned away," Wells explained. "At least we're not due the calamity of rain for a few more weeks. The moment a single drop touches the soil, the bloody plants spring up again."

The Indian Ocean, a glittering turquoise line, lay far off to their right, while to their left, the peaks of the Usagara highlands shimmered and rippled on the horizon.

"But let us not be diverted from our topic," Wells said. "I'm trying to recall your biographies. If I remember rightly, in 1859 you returned from your unsuccessful expedition to find the source of the Nile and more or less retreated from the public eye to work on various books, including your translation of *The Arabian Nights*, which, may I add, was a simply splendid achievement."

"*The Book of a Thousand Nights and a Night*," Burton corrected. "Thank you, but please say no more about it. I've not completed the damned thing yet. At least, I don't think I have."

He helped his companion past a fallen tree that was swarming with white ants, and muttered, "It's odd you say that, though, about my search for the source of the Nile. The moment you mentioned it, I remembered it, but I feel sure I made a second attempt."

"I don't think so. It certainly isn't recorded. The fountains of the Nile were discovered by—"

Burton stopped him.

"No! Don't tell me! I don't want to know. If I really am from 1863, and I return to it, perhaps I'll rewrite that particular item of history."

"You think you might get back to your own time? How?"

Burton shrugged.

"But isn't it obvious you won't?" Wells objected. "Otherwise we wouldn't be having this conversation, for you'd surely do something to prevent this war from ever happening."

"Ah, Bertie, there's the paradox," Burton answered. "If I go back and achieve what your history says I never achieved, you'll still be here aware that I never did it. However, I will now exist in a time where I did. And in my future there'll be a Herbert George Wells who knows it."

"Wait! Wait! I'm struggling to wrap my brain around that!"

"I agree; it's a strain on the grey matter, especially if, like mine, it's as full of holes as a Swiss cheese. These days, I hear myself speak but have barely a notion of what I'm talking about."

Burton pulled a handkerchief from his pocket and wiped the sweat from the back of his neck. "But something tells me that if you go back into the past and make an alteration, then a whole new sequence of events will spring from it, establishing an ever widening divergence from what had been the original course of history."

Wells whistled. "Yet that original has to still exist, for it's where you travelled back from."

"Precisely."

"So existence has been split into two by your act."

"Apparently."

"How godlike, the chronic argonaut," Wells mused.

"The what?"

"Hum. Just thinking out loud."

They joined a small group of officers who'd gathered at the top of the ridge. Wells indicated one of them and whispered: "That's Commander Aitken. He's in charge of this whole operation."

Burton tugged at his khaki uniform jacket, which he considered far too heavy for the climate. He felt smothered and uncomfortable. Perspiration was running into his eyes. He rubbed them. As they readjusted, the vista that sprawled beneath him swam into focus, and all his irritations were instantly forgotten.

Seen through the distorting lens of Africa's blistering heat, Dar es Salaam appeared to undulate and quiver like a mirage. It was a small white city, clinging to the shore of a natural harbour. Grand colonial buildings humped up from its centre and were clustered around the port—in which a German light cruiser was docked—while a tall metal structure towered above the western neighbourhoods. Otherwise, the settlement seemed very flat, with single-storey dwellings strung along tree-lined dirt roads and around the borders of small outlying farms.

A strip of tangled greenery surrounded the municipality— "They seem small from here, but those are the artillery plants," Wells observed—and beyond them, the German trenches criss-crossed the terrain up to a second band of foliage: the red weed. The British trenches occupied the space between the weed and the ridge.

Like a punch to the head, Burton suddenly recalled the Crimea, for, as in that terrible conflict, the earth here had been torn, gouged, and overturned by shells. Flooded by heavy rains some weeks ago, the horrible landscape before him had since been baked into distorted shapes by the relentless sunshine. It was also saturated with blood and peppered with chunks of rotting human and animal flesh, and the stench assailed Burton's nostrils from even this distance. Bits of smashed machinery rose from the churned ground like disinterred bones. It was unnatural. It was hideous. It was sickening.

He unhooked his canteen from his belt, took a swig of water, and spat dust from his mouth.

"That's our target," said Wells, pointing at the metal tower. "If we can bring it down, we'll destroy their radio communications."

"Radio?" Burton asked.

Wells smiled. "Well I never! How queer to meet a man who isn't familiar with something that everyone else takes for granted! But, of course, it was after your time, wasn't it!"

Burton glanced uneasily at the nearby officers, who were peering at the sea through binoculars.

"Keep your voice down, please, Bertie," he said. "And what was after my time?"

"The discovery of radio waves. The technique by which we transmit spoken words and other sounds through the atmosphere to literally anywhere in the world."

"A mediumistic procedure?"

"Not at all. It's similar to the telegraph but without the wires. It involves the modulation of oscillating electromagnetic fields."

"That's all mumbo-jumbo to me. What are they looking at?"

Wells turned to the officers, then raised his binoculars and followed the men's gaze.

"Ah ha!" he said. "The rotorships! Have a squint."

He passed the binoculars to Burton, who put them to his eyes and scanned the eastern sky, near the horizon, until two dark dots came into view. As they approached, he saw they were big rotorships, both with twelve flight pylons, with wings spinning at the top of the tall shafts. The black flat-bottomed vessels were rather more domed in shape than those from his own time, and he could see cannons poking out of portholes along their sides.

"*Astraea* and *Pegasus*," Wells said. "Cruiser class. The *Pegasus* is the one on the right."

"They're fast. What are those little things flying around them?"

"Hornets. One man fighters. They'll swoop in to shoot at the ground defences."

"Actual insects?"

"Yes. The usual routine. Breed 'em big, kill 'em, scrape 'em out, shove steam engines into the carapaces. The method hasn't changed since your day. Look out! The *Königsberg* is bringing her cannon to bear!"

Burton directed the glasses to the city's harbour and saw that the decks of the seagoing vessel were swarming with men. A gun turret, positioned in front of its three funnels, was turning to face the oncoming rotorships. A few moments later, orange light blazed from the muzzle. Repetitive booms, lagging a few seconds behind the discharges, rippled out over the landscape, becoming thin and echoey as they faded away.

He looked back at the rotorships, both almost upon the city now. Puffs of black smoke were exploding around them.

Hornets dived down at the light cruiser and raked her decks with their machine guns.

"Come on, lads!" Wells cheered.

Burton watched men ripped into tatters and knocked overboard as bullets tore into them. A loud report sounded. He lowered the binoculars and saw that metal and smoke had erupted from the side of the *Pegasus*.

"She's hit!" Wells cried.

The rotorship listed to her left. As her shadow passed over the *Königsberg*, small objects spilled from beneath her. They were bombs. With an ear-splitting roar, the German vessel disappeared into a ball of fire and smoke. Fragments of hull plating went spinning skyward. Another huge detonation sounded as the ship's munitions went up.

The Pegasus, rocked by the shockwave, keeled completely over onto her side and arced towards the ground. She hit the southern neighbourhoods of Dar es Salaam and ploughed through them, disintegrating, until, when she finally came to rest, she was nothing but an unrecognisable knot of twisted and tattered metal slumped at the end of a long burning furrow. Hundreds of buildings had been destroyed, maybe thousands of lives lost.

Wells opened his mouth to say something but his words were drowned by thunder as the *Astraea* started to dump her payload onto the middle of the city. The noise slapped again and again at Burton's ears as the colonial district was pummelled and decimated. Soon, all he could see was a blanket of black smoke through which the red lights of Hades flickered, and gliding along above it, silhouetted against the glaring white sky, the menacing rotorship, drawing closer and closer to where the tip of the radio tower emerged from the expanding inferno.

Wells stood on tiptoe and put his mouth to Burton's ear, which was ringing with such intensity that the explorer could barely hear the correspondent's soprano voice: "We had no choice but to do it. I wonder, though, will the human race ever transcend the animalistic impulses that lead to such behaviour?"

Burton yelled back: "I suspect animals would be most offended to be associated with an atrocity like this! What of the people down there? What of the Africans?"

"Casualties of war. As I said, we had no choice!"

"But this isn't their bloody conflict! It isn't their bloody conflict, damn it!"

A quick succession of blasts marked the end of the radio tower. The *Astraea* slid over the belt of red weed and sailed northward with hornets buzzing around her.

The attack was already over.

Silence rolled back in from the surrounding countryside, and was broken only by occasional small explosions.

"She's probably on her way to give Tanga some of the same treatment," Wells said, watching the rotorship receding into the distance.

Burton stood silently, struggling to stay on his feet. His legs were trembling violently, and his heart hammered in his chest.

"Bismillah!" he muttered. "Bismillah"

THE BAKER STREET DETECTIVE

➤● Macallister Fogg's Own Paper! ●◀

Issue 908. Every Thursday. Consolidated Press. One Penny.

THIS WEEK:

Macallister Fogg and his lady assistant, Mrs. Boswell,

INVESTIGATE

The Peril of the Gravity Pirates!

by T. H. Strongfellow

Plus the latest instalments of:

Doctor Tzu and the Singing Cobra by Cecil Barry

Fatty Cakehole's Dormitory Empire by Norman Pounder

"Take us up, Mr. Wenham, no higher than seven thousand feet, if you please." The order came from William Henson, the rotorship's first officer. He was a slender man, about fifty years old, with an extravagant moustache that curved around his cheeks to blend into bushy mutton-chop whiskers. He wore tiny wire-framed spectacles. They magnified his eyes while also accentuating his precise and somewhat stern manner.

He turned to Burton and Swinburne, who were standing next to Captain Lawless, having been invited up to the conning tower to witness the take-off. "We have to keep her low, gentlemen, on account of our ventilation problems. Until we get the heating pipes fixed, flying at any greater altitude will have us all shivering in our socks."

A vibration ran through the deck as the engines roared. There was no sensation of movement, but through the windows curving around the front and sides of the tower, Burton saw the horizon slip downward.

"Here we go," declared Francis Wenham, the helmsman. He was at a control console at the front of the cabin, manipulating three big levers and a number of wheels; a beefily-built man with pale blonde, rather untidy hair, and a wispy goatee beard.

"One thousand five hundred feet," murmured the man at the station beside him. "Swing her forty degrees to starboard, please."

"Forty degrees to starboard, aye, Mr. Playfair."

The horizon revolved around the ship.

Playfair turned to Henson and said, "Course set, sir."

"Thank you. Ahead, Mr. Wenham. Get her up to forty knots."

"Aye, sir."

"Flight time to London, three and a half hours," Playfair noted.

Swinburne eyed the sharp faced, dark eyed navigator. "I didn't see him consult his instruments," he muttered to Lawless. "Did he just do that calculation in his head?"

"Yes," the captain answered quietly. "He's a wizard with mathematics, that one."

The meteorologist—short, very stout, very hairy, and wearing his bulging uniform jacket tightly buttoned—announced: "Clear going until we reach the capital, sir. Fog there."

"Thank you, Mr. Bingham."

The captain turned to a tall heavily-bearded man who'd just entered the cabin and said: "Ah, there you are. Sir Richard, Mr. Swinburne, this is Doctor Barnaby Quaint, our steward and surgeon. He'll give you a tour of the ship, see that you're settled into your quarters, and will make sure that you have whatever you require."

"Is there a bar on board?" Swinburne asked.

Quaint smiled. "Yes, sir, in the lounge, though its closed at the moment. I dare say I could rustle you up a tipple, should you require it. Would you care to follow me, gentlemen?"

They took their leave of Lawless, left the command cabin, and descended a metal staircase. A short corridor led them past the captain's quarters on one side and the first officer's on the other, and through decorative double doors into the glass encased observation deck.

They were greeted by Detective Inspectors Trounce and Honesty, Commander Krishnamurthy, Constable Bhatti, and Mrs. Iris Angell, who was beside herself with excitement.

"Who'd have thought!" exclaimed Burton's housekeeper. "Dirty old Yorkshire—see how pretty it appears from up here, Sir Richard!"

He stepped to her side and looked out at the little villages and patchwork fields passing below.

"The northern counties have some of the most beautiful countryside in all of England," he said. "Did you think it would be different?"

"Yes!" she exclaimed. "I expected horrible factories everywhere!"

"You'll find plenty of William Blake's 'dark Satanic mills' in and around the manufacturing cities, Mrs. Angell, but as you can see, the horror of the North felt by those in the South is generally quite unjustified."

Burton watched the scenery slide by for a couple more minutes then moved over to where Detective Inspector Honesty was standing alone.

"Hello, old fellow," he said. "I didn't see much of you at Fryston. Are you all set for Africa?"

Honesty turned to him. "I am. Wife unhappy but duty calls. Must finish this business. Stop interference from the future." The detective gazed back out of the window and his pale grey eyes fixed on the horizon. "Africa. Exotic flora. Might collect specimens. Cultivate in greenhouse when we return."

"Are you an amateur horticulturalist? I didn't know."

Honesty looked back at Burton and the explorer noticed a strange light in the smaller man's eyes—an odd sort of remoteness about his manner.

"Should've been a landscape gardener. Always wanted to be. Joined the Force on account of my father. A Peeler. One of the originals. Very dedicated. Passionate about policing. Me—I'm just good at it. But gardening—well—" He paused and a small sigh escaped him. "There are different versions of history, Captain?"

"Yes."

"Maybe in one, I made another choice. *Thomas Manfred Honesty: Landscape Gardener.* Hope so."

He gave his attention back to the vista outside.

Burton patted the detective's shoulder and left him. He felt troubled by his friend's detached air. Honesty hadn't been quite himself since last September's battle with the Rakes, when he'd had his fingers broken and been throttled almost to death by an animated corpse. It was, Burton thought, enough to unnerve any man.

Trounce approached him.

"How long until we reach London? I'm eager to get back onto the trail of our murderer."

"A little over three hours." Burton lowered his voice. "I say, Trounce, what's your opinion of Honesty? Is he a hundred percent?"

Trounce glanced toward his colleague.

"I'd say he's the most determined of us all, Captain. He's a man who likes everything to be just so. The idea that an individual can hop back through time and turn it all on its head doesn't sit well with him."

Burton gave a small nod of understanding. "The steward is giving us a tour of the ship. Join us?"

"I will, thank you."

Leaving Honesty, Krishnamurthy, Bhatti and Mrs. Angell—all of whom had been around the vessel earlier that morning—Burton, Swinburne and Trounce followed Doctor Quaint back into the corridor. As they passed by the captain's rooms, a small, slightly pudgy boy emerged.

"All ship shape, Master Wilde?" the doctor asked.

"That it is, sir. Good morning to you, Captain Burton, Mr. Swinburne, Mr. Trounce. Welcome aboard!" The boy grinned, habitually raising his hand to his nose in order to conceal his rather crooked and yellowing teeth.

"Hallo, Quips!" said Burton.

Quaint addressed the explorer: "I understand Master Wilde is with us at your recommendation, sir?"

"He is, indeed."

"And I'm much obliged, so I am, Captain," Wilde said.

"By Jove, little 'un!" Trounce exclaimed. "If someone had told you a year ago that you'd be flying to Africa as a crew member aboard the biggest rotorship ever built, would you have believed them?"

"I can believe anything provided it is incredible, Mr. Trounce."

"Ha! Quite so! Quite so! And I daresay it's a great deal better than going to school, hey?"

"I wouldn't know, never having suffered such an indignity. While education may be an admirable thing, it is well to remember that nothing worth knowing can be taught. Now then, I must get myself up to the captain to have these acquisition orders signed. There's much to be done, so there is, if we're to depart the country without leaving unpaid debts behind us. I'll see you later, gentlemen!"

"Good lord!" Quaint said, as Wilde disappeared up the stairs to the conning tower. "Where does he get those nimble wits from?"

"I have no idea," Burton answered. "Perhaps his diet of butterscotch and gobstoppers has affected his brain."

They moved on down the corridor, passing the crew's quarters, and entered the lounge, a large space stretching from one side of the ship to the other. There were tables and chairs, a small dance floor and stage, and, to Swinburne's evident satisfaction, a bar in one corner.

"How many passengers can the *Orpheus* accommodate, Doctor?" Burton asked.

"Two hundred, sir. The smoking room is ahead of us, and beyond that the dining room, then a small parlour, and the first class cabins all the way to the stern, where the reading room is situated. From there we'll take the stairs down to the rear observation room, pass through the cargo hold to the galley and pantries, then the engine room, and on to the standard class cabins in the prow end of the ship. As you can see, those rooms have access to this lounge via staircases on the port and starboard sides. Of course, the ship has a number of other rooms, but those are the main ones."

"Phew!" Trounce gasped. "Mr. Brunel certainly likes to work on a grand scale!"

They continued their tour, marvelling at the opulence that surrounded them—for every fixture and fitting, and every item of decor, had been hand-crafted from the finest materials—and eventually came to the galley, where they found Isabella Mayson unpacking foodstuffs and stocking the larders.

"By heavens, Miss Mason!" Quaint cried out. "You're making fast progress! The last time I looked in, this room was chock-a-block with unopened boxes!"

"A place for everything and everything in its place, Doctor Quaint," the young woman responded. "We took a great many supplies on board in Yorkshire and we'll be adding more when we get to London. If I don't have the kitchen in order by then, it'll mean more work and delayed meals. We wouldn't want that, would we?"

"Certainly not!" Quaint agreed.

Miss Mayson smiled at the steward, and said: "I shall be serving an early lunch at half past twelve, Doctor."

"Good!" Swinburne interjected. "I'm famished!"

Quaint led them out of the galley, past cabins given over to various shipboard functions, and into the first of the huge engine room compartments. After Daniel Gooch had shown them around the massive twin turbines, they moved on to the standard class cabins, where they encountered Sister

Raghavendra, who was organising a small surgery. As Quaint explained, it was essential to have medical facilities aboard the ship, not only to cater for any passenger who might be taken ill, but also because some of the engineering duties were exceedingly hazardous. It was the job of the riggers, for example, to maintain the flight pylons, which sometimes meant crawling out onto them while the *Orpheus* was in mid-flight. They wore harnesses, of course, but a fall could still be damaging. Riggers had been known drop then swing into the side of their ship, suffering a crushing impact.

"Now that you have your bearings, gentlemen, I shall take my leave of you," the doctor said, as they reached a staircase at the prow of the vessel. "There is much to be done before our principal voyage begins, as I'm sure you appreciate." He looked down at Swinburne. "I have to pass back through the lounge, sir. If you'd care to accompany me, I'll organise that breakfast tipple for you."

"Bravo!" Swinburne cheered. "That'll be just the ticket!"

"And you, sir?" Quaint asked Burton.

"Too early for me. I'll retire to my quarters to go over the expedition inventory."

"Then I shall see you at lunch, sir."

§

The top ends of four colossal copper rods poked out of the dense fog that blanketed London. Guided by Francis

Wenham, HMR *Orpheus* slid into position between them and gently descended into the central courtyard of Battersea Power Station.

It was two o'clock in the afternoon.

"How times have changed," Swinburne commented as he and Sir Richard Francis Burton disembarked, wrapped tightly in their overcoats, top hats pressed tightly onto their heads. "Who'd have thought, a couple of years ago, that we'd end up working with Isambard Kingdom Brunel?"

"How times *have* changed," Burton echoed. "That's the problem."

Herbert Spencer, the clockwork philosopher, emerged from the pall to greet them.

He was a figure of polished brass, a machine, standing about five-feet-five-inches tall. His head was canister-shaped, with a bizarre-looking domed attachment on top of it that was somewhat reminiscent of a tiny church organ. The "face" beneath it was nothing more than three raised circular areas set vertically. The topmost resembled a tiny ship's porthole, through which a great many minuscule cogwheels could be glimpsed. The middle circle held a mesh grille, and the bottom one was simply a hole out of which three very fine five-inch-long wires projected.

Spencer's neck consisted of thin shafts and cables, swivel joints and hinges. His trunk was a slim cylinder with panels cut from it, revealing gears and springs, delicate crankshafts, gyroscopes, flywheels, and a pendulum. The thin but robust arms ended in three-fingered hands. The legs were sturdy and tubular; the feet oval-shaped.

He was an astonishing sight; and few who saw him now would believe that not so many weeks ago he'd been a very human, grubby, and tangle-bearded vagrant.

"Hallo Boss! Hallo Mr. Swinburne!" he hooted.

His strange voice came from the helmet-shaped apparatus, recently created and added to the brass man by Brunel. Spencer spoke through it clearly but with a piping effect that sounded similar to the woodwind section of a band.

Burton returned the greeting: "Hallo. How are you, Herbert?"

"I reckons I've a touch of the old arthritis in me left knee," the philosopher said. "But can't complain."

"A screw loose, more like!" Swinburne suggested.

"P'raps. I tells you, though; it's a strange thing to be mechanical. I fear me springs may snap or cogs grind to a halt at any bloomin' moment. Speaking o' which, I have good news—I'll be comin' to Africa, after all."

"How so?" Burton asked, as they crossed the courtyard. "Conditions will hardly be conducive to your functioning."

"Mr. Brunel's scientists have dreamed up a new material what they makes usin' a chemical process. They calls it polymethylene. It's brown, very flexible, but waxy in texture. It's also waterproof, an' can't be penetrated by dust. They've used it to tailor a number of one-piece suits for me, what'll entirely protect me from the climate."

"You're certain that you'll be shielded and that the material will endure? Remember, there are extremes of heat and cold, as well as mud and dust," Burton cautioned. "During my previous expedition the clothes literally rotted off my back."

They arrived at the tall doors of the main building. Spencer reached out and took hold of one of the handles. "The material will no doubt deteriorate over time, Boss," he said. "But they've supplied me with fifteen of the bloomin' outfits, so I daresay they'll last. Besides—" He gestured at the fog that surrounded them, "—if I can survive this funk, I can survive anythin'!"

"Then I'm delighted," Burton replied. "You were pivotal in our securing of the South American diamond, and your presence might be of crucial importance when—or, rather, *if*—we reach the African stone. Welcome to the team, Herbert!"

"Marvellous!" Swinburne added.

The clockwork man pulled the door far enough open for them to pass through.

"Enter, please, gents."

The two men stepped into the Technologists' headquarters and were almost blinded by the bright lights within.

Isambard Kingdom Brunel had built Battersea Power Station in 1837. At the time, he'd been full of strange ideas inspired by his acquaintance Henry Beresford, and had designed the station to generate something he referred to as "geothermal energy." The copper rods that stood in each corner of the edifice rose high above it like four tall chimneys, but they extended much farther in the opposite direction, plunging deep into the crust of the Earth. Brunel, just 31 years old in '37, and still rather prone to exaggeration, had announced that these rods would produce enough energy to provide the whole of London with electricity, which could then be adapted to provide lighting and heat. Unfortunately, since its construction, the only thing Battersea Power Station had ever managed to illuminate was itself, although it was rumoured that this might soon change, for Brunel was thought to have discovered a means to significantly increase the output of the copper rods.

Shielding their eyes, Burton and Swinburne looked into the station and observed a vast workshop. A number of globes hung from the high ceiling. Lightning bolts had somehow been trapped inside them, and they bathed the floor beneath in an incandescent glare, which reflected off the surfaces of megalithic machines—contrivances whose functions were baffling in the extreme. Electricity fizzed, crackled and buzzed across their surfaces, and shafts of it whipped and snapped across the open spaces, filling the place with the sharp tang of ozone.

Amongst all this, over to their right, there stood a bulky vehicle. Around twelve feet high and thirty-six in length, it was tubular in shape—the front half a cabin, the back half a powerful engine—and it was mounted on a large number of short jointed legs. Rows of legs also projected from its top and sides. At its rear, steam funnels stuck horizontally outward, while its front was dominated by a huge drill, which tapered from the outer edges of the vehicle to a point, the tip of which stood some eighteen feet in advance of the main body.

Spencer, noticing them looking at it, explained: "That's a Worm; one of the machines what they're usin' to dig the London Underground tunnels. They reckons underground trains will make it easier for people to move around the city, now that the streets are so congested with traffic. But you won't find me gettin' into one o' them trains. I'd be afraid o' suffocatin'!"

"You can't suffocate, Herbert," Swinburne objected.

"Aye, so you says!"

Another contrivance caught their eye. Surrounded by a group of technicians and engineers, it was a large barrel-shaped affair, on tripod legs, and with a myriad of mechanical arms, each ending in pliers or a blowtorch or a saw or some other tool. As Burton, Swinburne and Spencer entered, it swung towards them, lurched away from the Technologists, and stamped over.

"Greetings, gentlemen," it said, and its voice was identical to Herbert Spencer's, except pitched at a low baritone.

"Hello, Isambard," Burton answered, for, indeed, this hulking mechanism was the famous engineer—or, more accurately, it was the life maintaining apparatus that had encased him since 1859, earning him the nickname *the Steam Man*. The king's agent continued: "The crew of the *Orpheus* is standing ready to take delivery of the vehicles and further supplies. Is everything prepared?"

"Yes, Sir Richard. My people will tarry—harry—excuse me, *carry*—everything aboard."

"I say, Izzy!" Swinburne piped up, with a mischievous twinkle in his green eyes. "Has your new speech rendering device broken?"

"No," Brunel answered. "But it is not currently interacting sufficiently—effusively—expectantly—I mean, *efficiently*—with the calculating elephants—um—*elements*—of my cerebral impasse—er, *impulse*—calculators. Unanticipated variegations—vegetations—my apologies—*variations* are occurring in the calibration of the devices' sensory nodes."

"My hat!" Swinburne exclaimed. "The problem is obviously chronic! I didn't understand a single word you just said! It was absolute gibberish!"

"Algy," Burton muttered. "Behave yourself!"

"It's all right, Sir Pilchard—er, Sir Richard," Brunel interjected. "Mr. Spinbroom has not yet forgiven me for the way I treated him during the String Filled Sack affair. I mean the Spring Heeled Jack despair—um—*affair*. Kleep."

"Kleep?" Swinburne asked, trying to stifle a giggle.

"Random noise," Brunel replied. "A recurring poodle. I mean, problem."

The poet clutched his sides, bent over, and let loose a peal of shrill laughter.

Burton sighed and rolled his eyes.

"Mr. Brunel's speakin' apparatus is the same as me own," Herbert Spencer put in, raising a brass finger to touch the rounded arrangement of pipes on his head. "But, as you know, me intellect is knockin' around inside the structure o' black diamonds, whereas his ain't, and the instrument responds better to impulses from inorganic matter than from organic."

"Ah ha!" Swinburne cried out, wiping tears from his eyes. "So you still have fleshly form inside that big tank of yours, do you Izzy?"

"That's quite enough," Burton interrupted, pushing his diminutive assistant aside. He steered the conversation back to the business at hand: "Are we on schedule, Isambard?"

"Yes. We have to declare—compare—*repair* the ventilation and leaping—um, *heating*—system, but the League of Chimney Sweeps has guaranteed periphery—I mean, *delivery*—of a new section of pipe by six o'clock today, and the work itself will slake—*take*—but an hour or so."

Swinburne, who'd regained control of himself, asked: "Why can't you fabricate the pipe yourself?"

"Reg—parp—ulations," Brunel answered.

Burton explained: "The Beetle has recently secured the sole manufacturing and trading rights to any pipes through which his people must crawl to clean or service."

"That boy is a genius," Swinburne commented.

"Indeed," Burton agreed. "Very well, we'll leave you to it, Isambard. The ship's crew will help your people to load the supplies. The passengers will reconvene here tomorrow morning at nine."

"Would you like to suspect—*inspect*—the vehicles before you depart?"

"No time. We have a murder investigation under way. I have to go."

"Before you do, may I peek—*speak*—with you privately for a moment?"

"Certainly."

Burton followed Brunel and stood with him a short distance away. They conversed for a few minutes, then the Steam Man clanked off and rejoined the group of Technologists.

Burton returned.

"What was all that about?" Swinburne asked.

"He was telling me a few things about the babbage device that John Speke has fitted to his head. Let's go."

"Should I join you, Boss?" Spencer asked.

"No, Herbert. I'd like you to stay and check the inventory against the supplies loaded."

"Rightio."

Leaving the clockwork man, Burton and Swinburne walked out through the doors, crossed the courtyard, and joined Detective Inspectors Trounce and Honesty, Commander Krishnamurthy, Constable Bhatti, Isabella Mayson, Mrs. Angell and Fidget, and various other passengers, at the foot of the rotorship's boarding ramp. Crew members D'Aubigny, Bingham, and Butler were also there, having been granted a few hours shore leave.

The pea-souper swirled around them all, dusting their clothes and skin with pollutants, clogging their nostrils with soot.

"Are we all ready?" Burton asked his friends. "Then let us go and bid civilisation farewell, except for you, Mother Angell. I fully expect you to maintain its standards while we're gone."

The group walked out through the station gates and passed alongside the outer wall beside a patch of wasteland that stretched down to nearby railway lines—a location which held bad memories for the king's agent and his assistant, for two years ago they'd been pursued across it by wolf-men and had narrowly avoided being hit by a locomotive.

They followed a path down to Kirtling Street, which took them the short distance to Battersea Park Road. Here they waved down conveyances. Monckton Milnes's guests gradually disappeared, as they each caught cabs home. Mrs. Angell and Fidget climbed into a hansom, bound for 14 Montagu Place; Isabella Mayson took another, for Orange Street; and a growler stopped for Detective Inspector Honesty, Commander Krishnamurthy, and Constable Bhatti, ready to take them each in turn to their respective homes.

A fourth vehicle—a steam-horse-drawn growler—was hailed by Burton for himself, Swinburne, and Trounce.

"Scotland Yard, driver!" the latter ordered.

"Not to Otto Steinrück's house?" Burton asked, as he climbed into the carriage and settled himself on the seat.

"It's out in Ilford," came the reply. "Too far by cab, so I thought we'd each borrow one of the Yard's rotorchairs."

The growler swung out on to Nine Elms Lane and chugged along next to the Thames. Its passengers took out their handkerchiefs and held them over their noses. The stench from the river was so intense it made their eyes water.

Burton looked out of the window. Somewhere along this road there was a courtyard in which a young girl named Sarah Lovitt had been assaulted by Spring Heeled Jack back in 1839—just one of many attacks Edward Oxford had committed while searching for his ancestor. That was twenty-four years ago, and in that short time Oxford's influence had totally transformed the British Empire. That one man could affect such a change so quickly seemed utterly incredible to Burton but it wasn't without precedent; after all, history was replete with individuals who'd done the same—the Caesars, Ghengis Khans, and Napoleons. Oxford had caused the death of Queen Victoria. After that, his influence had been subtler; he'd simply made unguarded comments about the future to Henry Beresford. The Marquess had passed that information on to Isambard Kingdom Brunel, whose remarkable creative talents had been set alight by the hints and suggestions, leading to the creation of the political and cultural juggernaut that was the Technologist caste.

While Brunel's Engineers and Eugenicists succumbed to their inventive zeal, Oxford's presence in the form of Spring Heeled Jack had also inspired an opposing force: the Libertines, who sought to change social policies and create a new species of liberated man.

All of these elements had given rise to a condition of rapidly growing chaos, as scientific developments and social experimentation accelerated without check. For Charles

Darwin, the man they called "God's Executioner," who'd fallen under the sway of his cousin, the Eugenicist Francis Galton, the possibilities had been so overwhelming they'd pushed him beyond the bounds of sanity.

How many others? Burton thought. *How many have become something they should never have been?*

The growler turned left onto Vauxhall Bridge and joined the queue of vehicles waiting to pay the toll to cross.

"The devil take it!" Trounce grumbled. "For how long are we to sit here breathing in this funk?"

"I can barely see a thing," Swinburne said, leaning out and peering ahead. "There's no telling how far from the toll booths we are. Surely, Pouncer, you don't expect us to fly rotorchairs in this?"

"Oy!" the police officer objected. "Don't call me Pouncer! But you're right, of course. After all that fresh Yorkshire air, I forgot how damned impenetrable these London particulars can be."

Burton made a suggestion: "It's only a couple of miles to the Yard. Why don't we leg it there and borrow penny farthings instead?"

Trounce agreed, and moments later they were crossing the bridge on foot, cursing the stink, cursing the traffic, and cursing the fog.

"I tell you, Captain, I'll be delighted to leave this bloody cesspool of a city behind for a few months," Trounce declared.

S

It was six o'clock by the time they reached Ilford, and, though the fog was thinner there, the daylight was fading and the ill-lit town was wreathed in gloom.

They steered their velocipedes along the Cranbrook Road, then turned left into Grenfell Place.

"We're looking for number sixteen," Trounce said.

A minute later, they found it; an isolated house set back from the road and concealed by a gnarled and unnaturally twisted oak tree.

"By Jove!" Trounce exclaimed. "Why would anyone want this monstrosity in their front garden?"

They opened the gate, passed through, ducked under the branches, and walked along the path to the front door. No lights were showing in the house.

Trounce exercised the door knocker with his usual vigour but was met with nothing but silence.

"This is a murder investigation," he said, taking two steps back. "So I have no qualms about breaking in. Stand aside, would you, while I put my shoulder to it."

Burton held up a hand. "No need for that, old chap." He produced a picklock from his coat pocket and went to work on the keyhole. Moments later, there was a click.

"Open sesame!" Swinburne commanded, with an effusive wave of his arms.

"Go back to the gate and stand guard, would you, Algy?" Burton asked. "We'll need to light lamps, and if our strangler returns while we're here and sees the windows blazing, he'll do a runner before we've a chance to nab him. Yell if you see anyone acting in a suspicious manner."

The poet nodded and moved away while Burton and Trounce entered the house. The Scotland Yard man took out a box of lucifers, struck one, and put it to a wall lamp in the hallway. It illuminated three doors and a flight of stairs.

The first door opened onto a small lounge. Trounce got another lamp going and the two men saw five chairs positioned around a coffee table on which ashtrays and empty glasses stood.

"It looks like there was a meeting of some sort," Burton observed. He checked a bureau and found it empty, then the cupboards of an armoire and found the same.

The second door led to a dining room in which they found nothing of interest, and the third door into a kitchen. Its pantry was empty.

"I fear our quarry is long gone," Trounce muttered.

The bedrooms upstairs added weight to his suspicion, for the wardrobes were bare and there were no personal possessions to be found anywhere.

"Let's take another look at the lounge," Burton suggested.

They returned to that room and began a thorough search of it. The king's agent picked through the ashtrays, lifting cigar butts to his nose.

"Revealing," he murmured. "Four different Germanic brands and one English."

"Look at this, Captain."

Burton moved over to where his friend was squatting by the fireplace.

Trounce pointed at a reddish brown patch at the back of the hearth. "Is that dried blood?"

Burton crouched and examined the stain. "Yes, I think so. Well spotted. But how the blazes did blood get there?" He thought for a moment, then said: "Would you call Algy in, please?"

Trounce grunted, straightened, and left the room. While he was gone, Burton pulled the ashes and half burned coals out of the fireplace and pushed them to one side, careless of the mess he made on the hearthrug. He lifted out the grate and set that aside, too.

"There was a hansom outside," Swinburne said as he entered the room with Trounce behind him. "It trotted past in the normal manner. I don't think it was anything untoward. What's happening here?"

"You're the chimney expert," Burton said. "Have a look at this."

Swinburne cast his eyes over the fireplace. "It was recently cleaned," he noted.

"It was?"

"Yes. Look how thin the layer of soot is. Is that a bloodstain?"

"We think so."

"Give me your lantern, Richard."

Burton reached into his pocket and pulled out his clockwork lantern. He shook it open and wound it, handing it over to his assistant.

Swinburne removed his topper and laid it on the coffee table, then ducked down, stepped into the fireplace, and raised the light into the chimney.

"I'm going up," he said, and, bracing his legs against either side of the opening, he began to climb.

"Be careful, lad!" Trounce cautioned.

"Don't worry," Burton said. "Vincent Sneed trained him well."

"Don't mention that cad!" came Swinburne's hollow voice. "I say! There's a sort of niche up here and a little stash of food. There are more bloodstains, too. I'm going to go all the way up to the roof."

Little showers of soot fell into the hearth, but less than Burton would have expected; evidently the poet was correct, and the chimney was fairly clean.

Five minutes passed, then scrapes and trickles of black dust and an occasional grunt indicated that Swinburne was on his way back down. His feet appeared, then the poet in his entirety; his clothes and skin blackened, his green eyes sparkling from his sooty face.

"My guess is that a chimney sweep was hired to clean the chimney then came back later to steal food from the house," he said. "It's not uncommon. Most of the boys are half-starved and those that lodge with Master Sweeps are often so brutalised that they occasionally seek refuge for a night in suitable chimneys."

"Suitable chimneys?" Trounce asked. "What constitutes a suitable chimney?"

Swinburne turned off the lantern and handed it back to Burton. "One like this, with a niche in it and a shelf wide enough for the nipper to sleep on."

"And the blood?" Burton asked.

"They shot him."

"What?"

"Halfway up, there's a furrow in the brickwork with a bullet lodged at the end of it. That shot obviously missed. Another one didn't. There's blood smeared all the way to the top and a lot of it on the roof tiles. The lad got away by the looks of it, but I doubt he survived for long, the poor little blighter."

The three men were silent for a moment, then Swinburne said quietly: "And now I hate that Prussian swine even more."

They made a final search of the house in case they'd missed anything then turned off the lights, stepped out, and closed the front door behind them.

"I'll report to the Yard and will have a couple of constables sent over to keep watch on the place," Trounce said as they proceeded down the path.

"We have no choice but to leave the investigation in the hands of your colleagues now," Burton said. "Which means even if they catch the wretch, we won't hear about it for some considerable time. There is, however, one last thing I can do."

"What?"

The king's agent pulled open the gate and they crossed to where their velocipedes were parked.

"I can visit the Beetle. He may know something about the injured sweep."

They started the penny farthings' engines, mounted, and set off. As they turned back into Cranbrook Road and began to chug down the hill, Burton called: "We'll split up when we get to Mile End. I'll head off to Limehouse. Algy, you go home, get packed, and have a good night's sleep. Stay off the alcohol. Trounce, do what you have to do at the Yard then get yourself home to your wife. We'll reconvene at the *Orpheus* tomorrow morning."

This arrangement was followed, and just under an hour later, Burton was striding through the stifling fog along the banks of Limehouse Cut canal. The factories that lined it had finished production for the day, and the thousands of workers who toiled within them had dispersed, returning to their lodgings in the loathsome slum that was London's East End—or "the Cauldron" as it was more commonly known.

Burton had left his velocipede in the charge of a constable back on the High Road. It wouldn't do to bring such an expensive vehicle into this district. He'd left his top hat with the policeman, too. The men in this area were most often bare-headed or wore flat caps. Best not to stand out.

The king's agent did, however, carry his sword cane—with its silver panther head handle—held in such a manner so as to be able to quickly unsheathe the blade should it become necessary.

He arrived at a towering factory that, unlike the others, stood derelict. Nearly every one of its windows was cracked or broken, and its doors were boarded up. He circled around it until he came to a narrow dock at the side of the canal. In a niche in the building's wall, he found iron rungs set into the brickwork. He climbed them.

The edifice was seven storeys high, and by the time Burton reached the roof, he was breathing heavily. Hauling himself over the parapet, he sat and rested a moment.

There were two skylights set into the flat roof with eight chimneys rising around them. The third one from the eastern edge had rungs set into its side, and, after the king's agent had got his breath back, he began to ascend it. Halfway up, he stopped to rest again, then pressed on until he came to the top of the structure. He swung himself onto the lip of the chimney and sat with one leg to either side of it. He'd picked up a number of stones on his way here, and now he retrieved three of them from his pocket and dropped them one by one into the flue. This signal would summon the Beetle.

Burton had never actually seen the strange leader of the League of Chimney Sweeps. All he knew about him was that he was a boy, he lived in this chimney, and he had a voracious appetite for books. The Beetle had been of significant help during the strange affair of Spring Heeled Jack, when he'd arranged for Swinburne to pose as a sweep—a move that led directly to the exposure of Darwin and his cronies—and since then Burton had visited regularly, always bringing with him a supply of literature and poetry. The Beetle was especially desirous of anything written by Swinburne, whose talent he practically worshipped.

Burton wrapped his scarf around the lower half of his face and waited.

From this height there was usually a stunning view across London but today the king's agent could barely see his own hand in front of his face. The fog was dense and cold, and the "blacks" were falling—coal dust that coalesced with ice at a higher altitude and drifted down like dark snow.

He frowned. The Beetle should have responded by now.

"Hi!" he called into the flue. "Are you there, lad? It's Burton!"

There was no answer. He dropped three more stones into the darkness and sat patiently. The minutes ticked by and there was no sound of movement, no whispery voice from the shadows.

Burton called again, waited a little longer, then gave up.

Where was the Beetle?

§

Half an hour later, after retrieving his vehicle and headwear, Burton continued homeward. For a few minutes it seemed to him that a hansom was following, but when he reached the main thoroughfares, he became so ensnarled in traffic that he lost sight of it.

Central London had ground to a complete halt. The streets were jammed solid with a bizarre mishmash of technologies. There were horses pulling carts and carriages; prodigious drays harnessed to huge pantechnicons; steam-horse-drawn hansoms and growlers; velocipedes; and adapted insects, such as harvestmen and Folks' Wagon Beetles, silverfish racers and omnipedes. Burton even saw a farmer trying to drive a herd of goats through the streets to Covent Garden Market.

It seemed to the king's agent that the past, present and future had all been compressed into the capital's streets, as if the structure of time itself was deteriorating.

None of the vehicles or pedestrians were making any progress, being more engaged in battling one another than in moving forward. The horses were whinnying and shying away from the insects, the insects were getting tangled up in each other's legs and mounting the pavements in an attempt to pass one other, and among them all, cloaked in fog and steam, crowds of people were shouting and cursing and shaking their fists in fury.

Slowly, with many a diversion down dark and narrow side streets and alleyways, Burton made his way out of Cheapside, past the Bank of England, and along the Holborn road. Here, at the junction with Red Lion Street, he collided with another velocipede—whose driver had lost control after his vehicle's boiler burst and knocked the gyroscope out of kilter—and was almost forced into an enormously deep and wide hole in the road. Clutching at the barrier around the pit so as not to topple from his penny farthing, Burton cursed vehemently, then reached down and turned off his engine. The other man, who'd fallen onto the cobbles, picked himself up and kicked his machine. "Stupid bloody thing!" he cried out, then looked up at the king's agent. "Bless me, sir, you almost came a cropper! Pray forgive me!"

"It wasn't your fault," Burton said, dismounting. "Are you hurt?"

"I've ripped my trouser knee and knocked my elbow but nothing more life-threatening than that. What's this whacking great crater all about?"

"They're building a station here for the new London Underground railway system. The Technologists say it'll make moving around the city a lot easier."

"Well it couldn't be any more difficult," the man answered. "Strike a light! What was that?"

Something had whined past his ear and knocked off Burton's top hat.

"Get down!" the king's agent snapped, pushing the other to the ground.

"Hey up! What's your game?"

"Someone's shooting!"

"I beg your pardon? Did you say shooting?"

The explorer scanned the milling crowd, then reached for his hat and snatched it up from the road. There was a hole in its front, near the top edge. At the back, an exit hole was set a bit lower.

"The shot was fired from slightly above ground level," he murmured.

"Shot? Shot?" the man at his side stammered. "Why are we being shot at? I've never done anything! I'm just a bank clerk!"

"Not we—*me*."

"But why? Who are you?"

"Nobody. Pick up your boneshaker and get out of here."

"But—I—um—should I call for a policeman?"

"Just go!"

The man scuttled sideways on his hands and knees, pushed his penny farthing upright, and wheeled it away while crouching behind it, as if it might shelter him from further bullets. As he disappeared into the noisy throng, Burton also moved, sliding along the edge of the barrier with his eyes flicking left and right, trying to pierce the fog.

"Confound it!" he hissed. He had no idea where the shootist might be. In one of the nearby carriages, perhaps? On a velocipede? Not in a building, that much was certain, for the windows along this side of the street were nothing but faint rectangular smudges of light—no one could possibly have identified him through the intervening murk.

He decided to follow Falstaff's dictum that "discretion is the better part of valour," and, bending low, he retrieved his cane, abandoned his conveyance, and shouldered his way into the crowd. He ducked between the legs of a harvestman, squeezed past a brewery wagon, and hurried away as fast as the many obstructions would allow. It was a shame to leave the penny farthing behind but he couldn't risk climbing up onto its saddle again—that would make him far too visible.

It was past eleven o'clock by the time he finally arrived at 14 Montagu Place. As he stepped in, Mrs. Angell greeted him.

"Hallo!" he said, slipping his cane into an elephant's foot holder by the door. "Good show! You got home! What a state the streets are in!"

"It's pandemonium, Sir Richard," she agreed. "How are the delivery boys to do their job? We'll starve!"

"I'm halfway there already," he said, shrugging out of his coat and hanging it on the stand. "I haven't eaten since I don't know when!"

"Then you'll be pleased to hear that a bacon and egg pie has been waiting for you these three hours past. That should fill the hole in your stomach. I don't know what to do about the hole that seems to have found its way into your hat, though."

Burton took off his topper and eyed it ruefully. "Oh well, I don't suppose I'll need it where I'm going. Perhaps you'd consign it to the dustbin for me?"

"Most certainly not!" the old woman objected. "A fine headpiece like that should be repaired, not abandoned. What happened to it?"

"Someone took a pot-shot at me."

Mrs. Angell raised her hands to her face. "Oh my goodness! With a gun? Are you hurt?"

Burton placed the hat on the stand, then squatted to untie his boot laces.

"Not at all. The would-be assassin's aim was off."

He eased his feet out and stood in his stockinged feet.

"I missed a night's sleep and I'm weary to the bone," he said. "I'll change into something more comfortable and join you in the kitchen for supper, if you don't mind."

Mrs. Angell looked surprised. "Eat? In the kitchen? With me?"

Burton took his housekeeper by the shoulders and smiled fondly down at her. "My dear, dear woman," he said. "I shan't see you again for such a long time. How will I ever do without you? You've fed me and cleaned up after me; you've kept me on the straight and narrow when I would have strayed; you've put up with intruders and all manner of inconveniences; you didn't even complain when the Tichborne Claimant practically demolished the house. You are one of the world's wonders, and I'd be honoured to dine with you tonight."

With glistening eyes, Mrs. Angell said: "Then be my guest, Sir Richard. There is, however, a condition."

"A condition? What?"

"I shall boil plenty of water while we eat and, when we are finished, you'll carry it upstairs and take a bath. You reek of the Thames, sir."

§

Burton relaxed in a tin bathtub in front of the fireplace in his study. He'd shaved, clipped his drooping moustache, and scrubbed the soot and toxins from his skin.

He took a final puff at the stub of a pungent cheroot, cast it into the hearth, reached down to the floor and lifted a glass of brandy to his lips, drained it, then set it back down.

"Someone," he said to the room, "doesn't want me to go to Africa, that much is plain."

"Fuddle-witted ninny," murmured Pox, his messenger parakeet. The colourful bird was sleeping on a perch near a bookcase. Like all of her kind, she delivered insults even while unconscious.

Burton leaned back, rested his head on the lip of the tub, and turned it so that he might gaze into the flickering flames of the fire.

His eyelids felt heavy.

He closed them.

His breathing slowed and deepened.

His thoughts meandered.

In his mind's eye, faces formed and faded: Lieutenant William Stroyan, Sir Roderick Murchison, Ebenezer Smike, Thomas Honesty, Edwin Brundleweed. They shifted and blended. They congealed into a single countenance, gaunt and lined, with a blade-like nose, tight lips and insane, pain-filled eyes.

Spring Heeled Jack.

Gradually, the features grew smoother. The eyes became calmer. A younger man emerged from the terrible face.

"Oxford," Burton muttered in his sleep. "His name is Edward Oxford."

His name is Edward Oxford.

He is twenty-five years old and he's a genius—a physician, an engineer, a historian, and a philosopher.

He sits at a desk constructed from glass but, rather than being clear, it is somehow filled with writing and diagrams and pictures that move and wink and come and go. The surface of the desk is flat and thin, yet the information dancing within it—and Burton instinctively knows that it *is* information—appears to be three-dimensional. It's disconcerting, as if something impossibly big has been stored in something very small—like a *djan* in a lamp—but this doesn't appear to bother Oxford. In fact, the young man has some sort of control over the material, for sometimes he touches a finger to the glass or he murmurs something and the writing and outlines and images respond by folding or flipping or metamorphosing.

A large black diamond has been placed on the desk.

Burton recognises it as the South American Eye of Nāga, which he'd discovered last year beneath the Tichborne family's estate. The dream disagrees with him. The stone was not found in 1862, it says. It was found in 2068.

Original history!

Oxford is fascinated by it. The structure of the stone is unique.

"Even more sensitive than a CellComp," he whispers to himself. "More efficient than a ClusterComp. More capacity than GenMem."

What is he talking about? Burton wonders.

The dream twists away and repositions itself inside a day a few weeks later.

The diamond is filled with the remnant intelligences of a prehistoric race. They have inveigled their way into Oxford's mind.

He starts to think about time.

He becomes obsessed.

He becomes paranoid.

It happens that he shares his name with a distant ancestor who, in a fit of insanity, had attempted to assassinate Queen Victoria. A voice, from somewhere behind his conscious mind, insists: "That man besmirched your family's reputation. Change it. Correct it."

Why does this obscure fact suddenly matter? Why should he care about a forgotten incident that occurred near three hundred and fifty years ago?

It matters.

He cares.

He can think about little else.

The reptilian intelligence plants another seed.

Slowly, in Oxford's mind, a theory concerning the nature of time blossoms like a pervasively scented exotic flower. Its roots dig deeper. Its lianas entangle him. It consumes him.

He works tirelessly.

The dream convulses and fifteen years have passed.

Oxford has cut shards from the diamond and connected them to a chain of DNA-StringComps and BioProcs. They form the heart of what he calls a Nimtz Generator. It is a flat circular device. It will enable him to move through time.

To power it, he's invented the fish scale battery, and has fashioned thousands of these tiny solar energy collectors into a one-piece tight-fitting suit. He's also embedded an AugCom into a round black helmet. It will act as an interface between his brain and the generator. It will also protect him from the deep psychological shock that he somehow knows will occur to anyone who steps too far out of their native time period.

The boots of the costume are fitted with two-foot-high spring-loaded stilts. They appear wildly eccentric but they offer a simple solution to a complex problem, for when the bubble of energy generated by the Nimtz forms around the suit, it must touch nothing but air.

Oxford will literally jump through time.

It is the evening of February 15th, 2202. Nine o'clock. A Monday. His fortieth birthday.

Oxford dresses in attire suitable for the 1840s. He pulls his time suit on over the top of it and clips on his stilts. He attaches the Nimtz Generator to his chest and puts the helmet on his head. He picks up a top hat and strides out of his workshop and into the long garden beyond.

His wife comes out of the house, wiping her hands on a tea towel.

"You're going now?" she asks. "Supper is almost ready!"

"I am," he replies. "But don't worry. Even if I'm gone for years, I'll be back in five minutes."

"You won't return an old man, I hope!" she grumbles, and runs a hand over her distended belly. "This one will need an energetic young father."

He laughs. "Don't be silly. It won't take long."

Bending, he kisses her freckled nose.

He instructs the suit to take him to five-thirty on the afternoon of June 10th, 1840. Location: the upper corner of Green Park, London.

He looks at the sky.

"Am I really going to do this?" he asks himself.

"Do it!" a voice whispers in his head, and before he can consciously make a decision, he takes three long strides, jumps, hits the ground with knees bent, and leaps high into the air. A bubble forms around him and he vanishes with a small detonation, like a little clap of thunder.

§

Pop!

Sir Richard Francis Burton jerked awake and tepid water slopped over the edge of his bath.

He shivered, sat up, and looked around his study, trying to identify the source of the noise. His attention was drawn to a thin wisp of steam rising from a tubular contraption on one of his three desks. He reached for his *jubbah*—the long and loose outer garment he'd worn while on his pilgrimage to Mecca, which he now used as a night robe—then stood, stepped out of the bath, and wrapped the cloth around himself. He crossed to the desk. The glass and brass apparatus was his direct connection to the prime minister and the king. Burton retrieved a canister from it, snapped it open, and pulled out a sheet of paper. He read the words:

Be prepared to receive the prime minister at 2 a.m.

"Curse the man! That's all I need!"

Pox twitched a wing and chirped: "Stink fermenter!"

Burton looked at the clock on the mantelpiece. It was half past one.

Rapidly drying himself, he went into his dressing room and put on loose white cotton trousers and a shirt, wrapped the *jubbah* over the top of them, and slid his feet into pointed Arabian slippers. He wrapped a turban around his damp hair.

By two o'clock, the bathtub had been removed, another Manila cheroot had been smoked, and Burton had sat and pondered his strange dream. There was much about it that he didn't understand—the curious glass desk, the sparsely furnished room in which it stood, some of the words that Edward Oxford had uttered—yet it seemed vividly real.

Did I just glimpse a distant future? The one that was meant to be before Oxford interfered?

Hearing the coughing of steam engines and rumble of wheels in the street outside, he stepped to the window and looked out in time to see Lord Palmerston's armoured, six-wheeled mobile castle draw up.

He went downstairs and opened the front door.

Palmerston was standing on the step, with his odd-job men, Gregory Hare and Damien Burke, on either side of him.

"Do you consider that suitable attire, Captain Burton?" the prime minister asked.

"For two o'clock in the morning? Yes, sir," Burton replied, moving aside to let the men enter. "Do you consider it a suitable hour for visiting?"

"One cannot run an empire and maintain respectable hours, sir."

"Up to the study, if you please."

Burton closed the door and followed them upstairs, noting that the prime minister's men were dressed, as ever, in outlandishly old-fashioned outfits.

"Last time I saw this room," Palmerston said as he entered the bookcase-lined chamber, "it was all but destroyed."

"You're referring to the occasion when we were attacked and you hid in my storeroom?" Burton responded.

"Now, now, Captain. Let us not get off on the wrong foot."

Palmerston placed his hat on one of the desks and took off his calfskin gloves. His fingernails were painted black. He didn't remove his tightly buttoned velvet frock coat but smoothed it down then sat in Burton's favourite saddlebag armchair and crossed his legs. He pulled a silver snuffbox from his pocket and said: "We must talk. I would have been here earlier but the streets were impassable."

Burke and Hare each sat at a desk. Burton took the armchair opposite Palmerston, who asked: "Your expedition is equipped and ready for departure?"

"It is."

"Good. Good. All running smoothly, then?"

"Yes. Unless you count two attempts on my life, one of which resulted in the death of my good friend Thomas Bendyshe."

Palmerston jerked forward. "What did you say?"

"A man named Peter Pimlico tried to poison me. He was hired by a Prussian named Otto Steinrück, who then killed him by strangulation to keep him quiet. And, earlier this evening, somebody sent a bullet my way."

Damien Burke, tall, hunchbacked, extremely bald, and sporting the variety of side-whiskers known as "Piccadilly Weepers," cleared his throat and said: "This Germanic individual, Captain Burton—did you find out anything about him?"

"Only that he's portly, wears a large moustache, has pointed claw-like fingernails, and chews Kautabak tobacco."

Burke glanced at Gregory Hare, who was short and muscular, with white hair and a broad, pugnacious face. "Ah ha," he said. "Do you agree, Mr. Hare?"

"I do, Mr. Burke," Hare answered. "Ah ha."

"You know something?" Burton asked.

"Yes," Burke said. "I consider it highly likely that Otto Steinrück is not Otto Steinrück. It is almost certainly an alias. The man fits the description of a notorious Prussian spy named Count Ferdinand Graf von Zeppelin. You'll remember that last year he helped Richard Spruce and his

Eugenicist colleagues to flee the country. A very dangerous man, Captain."

Burton nodded. "And one bent on preventing me from going to Africa, it would seem. I'm certain he's still working with Spruce, too."

"Why so?"

"The dead man had a foul-looking plant sprouting from the roof of his mouth."

"Hmm. That's interesting."

Burke took a notebook from his pocket and scribbled something in it with a pencil.

Palmerston opened his snuffbox, took a pinch of brown powder, sprinkled it onto the back of his right hand, and raised it to his nose. He snorted it and his eyes momentarily widened.

It occurred to Burton that the prime minister's face had been stretched so taut by his Eugenicist treatments that those eyes appeared almost oriental.

"A complex situation," Palmerston muttered. "There are great moves being made, Captain; moves that will reshape the world, and you are in the thick of it."

"How so?"

"Tomorrow afternoon, I shall make an announcement to parliament. You'll be out of the country by then, so I came to give you the news personally. Excuse me—"

Palmerston turned his head to one side and let loose a prodigious sneeze. When he looked back, there were hundreds of deep wrinkles around his eyes and nose. Over the next few minutes, they slowly flattened out and disappeared.

"What news?" Burton asked.

"Lincoln has surrendered. America is ours."

Burton's jaw dropped. He fell back into his seat, speechless.

"Some time ago," Palmerston continued, "I told you that if this should occur I would demand of the confederates the abolition of slavery as repayment for our role in their victory. I fully intend to do that. But not just yet."

Finally, Burton found his voice, and asked: "Why not?"

"Because of *blut und eisen*."

"Blood and iron?"

"Three months ago, while you were clearing up the Tichborne business and our turncoat Eugenicists were defecting to Prussia, Chancellor Bismarck made a speech in which he declared his intentions to increase military spending and unify the Germanic territories. He said, and, believe me, I can quote this from memory, for it is seared into my mind: 'The position of Prussia in Germany will not be determined by its liberalism but by its power. Prussia must concentrate its strength and hold it for the favourable moment, which has already come and gone several times. Since the treaties of Vienna, our frontiers have been ill-designed for a healthy body politic. Not through speeches and majority decisions will the great questions of the day be decided—that was the great mistake of 1848 and 1849—but by blood and iron.'"

Burton said: "I read accounts of the speech in the newspapers. Is he warmongering?"

Palmerston clenched his fists. "Indisputably. It is the first blatant move towards the world war Countess Sabina has predicted. There is no doubt that Bismarck is seeking to establish a Germanic empire to rival our own. Empires require resources, Captain Burton, and there is one vast untapped resource remaining in the world. I refer to Africa."

"So you suspect Bismarck will try to establish a foothold there?"

"I think he intends to carve it up and suck it dry."

"But what has this to do with America's slaves?"

"If a united Germany can count Africa among its territories, and if war breaks out, it will find itself with an almost limitless source of expendable manpower."

"Expendable?"

"I believe the term is 'cannon fodder.'"

The king's agent felt ice in his veins. "You surely aren't suggesting—" he began.

Palmerston interrupted him. "If we are faced with such a situation, we will require our own disposable units."

"You mean America's slave population?"

"Yes. A little over four million individuals, though I'm including women in that number."

Burton's jaw flexed spasmodically. "Hellfire, man! You're talking about human beings! Families! You're not only suggesting support for state sanctioned slavery—you're talking about bloody genocide!"

"I mean to ensure the survival of the British Empire, whatever it takes."

"No!" Burton shouted. "No! No! No!" He slapped his hand down on the leather arm of his chair. "I won't stand for it! It's despicable!"

"You'll do whatever you're damned well ordered to do, Captain Burton," Palmerston said, softly. "And what you are ordered to do is help me to ensure that no such circumstance ever arises."

"Wha—what?"

"Your primary mission hasn't changed; you are to retrieve the Eye of Nāga, so that we might employ it to infiltrate and coerce the minds of our opponents. However, there is now a secondary purpose to your expedition. You are to employ your military and geographical experience to determine which are the most strategically advantageous African territories and how we might best secure them. I intend to claim that continent before Bismarck makes his move, and I'm relying on you to advise me how to do it."

Burton's heart hammered in his chest. His mind raced.

He looked into Lord Palmerston's impenetrable eyes.

"And if I do, sir, and if we make Africa a part of the British Empire, then what of the inhabitants? What of the Africans?"

The prime minister—returning Burton's gaze steadily and without blinking—replied: "They will be accorded the rights granted to all British subjects."

There was a moment of silence, broken only by Gregory Hare clearing his throat slightly, then Burton said: "You refer to the same rights enjoyed by those undernourished Britishers who toil in our factories and inhabit our slums?

The same given to those who beg on our street corners and doorsteps? The same extended to servant girls abused and impregnated by their employers then thrown onto the streets where their only means of survival is prostitution? Is this the marvellous civilisation that you, the great imperialist, have to offer Africa?"

Palmerston shot to his feet and yelled: "Shut the hell up, Burton! Am I to endure your insolence every time we meet? I'll not tolerate it! You have your orders!" He stamped to the door, snapping his fingers at Burke and Hare. They rose and followed. He ushered them out first, then, with his hand on the doorknob, turned to face the explorer.

"Do your bloody job, Captain!" he snarled.

The prime minister stepped out of the room and slammed the door shut behind him.

"Illiterate baboon," Pox squawked.

S

"In the maelstrom of making history," Bertie Wells said, "very little of it is accurately recorded. When the time finally comes for an account of the events that have passed, human nature takes over."

He and Burton were in an ambulance sharing that rarity of rarities, a scrounged cigar. The oxen-drawn vehicle was part of a convoy; a seemingly never-ending line of soldiers and vehicles moving up from the south toward the port of Tanga, some hundred miles north of Dar es Salaam.

It was early morning but already ferociously hot. The troops were dripping sweat. They were exhausted, ill, and miserable. Occasional bursts of chanting broke out—the usual sad native dirges—but quickly tailed off, overwhelmed by the rhythmic *tromp tromp tromp* of boots. At one point a company of Britishers broke into song, their mock cheerfulness shot through with resentful hatred. The tune was "*What a Friend We Have in Jesus*," but the lyrics were rather more colourful than those of the original hymn:

When this lousy war is over, no more soldiering for me,
When I get my civvy clothes on, oh how happy I shall be.
No more church parades on Sunday, no more begging for a pass.
You can tell the sergeant-major to stick his passes up his arse.

The sergeant-major in question harangued the men for a three-mile stretch after that.

Burton was sitting on the ambulance's tailgate, leaning against the side of the vehicle's open back. He couldn't stop scratching.

"Human nature?" he said. "What do you mean?"

Wells, perched on a bench just behind him, responded: "I'm of the opinion that we possess an in-built craving for narrative structure. We want everything to have a beginning, a middle, and an end. That way, we can make better sense of it." He looked down at Burton. "How many days did that uniform last before it got infested?"

"Four. The lice are eating me alive."

"Chin up, old man. It could be worse. Fever, trench foot, dysentery, having your bloody legs blown off—all the perils of wartime Africa."

"Bismillah! What are you people doing? You've created Hell from an Eden!"

"Is my generation responsible, Richard, or is yours? I've heard people say over and over that we are all products of the past. They'd lay the blame for this war squarely at their fathers' feet. In other words, welcome to the world you created."

"Absolutely not! None of my contemporaries intended for this *jahannam*!"

"As you say. Besides, I disagree with the philosophy of what you might term *sequentialism*. The problem, as I see it, is that we don't truly understand the nature of the past. We mythologise it. We create fictions about actions done to justify what we undertake in the present. We adjust the cause to better suit the effect. The truth is that the present is, and will always be, utter chaos. There is no story and no plan. We are victims of *zeitgeist*. I apologise for using a German word, but it's singularly appropriate. Are you familiar with it?"

"Yes. It translates as *ghost tide*, or, perhaps, *spirit of the age*, and refers to the ambience or socio-political climate of any given period."

"Exactly so, and in my view it's a phenomenon entirely independent of history. History doesn't create the zeitgeist, we create the history to try to explain the zeitgeist. We impose a sequential narrative to endow events with something that resembles meaning."

The ambulance jerked as its wheels bounced through a pothole. Burton's head banged against the vehicle's wooden side.

"Ouch!"

"How's your arm?" Wells asked.

"Aching. How's your leg?"

"Broken. How's your head?"

"Shut up."

"Have a cigar."

The war correspondent passed what remained of the "Hoffman" to the explorer, who glanced at its much-reduced length and muttered: "Your lungs are healthy, at least." He raised it to his lips and drew in the sweet smoke, savouring it while observing the column of men and vehicles that snaked back over the rolling landscape.

The supply wagons and ambulances were mostly towed by steam-horses or oxen. There were a few mangy looking non-mechanical horses in evidence, too, including mega-drays pulling huge artillery pieces. Harvestmen stalked along beside the troops, and Scorpion Tanks thumped through the dust with their tails curled over their cabins, the cannons at their ends slowly swinging back and forth.

"Hey! Private!" Burton called to a nearby Britisher. "Where are we?"

"In it up to our bloody eyeballs, chum!"

"Ha! And geographically?"

"I ain't got a bleedin' clue. Ask Kitchener!"

"We're almost there, sir," an African voice answered. "Tanga is a mile or so ahead."

"Much obliged!" Burton said. He turned Wells. "Did you hear that? We must be near your village. Shall we hop out here?"

"Hopping is my only option, unfortunately."

Burton slid from the tailgate into the ambulance, then moved to its front and banged his fist against the back of the driver's cabin. "Stop a moment would you?"

He returned to Wells and, as the vehicle halted, helped him down to the ground and handed him his crutches. The two men put on their helmets, moved to the side of the column, and walked slowly along beside it.

"So what's your point, Bertie?"

"My point?"

"About history."

"Oh. Just that we give too much credence to the idea that we can learn from the past. It's the present that teaches the lesson. The problem is that we're so caught up in doing it that we can never see the wood for the trees. I say! Are you all right?"

Burton had suddenly doubled over and was clutching the sides of his head.

"No!" he gasped. "Yes. I think—" He straightened and took a deep, shuddering breath. "Yes. Yes. I'm fine. I'm sorry. I just had a powerful recollection of—of—of a man constructed from brass."

"A statue?"

"No. A machine. But it was—it was—Herbert."

"What? Me?"

"No, sorry, not you Bertie. I mean, its—his—name is—was—is Herbert, too."

"A mechanical man named Herbert? Are you sure your malaria hasn't flared up again?"

Burton clicked his tongue. "My brain is so scrambled that the line between reality and fiction seems almost non-existent. I'm not sure what that particular memory signifies, if anything. Perhaps it'll make more sense later. Where's the village?"

Wells pointed to a vaguely defined path that disappeared into a dense jungle of thorny acacias. The trees were growing up a shallow slope, and Burton could just glimpse rooftops through the topmost leaves. "Along there," Wells said. "Kaltenberg is right on the edge of Tanga—practically an outlying district. It was built by the Germans in the European style, on slightly higher ground. The occupants fled into the town a few days ago. We'll get a good view of the action from up there."

"I gather the role of war correspondents is to climb hills and gaze down upon destruction?"

"Yes, that's about it."

They left the convoy and followed the dirt track. The boles of the trees crowded around them, blocking the convoy from sight. The sky flickered and flashed through the foliage just above their heads. Mosquitos whined past their ears.

"Who's Kitchener?" Burton asked.

"One of the military bigwigs. Or was. No one knows whether he's dead or alive. Damn this leg! And damn this heat. In fact, damn Africa and all that goes with it! I'm sorry, we'll have to slow down a little." Wells stopped, and, balancing himself on his crutches, struck a match and lit a cigarette. He took a pull at it then held it out to Burton, who said: "Thanks but I'll pass. My fondness for cheap cigars doesn't plummet to such depths. Besides, it would ruin the taste of my toffee."

"You have toffee?"

"I scrounged it from the ambulance driver. Four pieces. I'd offer you two but I fear they'd be wasted after that tobacco stick."

"You swine!"

Burton grinned.

"And don't do that with your ugly mug," Wells advised. "It makes you look monstrously Mephistophelian."

"You remind me of someone, Bertie."

"Who?"

"I don't recall."

They set off again, the war correspondent swinging himself along.

Burton said: "Remind me again why we're attacking Tanga."

"Firstly," Wells replied, "because we're trying to regain all the ports. Secondly, because we want to raid German supplies; and thirdly, and most importantly, because it's believed the commander of the *Schutztruppe*, Lieutenant Colonel Paul Emil von Lettow-Vorbeck, is holed up there, and we would dearly love to deprive him of his existence. The man is a veritable demon. He has a military mind to rival that of Napoleon Bonaparte!"

By the time they reached the first of the Kaltenberg cottages, both men were sweating profusely. "Do you remember snow?" Wells muttered as they moved out from beneath the acacias and into the village. "What I wouldn't give for a toboggan ride down a hill with a tumble at the bottom." He stopped, and said quietly: "Richard."

Burton followed his companion's gaze and saw, in a passageway between two cottages, the body of an Askari in British uniform. They approached and examined the corpse. A laceration curved diagonally across the African's face. The skin to either side of it was swollen and puckered.

"That's a lurcher sting," Wells observed. "He's recently dead, I'd say."

"This was a bad idea, Bertie. We should have stayed with the column."

Wells shook his head. "It's the job of a war correspondent to watch and report, Richard. When we reach the other end of the village, you'll find that it offers an unparalleled view across Tanga. We'll see far more from here than we would if we were in the thick of it. Not to mention the fact that we'll stand a better chance of staying alive."

The silence was suddenly broken by a rasping susurration, similar to the sound of a locust, but shockingly loud and menacing.

"Hum. I might be wrong," Wells added, his eyes widening. "Where did that noise come from?"

"I don't know."

They stepped out of the passage and immediately saw a lurcher flopping out of one of the cottages they'd just passed. It was a hideous thing—a tangle of thorny tentacles and thrashing tendrils. From its middle, a red, fleshy and pulsating bloom curled outward. Extending from within this, two very long spine-covered stalks rose into the air. They were rubbing together—a horribly frantic motion—producing the high-pitched ratcheting. The wriggling plant rolled forward on a knot of squirming white roots—and it moved fast.

"We've got to get out of here!" Burton cried out. "Drop your crutches, Bertie! I'm going to carry you!"

"But—"

Wells got no further. Burton kicked the crutches away, bent, and hoisted the shorter man up onto his shoulder. He started to run, heavy footed.

"Bloody hell!" he gasped. "This is a lot easier with Algy!"

"Who?"

"Um. Algy. Bismillah! That's who you put me in mind of! How in blazes could I have forgotten him?"

"I don't know and right now I don't care. Run!"

Burton pumped his legs, felt his thigh muscles burning, and heard the lurcher rapidly drawing closer behind him.

"It's on us!" Wells yelled.

The famous explorer glimpsed a house door standing ajar. He veered towards it and bowled through, dropping Wells, and banging the portal shut behind him. The lurcher slammed into it with terrific force, causing the frame to splinter around the lock. Burton quickly slid the bolts at the top and bottom into place. Thorns ripped at the wood outside.

"This door won't keep it out for long. Are you all right?"

"I landed on my leg," Wells groaned.

Burton helped the war correspondent to his feet. "Let's get upstairs. God, my head! I was just knocked sideways by memories!"

He gave support to his friend and they made their way up and through to the front bedroom. The other upper chamber was given over to storage.

The din of hammering tentacles continued below. Burton was breathing heavily. He lowered Wells onto a bed, then staggered back and leaned against a wall, pressing the palms of his hands into his eyes.

"Algernon," he whispered, and when he looked up, there were tears on his cheeks.

"What is it?" the shorter man asked.

Burton didn't answer. He was looking beyond his companion, at a dressing table mirror, and the face that stared back from it was that of a total stranger. It was all he could see. He fell into its black, despair-filled eyes and was overwhelmed by such a powerful sense of loss that his mind began to fracture.

"Richard!" Wells snapped. "Hey!"

The room sucked back into focus.

"Where am I?" Burton gasped. He felt hollow and disassociated.

Wordlessly, Wells pointed at the window.

After drawing a shuddering breath, Burton crossed to it, but he quickly stepped back when he saw thorny vines crawling over the glass.

"Manipulated and accelerated evolution," the war correspondent observed. "Another of the Eugenicists' ill-conceived monstrosities. That thing was once a man in a vehicle. Look at the damned thing now! So who's this Algy person?"

"Algernon Swinburne."

"The poet? Yes, of course, you knew him, didn't you?"

"He is—was—my assistant."

"Really? In what?"

"I have no idea. But I recall fleeing from a fire with him slung over my shoulder."

"Fire is what we need now. It's the only way we'll destroy the lurcher. Step a little farther back from the window, Richard. The stalks are strong enough to break through the glass."

Burton hastily retreated. He looked around the room at the furniture, the pictures and the ornaments. Everything was crawling with ants and cockroaches. Even this fact seemed to stir buried recollections. The name "Rigby" rose into his awareness then sank away again.

Wells said: "My leg is hurting like hell."

"Stay here while I have a poke about in the other room," Burton responded. He went out onto the landing and into the chamber beyond. Wells sat and massaged his right thigh.

A loud crack sounded from below as the front door split under the lurcher's continued assault.

Burton came back in.

"Any luck?" Wells asked.

"A whole bottle of it." Burton held up a wide-necked container. "Turpentine."

Wells pulled something from his jacket pocket. "And a box of four whole matches. Yours for the price of two pieces of toffee."

"Deal."

Burton crossed to the window and, after putting the bottle on the floor, used both hands to slide the sash up. It squealed loudly and jammed, with less than a foot of it open.

"Look out!" Wells cried out.

The explorer staggered back as two flailing stalks came smashing through the glass and wood. Splinters showered over both men. The spiny appendages coiled and slashed around the room, gouging the furniture and ripping long gashes across the walls.

Wells, acting without thinking, threw himself back onto the bed, clutched the thin mattress, and rolled, wrapping it around himself. He lunged upright and dived at the window, letting out an agonised scream as pain knifed through his wounded leg. He landed across the stalks, pinning them to the floor. They bucked under him, and curled back, slapping against the bedding, shredding it.

"Quick, man! I can't hold it!"

Burton sprang at the bottle, which was rolling over the floorboards, scooped it up, and untwisted the cap. Unable to get past Wells to the front of the window, he stuck his arm through it from the side and poured the turpentine, praying to Allah that it would land on the target.

"The lucifers, Bertie!"

"I dropped the bloody things!"

A ragged length of the mattress's cotton cover was ripped away from the foam beneath. It flew into the air as one of the stalks whipped up and back down, thumping across the correspondent's body.

Burton, having spotted the matchbox lying on the floor, scrambled across the room. He crawled and rolled on broken glass.

"Have you got them?" Wells yelled.

"Yes!"

Snatching up the length of torn material, Burton reeled back to the front wall, thudded against it, and slid into a crouch beside the window.

Wells was suddenly sent spinning into the air as the long stalks jerked violently and slid from the room.

The battering noises ceased.

Burton, with a puzzled expression, stood and cautiously peered out of the window. The stalks were nowhere in sight. Carefully, he leaned out and looked down.

The lurcher was below, quivering and jerking as if in the grip of a seizure.

"What's happened to it?" he murmured.

He pulled a match from the box, struck it, put the flame to the torn cotton, and dropped the burning cloth onto the plant, which immediately exploded into flames.

As he watched, the fire turned from blue to yellow and started to belch thick black smoke.

He turned and started to speak but realised that Wells was unconscious.

"Bertie, are you all right?"

The war correspondent shifted and groaned.

Pulling away the tattered mattress, Burton helped his companion to sit upright. Wells's uniformed was ripped and blood-stained.

"You're bleeding, Bertie."

"Nothing serious," his friend croaked. "So are you. Is it dead?"

"Yes. It was odd, though. The thing seemed to lose control of itself just before I set fire to it. Let's get out of here."

They limped from the bedroom and down the stairs, pulled open the wrecked front door, and tumbled out onto the street.

The lurcher had already been reduced to a twitching bonfire.

"Wait here," Burton said. "I'll get your crutches."

He retrieved them from outside the alley farther down the road and returned.

"You did exactly what he would have done," he said, handing over the sticks.

"Who?"

"Algernon Swinburne. He's the most fearless man I've ever known."

"That's where the comparison fails, then. I was scared out of my wits."

"You're a good chap, Bertie."

CHAPTER 4

Disaster!

1 Six-inch sextant. 1 Four-inch sextant. 1 Mercurial horizon. 1 Prismatic compass. 2 Pocket chronometers. 3 Thermometers to 212°.

3 Ditto smaller, in cylindrical brass cases. 2 Casella's apparatus for measuring heights by the boiling point: steam and 1 for water. 1 Book, having its pages divided into half-inch squares for mapping. Memorandum-books. 1 Nautical Almanac. 1 Thomson's Lunar Tables. 1 Galton's Art of Travel. 1 Admiralty Manual. 1 Tables of Logarithms. Hints to Travellers by the Royal Geographical Society.

—From Burton's inventory notes, African Expedition, 1863

The *Orpheus* was over southern France by the time Sir Richard Francis Burton woke up. After two nights in a row with virtually no sleep, he'd been oblivious for the first hours of the voyage.

Now he stood on the observation deck, enjoying the view and feeling an immense sense of release. Departure always lifted his spirits, and as the shackles and restraints of civilisation fell away, he was giving himself up to that which he liked best: the lure and promise of the unknown.

Algernon Swinburne entered and joined him at the window.

"What ho! What ho! And what ho again! But you missed a top nosh-up at lunch, Richard!"

"I've been dead to the world, Algy. What have you been doing, apart from lining your stomach, that is?"

"I've been looking for that little imp Willy Cornish, but it seems our funnel scrubbers are already crawling about in the pipes."

"Sweltering work, I imagine. He'll emerge eventually. No doubt you'll catch up with him later."

"I suppose. I say, there's a bit of a flap on with Mr. Gooch and his people."

"Why so?"

"The four stern engines have gone wonky. I think it's something to do with the doo-dah forcing the thingumajig to bang against the wotsitsname. There's not much poetry in engineering, is there?"

"Not a lot. Are you quite all right?"

"I'm fine. No, I'm not. Oh, blast it, I don't know, Richard."

"Thinking about Tom?"

Swinburne heaved a sigh. "Yes. They'll be burying him this afternoon."

The poet reached into his jacket and pulled out Apollo's gold-tipped arrow. He examined its point. "We didn't catch his killer, and we're going to be away for such a long time that we probably never will."

"Don't be so sure. I found out last night that Otto Steinrück is actually Count von Zeppelin."

"What? What? The spy?"

"Yes. I'll be very surprised if his and our paths don't cross again in due course."

Swinburne's face took on a ferocious expression. "Good!" he snarled. "Good!" He held up the arrow and, in a melodramatic tone, declared: "This is the arrow of justice! I shall carry it with me until Tom Bendyshe is avenged!"

Burton patted his friend's shoulder.

They stood and watched the scenery slipping by far below. Ahead, France's south coast was visible.

Swinburne said: "I think I'll go and do some work."

"*Atalanta in Calydon*?"

"No. I've started a little something entitled *A Lamentation*."

"In memoriam?"

"I'm not entirely sure. It might concern another matter entirely. It's hard to tell. It's coming out of here—" He tapped the middle of his chest. "Rather than here—" He put a finger to his head. "Maybe it'll make more sense to me when it's finished."

With that, he left the observation deck.

Burton's fathomless eyes fixed on the line of ocean at the horizon.

"Poems the poet cannot quite grasp. Dreams the dreamer cannot decipher. Mystery upon mystery. And still the Weaver plies his loom, whose warp and woof is wretched Man. Weaving the unpatterned dark design, so dark we doubt it owns a plan."

An hour passed, during which time he stood, motionless, lost in thought.

"Sir Richard," came a voice from behind him. He turned and saw Captain Lawless. "Do you feel a vibration beneath your feet?"

"I do," Burton answered. "Something to do with the stern engines?"

"Ah, you've heard. They're operating out of alignment with the forward engines and pushing us too hard. If we can't regulate our speed, we'll complete our voyage considerably ahead of schedule but in doing so the ship will have shaken herself half to pieces and won't be fit for the return journey. I don't much fancy being stuck in Zanzibar. I'm on my way down to engineering to see whether Mr. Gooch can cast some light on the matter. Would you care to accompany me?"

Burton nodded, and, minutes later, they found Daniel Gooch in an engineering compartment behind the furnace room. He'd removed a large metal panel from the floor and was on his knees peering into the exposed machinery beneath. When he heard the two men approaching, he looked up and said: "There's a bearing cradle missing."

"A what?" Burton asked.

"A bearing cradle. It's a metal ring, twelve inches in diameter, housing a cog mechanism and greased ball bearings. It's an essential component in the system that synchronises the engines. There are four bearing cradles on the ship, each governing four of the flight shafts. The one for the stern engines has gone. Someone has removed it."

"Are you suggesting we've been sabotaged, Mr. Gooch?" Lawless asked.

"Yes, sir. I am."

"By someone on board?"

"That's very likely the case, sir."

Nathaniel Lawless's pale grey eyes narrowed. He clenched his fists and addressed Burton. "I don't like the idea that one of my crew is a rogue, Sir Richard. Nor do I understand it. Why would anyone wish to interfere with your expedition?"

Burton clicked his teeth together. He glanced at Gooch, who got to his feet and stood with his metal arms poised over his shoulders, then turned back to Lawless. "How much do you know about my mission, Captain?"

"Only that you intend to discover the source of the River Nile. I've been instructed by Mr. Brunel to deliver you and your supplies to Zanzibar. I understand that the government has funded the entire undertaking. Is there something more?"

"There is."

"Then I ask you to tell me. You can count on my discretion. Mr. Gooch, would you leave us, please?"

"It's all right, Captain" Gooch said. "You have authority over me on this ship but, as a Technologist, I hold a more senior position and happen to know the details. I apologise for having kept them from you, but our superiors felt that certain aspects should remain hush hush."

Lawless looked from one man to the other. "That's all well and good, but if the *Orpheus* is in danger, I have the right to know why."

"Agreed," Burton said. "The truth, sir, is that while I hope to finally identify the source of the Nile, it is only a secondary consideration. The priority is to locate and retrieve a black diamond, known as the Eye of Nāga. In this endeavour, I am almost certainly opposed by a Prussian spy named Zeppelin."

Lawless's eyes widened. "Are you telling me that our saboteur is a Prussian agent?"

"In all probability, yes. I should say he was commissioned by Zeppelin to interfere with the ship."

Lawless raised a hand and ran it over his closely cropped white beard. His eyes flashed. "I'll keelhaul the bastard!"

"I'm not sure that's possible in a rotorship," Gooch muttered.

"I'll bloody well make it possible!"

"We have to catch him first," Burton observed.

"It's puzzling, though," said Gooch. "If the saboteur intends to delay your expedition, don't you think it rather peculiar that he's committed an act which actually causes the ship to fly faster—albeit destructively so; an act that'll cause you to arrive at Zanzibar considerably earlier than planned?"

Burton frowned. "That, Mr. Gooch, is a very good point. A very good point indeed!"

§

Burton spoke to Swinburne, Trounce, Honesty, Krishnamurthy, Bhatti, Spencer, Miss Mayson and Sister Raghavendra, and arranged for them to patrol the ship, keeping a close watch on the crew and their eyes peeled for suspicious behaviour. He then returned to his quarters, intending to update his journal. Pulling a key from his pocket, he unlocked the door, pushed it open, and stopped in his tracks.

There was something on the desk.

He stepped into the room and looked around. The cabin was rectangular and of a medium size. It was carpeted, wallpapered, and well furnished. One of the thick ventilation pipes ran across the ceiling and four oil lamps were suspended two to each side of it. There were two other doors, one to the small bedchamber and the other to a tiny washroom.

The afternoon sun was sending a shaft of Mediterranean brilliance in through the porthole. Its white glare reflected brightly off the object, which hadn't been on the desk when Burton left the cabin a couple of hours earlier. He'd locked the door behind him. There were no other means of ingress.

He picked the thing up, went back out into the corridor, closed and locked the door, then knelt and squinted at the keyhole. He stood and paced away, heading towards the prow of the rotorship. Doctor Quaint was coming the other way.

"Doctor," Burton said. "May I have a minute of your time?"

"Certainly. I say! What have you there?"

Burton held up the object. "A mystery, Doctor. It was on the desk in my quarters. Tell me; who else has a key?"

"To your cabin? Just Sister Raghavendra and myself." Quaint reached into his pocket and pulled out a crowded key ring. "As stewards, we have access to all the passenger rooms." He picked through the keys one by one. "Here it is. This is yours."

"And have you used it today?"

"No, sir, I have not."

"Could you prove that, should it be necessary?"

Quaint bristled slightly. "Sister Raghavendra will attest that I've been working with her all morning, throughout lunch, and up until a few minutes ago, when I left her in order to report to the captain. I've just come from the bridge."

"Thank you, Doctor. I'm sorry to have troubled you. I'd better see the captain myself, I think."

"Very well." Quaint glanced again at the object.

Burton left the steward and proceeded along the corridor and up the metal stairs to the conning tower. He stepped onto the bridge, which was occupied by a number of crew members. Captain Lawless turned as he entered, saw what he was holding, and uttered an exclamation.

"Great Scott! Where did you find that?"

"On the desk in my cabin, Captain. Am I correct in assuming it's the missing bearing cradle?"

"You are. Let me see."

Burton handed the metal ring to Lawless, who examined it closely before pronouncing it undamaged. He addressed

Oscar Wilde, who was cleaning a console at the back of the room.

"Master Wilde, would you run this down to the engine room, please? Ask Mr. Gooch to have it fitted as soon as we land at Cairo."

Wilde took the cradle and departed.

"In your cabin?" Lawless said. "How did it get there?"

"That's the question. I locked the door when I left and it was still locked when I returned. Doctor Quaint assures me that neither he nor Sister Raghavendra entered the room in my absence and I saw no indication that the lock had been picked. It doesn't mean it wasn't, but in my experience there are usually tiny scratches left after that manner of break in."

Lawless removed his captain's hat and rubbed his head. "Well whatever method your intruder used, this is rather an inept way to implicate you."

"It would only implicate me if the stewards had found the bearing cradle while servicing my cabin. And you'd think it would at least be hidden under my bunk, rather than placed on top of my desk in broad daylight. Besides which, it makes no sense that I would sabotage my own expedition."

Lawless hissed softly: "Curse it! I won't rest until we find this bloody traitor!"

"Nor I," Burton whispered back. "I have my people patrolling the ship. Our villain will find it hard to cause any further damage without being caught in the act!"

The explorer remained on the bridge for the next three hours. He kept a close eye on the men at their stations, but saw nothing suspicious.

The Mediterranean slid beneath the big rotorship.

A hollow whistle sounded.

Lawless crossed to a brass panel in the wall and pulled a domed lid from it. As it came away, a segmented tube followed behind. Lawless flipped the lid open, blew into the tube, put it to his ear, and listened awhile. He then moved it to his mouth and said: "Hold him. I'll be right down."

He clicked the lid back into the panel and said to Burton: "Apparently your assistant is causing merry mayhem in the engine room."

"How so?"

Captain Lawless ignored the question and turned to his First Officer. "Take command, please, Mr. Henson."

"Yes, sir."

"Mr. Playfair, how long to Cairo?"

"Two and a half hours, sir, unless we can slow her down. All four stern engines are already overheating, according to my instruments."

"Thank you. Mr. Bingham, report please."

The fat little meteorologist replied: "Clear sailing all the way, sir. Not a cloud in the sky. Breeze is north westerly, currently less than five knots but building."

"Mr. Wenham?"

"Steady going, sir."

"Good. Follow me, Sir Richard."

The aeronaut and explorer left the bridge, descended through the conning tower, and entered the corridor that ran the length of the rotorship.

"Mr. Swinburne claims to have caught our saboteur," Lawless said.

"Ah!" Burton replied.

They entered the lounge and descended the port side staircase, then moved past the standard class cabins and on into the first of the engine room compartments. The rumble of the turbines sounded from the next chamber, muffled by thickly insulated walls.

Peering past pipes and four wide rotating pillars, Burton saw Trounce and Honesty gripping the arms of a very small person. Engineers were gathered around them, and Swinburne was dancing in front of the police officers and their captive, shrieking at the top of his voice.

"Tobias Threadneedle, my eye!" he screeched. "Liar! Brute! Traitor! Impostor!"

"What are you doing down here, Algy?" Burton asked, as he and Lawless joined the group. "I thought you were working?"

"I found myself unable to write, Richard. So I came in search of inspiration, and what I found instead—" Swinburne raised his voice to a scream and pointed his finger, "—is the one and only Vincent Sneed—otherwise known as the Conk!"

Burton looked down at the short wiry individual held in the grip of the two Scotland Yard men. He wasn't much bigger than a child, and owned a very unprepossessing stoat-like face, dominated by a perfectly huge nose. A nicotine-stained and ragged moustache concealed his lipless mouth. His thin black hair was long, greasy, and combed backwards over his narrow skull. He was pockmarked and sly-looking, and his beady little eyes—positioned almost on the sides of his gargantuan proboscis rather than to either side of it in the normal way—were flicking back and forth in a panicked manner.

"I bloody aren't!" he protested. "Me name's Threadneedle. Arsk 'im!" He nodded to a small boy standing nearby, a ragamuffin with sandy blonde hair.

Captain Lawless said: "And who are you, my lad?"

"Willy Cornish, sir," the boy answered nervously.

Daniel Gooch stepped forward, his mechanical arms slowly undulating to either side of him. "They are the ship's funnel scrubbers, Captain."

Willy Cornish nodded and pointed at the prisoner. "That's right, sir. And he's who he says he is—Tobias Threadneedle."

Swinburne let loose a tremendous howl and hopped up and down like a madman. "Willy! You know perfectly well this is Sneed!"

Cornish shifted uncomfortably and wrung his hands. "No, Carrots," he said, employing the nickname he'd given the poet during the time they'd spent together sweeping chimneys. "I know he looks like old Sneed, but he's Mr. Threadneedle, and he's all right, he is."

"All right? He's a rogue! A bully! A snake in the grass!"

"I ain't none o' them things!" the captive cried out, struggling to free himself.

"Here, less of that!" Trounce snapped.

"I'll have the cuffs on you!" Honesty threatened.

"I ain't done nuffink!" the prisoner protested.

"You sabotaged the ship!" Swinburne shouted.

"I bloody didn't!"

"You bloody did!"

"I bloody didn't!"

"SHUT UP!" Lawless roared. "You—" He jabbed a finger at Swinburne. "—Calm down and explain."

"The explanation," Swinburne answered, "is that while this hound may be calling himself Tobias Threadneedle, he is actually, and without doubt, a scurrilous rogue by the name of Vincent Sneed. I worked side by side with him the year before last and he treated me abominably. I cannot be mistaken. Look at that nose of his! How many men do you think there are walking around with such a perfectly enormous hooter?"

"Oy!" the prisoner objected.

"But you say Mr. Swinburne is mistaken?" Lawless demanded of Cornish.

"Y-yes, sir," the boy stuttered. "I kn-know Mr. Sneed, and this ain't him."

Swinburne groaned and slapped a hand to his forehead. "Why, Willy? Why are you supporting this blackguard?"

"Stop calling me them bleedin' names you damned rat!" the accused man cried out.

"Algy," Burton said. "Even if this is Mr. Sneed—"

"It is!"

"—What makes you think it was he who sabotaged the ship?"

"Because he's a villain!"

"So your allegation is based on supposition rather than evidence?"

Swinburne sighed and muttered: "Yes, Richard. But isn't it enough that he's lying to us?"

Burton turned to Captain Lawless. "Is there a secure room available? I'd like to keep this man under guard while we get to the bottom of this."

"Use the first of the class two passenger cabins," Lawless said, pointing back at the corridor they'd come through. "I have to get back to the bridge. I'll send the steward down with the key. Report to me when this is sorted out, please."

With that, the captain gave a last glance at the prisoner then marched away.

Burton addressed his assistant: "Algy, where is Herbert?"

"Holed up in his cabin, working on a philosophical treatise."

"Would you fetch him, please?"

The poet shifted his weight from one foot to the other, glowered at the big nosed man, frowned at Willy Cornish, then nodded and followed after Lawless.

Burton positioned himself in front of the individual who called himself Tobias Threadneedle and said: "Did you take part in a riot at Speaker's Corner last summer?"

"No!" the man answered. He couldn't meet Burton's eyes, and kept raising his own to the ceiling, anxiously scanning the pipes and machinery above. The way he squirmed in Trounce and Honesty's grip suggested that he wasn't telling the truth.

"The two men holding you are police officers," Burton revealed.

Trounce added: "And we won't hesitate to arrest you and deliver you to a Cairo gaol if you're what Mr. Swinburne says you are!"

"Egyptian prison," Honesty murmured. "Very nasty. Foul places."

"Oh please mother! I ain't done nuffink!" their captive wailed. "I'm just a bleedin' funnel scrubber!"

"Sneed was at the riot," Burton stated. "As were these two fellows and myself. My assistant got into a scrap with him. None of us saw it, but our colleague, Mr. Spencer, did. He's on his way down now, and he'll either endorse Mr. Swinburne's assertion, or he won't. If you're Tobias Threadneedle, you have nothing to worry about. If you're Vincent Sneed, things are about to go very badly for you."

The prisoner let out a keening whine of despair.

Burton turned to Willy Cornish.

"I've heard good things about you, young man. I hope you're not telling fibs. I would be very disappointed indeed."

Willy burst into tears and buried his face in the crook of his arm.

Daniel Gooch approached Burton and said, in a low voice: "That bearing cradle, Sir Richard; I understand it appeared in your cabin under mysterious circumstances?"

"Yes."

"It's this fellow's duty—" One of Gooch's mechanical arms gestured towards Threadneedle, "—to keep the pipes clear on that side of the ship. He could have opened the ventilation panel in the pipe and entered your quarters through it."

"I see. Thank you, Mr. Gooch."

A few tense minutes passed while they waited for Herbert Spencer's arrival. When the clockwork philosopher entered the room—clanking along beside Swinburne, and with Pox squatting on his head—Threadneedle's little eyes widened and he stuttered: "Wha-wha-what's that thing?"

"Tosspot!" Pox squawked.

"Herbert," Burton said. "Have you seen this fellow before?"

The brass man stepped over to Threadneedle and nodded. "Yus, Boss. He were at the riot last summer. He got into a fight with Mr. Swinburne. He's Vincent Sneed."

The prisoner groaned and slumped.

Doctor Quaint walked in, glanced curiously at the scene, and handed a key to Burton. "Second class cabin number one," he said.

"Thank you, Doctor." Burton addressed the Yard men: "Let us secure Mr. Sneed, gentlemen."

He led the way to the cabin, followed by the policemen and their prisoner.

Swinburne turned to Willy Cornish and placed a hand on the boy's shoulder. "Why were you protecting him, Willy? Has he threatened you?"

Willy looked up, his eyes swimming in tears. "I can't say, Carrots. I would, but I just can't!"

Swinburne shook his head and chewed his bottom lip. "There's something very wrong about all of this," he grumbled. "But how the blazes am I to get to the facts of the matter if you won't help?"

With a cry of anguish, Willy suddenly sped away, ducked under the arms of the engineers who tried to stop him, and leaped onto machinery lining one of the walls. He clambered up it like a little monkey until he reached a ventilation panel. Swinging it open, he disappeared into the pipe behind.

"My hat!" the poet muttered. "What on earth has got into him?"

§

The *Orpheus* landed at the Cairo Airfield at seven in the evening, and the crew got to work taking on a fresh load of Formby coal and refilling the water tanks.

Vincent Sneed had been left alone to stew in Standard Class Cabin 1. He was slumped on the bunk when a key turned in the lock and the door opened. Sir Richard Francis Burton entered followed by Detective Inspectors Trounce and Honesty and a tall dark skinned man wearing a uniform with epaulets and a sash. His face was eagle-like, adorned with a moustache and imperial, and his eyes were black. There was a fez on his head.

"Mr. Sneed," Burton said. "This is Al-Mustazi, the Commissioner of the city police. He has men waiting outside. They will take you into custody until the British consul gets around to dealing with you. That could take a good few weeks, during which time you'll have to survive as best you can in Cairo's prison. I know you were born and raised in the Cauldron, and I know from personal experience what a hell hole that part of London is, but I can assure you that it will seem like Shangri-La in comparison to the conditions you are to experience shortly."

Sneed looked up, his little ferrety eyes filled with wretchedness. "I ain't done nuffink," he keened.

"Do you still maintain that your name is Tobias Threadneedle?"

The funnel scrubber swallowed, his Adam's apple bobbing on his scrawny neck.

"Yes," he whispered.

"Even though you've been identified by two people as Vincent Sneed?"

"Yes."

"Did you break into my quarters and deposit a bearing cradle in them?"

Burton noted that the little man's hands were trembling. He saw the eyes flick to the left and right, then up at the ceiling.

"I—I ain't done nuffink! Nuffink!"

Burton sighed. "Mr. Sneed, many a man has lied to me in the past and I have a practiced eye. I can see by the way you hold yourself, by your every movement and expression, that you're not telling me the truth. I shall give you one final chance. Admit who you are, tell me why you placed the bearing cradle on my desk, then I shall see to it that you are shipped back to London with due dispatch. I'll even ask that no charges are brought against you. Obviously, you'll never work as a funnel scrubber again, but you can, at least, go back to being a master sweep."

A tear trickled down Sneed's cheek. "You don't understand," he said. "I knows I've been a bad 'un. P'raps a bit too strict, like, wiv the nippers. But I were only tryin' to get good work out o' them. I didn't mean no 'arm to that carrot top. I were just trainin' 'im. An'—" he sucked in a shuddery breath and swallowed again. "—An' I don't mean no 'arm now, neither. I ain't done nuffink! I ain't done nuffink!"

"So you admit to the actions of Vincent Sneed yet still say you aren't him?"

The little man wrung his hands together then raised them to cover his face.

"Yes," he groaned.

"Does the name Zeppelin mean anything to you?"

Sneed parted his fingers and looked out from behind them. "Zephram?"

"Zeppelin."

"I don't know no Zeppelin."

Burton turned to Trounce and Honesty. "Would you hand the prisoner over to your Egyptian colleagues, please?"

The two detectives nodded, stepped forward, and hoisted Sneed up off the bed.

"No!" he screeched, writhing in their grip. "Get yer 'ands off me!"

"No nonsense, if you please!" Trounce snapped.

They bundled him out of the cabin, to where four Egyptian constables waited. Sneed howled.

Burton, speaking fluent Arabic in the local dialect, quietly addressed Al-Mustazi: "Despite my threats to the man, I'd prefer it if you kept him from the worst of it. I sent my parakeet to the consul as soon as we landed with a request that the prisoner be processed with due dispatch. He'll be handed over to British authorities and sent home in a few days but there's no need to tell him that. Let him think he's going to be in Cairo prison for the long haul, it may teach him a lesson."

Al-Mustazi murmured an acknowledgement, bowed and departed.

Burton left the cabin and met Trounce and Honesty in the corridor. They headed up to the passenger lounge.

"Strange!" said Honesty. "Why so stubborn?"

"It's odd, I'll admit," Burton replied. "And there was something else rather peculiar, too. He kept glancing up at the ceiling."

"I noticed that," Trounce grunted. "I wonder why?"

The three men joined Swinburne, Krishnamurthy, Bhatti, and Herbert Spencer in the lounge. The clockwork philosopher was incapable of drinking or smoking but he enjoyed company and needed the mental relaxation, despite that his mind was an electrical field processed by a machine. With Pox on his head, he sat at the bar with the men, who sipped at their brandy and sodas and watched the sun through the portholes as it sank down behind the city's houses and minarets. Burton smoked one of his disreputable Manila cheroots, Trounce opted for a rather more expensive *Flor de Dindigul* Indian cigar, while Honesty and Krishnamurthy puffed at their pipes. Neither Swinburne nor Bhatti smoked. The poet compensated for it by consuming twice as much brandy.

"Steady on," Burton advised him.

"I need it," his assistant answered. "I'm frustrated. Willy Cornish is a splendid young man, and I can't for the life of me think why he would defend a scurrilous miscreant like Sneed. And now he's vanished into the pipes and probably won't emerge until he's starving!"

"Needs interrogating!" Honesty snapped. "Spill the beans. Tell us what Zeppelin is up to."

"Dribbly snot rag!" Pox cawed.

"I don't understand it," Krishnamurthy said. "Why would the Prussian hire a villain Mr. Swinburne could recognise in an instant?"

"Perhaps he didn't know that we'd encountered Sneed before," Bhatti suggested.

Trounce snorted. "Pah! Too much of a coincidence! There's more to it, mark my words, lad!"

Burton nodded thoughtfully. "I agree," he murmured. "There's a deeper mystery here."

Doctor Quaint and Sister Raghavendra entered the chamber and began to light the oil lamps. Burton stood and wandered over to the young woman.

"Hello, Sadhvi. Have you settled into your duties?"

"Hello Captain Burton. Yes. It's been a busy day. I'll go down to the kitchen in a minute to help Mr. Butler and Miss Mayson with the supper, then once that's cooked and eaten and tidied, I'll retire to my cabin for a well-earned rest. Incidentally, I brought with me a volume of Mr. Swinburne's *Poems and Ballads* to read but I seem to have misplaced it. Might you ask him if he has a spare copy?"

"You can borrow mine. I'll have Quips deliver it to you. I should warn you, though; it's a mite vivid!"

"So I've heard, but I'm from India, Captain. I don't suffer the modesties, embarrassments or fainting fits of your English ladies!"

Burton smiled. "Then you are most fortunate!"

On his way back to his friends, halfway across the small dance floor, the king's agent suddenly stopped and gazed up at the ceiling.

"By James!" he whispered. "Could it be? It would certainly explain a lot!"

When he sat down and picked up his drink, the others noticed that he wore a distracted expression.

"What's on your mind, Captain?" Bhatti asked.

"Hmm? Oh, I'm just—just thinking about—about—um—Christopher Rigby."

"Yikes!" Swinburne exclaimed. "He's going to be nothing but trouble!"

"Who's Rigby?" Herbert Spencer asked.

"Malodorous horse bucket!" Pox whistled.

"The parakeet has it!" Swinburne declared. "Lieutenant Christopher Palmer Rigby is the consul at Zanzibar and a fat-headed ninny of the first order. Richard repeatedly knocked him off the top spot in language examinations back when they were stationed in India, and Rigby, sore loser that he is, has never forgotten it. The rotter's made a career of besmirching our friend's reputation. I'd like to punch the hound right on the nose!"

"Thank you, Algy," Burton said. He explained further: "Rigby and I were in the East India Company's 18th Bombay Native Infantry at Scinde, and he formed an immediate and irrational hatred of me from the outset. He'll cause problems for us when we land in Africa, of that I'm certain."

"King's agent!" Honesty barked. "Authority!"

"Possessing authority is one thing," Burton replied. "But expecting a man like Rigby to respect it is quite another."

Over the next hour, he barely said another word, and when they attended the Captain's table for supper, the explorer seemed so preoccupied that his bearing came perilously close to impoliteness. Afterwards, he muttered a few words about writing up his journals and retired to his cabin.

He lit one lamp and turned it down low, then got undressed, washed, put on his pyjamas, and wrapped himself in his *jubbah*. He lit a cheroot and relaxed in an armchair, his eyes focused inward, his mind working on a Sufi meditation exercise.

He finished the cigar.

A couple of hours passed.

He didn't move.

Then: *There!*

He'd heard a faint noise, a tiny rasping sound.

He waited.

Again, an almost imperceptible scrape.

He allowed a few minutes to tick by.

"You should have asked before borrowing Sister Raghavendra's copy of *Poems and Ballads*."

Silence.

He spoke again. "You made a scapegoat of Vincent Sneed. I have no fondness for the fellow, but why? What was the point?"

Thirty seconds or so passed.

A small, whispery voice said: "Distraction, Captain Burton."

"There you are! Hello, lad! I take it Sneed and Willy Cornish smuggled you onto the ship in the replacement section of pipe?"

"Yes. I had ordered the previous two funnel scrubbers to purposely damage a section in order to facilitate my presence here."

"So the Beetle, the chief of the League of Chimney Sweeps, finds himself en route to Africa. A bizarre circumstance indeed, and I imagine you must have a very good reason for leaving your chimney. Distraction, you say? Who are you trying to distract, and from what?"

Burton stood and moved to the middle of the room. He looked up at the grille in the thick ventilation pipe. Vaguely, he could discern something moving behind it.

"Don't turn the lamps up," came the whisper.

"I don't intend to. I know how you abhor light."

"One of my boys was killed."

"Who?"

"Bingo Stokes. He was ten years old, and one of the few not an orphan. But his father mistreated him terribly, and Bingo often sought refuge in a chimney."

"Ah. Now I understand. He cleaned the chimney of a house in Ilford, then went back there to steal food and spend a night in the flue."

"That is correct, Captain. And while he was there, he overheard four men plotting. Three were Prussians, but, fortunately, they spoke in English on account of the fourth man. That individual was instructed to bring down this ship, if he couldn't kill you first. Unfortunately, Bingo's presence was detected, and though he got away, he was shot. By the time he reached me, it was too late to save him. He bled to death, but not before repeating to me everything he'd heard."

"So there is still a saboteur at loose?"

"Yes, but I do not know who it is. I arranged to be smuggled aboard and I instructed Vincent Sneed to steal the bearing cradle."

"You're conversant with the engineering of the *Orpheus*?"

"I had already read a great deal of material pertaining to her construction."

Burton thought for a moment, then said: "So you alerted us to the fact that a saboteur was aboard by arranging a fairly harmless act of sabotage yourself?"

"Exactly, and in doing so, I made it difficult, if not impossible, for the Prussian agent to act, for now your people were all on the lookout for suspicious behaviour. The first leg of your voyage was thus protected. I then placed the cradle in your room, knowing that Sneed would be recognised and accused."

"Why do that?"

"Because now Sneed's been dealt with, your enemy will think that you consider yourselves safe. He'll be of the opinion that he can act with impunity when, in truth, you'll be watching out for him."

Burton pondered this, then said: "You've done me a service, and I thank you, but I don't understand. Why such an extravagant scheme when you could've got a message to me before the *Orpheus* left Battersea?"

"If I had, what would you have done?"

"I'd have dismissed the entire crew, hired a new one, and had every inch of the ship thoroughly checked."

"And how long would that have taken?"

"Perhaps four days. Maybe five or six."

"Bingo Stokes learned something else. The man who owned the house, Steinrück, was taking care of some business in Yorkshire—"

"His real name is Zeppelin and he went there to arrange my poisoning."

"I see. I'm glad he failed. Upon completing this business, he was going to fly to Prussia to join an expedition to central Africa led by Lieutenant John Speke. I realised, therefore, that warning you would result in a delay you can ill afford, for you are in a race."

"Bismillah!" Burton cursed. "I thought a rival expedition might be a possibility! So Speke and Zeppelin are already on their way?"

"They are, and it is why I chose the removal of the bearing cradle as my means of false sabotage, for I knew that it would result in a dangerous turn of speed. Maybe it will get you ahead in the game."

Burton smacked a fist into his palm and paced up and down.

"Damnation!" he muttered.

"You have no time for this stopover in Cairo," the Beetle urged. "You must get this ship back into the air at once. The saboteur will make a move but he will undoubtedly lack the appropriate caution. Catch him, then catch up with your opponents."

Burton hurried across the room and snatched up his clothes. "What of you?" he asked, as he started to dress.

"I will watch and listen and try to identify the agent. After you are delivered to Zanzibar, I'll remain with the ship while it returns to London. Willy Cornish—who, incidentally, has been following my orders—will facilitate my return to Limehouse."

"And Sneed?"

"He has a history of bullying my lads. This was his chance to redeem himself. He performed his part well and will be compensated for the inconvenience he is currently suffering."

Burton quickly buttoned up his clothes and tied his bootlaces. He stepped to the door and grasped its handle. "I have to tell my people what you've done, then get us moving," he said. "Thank you, lad. I'm in your debt."

§

First Officer William Henson had just dropped off to sleep when a hammering at his cabin door waked him. Swearing under his breath, he pulled on a gown, yanked open the door, and was confronted by the Captain.

"Sleep is cancelled, Mr. Henson. I need all hands on deck."

"Right away, sir. Is there a problem?"

"A change of schedule. No layover in Cairo. We're departing immediately. Mr. Gooch and the riggers will be recalibrating the four stern engines while we're in mid-flight. That means four external doors are going to be wide open in the sides of the engineering bay. We'll keep a low altitude, of course, but nevertheless I feel uneasy flying so exposed. I'd like you to oversee things down there until we're properly sealed up again."

"Certainly, sir, though I'm sure Mr. Gooch—"

"—will have everything under control. I don't doubt it, Henson, but since we have only three riggers and there are four engines that require attention, Mr. Gooch will be out on one of the flight pylons."

"Ah. I see. I'll get down there at once."

"You can shave and tidy yourself up first. There are some internal repairs and adjustments to be made before Gooch and his team go outside. Get down there within the hour, please."

"Yes, sir."

Henson's door was the first of a number to be knocked upon over the course of the next few minutes, and in very short measure the majority of the *Orpheus's* aeronauts found themselves unexpectedly back on duty.

It was a few minutes past midnight.

The rotorship's flight crew gathered on the bridge. Sir Richard Francis Burton was there, watching each of them carefully. They looked bleary eyed and dishevelled. Captain Lawless did not. His uniform was buttoned, his eyes were bright, and he was all efficiency.

"What's going on, sir?" Arthur Bingham, the meteorologist, asked.

"I'll have your report, Mr. Bingham, not your questions," Lawless snapped.

"Yes, sir. A wind has picked up. Rather strong. Easterly, currently at a steady twenty knots. No cloud."

"You heard that, Mr. Playfair?"

"Yes, sir," the navigator responded. "Taken into account. Course plotted to Aden."

"Good man. Mr. Pryce, call down to Mr. Gooch and have him start the engines."

"Aye, sir." Wordsworth Pryce, the second officer, moved to the speaking tubes. Moments later, a vibration ran through the rotorship.

"Engage the wings, Mr. Wenham."

"Engaging. Opening. Rotating ... and ... up to speed."

"Take us to two thousand feet."

On an expanding cone of steam, the *Orpheus* rose into the night sky and began to power into the south east, leaving the ill-lit city of Cairo behind her. Above, the Milky Way arced across the heavens, but below, the narrow Red Sea and the lands to either side of it were wreathed in darkness, so that it seemed the ship was sailing through an empty void.

With her stern engines still operating abnormally, the huge vessel rattled and shook as she ate up the miles, speeding at almost 150 knots towards Aden, on the tip of the Arabian peninsular.

In the engine room, the bearing cradle had been refitted, but it took Daniel Gooch and his fellow engineers almost four hours to reset the synchronisation system, which they achieved by shutting down the four rear engines one at a time while adjusting the various components to which the cradle was connected.

Now, it just remained to recalibrate each of those stern-most engines.

Gooch, and the riggers Gordon Champion, Alexander Priestley, and Winford Doe, positioned themselves at the four hull doors and buckled themselves into harnesses. They clipped safety straps to brackets above the portals.

First Officer Henson pulled a speaking tube from the wall.

On the bridge, his call was answered by Oscar Wilde, who said: "Captain Lawless. Mr. Henson is asking permission to open the external doors."

Lawless was standing by the window with Sir Richard Francis Burton. They were watching *al-fajr al-kaadhib*, the zodiacal light, which was rising column-like, in the western sky. He said: "Tell him permission is granted, Master Wilde."

"Aye, sir," the boy replied. He relayed the message down to the engine room.

Lawless stepped over to the helmsman and stood beside him, quietly ordering: "Steady as she goes, please, Mr. Wenham."

"Aye aye, sir, but—" Wenham hesitated.

"What is it?"

"I—um—I think—" The helmsman turned to Cedric Playfair, the navigator. "Shouldn't we still be over the Red Sea?"

"Yes," Playfair answered, glancing at his instruments.

"Then why is there desert below us?"

Lawless and Playfair both looked up and saw what Wenham had spotted—that the vaguest glimmers of light were skimming not over water, but sand dunes.

"Impossible!" Playfair gasped.

Burton joined them and watched as the navigator checked over his console.

"The compass says we're travelling south-south-east," Playfair muttered. "But if that were true, we'd be where we should be." He tapped the instrument, then bent, opened a panel in the console, reached in, and felt about, muttering: "Maybe something is interfering with—hello! What's this?" He pulled out a small block of metal, and as he did so, the compass needle swung from SSE to SE.

"A magnet!" Burton observed.

"How the devil—?" Playfair exclaimed.

Lawless clenched his teeth and bunched his fists.

"But it shouldn't make any difference!" Francis Wenham objected. "That compass is just for reference. It isn't used to set the course."

"He's right, sir," Playfair put in. "Mr. Wenham follows the instrumentation on his own console. It indicates the degrees to port or starboard he should steer the ship to maintain the course I set. Taking into account the compensation I calculated, if he's followed his indicators exactly, we should be slap bang over the Red Sea."

"And I have done," Wenham noted.

"Compensation?" Burton asked.

"For the wind, sir," Playfair replied.

Burton stepped back to the window. He turned and gestured for Oscar Wilde to join him.

"Yes, sir?" the boy asked.

"Can you find me some field glasses?"

"Right over here," said Wilde, crossing to a wall cabinet. He came back with a large-lensed brass device. Burton took it and raised it to his face, clipping its bracket over his head. He turned back to the window, and with the fingers of both hands, rotated the focusing wheels on either side of the apparatus.

The land below was wreathed in darkness, with just the tips of dunes visible in the faint light of *al-fajr al-kaadhib.* The field glasses threw them into sharp relief.

"Captain Lawless," Burton murmured. "I have a reasonably clear view of the sand dunes below us."

"What of it, Sir Richard?"

"They are entirely motionless. There is no sand rippling across their surface or spraying from their peaks. In other words, the strong wind Mr. Playfair just mentioned is nonexistent, at least at ground level, and since we're flying low—"

"If I've been taking into account a wind that isn't actually blowing, it would certainly explain our position," Playfair put in.

"Mr. Bingham!" Lawless roared, but when he turned to the meteorologist's position, he saw that it was unoccupied. "Where the devil is he?" he demanded.

"Mr. Bingham left the bridge some little time ago, so he did, sir," said Oscar Wilde.

"Playfair, Wenham, get us back on course! Sir Richard, come with me. We have to find my meteorologist. He has some explaining to do!"

Some minutes later, they located Arthur Bingham in the engine room, standing with Daniel Gooch, Shyamji Bhatti, and Winford Doe, near one of the open hull doors. Doe was unbuckling his harness.

"Hallo, Captain Burton, Captain Lawless!" Bhatti called as they approached.

Gooch turned and said: "Almost done, Captain. Mr. Champion is just putting the finishing touches to the last of our wayward engines."

Lawless ignored the chief engineer and glared at the short, fat meteorologist. "You appear to have deserted your post without permission, Bingham."

"I—I just came down to watch Mr. Gooch at—at work, sir," Bingham responded.

"Worried he'd be blown off the pylon by the high winds, were you?"

Bingham took a couple of steps backward.

"Is there a problem?" Gooch asked.

Lawless's eyes flashed angrily. "There most certainly is!"

Bingham pulled a pistol from his pocket and brandished it at them. "Get back, all of you!"

"Bloody traitor!" Lawless snapped.

"Hey! Drop that!" Bhatti cried out.

Bingham swung the pistol towards the constable, then pointed it at Burton, then at Lawless. His lips thinned against his teeth and his eyes flashed threateningly.

Lawless said: "Why?"

"Because I have a wife and two children," the meteorologist snarled. "And I also happen to have a tumour in my gut and not many months to live. A certain party has agreed to pay my family a large amount of money in return for the sacrifice I'm about to make." He directed his gun back at the king's agent. "I wouldn't have to do it at all but for you, Burton. I followed you to Ilford and back and took a pot shot at you."

"You ruined a perfectly good hat."

"It's a crying shame I didn't spoil the head it was adorning. If you'd have been decent enough to die then, this ship and its crew would have been spared."

"You're not the only man Zeppelin hired to kill me," Burton revealed. "The other was promised money and received instead the Count's hands around his neck."

"Ah, so you know my employer, then! But what do you mean?"

"My other would-be assassin was strangled to death, Bingham. Had you managed to put a bullet in me, I have little doubt that Zeppelin's associates would have then put one in you. As for money being paid to your family, you can forget it. The Prussians will feel no obligation to you once you're dead."

"Shut your mouth!" Bingham yelled. His finger whitened on the trigger as he jerked his pistol back and forth between Burton, Lawless, and Bhatti.

"Give it up, man!" the latter advised. "Don't leave your family stained with the name of a traitor!"

The meteorologist backed away a step. "Not another word out of you!" he spat at Bhatti. "As for you, Burton, they want an end to your little jaunt to Africa, and this—" With his free hand, Bingham undid his tightly buttoned jacket and pulled it open. He wasn't the fat man they thought he was. He was a slim man made bulky by a vest fashioned from sticks of dynamite. "—this will ensure they get what they want!"

"Hell's teeth!" Captain Lawless shouted. "Are you bloody insane, man?"

Bingham sneered nastily. "Blame your friend, here, Lawless. He's left me with no choice but to eliminate you all."

"You do have a choice," Burton said. "Shoot me now and spare the ship."

"No. I've overheard you and your companions enough to know that, now they're on their way to Africa, they'd continue your mission. This is it for all of you."

He placed his left index finger over a button in the middle of his chest.

"Bingham! There are women and children on board!" Lawless bellowed.

"To protect my own woman, and my own children, I would do anything, even—"

Shyamji Bhatti suddenly threw himself at the meteorologist, thudded into him, and with his arms wrapped around the saboteur, allowed his momentum to send them both toppling out of the open hull door. There came a blinding flash from outside and a tremendous discharge. The floor swung upwards and slapped into the side of Burton's head, stunning him and sending him sliding across its metal surface. Bells jangled in his ears. Through the clamour, as if from a far off place, he heard someone yell: "We're going down!"

"A Phenomenal Success."

FLOR DE DINDIGUL

A Medium-Mild Indian Cigar

"WILL BEAR FAVOURABLE COMPARISON WITH CHOICE HAVANAS, WHILE THE COST IS ABOUT ONE-THIRD."

Indian Tobacco, grown by Messrs. Slightly & Co. is eugenically enhanced for exquisitely choice flavour and delicate aroma.

A DELIGHTFUL WHIFF

22/- per 100 from all good Tobacconists.

Sir Richard Francis Burton was leaning against a palm tree just beyond the final cottage of Kaltenberg. Beside him, Bertie Wells, sitting on a rock, was dabbing at a small wound on the back of his neck with a handkerchief. Burton had just used a penknife to dig a jigger flea out from beneath the war correspondent's skin.

From the trees around them, the shrieks and cackles of birds and monkeys blended into a cacophonous racket.

High overhead, eagles wheeled majestically through the dazzling sky.

The terrain in front of the two men angled down to the outlying houses and huts of Tanga.

Burton squinted, looking across the rooftops of the sprawling town to the ocean beyond. It was like peering through glass; the atmosphere was solid with heat. The humidity pressed against him, making his skin prickle. Respiration required a conscious effort, with each scalding breath having to be sucked in, the air resisting, as if too lethargic to move.

Wells pointed at a large building in the western part of the seaport. "That's the railway terminal. Two major lines run from it; the Tanganyika, all the way west to the lake; and the Usambara, up to Kilimanjaro."

"Language is an astonishingly liquid affair," Burton muttered. "We pronounced it Kilima Njaro in my day. Like the natives."

"Perhaps some still do," Wells replied. "But it's the fluid quality that makes language an excellent tool for imperialists. Force people to speak like you and soon enough they'll be thinking like you. Rename their villages, towns and mountains, and, before they know it, they're inhabiting your territory. So Kilimanjaro it is. Anyway, as I was saying, that's the station and our forces need to capture or destroy it to slow down the movement of German troops and supplies." He indicated a twin funnelled warship lying at anchor in the bay. "And that's HMS *Fox*. She's almost two decades obsolete but such is our desperation that we have to resort to whatever's available. She's been sweeping the harbour for mines. Look at her flags. Do you understand the signal?"

"No."

"It's a demand for surrender. The British Indian Expeditionary Force transports have already offloaded the troops onto the beaches. They're awaiting the order to attack. The *Fox's* captain will lead the assault. He's probably waiting for Aitken to get our lot to get into position. It won't be long now."

Burton frowned. "The town seems uninhabited."

Wells looked at his blood-stained handkerchief and pushed it into a pocket. "They're all hiding indoors," he said. "They've known the attack was coming for a couple of days."

Burton closed his eyes, removed his helmet, and massaged his scalp with his fingertips.

Wells looked at him and asked: "Is that tattoo of yours hurting?"

"No. It's just that—I don't know—I feel like I should be somewhere else."

"Ha! Don't we all!"

They lapsed into silence, broken a few minutes later when Wells said: "I have a theory about it. Your tattoo, I mean. It seems African in pattern. You still don't recall how you got it?"

"No."

"I think perhaps you were captured and tortured by some obscure tribe. There are still a few independent ones scattered about, especially up around the Blood Jungle where you were found. Certainly the state you were in suggests some sort of trauma in addition to the malaria and shell shock, and the tattoo possesses a ritualistic look about it."

"It's possible, I suppose, but your theory doesn't ring any bells. Why is it called the Blood Jungle?"

"Because it's red. It's the thickest and most impassable jungle on the whole continent. The Germans have been trying to burn it away for I don't know how long but it grows back faster than they can destroy it."

An hour passed before, in the distance, a bugle sounded. Others took up its call; then more, much closer.

Wells used a crutch to lever himself to his feet. He leaned on it, raised his binoculars, and said: "Here we go. Stay on your toes, we're closer to the action than I'd like."

A single shot echoed from afar and, instantly, the birds in the trees became silent. For a moment there was no sound at all, then came a staccato roar as thousands of firearms let loose their bullets. An explosion shook the port.

Below and to his left, Burton saw a long line of British Askaris emerging from the undergrowth, moving cautiously into the town. They had hardly set foot past the outermost shack before they were caught in a hail of gunfire from windows and doorways. As men fell and others scattered for cover, Wells let loose a cry: "Bloody hell!"

A stray bullet whistled past him and thudded into a tree.

"Get down!" Burton snapped. The two observers dived onto to the ground and lay prone, watching in horror as the Askaris were shredded by the crossfire. It fast became apparent that armed men inhabited all the houses and huts. Tanga wasn't a town waiting to be conquered—it was a trap.

A squadron of Askaris ran forward, threw themselves flat, and lobbed grenades. Explosions tore apart wooden residences and sent smoke rolling through the air. Similar scenes unfolded all along the southern outskirts of the town as the allied forces pressed forward. Hundreds of men were falling, but by sheer weight of numbers, they slowly advanced.

A sequence of blasts assaulted Burton's eardrums as HMS *Fox* launched shells into the middle of the settlement. Colonial houses erupted into clouds of brickwork, masonry and glass.

"There goes the Hun administration!" Wells shouted. "If we're lucky, Lettow-Vorbeck was in one of those buildings!"

A Scorpion tank scuttled out of the smoke and into a street just below them. The cannon on its tail sent shell after shell into the houses, many of which were now burning. When a German soldier raced from a doorway, one of the Scorpion's claws whipped forward, closed around him, and snipped him in half.

Harvestmen were entering the town, too, firing their Gatling guns and wailing their uncanny "Ulla! Ulla!"

Forty minutes later, the last of the troops with whom Burton and Wells had travelled moved past the observation point and pushed on into the more central districts of Tanga. As the clamour attested, the battle was far from over, but it had passed beyond Burton and Wells' view now, so they were forced to judge its progress by the sounds and eruptions of smoke. A particularly unbridled sequence of detonations occurred in the eastern part of the town, and, shortly afterwards, a Union Jack was spotted there by Wells as it was hoisted up a flagpole at the top of a large building.

"That's the Hotel Nietzsche!" Wells exclaimed.

Pain lanced through Burton's head.

"Nietzsche!" he gasped. "I know that name! Who is he?"

"Bismarck's advisor," Wells replied. "The second most powerful man in the Greater German Empire!"

"He—he's going to—he's going to betray Bismarck!" Burton said, hoarsely. "He's going to take over the empire! This year!"

Wells regarded his companion, a confused expression on his face. "How can you possibly know that? You're from the past not the future."

Burton was panting with the effort of remembering.

"I—it—something—something to do with Rasputin."

"If Ras—"

"Wait!" Burton interrupted. "1914. It's 1914! Rasputin will die this year. I killed him!"

"You're not making any sense, man!"

Burton hung his head and ground his teeth in frustration. A tiny patch of soil just in front of his face suddenly bulged upward and a green shoot sprouted out of it. He watched in astonishment as a plant grew rapidly before his eyes. It budded and its flower opened, all at a phenomenal speed.

It was a red poppy.

Wells suddenly clutched at the explorer's arm. "What's that over there?"

Burton looked up and saw, writhing into the air from various places around the town, thick black smudges, twisting and spiralling as if alive. They expanded outwards, flattened, then sank down into the streets. From amidst the continuing gunfire, distant screams arose.

"What the hell?" Wells whispered.

Some minutes later, British troops came running out from between the burning buildings. They'd dropped their rifles and were waving their arms wildly, yelling in agony, many of them dropping to the ground, twitching, then lying still. One, an Askari, scrambled up the slope and fell in front of the two onlookers. He contorted and thrashed, then a rattle came from his throat, his eyes turned upward, and he died.

He was covered in bees.

"We've got to get out of here!" Wells shouted. "This is Eugenicist deviltry!"

Many more men were now climbing the incline towards them, all screaming.

Burton hauled Wells to his feet, handed him his crutches, then guided him from the observation point back into Kaltenberg. Behind them, gunfire was drawing closer.

"Counterattack!" Wells said. "Go on ahead, Richard. Get out of here. Don't let me slow you down."

"Don't be a blessed fool!" Burton growled. "What manner of ridiculous war is this that our forces can be routed by bees?"

Even as he spoke, one of the insects landed on the back of his hand and stung him. Then another, on his neck. And another, on his jaw. The pain was a hundred times worse than a normal sting, and he yelled, slapping the insects away. Almost immediately his senses began to swim and his heart fluttered as the venom entered his system. He staggered but found himself supported on either side by a couple of British Tommies who began to drag him along.

"Come on, chum!" said one. "Move yer bleedin' arse!"

"Bertie!" Burton shouted, but it came out slurred.

"Never mind your pal," the other soldier snapped. "He's bein' taken care of. Keep movin'. Have you been stung?"

"Yes." Burton's legs had stopped functioning and he had tunnel vision; all he could see was the ground speeding by. There was a buzzing in his ears.

The soldiers' voices came from a long way away: "He's snuffed it. Drop him."

"No. He's just passed out."

"He's slowing us down. Aah! I've been stung!"

"I'll not leave a man. Not while he still lives. Help me, damn it!"

A shot. The whine of a bullet.

"They're on us!"

"Run! Run!"

§

Burton's senses came swimming back. Two men were dragging him along.

"I can walk," he mumbled, and, regaining his feet, he stood and opened his eyes.

Light blinded him. It glared down from the sky and glared up from the sand.

He raised a hand for shade and felt a big bump over his right eyebrow. It was sticky with blood.

"Are you dizzy, Captain?" asked Wordsworth Pryce, the Second Officer of the *Orpheus*.

"You took quite a knock," observed another. Burton recognised the voice as that of Cyril Goodenough, one of the engineers.

His vision blurred and swirled then popped back into focus. He looked around, and croaked: "I'm fine. Somewhat dazed. We crashed?"

"The bomb destroyed our starboard engines," Pryce replied. "It's a good job we were flying low. Nevertheless, we turned right over and came down with one hell of a thump."

Burton saw the *Orpheus*.

The huge rotorship was upside down, slumped on desert dunes, its back broken, its flight pylons snapped and scattered. Steam was pouring from it and rising straight up into a clear blue morning sky. The sun was not long risen, but the heat was already intense. Long shadows extended from the wreckage, from the figures climbing out of it, and from the bodies they were lining up on the ground some way from the ship.

William Trounce was suddenly at his side. The detective's jacket and shirt were badly torn and bloodied but his wounds—lacerations, grazes and bruises—were superficial; no broken bones.

"I think we've got everyone out now except the Beetle," he said. "The boy is still in there somewhere."

"What state are we in?" Burton asked, dreading the answer.

"Thirteen dead. Officer Henson; Helmsman Wenham and his assistant D'Aubigny; Navigator Playfair; riggers Champion, Priestley, and Doe; the two firemen, Gerrard and Etheridge; Stoker Reece-Jones; and, of course, that cur Arthur Bingham. I'm afraid Daniel Gooch bought it, too."

Burton groaned.

"I'm told Constable Bhatti died a hero's death, heaven bless him," Trounce said.

"He did. There'd probably be no survivors at all but for his sacrifice. What of the wounded?"

"Tom Honesty is still unconscious. Captain Lawless was pierced through the left side. Engineer Henderson and the Quartermaster, Butler, are both in critical condition with multiple broken bones and internal injuries. Miss Mayson has just had a dislocated arm snapped back into place. She'll be all right. Everyone else is battered, cut and bruised in various degrees. Swinburne is fine. Mr. Spencer has a badly dented and twisted leg. Sister Raghavendra is unharmed, as are Masters Wilde and Cornish. Krishnamurthy was banged around pretty badly but has no serious injuries. He's devastated at the loss of his cousin, of course." Trounce paused, then said quietly: "What a confounded mess."

"And one that's fast heating up," added Pryce. "We're slap bang in the middle of a desert."

"I suppose the captain is out of action," Burton said to him. "Which makes you the commanding officer. I suggest you order the wreck stripped of everything useful. As a matter of urgency, we should employ whatever suitable material we can find to build a shaded area beside it. Please tell me the ship's water tanks are intact."

"Half of them are. There'll be plenty enough water."

"Well, that's something, at least. Have some of it put into containers."

"I'll organise it at once."

Pryce strode off.

Trounce cleared his throat. "Um. Captain, this heat—it's not—that is to say, how should we treat our—um—what should we do with the dead?"

The muscles to either side of Burton's jaw flexed. His closed his eyes for a moment, then opened them and looked at his friend. "We can't bury them, William. These sands are permanently shifting. We can't leave them in the open; there are scavengers. Our only option is a pyre."

Trounce considered this for a moment, gave a brusque nod, said, "I'll get it done," and walked away.

Burton turned to Engineer Goodenough: "What of the cargo hold and the expedition's equipment?"

"It's intact, sir. The vehicles are relatively undamaged. Overturned, of course. They just need to be righted. Your supplies look like they got caught up in a tornado but I daresay we can sort them out. I'll see to it."

"Thank you. I'll round up some help for you."

Burton walked over to where Doctor Quaint and Sister Raghavendra were treating the wounded. Thomas Honesty was sitting up now but obviously hadn't fully regained his wits; his eyes were glazed, his mouth hanging slackly open. There was blood all over his face.

The doctor looked up from Charles Henderson, who was semi-conscious and moaning softly, and said: "Almost everyone on the bridge was killed. As for the rest, the extent of their injuries depended on where they were when the ship hit the ground." He stood, drew Burton aside, and continued in a low voice: "If we don't get the wounded to a hospital, they won't make it."

Burton examined the landscape. To the north, behind the fallen *Orpheus*, to the east, and to the south, pale sand undulated all the way to the horizon in a sequence of large dunes. To the west, a thin strip of green and brown terrain clung to the hilly horizon.

"If I can recover my instruments from the hold—and if they're undamaged—I can establish our position, Doctor. Then we can work out how to get to the nearest settlement."

"But, as I say," Quaint replied, "these men need a hospital."

"I assure you, Doctor, the Arabians are masters at the medical arts. They invented surgery."

"Very well. I'll trust your judgement, sir."

Burton looked at the Sister. She gave a slight jerk of her head, to indicate that she was all right. He moved away, feeling oddly detached. The front of his skull was throbbing, and the dry heat of the Arabian peninsular was beginning to suck the moisture out of him. He knew that within a couple of hours it would become a furnace. Shelter was the priority, now. The inside of the *Orpheus* wouldn't do—the sun would soon make a giant oven of it.

Swinburne approached with Oscar Wilde and Willy Cornish in tow. The two youngsters were wide-eyed and pale faced. Wilde was cradling his right arm.

"Are you hurt, Quips?"

"Just a sprain, Captain Burton. I'm thinking it's my wits that are more shaken than my body. I'd only just left the bridge when the ship went down. Escaped by the skin of my teeth, so I did."

"And you, Master Cornish?"

"I bumped my head, Mr. Burton. Really hard."

"Me too. How is it now?"

"Not so bad, sir."

"Good boy. Algy, you appear to have escaped without a scratch."

"Don't ask me how," Swinburne replied, glancing across at the Sister's patients. "My hat! I was bounced around like a rubber ball. What infamy, Richard, that our enemies are prepared to kill innocent men, women and children in order to stop our expedition."

"All the more reason why we must succeed," Burton growled. He regarded the stricken *Orpheus*. "Algy, when the engineers have made it safe, I want you and the boys to search the ship. Locate the Beetle."

"Is he alive, Mr. Burton?" Cornish asked, anxiously.

"I don't know. But if he is, we need to get him out of there before he gets cooked. Good Lord! What on earth is that?"

Burton gaped at an approaching figure. It looked something like an upright brown bear, but baggy and shiny and possessed of a strange, narrow head, upon which Pox squatted. The thing moved with an ungainly lurching motion, swaying unevenly to from side to side as it drew closer. The parakeet held out first one wing, then the other, to stay balanced.

"Cripes! A monster!" Cornish exclaimed, diving behind Burton and clinging to his legs.

"Pestilent stench monkey!" Pox whistled.

"Hallo, Boss," the creature beneath the bird hooted.

"Is that you, Herbert?"

"Aye. I've busted me arthritic leg. Got a whackin' great dent in it. Can't hardly walk straight! Otherwise I came through with just a scratch or two. I'm itchin' all over, though. It's these blinkin' polymethylene togs."

Swinburne snorted. "You can't possibly itch, Herbert. You're made of brass!"

"I know. But I tells you, I itch!"

Herbert was completely enveloped by the suit. Gloves encased his three-fingered hands, and his flat-iron shaped feet were booted. The voluminous material billowed around his limbs and torso but was wrapped tightly against his head and held in place by two elasticated belts. There were three openings in the suit, through which the circular features of his "face" could be seen.

"I can't say your outfit is worthy of Savile Row," Burton noted. "But it looks functional and you're protected from wind-borne sand. Come on, let's give the crew a helping hand."

They moved to the back of the steaming hulk, from which supplies were being unloaded, and started to sort through them. Thirty minutes later, Swinburne, Cornish and Wilde were given the all clear to enter the ship. They began their search for the Beetle.

Burton, meanwhile, found his surveying equipment, climbed to the top of a nearby dune, and took readings. He returned and approached Wordsworth Pryce, announcing: "We're about a hundred miles to the north east of Mecca. Unfortunately, that city is forbidden to us. However, I'm familiar with this area. If the expedition travels south for a hundred and eighty miles, we'll come to the town of Al

Basah, where we should be able to join a fast caravan that'll take us all the way to Aden."

Pryce looked surprised. "Surely you don't mean to continue with your expedition? What about your supplies? How will you transport them?"

"We have no choice but to keep going. Our mission is of crucial importance. The supplies will have to be abandoned, apart from whatever we can realistically carry. We'll purchase what we can when we get to Aden, then more at Zanzibar. There's also a large shipment awaiting us in the Dut'humi Hills in Africa."

Pryce shook his head. "But travelling nearly two hundred miles through this desert? The injured will never survive it."

"They won't have to. I want you and your men to use the vehicles to transport them westward, until you encounter the ocean, then south along the coast to Jeddah, which has excellent medical facilities and a British Consulate. It's not far. If we work fast, you'll be ready to leave at sunset and you'll arrive there before dawn."

"But Captain Burton!" Pryce objected. "What about you and your people? You can't possibly walk to Al Basah!"

"If they don't receive proper attention soon, Lawless, Henderson and Butler will die. Take the vehicles. I'm an experienced desert traveller and I happen to know that there's a chain of oases between here and the town. They're frequented by traders and there's a very high probability that we'll join a caravan within hours of setting forth."

The aeronaut gripped Burton by the arm. "Come with us, sir! You can get a ship and sail from Jeddah to Aden."

"We'll not all fit into the vehicles, Mr. Pryce. And strange as it might seem, caravans journey south far more frequently than ships do. Vessels sailing from Jeddah are normally bound for Cairo. We might wait for months for one that's going to Aden. But in Al Basah, camel trains leave on a daily basis and travel rapidly down through central Arabia. We might reach Aden in less than two months."

"Two months! But by golly, sir; that's a huge delay!"

Burton shook his head. "It might seem so, but it's nothing compared to the hold ups I experienced during my first expedition. Believe me, Pryce, Speke will be encountering many similar hindrances. I remain confident that we can catch him up, despite this setback. Now, let's get those vehicles out of the cargo hold."

Frantic hours followed. Supplies were sorted and stacked beneath makeshift awnings, food and water was distributed, and two travois were constructed for Burton and his team to use to transport whatever they could manage.

The Beetle was finally located in a pipe in the heart of the wreck, which the desert heat had not yet reached. He was uninjured but hungry. Burton took him a bag of sausage rolls, some sliced meat, half a loaf of bread, and a canteen of water. He held the comestibles up to a panel in the pipe. It swung open, and a small pale blue and mottled hand reached out and drew them into the darkness.

"Thank you, Captain," came a whisper. "And I'm very sorry."

"Sorry?"

"If I had warned you about the saboteur in London, you might have lost a week. Instead, my scheme has cost you the expedition."

"No, lad. As I just informed Mr. Pryce, this crash has put us maybe two months behind Speke."

"Then he has won!"

"Not a bit of it. Time in Africa is not the same as time in England. Where we can measure a journey in hours and days, in Africa, they must be measured in weeks and months and even years. And Speke is in incompetent traveller. He is certain to make mistakes, and they will cost him as much time as we have lost today."

"I hope so. And what of me, Captain? I appear to be somewhat disadvantaged."

"We've arranged transportation for you, lad."

"How so?"

"If you follow this pipe towards the stern and turn right at the second junction, you'll find that it ends at a grille. When you are there, signal by tapping. The engineers will then saw through the pipe behind you, leaving you in a six-foot long section, the cut end of which they'll immediately seal."

"I do not want them to see me."

"They shan't. I'll be there to ensure your continued privacy."

"That is good of you. What will then happen?"

"The pipe will be loaded aboard one of our vehicles in the custody of William Cornish and Oscar Wilde. You'll travel to Jeddah by night—which will be cold, but that's better than being baked alive. It may take some time for Officer Pryce to arrange, but from the port you'll sail with the boys and the crew of the *Orpheus* to Cairo, and from there home to London. All those who'll accompany you have pledged to guard you en route. It will mean a long time in a cramped pipe, but you'll get home."

"That is most satisfactory, Captain. Thank you."

A little later, after Bloodmann and Bolling had cut and sealed the pipe, they and Burton carried it into the long tent-like structure that had been erected beside the ship. The six members of the explorer's expedition were resting there: Swinburne, Trounce, Honesty, Spencer, Krishnamurthy, and Sister Raghavendra; and so were the other nine surviving crew members: Pryce, Goodenough, Quaint, Beadle, Miss Mayson, the boys—Cornish and Wilde—and the injured men, Lawless, Henderson, and Butler.

Those who were conscious had a haunted look about their eyes—they'd all seen the tall column of smoke rising up from the other side of a nearby dune. They knew what it meant. They sat, silently bidding their friends goodbye.

Then they slept.

For the next few hours, the hottest of the day, the clockwork man kept lone vigil over the camp.

There wasn't a single sound from outside, but inside, the exhausted survivors shifted restlessly and gave forth occasional moans, for even in their trauma-filled dreams, they could feel the arid air scorching their lungs.

Five hours later, when they awoke, they felt as desiccated as Egyptian mummies.

"By Jove!" Trounce croaked. "How can anyone live in this?"

"Are Arabs flameproof?" Krishnamurthy asked.

"It will cool rapidly over the next hour," Burton declared, pushing canvas aside and squinting out at the setting sun. "Then you'll be complaining about the cold."

"Can't imagine cold. Not now!" Honesty confessed.

"This is a land of extremes, old chap, and we have to take advantage of those few hours, twice a day, when the climate shows an iota of mercy."

One such period was soon upon them, and after a hasty meal, they stocked the two conveyances with fuel and food and water, and the aeronauts prepared to take their leave.

The vehicles were extraordinary. They were crabs—of the variety *Liocarcinus vernalis*—grown to gigantic size, their shells cleaned out and fitted with steam machinery, controls, chairs and storage cabinets. They walked forward, rather than sideways, as they had done when alive, and their claws had been fitted with razor-sharp blades, designed to slice and rip through jungle.

Wordsworth Pryce reached up to the underbelly of one of them and opened a hatch. It hinged down. On its inside surface, steps unfolded. One by one, Captain Lawless, Charles

Henderson, and Frederick Butler were born up on stretchers by Doctor Quaint and Cyril Goodenough.

"I'm not at all happy about this, Captain," Pryce said to Burton. "Could you not wait it out here? Myself and one of my men could drive back to you and ferry you south."

"That would mean us tarrying for two days," Burton replied. "And in that time, we could be well on our way. The Al Atif oasis is about five hours walk from here. The chances are good that we'll be able to join a caravan to Al Basah from there. And you must bear in mind that, in travelling westward, you'll soon find yourself on firmer terrain, easy for the crabs to traverse. Southward lies only sand. It would quickly infiltrate the machinery and the vehicles would be rendered inoperable in short order. No, Mr. Pryce, this is the best way."

Pryce shook the explorer's hand. "Very well, Captain Burton. I wish you luck, and rest assured that the Beetle's privacy will be protected and he'll be escorted all the way back to his chimney in Limehouse."

With that, Pryce boarded the vehicle and pulled up the hatch.

Burton paced across to the second crab, into which Bolling and Bloodmann had just carried the Beetle's section of pipe. The stoker, Thomas Beadle, joined them.

Willy Cornish and Oscar Wilde lingered a moment to say goodbye.

"Quips, I'm sorry I dragged you into this," Burton said. "I thought I was doing you a favour."

Wilde smiled. "Don't you be worrying yourself, Captain. Experience is one thing you can't get for nothing, and if this is the price, I'm happy to pay it, for I'm having the experience of a lifetime, so I am!"

The boys entered the crab.

Burton turned to Isabella Mayson.

"Are you sure you want to remain behind, Miss Mayson? I warn you that we have many months of severe hardship ahead of us."

"There is barely room for another aboard the vehicles, Sir Richard," she replied. "And your expedition needs to be fed—a responsibility I'm happy to make my own. Besides, it will be better for Sadhvi to have another woman present. We must, at very least, tip our heads at propriety, do you not think?"

Burton pushed up the hatch and clicked it shut, then stood back as the two crabs shuddered into life with coughs and growls. Steam plumed from their funnels, and Wilde and Cornish and Doctor Barnaby Quaint waved from the windows as the two outlandish machines stalked away.

The sun sank.

Beside the *Orpheus*, eight people remained, standing in the gathering twilight watching their friends recede into the distance.

Pox the parakeet sang, "Crapulous knobble thwacker!" and Burton muttered: "I couldn't have put it better myself."

∫

One foot in front of the other.

Step. Step. Step. Step.

Eyes on the ground.

Ignore the cold.

"How far?" Krishnamurthy mumbled.

"Soon. By sunrise," Burton replied.

They were dragging a travois over the sand. It was loaded with food and water, cooking pots and lanterns, rifles and ammunition, tents, clothing, instruments, and other equipment. Krishnamurthy was certain it was getting heavier.

The Milky Way was splattered overhead, dazzling, deep, and endless. The full moon had risen and was riding low in the sky. The dunes swelled in the silvery light.

Step. Step. Step. Step.

A second travois was pulled by Trounce and Honesty.

The two women trudged along beside it.

Herbert Spencer, in his protective suit, limped a little way behind.

"Tired," Honesty said. "Four hours walking."

Trounce gave a guttural response.

Ahead, Algernon Swinburne reached the peak of the next dune and stood with his rifle resting over his shoulder. He looked back at his companions, waited for them to catch up a little, then disappeared over the sandy peak. Before the others had reached the base of the upward slope, the eastern sky suddenly brightened.

To Burton, the quickness of dawn in this part of the world came as no surprise; to the others, it was breath-taking. One minute they were enveloped by the frigid luminescence of the night, and the next the sky paled, the stars faded, and brilliant rays of sunshine transformed the landscape. The desert metamorphosed from cold naked bone to hot dry flesh.

They slogged across it.

Step. Step. Step. Step.

"Cover your eyes," Burton called.

On his recommendation, they were each wearing a *keffiyeh*—a square headscarf of brightly striped material, secured on the crown with a circlet, or *agal*—which they now pulled down across their faces. The light glared through the material but didn't blind them, and, as they came to the top of the dune, they could clearly see through the weave that the redheaded poet had reached its base and was starting up the next one.

"I can feel heat!" Krishnamurthy exclaimed. "Already!"

"It will be unbearable within the next two hours," Burton predicted. "But by that time we'll be encamped at Al Atif."

A few yards away, Honesty glanced toward the huge molten globe of the sun and whispered: "*Gladiolus gandavensi.*"

"What?" Trounce asked.

"A plant. Not a hardy one. Dislikes winter. Roots best kept in sand until mid-March. Then potted individually. You have to nurture them, William. Start them off in a greenhouse."

It was the first time, in all the years they'd worked together, that Thomas Honesty had used Detective Inspector Trounce's first name.

"I say, Honesty. Are you all right, old fellow?"

The small, dapper man smiled. "Thinking about my garden. What I'll do when we get back. Do you like gardening?"

"My wife takes care of it. We only have a small patch, and it's given over to cabbages and potatoes."

"Ah. Practical."

Step. Step. Step. Step.

"William."

"Yes?"

"I was wrong."

"Wrong?"

"About Spring Heeled Jack. Didn't believe you."

"Nor did anybody else."

"But you were right. He was at Victoria's assassination."

"Yes, he was."

"Will you forgive me? Misjudged you."

"Already done, old fellow. Some considerable time ago."

"When we get back, there's something I'd like."

"What?"

"You and Mrs. Trounce. Come over. Have tea with Vera and me. In the garden."

"We'd be honoured."

"Maybe the gladioli will be out."

"That'll be nice."

"Ahoy there!" Swinburne shouted. "I see palms!"

"The oasis," Burton said.

"Praise be!" Krishnamurthy gasped.

"Arse!" Pox squawked.

They climbed up to the poet and stopped beside him. He pointed at a distant strip of blinding light. They squinted and saw through their lashes and *keffiyehs* that it was dotted with wavering palm trees.

"Please, Captain Burton, don't tell us that's a mirage!" Sister Raghavendra said.

"No," Burton responded. "That's real enough. It's just where it ought to be. Let's push on."

They each took a gulp of water from their flasks, then returned to the hard work of placing one foot in front of the other, on and on and on, not daring to look up in case the oasis was farther away than they hoped.

Step. Step. Step. Step.

Another hour passed, and the temperature soared, sucking away what little strength remained in them.

Then, suddenly, they were in shade, green vegetation closed around them, and when they finally raised their eyes, they saw a long narrow lake just a few yards ahead.

"Thank goodness!" Isabella Mayson exclaimed, sinking to the ground. "Let me catch my breath, then I'll prepare some food while you gentlemen put up an awning."

Forty minutes later, they were tucking into a meal of preserved sausages and bread and pickles, which they washed down with fresh water and a glass each of red wine—an indulgence Swinburne had insisted on bringing, despite Burton's directive that they keep their loads as light as possible.

They sighed and lay down.

"My feet have never ached so much," Trounce observed. "Not even when I was a bobby on the beat."

Herbert Spencer, sitting with his back against the bole of a palm tree, watched Pox flutter up into its leaves. The colourful bird hunkered down and went to sleep. The clockwork philosopher made a tooting sound that might have been a sigh. "For all your complaints, Mr. Trounce" he said, "at least you can enjoy the satisfaction of a good meal. All I ever get these days is a touch of oil applied to me cogs n' springs, an' that always gives me indigestion."

Trounce replied with a long drawn out snore, then rolled onto his side and fell silent.

Peace settled over the camp, and into it, Swinburne said softly:

"Here life has death for neighbour,
And far from eye or ear
Wan waves and wet winds labour,
Weak ships and spirits steer;
They drive adrift, and whither
They wot not who make thither;
But no such winds blow hither,
And no such things grow here."

"That's beautiful, Mr. Swinburne," Sister Raghavendra whispered.

The sun climbed and the heat intensified.

Three hours passed.

They were too tired to dream.

Herbert Spencer's polymethylene-wrapped canister shaped head slowly turned until the three vertical circles of his face were directed at the king's agent. He watched the sleeping man for many minutes. Very quietly, the pipes on his head wheezed: "Time, Boss, is that which a man is always trying to kill, but which ends in killing him." Then he looked away, and sibilated: "But for us, only equivalence can lead to destruction—or transcendence."

He sat, motionless.

§

"Wake up! Wake up! We're attacked!"

Herbert Spencer's trumpeting shocked them all out of their sleep.

"We're attacked! We're attacked!"

"What the devil—?" Trounce gasped, staggering to his feet.

"Grab your rifle," Burton snapped. "Look sharp and arm to defend the camp!"

He winced, realising that he'd uttered the very same words back in '55 at Berbera; the day a spear had transfixed his face;

the day his friend William Stroyan had been killed; the day John Speke had begun to hate him.

There was a thud, and Trounce went down.

A wild-looking man stepped over him and jabbed the butt of a matchlock at Burton's head. The king's agent deflected it with his forearm, lunged in, and buried his fist in his assailant's stomach.

From behind, an arm closed around the explorer's neck and the point of a dagger touched his face just below the right eye.

"Remain very still," a voice snarled in his ear. Burton recognised the language as Balochi—a mix of Persian and Kurdish.

He froze, tense in the man's grip, and watched as brigands rounded up his companions. They were big men with intimidating beards and flowing robes, wide blue pantaloons, and colourful sashes around their waists. They were armed with matchlocks, daggers, swords and shields.

Herbert Spencer—who they obviously regarded as some sort of exotic animal—was surrounded and roped. With his enormous strength, he yanked his captives this way and that, throwing them off their feet, until one of the bandits raised a gun and fired a shot at him, at which point Burton, afraid that his friend would be damaged, called: "Stop struggling, Herbert!"

The brass man became still, and his attackers wound him around and around with the ropes then bound him to a tree trunk.

"Goat ticklers!" Pox screeched from somewhere overhead.

Burton was dragged over to the others. The two women were pulled aside, and, with their arms held tightly behind their backs, were forced to watch as the men were lined up and pushed to their knees.

"I say!" Swinburne screeched. "What the dickens do you think you're playing at? Unhand me at once, you scoundrels!"

A heavily built warrior strode over. He sneered down at the diminutive poet and spat: "*Kafir!*"

"Bless you!" the poet replied. "Do you not have a handkerchief?"

The big man cast his eyes from Swinburne to Honesty, then to Trounce, Burton and Krishnamurthy.

"Who leads?" he demanded.

"I do," said Burton, in Balochi.

The man moved to stand in front of him.

"Thou has knowledge of my language?"

"Aye, and I say to thee that there be no majesty and there be no might save in Allah, the Glorious, the Great, and in his name we ask for thy mercy and thy assistance, for we have suffered severe misfortune and have a long journey before us."

The Baloch threw his head back and loosed a roar of laughter. He squatted and looked into Burton's eyes.

"Thou speakest very prettily, Scar Face. I am Jemadar Darwaas. I lead the Disciples of Ramman. Who art thou?"

"Some call me Abdullah the Dervish."

"Is that so?" Darwaas pointed at Herbert Spencer. "And what is that?"

"It is a man of brass. A machine in which a human spirit is housed."

"So! A whole man in a whole mechanism this time! Like Aladdin's djan?"

"Like that, aye. He is concealed within material that protects him from the sand, for if grains of it got into him, he would die."

While he spoke, Burton took stock of the men into whose clutches his expedition had fallen. He judged there to be about sixty of them—all hardened desert warriors—marauders from Belochistan a thousand miles to the northeast.

"Thou art a storyteller, Abdullah."

"I speak the truth."

"Then I would cut through the material and look upon this miraculous brass man of thine."

"In doing so, thou shall kill him," Burton advised. "And what would he then be worth?"

Jemadar Darwaas grinned through his beard. "Ah," he said. "Now, O Abdullah, thou art truly speaking my language! He has value, eh?"

"The British government would pay a substantial ransom for him, and for these others, too," Burton said, indicating his companions with a jerk of his head. "Especially for the women, if they are unharmed."

Darwaas grunted. He drew his dagger and held it up, examining its sharp point. His eyes flicked from the blade to Burton's dark eyes. With a fluid motion, he stood, paced away, and began to speak in low tones with a group of his men.

William Trounce leaned close to Burton and whispered: "What was all that about?"

"I'm trying to talk him into holding us for ransom."

"Why do that?"

"Because it'll buy us some time," the king's agent replied.

Less than half an hour later, the brigands finished setting up their camp on the edge of the oasis, and the two women were taken to it and placed in a guarded tent.

Darwaas returned to the remaining captives, drew his scimitar, and levelled the point at Burton's face.

"Thy people will be held until the British consul in Jeddah pays for their release," he said. "But thee, Abdullah the Dervish, thee I shall fight."

"Fight? For what purpose?"

"For no purpose other than I desire it."

The Jemadar ordered his men to clear a circular area. The prisoners were dragged to its boundary and the bandits gathered around. Burton was yanked up and pushed forward. A warrior threw down a scimitar. It landed at the explorer's feet, and he bent, picked it up, and noted that it was a well-balanced blade.

Sir Richard Francis Burton was a master swordsman, but he much preferred fighting with a point than with an edge. The point demanded skill and finesse; the edge required mainly strength, speed and brutality, though there were also a few techniques associated with it, which, fortunately, he was well schooled in.

He held the blade, narrowed his eyes at his opponent, and sighed.

Before leaving the wreck of the *Orpheus*, he'd attached to his belt a leather holster, and in that holster there was a very odd-looking pistol. It was green and organic—actually a eugenically altered cactus—and it fired venomous spines that could knock a man unconscious in an instant. His captives had not removed it, and he wished he could draw it now, for he would far prefer to render the leader of the Disciples of Ramman senseless than to hack at him with a blade. Sword cuts, unless they were to the head, neck or stomach, very rarely killed quickly. Instead, they condemned the victim to hours—even days—of excruciating agony, often followed by infection and a lingering death. He knew, however, that the moment he went for his gun, matchlocks would be jerked up and fired at him.

Jemadar Darwaas stepped closer and brandished his scimitar. "How didst thou come by that scar on thy face, Abdullah?" he asked.

"A spear," Burton responded. "Thrust by an Abyssinian."

"Didst thou kill him?"

"No."

"That was a mistake. My people say: 'When thy enemies attack—'"

"'—bathe in their blood,'" Burton finished.

"Ha! Thy knowledge is impressive. Hast thou lived among Allah's children?"

"I am *Hajji*."

"What? A pilgrim? A believer? I did not know. Now I shall honour thee doubly after I have spilled thy guts."

Darwaas suddenly lunged forward and swung his sword at Burton's head. The king's agent deflected it with ease and slashed back at his opponent, slicing through the front of Darwaas's robe. The Baloch jumped back and exclaimed: "Thou art practiced with the sword, then?"

"Aye," said Burton, circling slowly. "And these are designed for fighting from horseback, not for face to face combat. Nevertheless, there are tactics that a man can employ with them when on foot. For example—" He paced forward, ducked, and, balancing on one heel, whipped around in a full circle, using his momentum to sweep his scimitar upwards at a twenty degree angle. Darwaas barely had time to react, only just managing to place his weapon between himself and Burton's blade, and when the two scimitars clanged together, his own was forced back hard against him, sending him staggering.

Burton immediately pressed his advantage, striking at his opponent's right side—a blow that was, again, turned aside with difficulty.

Darwaas teetered off balance, stumbled, and gasped: "By Allah! Thou art considerably more than I expected!"

"A man should not be precipitous in his choice of enemy," Burton advised. "And I am puzzled that thou hath chosen me. Wert thou paid to do so?"

"Aye, 'tis the case."

"When I told thee of the man of brass, thou didst exclaim 'a whole man in a whole mechanism this time!' Perhaps, then, thou hast seen a man partially of metal? Mayhap it was his head that was half of brass, and this man was your paymaster?"

John Speke.

"I do not deny it. Enough talk. Let us fight."

Burton transferred his scimitar to his left hand. "Keep thy body loose, Jemadar, and control thy blade with the wrist, not with the entire arm. Now, strike at me."

"Art thou so confident?"

"Strike!"

The Jemadar gave a grimace. The duel wasn't going at all the way he'd have liked. He spat onto the sand and crouched a little, his sword arm held out. The two men moved around one another, their dark eyes locked.

With such speed that the movement was almost a blur, Darwaas launched himself at Burton and sliced sideways. His blade hit his adversary just below chest level, but Burton was braced against it, with his own weapon shielding him closely, held point downward, tight against his body from shoulder to mid-thigh. He immediately swept it out, up and around, hooking it beneath the bandit's scimitar. He stepped in with knees bent and pushed upward. Darwaas's sword was instantly levered right out of his hand.

The gathered Baloch men cried out in amazement as their leader's weapon went spinning away, landing at the edge of the arena.

Darwaas stood stunned.

"The sword should be held against the body in defence," Burton stated. "Else, as thou saw, in being knocked backwards, it can do as much damage as the attacking blade. Also, this means that, for the defender, the muscles of the shoulders, arms and wrists are relaxed—are not employed in resisting the offensive—and are thus free to fully power the counter attack."

Darwaas's face blackened. "Dost thou mean to humiliate me, dog?"

Burton shook his head. "I did not seek to fight thee, Jemadar. I desire only to—"

"Richard!" Swinburne shrieked.

Something impacted against the back of Burton's head. The world reeled around him and vanished.

§

A conflagration raged in his skull, needled his eyelids, clawed at his skin. He tried to move and found that he couldn't. Thirst consumed him.

He forced his eyes open and squinted up at the pitiless sun. Turning his head, he saw that he was on his back, with limbs spread out, and wrists and ankles bound with cord to wooden stakes, driven deeply into the ground.

Dunes rose to either side.

He opened his mouth to shout for help but only a rattle emerged.

Grains of sand, riding a hot, slow breeze, blew against the side of his face.

He experienced a strange sense of deja vu.

Is this a dream?

Jemadar Darwaas entered his field of vision.

"Art thou comfortable?" he asked. "Thy head aches, I fancy? My *moollah*—lieutenant—struck thee with a knob stick." The bandit chuckled. "By Allah, he knows how I hate to be bested! Thou art a fine swordsman, Abdullah! Mayhap the tales told of thy race are true, for it is said that the British are undefeated in battle. Praise be to Allah that the lands of my people have no resources that thy people covet!" Darwaas held his arms out wide as if to embrace the entire desert. He grinned wickedly. "Let us see," he said, "how that land now judges thee, Britisher."

He turned away and climbed to the top of a dune, looked back once, spat, then descended the other side of the mound and passed out of sight.

Burton felt his flesh cracking.

It was mid afternoon and the heat wouldn't abate for at least another three hours. If he survived it, he'd then have to endure the severe chill of night.

He moved his tongue in his mouth. It felt like a stone.

There was a spell of nothingness.

He sucked in a burning breath and realised that he'd been unconscious.

Think. Think, and hang on to the thoughts. John Speke and Count Zeppelin obviously stopped here and warned the bandits to look out for a crashed rotorship and to kill any survivors. How far ahead are they? Already at Aden, perhaps?

Think, and keep thinking!

Awareness slipped to one side and skidded into oblivion.

Awake.

Where?

He tried to form words, to call for help, but the slightest movement of his mouth increased the pain a thousandfold. The agony flared; an unbearable brilliance.

He sank into the centre of an inferno.

Flames.

Flames in a stone bowl hanging by chains from a ceiling so high that it is lost in shadows. Columns. A monolithic temple. It is on a hill in the centre of Kantapuranam, the capital city of Kumari Kandam, the land of the reptilian Nāga.

A man steps forward.

He is Brahmin Kaundinya, and he is wedded to the monarch's daughter, their union a symbolic pact to mark the end of conflict between the lizard race and humans. He has lived a year among them, and is now standing before K'k'thyima, the high priest.

Thin blue smoke from burning incense curls around the human's legs. Onlookers watch attentively. There are at least a thousand of them gathered in the temple, and many millions more in attendance mentally but not physically.

The man bows his respect to the priest.

"Not to me, soft skin," K'k'thyima hisses. "To the Joined." With a three-fingered clawed hand, he gestures to his right.

Kaundinya turns to a huge black diamond, which rests on a plinth of gold.

One of the three Eyes of Nāga.

Kaundinya bows again.

K'k'thyima says: "Thy wife may step to thy side."

The man turns around to look at his mate. "Come, and speak for me, that all may know my character," he says, following the ritual.

She moves to him. Like all of her race, she is about half his height; her skin segmented into a mosaic of leathery black, yellow and green; her limbs short and thick; her head confusing to the human, for sometimes it seems to be one of seven heads, other times one of five, and occasionally the sole one. She is wearing extravagant jewellery and a chain mail tunic.

"Husband," she says. "I am willing to speak."

The High Priest, who also appears to have multiple heads, orders a human prisoner to be brought forward. As the man is escorted to the plinth, Kaundinya is addressed.

"Thou came as an emissary, O Kaundinya. Thou came to broker peace between the race of soft skins and the race of Nāga. Thou hast lived among us as one of us, and thou hast been husband to Kuma K'sss'amaya."

He turns to the female.

"Hast thou, my Kuma, been satisfied with the conduct of thy husband?"

"I have," she answers. "With intervention from our wise ones, that which divides our species was bridged, and the human gave to me a child. He is an attentive and dutiful father. He has respected our ways. He has learned much and has not judged. He brings peace."

The crowd emits an approving sibilance.

Kaundinya watches the High Priest. A single head swims into focus. Its yellow eyes blink, their membranes sliding sideways; a sign of satisfaction. The head blurs. There are seven heads. There are five. There is one. There are seven.

"Pay honour to the Joined," K'k'thyima orders.

A blade slices through the prisoner's neck and his blood spurts over the irregular facets of the giant gemstone. He convulses and dies and his corpse is dragged out of the chamber.

"A sacrifice is always necessary, O Kaundinya, but the essence of he who gave his life will live on in the Eye."

The priest performs a number of ritualistic gestures, almost a dance, and intones: "The multitude are one. Individual thoughts are one thought. Separate intentions are one intention. The words of one are the words of all. The days that have been and the days that will come are eternally now."

He steps to the stone, leans over it, and, with one of his long forked tongues, licks blood from its surface. He then dips the same tongue into a bowl containing black diamond dust.

With the organ extended, he returns to Kaundinya—who bows down—and runs it delicately over the human's shaven scalp, leaving a swirling, glittering hieroglyph.

K'k'thyima steps back. Kaundinya straightens.

The High Priest says: "Thou art invited into the Great Fusion, O Emissary. Dost thou accept the Joining?"

"I accept."

The crowd emits a throbbing susurration, a repetitive refrain. All the gathered priests extend and quiver their multiple neck crests, a dazzling display of vibrating colour.

From somewhere, a throbbing rhythm pulses and a melody of heart-wrenching beauty swells through the temple. Layer after layer is added to it. Its refrains are bafflingly complex, and they are constructed from tones that no human instrument has ever produced; tones that no human being can even properly comprehend.

Kaundinya tries to meet K'k'thyima's eyes but is unable to focus on any single head. He feels the music and the lizard's mesmeric power overwhelming all but one tiny and very well concealed part of his consciousness, and he allows it.

He looks at the black diamond. His eyes fixate upon it. He feels himself pulled into its depths. The essence of his individuality seems to break apart, distributing itself among the planes and lines and points and angles of the great stone.

Kaundinya remains passive as thousands upon thousands of other minds touch his. He loses his sense of independence and becomes enmeshed, soaking into a vast multiple consciousness.

He wills his identity farther and farther into the diamond. He fills it; exists in every part of it; becomes an ingredient in its very existence.

He is one with the Nāga.

He exists with them in the Eternal Now.

All but one tiny part of him.

Kaundinya is no ordinary man. Through rigorous education, meditation, and ritual, he has attained the absolute pinnacle of intellectual order and emotional discipline. Here, at the dawn of human history, his self-control is unmatched; and it will remain so until the end of that history.

The Nāga have been surreptitiously probing his mind from the moment he started to live among them. They have found only good intentions, only a desire for peace between the human race and their own.

Kaundinya's true purpose has never been exposed.

Now, the moment has arrived.

He flexes the one small knot of awareness that has not melted into the Joined and turns it inward, probing deep into the physical matter of his own brain.

He locates a major blood vessel and he wrenches at it.

A massive haemorrhage kills him in an instant, and at the moment his consciousness is destroyed, it sends an inexorable shockwave through the structure of the diamond.

The stone fractures and explodes into seven fragments.

The Joined are ripped apart.

Millions of Nāga drop dead.

The retorts of the shattering gem echo through the temple like rifle fire. The pieces fall from the plinth to the floor, their facets glinting like stars.

Rifle fire and stars.

Rifle fire. Stars.

Rifle fire. Stars.

Sir Richard Francis Burton opened his eyes.

It was night.

Stars filled the sky.

Rifle fire echoed across the desert.

A man screamed.

A camel brayed.

Voices argued in one of the languages of the Arabian Peninsula.

His eyelids scraped shut, time overbalanced and dropped away, and he opened them again and saw the dawn.

A figure climbed into view and stood looking down at him. A breeze tugged at her robes—for it was undoubtedly a woman, Burton could tell that from the curve of her hip, against which she rested the butt of her rifle.

"No," she said, in English. "It cannot possibly be you."

Her voice was deep and warm but filled with shock.

He tried to speak but his tongue wouldn't move. His skin was afire, yet the core of him, having suffered the night, was as cold as ice. He could feel nothing but pain.

The woman slipped and slithered down the sand then strode to his side and knelt, laying her weapon to one side. Her face was concealed by a *keffiyeh* and remained in shadow—silhouetted against the deep orange sky. She unhooked a flask from her belt, unscrewed its top, and dribbled water onto his lips. It trickled into his mouth, through his teeth, over his tongue, and was so good that he passed out from the sheer relief of it.

When awareness returned, he was inside a tent and sunlight was beating against its roof. Sister Raghavendra smiled down at him.

"Lie still, Sir Richard," she said. "I have to apply more ointment to your skin."

"Give him warm water mixed with a spoonful of honey, please, Sadhvi."

The voice was the same melodious one he'd heard before. Impossibly familiar.

He tried to look but a stab of pain prevented him from turning his head.

Sister Raghavendra drizzled sweet liquid into his mouth.

"We were rescued," she said.

Consciousness escaped him yet again, only to be summoned back by the tinkle of camel bells and the flapping of the tent's canvas as it was battered by the *simoon*—the strong hot desert wind.

He'd been propped up into a semi-reclining position, with his back and head supported by soft pillows. Sadhvi Raghavendra was sitting to his left, Algernon Swinburne to his right. The owner of the deep female voice was standing at his feet, with her face still concealed by her Arabian headdress.

She was a tall woman, slender but curvaceous, and she radiated confidence and power. Her large clear eyes, above the scarf, were of a scintillating blue.

She reached up, pulled the material aside, smiled prettily, and said: "Are you *compos mentis*? You've been ranting about reptiles and temples and diamonds."

He tested his voice. "I think—" and found that it worked, albeit harshly. "I think my mind is in better order, though my body is burned to a crisp. Hello, Isabel."

"Hello, Dick."

Isabel Arundell, who'd once been his fiancé, was wearing a long white cotton shirt, white pantaloons, and an *abba*—a short-sleeved cloak of dark green woven from the finest of wools. A sword, a dagger, and a flintlock pistol were held in place by a multi-coloured sash circling her slender waist. She manoeuvred them out of the way as she lowered herself onto a cushion and sat with her legs tucked to one side.

Burton rasped: "I thought you were running around with Jane Digby in Damascus."

Sadhvi handed him a canteen. He drank from it sparingly, knowing from experience that gulps would cause excruciating stomach cramps.

"We parted ways," Isabel replied. "I found her morals to be wanting."

"My hat, Richard!" Swinburne piped up. "We've experienced a miraculous intervention! Miss Arundell is leading a merry band of Amazonian warriors. They came galloping to our rescue on the most beautiful horses you've ever seen and gave the Disciples of Ramman a proper thrashing!"

Burton looked from his assistant back to Isabel, a question in his eyes.

She smiled again and said: "I seem to have acquired the habit of collecting about me women who've suffered at the hands of their husbands. When I opened a refuge in Damascus, there were objections from those same men. The continued existence of the place soon became untenable, so my companions and I left the city to live as Bedouins. We travelled south, through Syria, collecting more women on the way, until we arrived in Arabia, where we've survived by raiding the bandits who plunder the caravans."

"Extraordinary!" Burton wheezed. "How many of you are there?"

"A little over two hundred."

"Great heavens!"

"We saw a plume of steam, went to investigate, and discovered your downed ship. It was abandoned and a lot of supplies had been left behind. Don't worry; we have them with us. Then we followed your trail and happened upon the brigands."

"The women are armed to the teeth!" Swinburne enthused. "And they revere Miss Arundell as if she were the Goddess herself! Guess what they call her!"

"Please, Algernon!" Isabel protested.

"What?" Burton asked.

"Al-Manat!"

THE SECOND PART

The Perilous Safari

Hardly we find the path of love, to sink the self, forget the "I,"
When sad suspicion grips the heart, when Man, the Man begins to die:
How Thought is imp'otent to divine the secret which the gods defend,
The Why of birth and life and death, that Isis-veil no hand may rend.
Eternal Morrows make our day; our is is aye to be till when
Night closes in; 'tis all a dream, and yet we die, — and then and then?
And still the Weaver plies his loom, whose warp and woof is wretched Man
Weaving th' unpattern'd dark design, so dark we doubt it owns a plan.
Cease, Man, to mourn, to weep, to wail; enjoy thy shining hour of sun;
We dance along Death's icy brink, but is the dance less full of fun?

—Sir Richard Francis Burton, The Kasîdah of Hâjî Abdû El-Yezdî

CHAPTER 6

The Expedition Commences

It only requires a scientist to be told what variety of thing to look for, and where best to look, and it is inevitable that the thing will be found. So it was in the earliest days of Eugenics. The hints had been of the vaguest. They were passed from a madman to a drunkard, and from the drunkard to an engineer, and from the engineer to a naturalist, and from the naturalist to Mr. Francis Galton. Whether they seeded themselves in Mr. Galton's brain in anything resembling their original form seems doubtful—we all know how information is corrupted by travel—and yet, in that magnificent, terrifying mind of his, they blossomed, and he dazzled us all with his brilliance. Mr. Charles Darwin, in particular, was enthused to the point where, I regret to say, moral and ethical boundaries ceased to exist for him. To some extent, this happened to all of us in that little band of scientists. Unquestionably, I am now ashamed of certain of my actions whilst under the influence of that great wave of fervour and creativity that overtook us. And I feel somewhat responsible, too, for the dark turn Eugenics very quickly took after it was established as a unique scientific discipline, for it was I who, under Mr. Galton's direction, conjoined his and Mr. Darwin's brains, using techniques that I have since discovered are many, many decades ahead of their proper time. The thing that Darwin/Galton became, as a consequence of that operation, I now regard as a monstrosity, but while it existed I was in its thrall, and much against my better judgement, I was a principal in the horrible path that Eugenics trod. Oh that I could travel back and change everything! The death of Darwin/Galton liberated me and restored my proper senses, but with them I now suffer to witness the villainies of Eugenics; I see the terrifying speed at which its ghastly techniques develop; I see how it has moved so far beyond the original concept of guided evolution that it now perverts life dreadfully. Perhaps it is true that, as many claim, Mr. Darwin killed God. The existence of Eugenics rather suggests to me, I fear, that he did not, at the same time, succeed in destroying the Devil.

—From The Eugenicists; Their History and Their Crimes by Florence Nightingale, 1865

Edward Oxford thudded onto grass and bounced on his spring-heeled boots. Glancing around he saw a rolling park surrounded by tall glass buildings whose sides flashed with advertising, and in the near distance, the ancient form of the Monarchy Museum, once known as Buckingham Palace, in which the relics of England's defunct royal families were displayed. A sonic boom echoed as a shuttle headed into orbit. People buzzed overhead in their personal fliers. His AugCom was functioning.

He checked that he was still holding the top hat he'd carried with him, then ran into the wooded corner of the park, not noticing that, in the long grass to his left, a white-haired man was lying unconscious with a sniper rifle, a jewel case, and a portmanteau bag at his side.

Oxford ducked into the trees, and pushed through the undergrowth until he felt safe from prying eyes. He detached the Nimtz generator from his chest and put it on the ground, pulled off his stilted boots and placed them beside it, then stripped off his fish scale battery suit and draped it over a low branch. Reaching up to his helmet, he hesitated, then switched off the AugCom and removed the headgear. A foul stench assaulted his nostrils, a mix of raw sewerage, rotting fish and burning fossil fuels. He started to cough. The air was thick and gritty. It irritated his eyes and scraped his windpipe. He fell to his knees and clutched at his throat, gasping for oxygen. Then he remembered that he'd prepared for this and fumbled in his jacket pocket, pulling out a small instrument that he quickly applied to the side of his neck. He pressed the switch, it hissed, he felt a slight stinging sensation, and instantly he could breathe again. He put the instrument away and rested for a moment. The inability to catch his breath had been a perceptive disorder rather than a physical one. The helmet had protected him from the idea that the atmosphere was unbreathable; now a sedative was doing the job.

Unfamiliar sounds reached him from the nearby road: horses' hooves, the rumble of wheels, the shouts of hawkers.

He stood and straightened the reproduction mid-Victorian era clothes that he'd worn beneath his time suit, placed the top hat on his head, and made his way to the edge of the thicket. As he emerged from the trees, a transformed world assailed his senses, and he was immediately shaken by a profound uneasiness.

There were no AugCom illusions now, and only the grass was familiar. Through dense, filthy air, he saw a massive expanse of empty sky. The tall glass towers of his own age were absent, and London clung to the ground. To his left, Buckingham Palace, now partially hidden by a high wall, looked brand new. Quaintly costumed people were walking in the park—no, he reminded himself, not costumed; they always dressed this way!—and their slow pace appeared entirely unnatural.

Despite the background murmur, London slumbered under a blanket of silence.

He started to walk down the slope toward the base of Constitution Hill, struggling to overcome his growing sense of dislocation.

Behind him, unseen, the unconscious man regained his wits, snatched up his things, staggered to his feet, and stumbled into the trees.

"Steady Edward," Oxford muttered to himself. "Hang on, hang on. Don't let it overwhelm you. This is neither a dream nor an illusion, so stay focused, get the job done, then get back to your suit!"

He reached the wide path. The Queen's carriage would pass this way soon. My God! He was going to see Queen Victoria! He looked around. Every single person was wearing a hat or bonnet. Most of the men were bearded or had moustaches. The women held parasols.

Slow motion. It was all in slow motion.

He examined faces. Which belonged to his ancestor? He'd never seen a photograph of the original Edward Oxford—there were none—but he hoped to recognise some sort of family resemblance.

He stepped over the low wrought-iron fence lining the path, crossed to the other side, turned around to face the hill, and loitered near a tree. People started to gather along the route. He heard a remarkable range of accents and they all seemed ridiculously exaggerated. Some, which he identified as working class, were incomprehensible, while the upper classes spoke with a precision and clarity that seemed wholly artificial. Details kept catching his eye, holding his attention with hypnotic force: the prevalence of litter and dog shit on the grass; the stains and worn patches on people's clothing; rotten teeth and rickets-twisted legs; accentuated mannerisms and lace-edged handkerchiefs; pockmarks and consumptive coughs.

"Focus!" he whispered.

He noticed a man across the way, standing in a relaxed but rather arrogant manner and looking straight at him with a knowing smile on his round face. He had a lean figure and a very large moustache.

Can he see that I don't belong here?

A cheer went up. The queen's carriage had just emerged from the palace gates, its four horses guided by a postilion. Two outriders trotted along ahead of the vehicle; two more behind.

Where was his ancestor? Where was the gunman?

Ahead of him, an individual wearing a top hat, blue frock-coat, and white breeches, reached under his coat and moved closer to the path. Slowly, the royal carriage approached.

Is that him?

Moments later, the forward outriders came alongside. The blue-coated man stepped over the fence, and, as the queen and her husband passed, he took three strides to keep up with their vehicle, then whipped out a flintlock pistol and fired it at them. He threw down the smoking weapon and drew a second.

Oxford yelled "No, Edward!" and ran forward.

$\mathcal{S}$

They detected Zanzibar first with their nostrils, for, prior to the island darkening the horizon, the sultry breeze became laden with the scent of cloves. Then the long strip of land hove into view at the edge of the sapphire sea, and its coral-sand beaches seemed turned to burnished gold by the fierce sun.

"By Jove," William Trounce whispered. "What's the word for it? Sleepy?"

"Tranquil," Krishnamurthy suggested.

"Languidly basking in sensuous repose," Swinburne corrected.

"Whatever it is," said Trounce, "it's splendid. I feel as if I'm inside one of Captain Burton's tales of the Arabian Nights."

"More so than when you were actually in Arabia?" the poet enquired.

"Great heavens, yes! That was just sand, sand, and more sand. This is ... romantic!"

"Seven weeks!" Krishnamurthy grunted. "Seven weeks on a blasted camel. My posterior will never recover."

Ahead, the land swelled seductively, coloured a reddish brown beneath its veils of green, which wavered and rippled behind the heavy curtain of air.

"What do you think, Algy?" Trounce asked. The members of Burton's expedition were all on first name terms now—one of the more positive effects of their gruelling trek through central Arabia. They were also all burned a deep brown, with the exception of Swinburne, whose skin was almost as crimson as his hair had been before the sun bleached it the colour of straw.

The poet looked up at the detective, then followed his gaze to the prow of the ship—the Indian Navy sloop of war, *Elphinstone*—where he saw Sir Richard Francis Burton standing with Isabel Arundell.

"If you're asking me whether the romance of Zanzibar is infectious, Pouncer, then I take it that you haven't read Richard's account of his first expedition."

"There's little time for reading at Scotland Yard, lad. And, for the umpteenth time, don't call me Pouncer."

Swinburne grinned, cheekily. "Apparently, the island's infections are nothing to celebrate. By the same token, I'd suggest that Richard and Isabel's relationship is probably not exactly as it appears from here."

He was correct. In fact, had he been able to eavesdrop upon their conversation, Swinburne would have reported to Trounce that Isabel was giving Burton "what for."

"You're a pig-headed, self-absorbed, stubborn fool," she said. "You have never failed to underestimate me or to overestimate yourself."

Burton fished a cigar from his pocket.

"Do you mind if I smoke?" he asked.

"You'll not drive me away with tobacco fumes."

He put a flame to the Manila, inhaled the aromatic smoke, and gazed down at the water that gurgled and sparkled against the hull below. A few yards away, a shoal of flying fish shot out of the sea and glided some considerable distance before plunging back in.

Isabel pulled a small straw-coloured cylinder from a pouch at her waist and raised it to her lips. She struck a lucifer and lit its tip.

Burton smelled the tart fumes of Latakia and looked at her, raising his eyebrows.

"Good grief! Surely that's not a cigarette?"

"All the rage since the Crimea," came her murmured reply. "Do you object to a woman smoking?"

"I—well—that is to say—"

"Oh stop stammering like an idiot, Dick. Let's set it out plainly, shall we? You disapprove of my lifestyle."

"Nonsense! I simply asked you why you have chosen to live as a Bedouin when you belong to the House of Wardour, one of the richest families in Britain."

"The implication being?"

"That you could have Society at your feet; that the comforts and advantages of an aristocratic life are yours to enjoy. You aren't Jane Digby, Isabel. She fled England after her scandalous behaviour made it impossible for her to remain. Not so, you. So why endure the hardships and dangers of the nomadic life?"

"Hypocrite!"

"What?"

"How often have you railed against the constrictions and restraints of the Society you now endorse? How often have you purposely provoked outrage and challenged social proprieties at dinner tables with your shocking anecdotes? How often have you styled yourself the outsider, the man who doesn't fit in, the noble savage in civilised clothing? You glory in it, and yet you denounce Miss Digby! Really! They call you Ruffian Dick. I call you Poseur Dick!"

"Oh stop it, and tell me why you've settled upon this extraordinary lifestyle."

"Because I'm a woman."

"Indubitably. How is that an answer?"

"Just this: I accepted your proposal of marriage not just because I loved you, but because I saw in you the solution to my problem, and in me the solution to yours."

"Mine?"

"When we met, you had no security. You were adrift. I could have given you a sense of belonging."

A breath of wind pushed at them, driving away the scent of cloves and replacing it with the odour of putrefying fish. Burton wrinkled his nose, puffed at his cigar, and looked at the looming island.

"And in you," Isabel continued, "I might have found liberation from the suffocating corsets of the English gentlewoman. I mean that metaphorically, of course." She gave him a sideways glance. "Well, perhaps not entirely metaphorically."

Burton gave a savage smile and turned his attention back to her.

"What I mean to say," Isabel continued, "is that I require something the Empire is not willing to give to a woman."

"You mean liberty?"

"And equality. I am not one to be laced up and condemned to the parlour to while away my days crocheting antimacassars. Why should I allow my behaviour to be dictated by the protocols of a society in which I'm granted neither a voice nor representation?"

"I hardy think Bedouin women have a better time of it," Burton murmured.

"That's true. But at least they don't pretend otherwise. Besides, I'm not a Bedouin woman, am I? And the Arabs don't know what to make of me. To them, I'm a curiosity, whose foreign ways can be neither understood nor judged. I've found a niche where the only rules that apply are the ones I make myself."

"And you're happy?"

"Yes."

"In that case, Isabel—believe me—I don't disapprove. I detected both courage and resourcefulness in you very soon after our initial meeting, and I've always admired you for them. I salute your spirit of independence. And, incidentally, while it may be true that I was at one time uncertain of myself, I assure you that it's not now the case. As the king's agent, I have a purpose. I no longer feel that I don't belong."

She sought his eyes. "But still there's no room for a wife."

He took another drag at his cigar, then looked at it with dissatisfaction and flicked it over the side of the ship. "When I called off our engagement, it was because I thought my new role would be dangerous for anyone too closely associated with me. Now I know for certain that I was right."

"Very well," she said. "And accepted. But if I can't support you as Isabel the wife, I shall most certainly do so as Al-Manat, the warrior."

"I don't want you in harm's way, Isabel. It was good of you to escort us through the desert to Aden, but there was no need for the Daughters of Al-Manat to sail with us."

"We will march with you to the Mountains of the Moon."

Burton shook his head. "No, you won't."

"Do you still imagine that, as my husband, you would have been in a position to command me? If so, I must disillusion you. Besides which, you are not my husband, and I take orders from no one. If I see fit to lead my women alongside your expedition, what can you do to stop me?"

"Nothing."

"Then our conversation is done."

With that, Isabel dropped her cigarette, crushed it beneath her heel, and paced away.

The *Elphinstone* manoeuvred through sharp coral reefs and steered towards a white Arabic town, dominated by a plain square fort, which rose from among the clove shrubs, the coco-trees, and the tall luxuriant palms. Though the sun was high in the azure sky, the light it cast over the settlement was hazy and mellow, perhaps an effect of the high humidity, making the place appear beautiful in the extreme. However, twenty minutes later, when the steamer glided past the guard ship and into the mirror-smooth harbour waters where the rank stench of rotting molluscs and copra became overwhelming, the illusion broke. The idyllic landscape, seen up close, proved anything but. The shoreline was marked by a thick line of refuse, including three bloated human corpses upon which cur dogs were chewing, and the buildings were revealed to be in dire need of renovation.

Small fishing vessels now swarmed around the arriving sloop, and from them men shouted greetings and questions, and requested gifts, and demanded *bakhshish*, and offered fish and tobacco and alcohol at exorbitant prices. They were a mix of many races; those with the blackest skin wore wide brimmed straw hats, while those of a browner cast wore the Arabic fez. Their clothing was otherwise the same; the colourful cotton robes common to so much of Africa.

Burton watched the familiar details unfold, and thought: *I no longer feel that I don't belong.*

He'd been reflecting upon that statement ever since he'd made it. Now, while deck hands milled around making preparations to secure the vessel, it occurred to him that he hadn't adapted himself to British society at all—rather, British society was changing at such a pace, and with so little planning and forethought, that it had become extremely volatile, and, while this precarious state caused most of its people to feel unsettled, for some reason Burton couldn't comprehend, it was an environment he practically relished.

He stretched, turned, and walked over to Swinburne, Trounce, and Krishnamurthy.

Trounce grumbled: "It's not quite the paradise I thought, Richard."

Burton examined the flat-roofed residences, the Imam's palace and the smart-looking Consulates. Beyond them, and ill concealed by them, the decrepit hovels of the inner-town slumped in a mouldy heap.

"Zanzibar city, to become picturesque or pleasing," he said, "must be viewed, like Stanbul, from afar."

"And even then," Swinburne added, "with a peg firmly affixed to one's nose."

The ship's anchors dropped, and, with gulls and gannets wheeling and shrieking overhead, she came to a stop in the bay, nestling among the dhows and half a dozen square-rigged merchantmen. The British collier ship, *Blackburn*, was also there, waiting forlornly for the *Orpheus*.

As tradition demanded, the *Elphinstone* loosed a twenty-one-gun salute, and the detonations momentarily silenced the seabirds before rolling away into the distance. Strangely, no response came, either in the form of raised bunting or returned cannon fire.

"That's a curious omission. I wonder what's happening," Burton muttered. He turned to his friends, and said: "The captain will order a boat lowered soon. Let's get ourselves ashore."

They had spent seven weeks in the Arabian desert, two weeks in Aden, and ten days at sea. The expedition was considerably behind schedule. It was now the 25th of March.

Time to disembark.

Time to set foot on African soil.

§

Burton, Swinburne, Trounce, Honesty and Krishnamurthy were met at the dock by a half-caste Arab who placed his hand over his heart, bowed, and introduced himself, in the Kisawahili tongue, as Saíd bin Sálim el Lamki, el Hináwi. He was of a short, thin and delicate build, with scant mustachios and a weak beard. His skin was yellowish brown, his nose long, and his teeth dyed bright crimson by his habitual chewing of betel. His manner was extremely polite. He said: "Draw near, Englishmen. I am wazir to His Royal Highness Prince Sayyid Majid bin Said Al-Busaid, Imam of Muscat and Sultan of Zanzibar, may Allah bless him and speed his recovery."

Burton answered, in the same language: "We met when I was here last, some seven years ago. Thou wert of great help to me then."

"I was honoured, Sir Richard, and am more so that thou doth remember me. I would assist thee again, and will begin by advising thee to accompany me to the palace before thou visits the Consulate."

"Is there a problem?"

"Aye, there may be, but I should leave it for Prince Sayyid to explain. He is looking forward to seeing thee."

Eight men had accompanied Saíd. They were *Askaris*—a title created some years ago by the prince's grandfather, Sultan bin Hamid, to distinguish those Africans who took military service with him. Through means of immoderately wielded staffs, they now kept the hordes of onlookers, beggars and merchants away from the group as it moved into the town.

"His Highness has been ill?" Burton enquired.

"With smallpox," Saíd answered. "But by Allah's grace, the worst of it has passed."

They entered a deep and winding alley, one of the hundreds of capricious and disorderly lanes that threaded through the town like a tangled skein. Some of the bigger streets were provided with gutters, but most were not, and the ground was liberally puddled with festering impurities, heaps of offal, and the rubble of collapsed walls. Naked children played in this filth, poultry and dogs roamed freely through it, and donkeys and cattle splashed it up the sides of the buildings to either side.

The fetor given off by the streets, mingled with the ubiquitous odour of rotting fish and copra, made the air almost unbreathable for the visitors. All of them walked with handkerchiefs pressed against their noses.

Their eyes, too, were assaulted.

Initially, it was the architecture that befuddled Burton's companions, for they had seen nothing like it before. Built from coral-rag cemented with lime, the masonry of the shuttered dwellings and public establishments to either side of the alleys showed not a single straight line, no two of their arches were the same, and the buildings were so irregular in their placement that the spaces between them were sometimes so wide as to not seem thoroughfares at all, and often so narrow that they could barely be navigated.

Slips of paper, upon which sentences from the Koran had been scribbled, were pinned over every doorway.

"What are they for?" Krishnamurthy asked.

"To ward off witchcraft," Burton revealed.

As for the inhabitants of Zanzibar, they appeared a confusing and noisy mélange of Africans and Arabs, Chinamen and Indians. The Britishers saw among them sailors and market traders and day-labourers and hawkers and date-gleaners and fishermen and idlers. They saw rich men and poor men. They saw cripples and beggars and prostitutes and thieves.

And they saw slaves.

Swinburne was the first to witness the island's most notorious industry. As he and his friends were escorted through the crowded and chaotic Salt Bazaar—thick with musky, spicy scents, and where Saíd's men swung their staffs with even less restraint—the little poet let out a terrific yell of indignation. Burton, following his assistant's shocked stare, saw a chain gang of slaves, being driven forward by the whip, approaching them through the crowd to the right.

Swinburne hollered: "This is atrocious, Richard! Why has our Navy not stopped it?"

"They can't be everywhere at once," the king's agent replied. "For all our successes on the west coast of Africa, here in the east the miserable trade goes on."

The poet, gesticulating wildly in his frustration, made a move towards the slaves but was held back by his friend, who said: "Don't be a fool, Algy. More than forty thousand slaves pass through Zanzibar every year, you'll not change anything by causing trouble for us now."

Swinburne watched miserably as the captive men and women were herded past like animals, and he was uncharacteristically silent for a considerable time afterwards.

Saíd led them into the main street leading up to the palace.

As they neared the blocky, high-windowed edifice, Thomas Honesty remarked on the tall purple clouds that had suddenly boiled up in the southeastern sky.

"It's the *Msika*," Burton told him. "The greater rain. This is the worst season to commence an expedition, but it lasts for two months and we can't delay."

"We're English," Honesty said, in his usual jerky manner. "Conditioned to rain."

"Not such as Africa has to offer, old thing. You'll see."

The palace, when they came to it, looked little better than a barracks. Roofed with mouldering red tiles, it was double storied, square, and unencumbered by adornment.

They were ushered through the big entrance doors into a pleasant vestibule, then up a staircase and into a parlour. Saíd left them for a few moments before returning to announce that the prince was ready to receive them. The four men were then escorted into a long and narrow room, furnished with silk hangings, divans, tables, lamps, a plethora of cushions, and with colourful birds singing in its rafters.

Prince Sayyid Majid greeted them in the European manner, with a hearty handshake for each. He was a young man, thin, and possessed of a pleasant, though terribly pockmarked countenance.

They sat with him on the floor, around a low table, and waited while two slaves served sweetmeats, biscuits, and glasses of sherbet.

"It pleases me to see thee again, Captain Burton," the Prince intoned, in high-spoken Arabic.

Burton gave a bow of his head, and employing the same language, replied: "Much time has passed, O Prince. Thou wert little more than a child when I last visited the island. It pained me to hear of thy father's death."

"He taught me much and I think of him every day. May Allah grant that I never disgrace his name. I intend to continue his efforts to improve the island. Already I have cleared more land for *shambas*—plantations."

"And of thy father's intention to end the slave trade, O Prince—hast thou made progress in this?"

Sayyid Majid took a sip of his sherbet, then frowned. "There is one who opposes me—a man named el Murgebi, though most know him as Tippu Tip. His caravans penetrate far into the interior and he brings back many slaves. This man has become rich and powerful, and I can do little against him, for his supporters outnumber my own. Nevertheless—" The prince sighed and touched his nose with his right forefinger—a gesture Burton knew meant, "it is my obligation."

They talked a little more of the island's politics, until, after a few minutes, the prince revealed: "A very large force of Europeans has made its base on the mainland, Captain, in the village of Mzizima, directly south of here. Thy friend, Lieutenant Speke, was among them."

"He's no longer a friend of mine," Burton declared.

"Ah. Friendship is like a glass ornament; once it is broken, it can rarely be put back together the same way. I believe the men are of the Almaniya race."

"Germanic? Yes, I think that likely. Thou sayest Speke *was* with them? Is he no longer?"

"He and a number of men left Mzizima and are currently moving toward the central territories."

"Then I must follow them at the earliest opportunity."

The prince sighed. "The rains will make that difficult, and it pains me to tell thee, Captain, but also, thou hast been betrayed by Consul Rigby."

Burton's hands curled into fists.

The prince continued: "The British government shipped supplies here some weeks ago and instructed him to hire Wanyamwezi porters to transport them to the Dut'humi Hills, where they were to await thy arrival. The supplies consisted of trading goods—bales of cotton, rolls of brass wire, beads, the usual things—plus food, instruments, weapons and ammunition, and two of the spider machines—they are called harvestmen?"

"Yes."

"The men were never hired, and the goods never transported. A month ago, when the Almaniyas arrived, the Consul handed the supplies over to them."

"Bismillah! The traitorous hound! Ever has Rigby sought to stand in my way, but I tell thee, Prince Sayyid, this time he hath defied those to whom he owes his position. This will ruin him."

"Aye, Captain, mayhap. But that is for the future. For now, we must put our energy into overcoming the obstacles this man hath set in thy path. To that end, I offer my resources. Tell me what I can do."

Over the next hour, Burton and the prince made plans, with the king's agent occasionally breaking off to translate for his companions.

By mid afternoon, they all had tasks assigned to them. Honesty and Krishnamurthy headed back to the *Elphinstone* to join Herbert Spencer, Isabella Mayson, and Sadhvi Raghavendra in overseeing the transference of the expedition's supplies and equipment to a corvette named *Artémis*. William

Trounce, Isabel Arundell and her followers were taken by Saíd bin Sálim to the prince's country ranch, there to select horses from his extensive stud, which, in the morning, they'd ship over to the mainland aboard a cargo carrier, the *Ann Lacey*.

Sir Richard Francis Burton and Algernon Swinburne, meanwhile, paid a visit to the British Consulate.

It was nine o'clock in the evening by the time they left the prince's palace. The rain had just ceased and the town was dripping. The filth, rather than being washed away, had merely been rearranged.

The king's agent and his assistant picked their way cautiously through foul alleyways until they arrived at their destination. Its gates, to their surprise, were open and unguarded.

They passed through, crossed the small courtyard, and pushed open the entrance doors. The building was unlit and silent.

"This isn't right," Burton whispered.

"Does Rigby live here?" Swinburne asked.

"Yes, in the upstairs apartments, but let's check his office first."

The ground floor consisted of the entrance hall, a waiting room, a sparsely furnished parlour, a records office and a clerks' office, a library, and the main consulting room. All were empty and dark.

In the library, Burton, upon detecting a faint rustling, drew out his clockwork lantern, shook it open, wound it, and cast its light around.

The bookshelves were teeming with ants and termites.

"My hat!" Swinburne exclaimed. "What an infestation! What on earth has attracted them, Richard?"

"I don't know, but this is certainly excessive, even for Africa."

They moved back into the entrance hall and started up the stairs. Halfway up, there was a small landing, where the steps made a turn to the right. The body of a man lay at an awkward angle upon it. Burton held his lantern over the face. He could see from the man's physiognomy that his skin would have been black in life; in death, it was a horrible ashen grey and had shrunk against the bones beneath. The lips had pulled back, exposing all the teeth, and the eyes had withdrawn to the back of the sockets.

The king's agent reached down and pressed a finger against the face.

"It feels like wood," he said. "Like all the blood and moisture has been sucked out of it."

"And that's how." Swinburne pointed to the dead man's left arm. Burton moved the light to better illuminate it. He saw that a leafy vine of a purplish hue was coiled around the wrist, and that the end of it, which was splayed flat and covered in three-inch long thorns of wicked appearance, was pressed against the forearm and had pierced the skin many times over.

Talking a dagger from his belt, he carefully probed at the plant. Its leaves were dry and fell away at his touch. The vine itself was hard and desiccated. Raising the lantern, he followed its course and saw that it coiled away up the stairs and disappeared around a corner.

"Be careful, Algy," he said, and started towards the upper floor.

Swinburne followed, noting that the steps were swarming with beetles and cockroaches.

When they reached the hallway at the top, they saw that the vine twisted through an open doorway into a faintly illuminated chamber just ahead. Only a small part of the room was visible—the bulk of it obviously lay to the left of the portal—but the end they could see was so seething with insects that every surface seemed alive. Vines were clinging to the walls and floor and ceiling, too. Loops of vegetation hung down like jungle creepers, and through and around it, glowing softly, hundreds of fireflies were flitting.

Muttering an imprecation, Burton moved forward with Swinburne at his heels. They traversed the corridor then passed through the doorway, and, with insects crunching underfoot, turned and tried to interpret what they saw. It was difficult. No item of furniture could be properly discerned, for everything was crawling with life and half-concealed behind a tangle of thorny but dead-looking foliage. Furthermore, Burton's lantern caused the great many shadows to deepen, while the myriad fireflies made them wriggle and writhe, so that the entire space seemed to squirm disconcertingly around the two men.

There was a shuttered window in the far wall. In front of it, what seemed to be the squat and bulky main trunk of a plant humped up from the floor. Burton, ducking under a dangling creeper, stepped closer to it. He saw that it had corners and realised that what he was looking at was actually a desk, though it was hardly recognisable as such, distorted as it was by all the knotted limbs of the growth that covered it.

His lantern picked out a gnarl of woody protrusions that caught and held his attention. A few moments passed before he realised why they did. It was because they resembled a hand.

The hairs at the nape of his neck stood on end.

He slowly raised the lantern and leaned closer. The protuberances grew from the end of a thick, vine-tangled branch which, a little way along its length, bent elbow-like upwards before joining a hideously warped trunk—positioned just behind the desk—over which centipedes, spiders, ants, beetles, and termites scuttled in profusion. The insects were flooding in a downward direction. Burton followed their course upward, to where the trunk suddenly narrowed before then widening into a large nodule which angled backward slightly. There was a hole in it, and from this the creatures were vomiting.

Burton knew what he was going to see next, and with every fibre of his being he didn't want to set eyes on it, but the compulsion to lift the lantern higher couldn't be resisted, and its light crept upwards from the hole, over the deformed nose and cheekbones, and illuminated Christopher Rigby's living eyes, which burned with hatred in his transfigured and paralysed face.

Burton's shock rendered him voiceless; he could only crouch and stare, his whole body trembling, his senses blasted by the appalling thing before him.

Rigby had been sitting at his desk when the metamorphosis came upon him. It had turned his flesh into plant tissue. Roots and creepers and vines and lianas had grown from him. Repulsive thorny leaves had sprouted. And, to judge from the corpse on the stairs, the thing he'd become was carnivorous, for it had sucked the blood from that unfortunate individual.

Now, though, with the exception of those demonic eyes, Rigby seemed to be dead, for he was withered and dried out, the majority of his leaves had fallen, and his body was riddled with termite holes.

Burton straightened. The eyes followed him. He noted that Rigby's neck had been crushed, then saw the same claw marks he'd noted on the corpse of Peter Pimlico, but they were deeper, more savage.

"The Devil take him, Algy," he muttered. "This is Zeppelin's doing."

Swinburne didn't reply.

Burton turned, and for a second he thought his assistant had left the room. Then a flash of red drew his attention to the ceiling. To his horror, he saw the poet up there, flat against it, entwined by creepers.

"Algy!" he yelled, but his friend was limp, unconscious, and the explorer spotted a thorny extension pressed against the side of the small man's neck.

Spinning back to face Rigby, he yelled: "Let him go, damn you!"

A thick fountain of insects suddenly erupted from the consul's mouth, spraying into the air and landing on the desk, floor, and on Burton. The head creaked slowly into an upright position.

"You!" Rigby whispered. His voice sounded like dry leaves being disturbed by a breeze. "I have waited for so long."

"Release him!" Burton demanded. "Maybe I can help you, Rigby!"

"I don't want your help, Burton. I only want your blood!"

A liana dropped from above and encircled the explorer's neck. Burton, realising that he still held his dagger, brought it up, sliced through the creeper, and pulled it away from his skin.

"Zeppelin did this to you, didn't he?"

"Yes."

"A Prussian, Rigby! He's working against the Empire and I've been sent to stop him. You're British, man! Do your duty! Help me!"

"Were it anyone else, Burton, I would. But you, never! I'll die a traitor rather than aid you!"

Leafy tendrils wound around Burton's calves. He felt thorns cutting through his trouser legs, piercing his skin. He ducked as a spiny appendage whipped past his face.

There was no time for persuasion. No time for discussion. Swinburne was being bled to death and, at any moment, Burton himself would likely be overwhelmed.

He jabbed his dagger into his lantern, ripped the side of it open, then prodded the point of the weapon into the oil sack. Liquid spurted out and instantly ignited.

"Don't!" the consul rasped.

"I've suffered your jealousy and enmity for too many years, Rigby. It ends here."

Burton slammed the burning lantern onto the desk. Immediately, the burning oil splashing outward and the tinder dry plant burst into flames, sending the king's agent reeling backwards. The vines around his legs tripped him but then slithered away, thrashing back and forth.

Swinburne dropped and thudded onto the floor. Burton crawled on hands and knees over to him, feeling the spreading inferno scorching the hairs on the back of his head. With Rigby's screams ringing in his ears, he tore vines away from the poet, grasped him by the collar, and dragged him through the scuttling insects and out of the room.

The fire was expanding with frightening speed. It tore along the walls and over the ceiling, raged past the two men, and filled the corridor with roiling black smoke.

Holding his breath and staying low, Burton reached the top of the stairs and practically fell down them. He rolled onto the cadaver on the landing, then Swinburne rolled onto him, then all three tumbled down the remaining steps. The corpse's limbs broke like snapping twigs as it fell.

A blazing roof beam crashed onto the landing they'd just vacated, showering sparks and fragments of flaming wood onto them.

Burton stood, hoisted Swinburne onto his shoulder, and staggered across the reception hall, out into the courtyard, and through the Consulate's gate.

He turned and looked back. There would be no saving the building, that much was plain, and Christopher Rigby, who'd hated him implacably for two decades, was being cremated inside it.

Burton felt no satisfaction at that.

He carried Swinburne back towards the Imam's palace.

§

Early the following day, on the east African coast below Zanzibar, two ships dropped anchor off a long low, bush-covered sand spit some twenty miles south of the ivory and copra trading town of Bagamoyo.

The *Artémis* and *Ann Lacy* lowered their boats and began the long task of transporting men, mules, horses and supplies to the mainland. In this, they were assisted by a hundred and twenty Wasawahili porters, who waited on the shore having been transported in a dhow from Bagamoyo by Saíd bin Sálim and his eight staff-wielding Askaris.

This part of the coast was known as the Mrima, or "hill land." Cut by deep bays, lagoons and backwaters, its banks were thickly lined by forests of white and red mangroves, the tangled roots of which made passage through to the more open land beyond extremely difficult. There was, however, a humped shelf of black rock that cut through the trees and formed a path from the spit. Burton ordered that this be strewn with sand—and straw from the *Ann Lacey's* hold— so the horses might traverse it without slipping. One by one, eighty of the fine Arabian mounts were lowered by harness from the cargo vessel to the boat, then landed two at a time on the spit and led across the rock and through the mangroves to an encampment; an extensive patch of white sand bordered by a wall of verdure on three sides and by a low hill, held together by tough and bright-flowered creepers, to landward. Beyond this, more grass-covered hills swelled between mosquito-infested creeks, lagoons, and black fetid ooze.

The eighty horses were the first of four livestock shipments, and once they were ashore, the *Ann Lacey* steamed away to pick up the next consignment from Zanzibar.

Meanwhile, *Artémis* offloaded seventy bundles of trading specie, crates of food and books and equipment, rowtie tents, weapons, ammunition, and all the other paraphernalia necessary for the safari.

Amid the perpetual whine and buzz of insects, Burton directed the construction of the camp. As soon as the first rowtie was erected, Algernon Swinburne was carried by litter into it and made comfortable on a bunk.

"He's still unconscious," Sister Raghavendra told the king's agent. "He lost a lot of blood and also took a nasty knock to the head, but he'll get over it. I have no doubt he'll be bouncing around again in due course. His durability is astonishing. I remember remarking upon it that time he was assaulted by Laurence Oliphant. Nevertheless, I should allow him a week of undisturbed bed rest."

Burton shook his head. "I'm sorry, Sadhvi, but that won't be possible. We can't tarry here. We have to strike camp and start moving at the first glimmer of dawn tomorrow. But I'll assign porters to his stretcher. We'll carry Algy along for as long as he needs."

"Very well. I'll stay close to him."

Saíd bin Sálim had been appointed *ras kafilah*—or guide—to the expedition. Thankfully, despite sharing the same name, he was not the man who'd acted in that capacity during Burton's first exploration back in '57. That particular Saíd had caused nothing but trouble, whereas the current *ras kafilah* immediately demonstrated his worth by assigning tasks to the Wasawahili and ensuring they earned their pay. In this, his eight "bully boys," as Trounce called them, were instrumental. With surprising rapidity, the camp was organised.

By the time the sun had set, two hundred and fifty horses and twenty mules were corralled at the southern end of the clearing; a semi-circle of rowtie tents had been erected at the northern end; the east side was crowded with *beit sha'ar*— Arabian goat hair tents—occupied by the two hundred Daughters of Al-Manat; and the west side by the porters, who sat or lay wrapped in blankets. Guards were posted, fires were lit, and chickens and vegetables and porridge were cooked and consumed.

The silence of the tropical night settled over the expedition, shattered now and then by the bellow of a bull-crocodile or the outré cry of a nocturnal heron. The atmosphere was stifling, the mosquitoes indefatigable.

Burton, his friends—with the exception of Swinburne—and Saíd, had gathered in the main tent. The Englishmen wore light trousers and collarless shirts, unbuttoned at the neck and with sleeves rolled up. Isabella Mayson and Sister Raghavendra had donned summer dresses of a modest cut. Saíd and Isabel Arundell were in their Arabian robes. Herbert Spencer still wore his polymethylene suit but had wrapped around it the full robes of a Bedouin, with his head completely concealed within a *keffiyeh*. He'd taken to walking with a staff, not only to compensate for his damaged leg, but also because it added to the impression that he was a leper—a disguise that caused the Wasawahili porters to give him a wide berth. Had they been aware of what really lay beneath those robes, superstitious dread would have caused them to desert in droves.

The group was sitting around a table upon which Burton had spread a large map. They examined it by the light of an oil lamp against which a repulsive moth was bumping.

"This was drawn up in 1844 by a French naval officer named Maizan," Burton told them. "As you can see, I have added extensive corrections and annotations. We are here—" He pointed to a spot on the map, then to another, farther inland. "—And this is the village of Kuingani. And beyond that, here we have the village of Bomani, and here, Mkwaju.

If you march at two and a half miles per hour and don't stop at the first two villages, you'll reach the third in about four and a half to five hours."

Thomas Honesty shrugged. "Seems too slow."

"Don't underestimate the terrain," Burton replied. "You'll find it hard going. The pace I suggest won't be easy. And in addition to the difficulties of swamp and jungle, the hills that extend back from here, and which rise up along the length of the coast, belong to the Wamrima tribes. They are generally hostile and uncooperative."

"Who wouldn't be with slavers preying on them?" Isabella Mayson murmured.

"Quite so. My point is: strike camp at the crack of dawn, press on as hard as you can, stay alert, and keep your weapons to hand. Don't take any nonsense from the villagers. They will undoubtedly try to charge you an extortionate tax for passing through their territory. They refer to it as *hongo*—meaning 'tribute'—and they'll do everything possible to hamper your progress if they aren't satisfied with what they get. Pay only as Saíd advises—which will, anyway, be over the odds."

He said something to the guide in Arabic. Saíd looked at Krishnamurthy and addressed him in fluent Hindustani: "I speak thy tongue, sir."

"Ah, good, that's excellent!" Krishnamurthy responded.

Burton continued: "When you reach Mkwaju, rest and eat, but be ready to move on at a moment's notice. If everything goes to plan, by the time we catch up with you, it'll be the hottest part of the day. Despite that, we'll have to start moving again. I want to reach Nzasa, here—" He tapped another mark on the map. "That's another three and a half hour march. By the time we get there, I'm pretty sure we'll be too done in to go any farther, and the day's rains will be on their way, so this is where we'll camp for the night."

They talked for a little while longer, then Burton stood, stretched, and fished a cigar from his pocket. He addressed Isabel Arundell and William Trounce: "It's a new moon tonight, so we'll be operating by starlight alone. Isabel, when your women are done with their evening prayers, please begin your preparations. William, come have a smoke with me. The rest of you: bed—that's an order!"

"I'll work on me book, Boss," Herbert Spencer said. "Sleep is another pleasure I'm denied nowadays, but it ain't all bad; my *First Principles of Philosophy* is comin' on a treat!"

They bid each other goodnight.

Burton and Trounce stepped outside, lit up, and strolled slowly around the camp, sending plumes of blue tobacco smoke into the heavy air. It did nothing to drive away the mosquitoes. Trounce slapped at one that was attacking his forearm. "Bloody things!"

"They gather especially around swampy ground," Burton told him. "The places where miasmic gases cause malaria. The areas where the mosquitoes are thickest are the same areas where you're most likely to succumb."

"How long before I do?"

"The seasoning fever usually sets in fairly quickly. A fortnight at most, old chap, then you'll be sweating it out and gibbering like a loon for a month. I'm afraid it's inevitable."

Trounce grunted. "I hope Sadhvi is as good a nurse as you say she is!"

They watched Isabel's women saddling their horses, then discarded their cigar stubs, walked back to the main tent, and retrieved their shoulder bags and rifles.

"All right," said Burton. "Let's get on with it."

Ten minutes later, the two men were riding at Isabel's side and leading two hundred mounted Amazons up the hill. When they reached its brow, Trounce pulled his horse around—like Honesty and Krishnamurthy, he'd learned to ride during their trek through Arabia—and looked down at the camp. It seemed a tiny island, hemmed in on three sides by riotous vegetation, with the Indian Ocean glittering in the starlight beyond, and, behind him, the seemingly endless expanse of unexplored Africa.

"I feel that we're up against impossible odds," he said to Burton.

The king's agent replied: "We probably are."

§

Mzizima village was five miles south of the camp. Originally, it had been composed of thatch-roofed beehive huts and a *bandani*—a wall-less palaver house; just a thatched roof standing upon six vertical beams—which were all positioned in an orderless cluster around an open central space. Surrounding the village, amid cocoa, mango, and pawpaw trees, there had been fields of rice, holcus, sugar cane, and peas, separated by clumps of basil and sage. This cultivated land stretched to the edge of a mangrove forest in the south, to the hills in the west, and to a small natural bay on the coast.

In the distant past, the Wamrima inhabitants had been farmers of the land and fishers of the sea, but the slave trade had made lying, thieving, shirking and evasiveness the tools of survival, reducing a once prosperous village to a clump of hovels occupied by men and women who, in the knowledge that life could be literally or metaphorically taken from them at any moment, did not bother to apply themselves to the business of living.

And now the Prussians had come.

It was four o'clock in the morning. Sir Richard Francis Burton was lying on his stomach at the top of a bushy ridge to the north, and was using the field glasses he'd retrieved from the *Orpheus* to spy upon the settlement. Only a few of its original structures remained—the palaver house being one of them—and in their place wood-built barracks of a distinctly European design had been erected. There were six of these, plus six more half-built, and beyond them a sea of tents that spread out into the once-cultivated fields. The canvas dwellings were especially numerous farther to the south, where mangroves had obviously been chopped and burned away. More half-erected wooden buildings were visible there, too.

"It looks like they're planning a permanent camp here," Trounce whispered. "Building a village a little to the south of the original one."

Burton grunted an agreement.

By the bright light of the stars, he could see that his stolen supplies were stacked up in the *bandani*. One of his harvestman vehicles squatted beside the structure. The other one was closer to his and Trounce's position, standing motionless at the outer edge of the tented area just in front of the ridge, obviously left there by its driver. A guard was standing beside it, with a rifle over his shoulder and a pipe in his mouth.

Mzizma was silent, with only a few men on patrol. Of the Wamrima, there was no sign, and Burton felt certain that the villagers had either been pressed into service as lackeys or killed.

"What the bloody hell is that?" Trounce hissed, pointing to the other side of the encampment.

Burton focused his glasses on the thing that flopped along there. Even before he caught a clear view of it, its shadowy shape caused him to shudder. Then it floundered into an area of silvery luminescence and he saw that it was a huge plant, propelling itself along on thick white roots. To Burton's astonishment, there was a man sitting in the thing, cocooned in a fleshy bloom and surrounded by flailing tendrils. He appeared to be steering the plant by thought alone, for there were coiling threadlike appendages embedded into the skin of his scalp, and when he moved his head, the grotesque vehicle turned in the direction he was looking.

"There are others," Trounce said. "They're patrolling the outer perimeter."

A few minutes later, it became apparent why.

One of the plants suddenly lunged forward and grabbed at something. A man, screaming wildly, was yanked out of the undergrowth and hoisted into the air. It was a Wamrima native, obviously trying to escape, and now he paid the price. Held aloft by creepers entangled around his wrists, he was mercilessly whipped by the plant's spine encrusted limbs, until his naked back was streaming blood, then he was cast back into the camp—sent spinning through the air to land in a heap between tents, where he lay insensible.

"This complicates matters," Burton said.

"Should we call it off?"

"No. We'll need those supplies if we're to catch up with Speke. He's got a tremendous lead on us but, if we have all our resources, we can cut straight through all the circumstances that will slow him down."

"What circumstances?"

"Mainly the obstructions the natives will throw in his path. I'm counting on his incompetence as an expedition leader, inability to communicate in any language other than English, and the fact that, believing us blown up on the *Orpheus*, he has no idea we're on his tail."

Fifteen minutes later, Pox swooped out of the sky and landed on Burton's shoulder.

"Message from Isabel Arundell!" the parakeet announced.

"Shhh!" Burton hissed, but it was an instruction the bird didn't understand.

"In position, you lumpish clotpole. Awaiting the word. Message ends."

"The guard by the harvestman is looking this way," Trounce said, softly.

"Message to Isabel Arundell," Burton whispered. "Consider the word received. Beware. There are Eugenicist plants. Message ends."

Pox gave a squawk and flew away.

"It's all right," Trounce said. "He just saw Pox. Probably thinks it's nothing but a noisy jungle bird. He's giving his attention back to his pipe."

"I think its time to take care of him, anyway," Burton said.

He pulled his spine shooter from its holster.

Steadying the cactus gun on his left forearm, he took careful aim and gently squeezed the nodule that functioned as a trigger. With a soft *phut!*, the pistol fired.

Seven spines thudded into the guard's chest. He looked down at them, muttered, "Was sind diese?" then crumpled to the ground.

"Quietly now," Burton hissed. "To the outer tents. Stay low."

The two men slipped over the brow of the ridge and slithered silently down to the perimeter of the camp. They crouched in the dark shadow of a tent and waited.

When it happened, it did so with such suddenness that even Burton and Trounce, who were expecting it, were taken by surprise. One minute, there was nothing but the sound of snoring men under canvas, the next the night was rent by rifle fire, the pounding of horses' hooves, and the ululation of women.

The Daughters of Al-Manat came thundering over the crest of the hill on the north western border of the camp, and even before a warning shout could be raised by the guards, they had stampeded over tents, had set burning brands to three of the barracks, and had wheeled their horses and raced back up the hill and out of sight.

The Prussian guards barely got a shot off, so panicked were they at this unexpected onslaught.

"Wir wurden angegriffen! Wir wurden angegriffen!" they bellowed. "Verteidigt das lager!"

Men blundered out of the burning buildings, came running out of the others, and emerged from the tents, rubbing their eyes and peering around in confusion. Gunfire banged and flashed from the summit of the hill. Many of the soldiers fell to the ground with bullets in them.

Snatching up their rifles, the Prussians raced to meet the attacking forces. Burton grabbed Trounce by the arm and pointed to the Eugenicist plant vehicles. They, too, were lumbering to the north westernmost part of the settlement.

The gunfire from one particular area of the hills intensified. The Prussians returned it, shooting blind. While their attention was thus engaged, twenty riders burst out of the verdure a little farther to the south, dashed across an overgrown field, and put torches to two of the plant creatures. Burton could barely repress a cheer when the starlight revealed that Isabel Arundell was the leader of this cavalry charge. She held a pistol in one hand and a spear in the other, and, expertly controlling her mount with her knees, she sent her charge leaping across tents to another of the Eugenicist creations. Plunging her spear into the densest part of it, she reared her horse away from its lashing tendrils, brought her pistol to bear, and shot the plant's driver through the head. She barked a command, galloped away with her band following, and disappeared into the darkness.

The part of Mzizima closest to Burton and Trounce was almost entirely abandoned now.

"Let's move," Burton urged. "We have to get this done before the southern part of the camp joins the fray." He and Trounce crept forward until they reached the nearest of the two harvestmen. The explorer reached up to where he expected to find a small hatch in the machine's belly. In London, harvestmen were primarily employed to transport goods, which they carried in netting suspended from their bellies. It had been his intention to reclaim the two vehicles, load them up with the supplies, and walk them away while the Prussians were distracted. He now encountered a serious setback.

"Damn!" he said. "They've removed the confounded net! It's been replaced by a bracket. Looks like they intend to fix something else on the underside of the body."

"How will we transport our stuff?" Trounce asked.

"I don't know. Let's get to it first. Speed is of the essence!"

They ran forward, unnoticed amid the confusion.

One of the barracks, consumed by flames, collapsed, sending out a shower of sparks. Men yelled. Rifles cracked.

Pox fluttered onto Burton's shoulder.

"Message from Isabel churlish bladder prodder Arundell. Hurry up, you foot licker! Message ends."

The second harvester, standing beside the *bandani*, was intact. Burton pulled down its net and spread it out.

"Start loading it. As many crates as you can. Ignore the specie; it's the equipment we need."

"Was sind Sie Mannhandeln?" a voice demanded.

Burton whirled, raised his spine shooter, and shot the inquisitor down.

"Message to Isabel Arundell," he said. "We're loading the equipment now. There's only one harvestman. Maximum distraction, if you please. Message ends."

Pox departed.

Moments later, the Daughters of Al-Manat came pelting back down the hill with guns blazing. As they engaged at close quarters with the Prussians, Burton and Trounce lifted crate after crate from the *bandani* into the netting. At one point, the king's agent sensed movement at the periphery of his vision, looked up, and noted ten or twelve Africans running up the slope of the ridge and disappearing into the undergrowth.

"Good for you!" he grunted.

Two more soldiers noticed the Englishmen and both went down with venomous cactus spines in them.

"That's as much as she can take," Burton panted. They'd loaded about a third of the stolen supplies. "Get into her, stay low, and drive back the way we came. If I haven't caught up with you by the time you reach the sand spit, wait for me there."

William Trounce uttered an acknowledgement, climbed the rungs on one of the harvestman's legs, and settled into the driver's seat. He started the engine. Its roar was drowned by the gunfire, but as the harvestman stalked away, with its loaded net swinging underneath and Burton running in its wake, its trail of steam was noticed, and three of the Prussian plant vehicles started to converge on it.

"Keep going!" Burton yelled. "Get out of here!"

They came abreast the other harvestman, and the king's agent quickly clambered up its leg, slipped into position, grabbed the control levers, and prayed to Allah that the machine was operational.

It was.

The engine clattered into life behind his seat, and he sent the conveyance striding into the path of the nearest plant. He raised his cactus gun and fired spines at the Prussian who was nestled in its bloom. They had no effect.

"Immune to the venom?" he muttered. "Maybe you're half plant yourself!"

Burton sent his steam-powered spider crashing into the mutated flora. Tendrils wrapped themselves around his machine's legs and started heaving at it, attempting to turn it over. He repeatedly shot spines at its driver until the Prussian's face resembled a porcupine. The man remained conscious, snarled at the Britisher, and sent a vine whipping at the explorer's hand. It caught the cactus gun with such viciousness that the barrel was sliced completely in half. Burton cursed and dropped it.

The harvestman was jolted from side to side. Its carapace was battered and scored by swishing barbed limbs, and Burton felt it slewing sideways beneath him. Desperately hauling at its levers, he caused its front two legs to rise up and brought them sweeping down onto the soldier's chest. The man died instantly, his heart pierced through, and the plant bucked and threshed wildly, causing the harvestman to topple over. In the instant before it hit the ground, Burton dived out of it, rolled, and started running. He reached the bottom of the slope but it was too late; the two other plants were looming over him. Putting his head down, he pumped his legs as fast as he could and started up the hill. Creepers coiled at the periphery of his vision, reaching out to grab him. Suddenly, one hooked under his left arm and wrenched him into the air. Expecting to be flayed or ripped apart, Burton instead found himself flying over the ground and bumping against the side of a horse. He realised that it wasn't a creeper but a hand holding him. Unable to manoeuvre himself into a position where he could see his rescuer, he clutched at the rider's ankle in an attempt to steady himself—a female ankle!

The horse dashed up to the top of the ridge and skidded to a stop beside Trounce's harvestman. Burton was dropped unceremoniously onto the ground.

"William! Stop!" The commanding voice belonged to Isabel Arundell.

Trounce brought his machine to a halt.

"Get onto the net, Dick!" Isabel barked.

Burton looked up at her just as a bullet tore through a fold in her Bedouin robes, missing her flesh by less than an inch. She turned in her saddle, levelled her revolver, and fired six shots back into the camp.

"Move! Damn it!" she yelled.

Burton snapped back into action. Three paces took him beneath the harvestman. He jumped up, gripped the net, and clambered onto it.

"Go, William!" Isabel shouted. "As fast as possible! Don't stop and don't look back! We'll keep the Prussians occupied for as long as we can."

"Isabel—" Burton began, but she cut him off: "We'll catch up with your expedition later. Get going!"

She reared her horse around, and, as she sent it plunging down the slope, she pulled a spear from over her shoulder and jabbed its point into one of the plant vehicles.

Trounce pulled back on a lever, his harvestman coughed and sent out a plume of steam, then went striding into the night with Burton swinging underneath.

§

William Trounce didn't stop the harvestman until he'd travelled half the distance back to the expedition's campsite. There'd been no pursuit. Distant gunshots peppered the night.

He manoeuvred one of the spider's long legs inwards until it was within Burton's reach. The king's agent climbed up it to the one-man cabin and sat on the edge of it with his legs inside and feet hooked under the seat.

"All right," he said, and Trounce got the vehicle moving again.

It was slow going. The harvestman was far heavier than a horse, and the pointed end of its legs frequently sank deep into the sodden earth. By the time they reached the sand spit, the sun had risen, the vegetation was dripping with dew, and the land was steaming.

The sandy clearing where they'd camped was empty.

"Good," Burton said. "They're on their way. Maybe we can catch up with them before they reach Nzasa."

Pox glided down and landed on Trounce's head.

"Hey there! Get off!" the Scotland Yard man protested. The bird ignored him.

"Message from Isabel Arundell. We're going to withdraw and recoup. Eleven of my women killed, three injured. We shall wage an idle-headed guerrilla campaign over the next few days to prevent them following you. We'll catch up presently. Travel safely, wobble paunch! Message ends."

"An idle-headed guerrilla campaign?" Trounce asked, in a puzzled tone.

"I think there's a parakeet insertion there," Burton said.

"Oh. Can you get the bloody parrot off my head please?"

"Message for Isabel Arundell," Burton said. "My gratitude, but don't take risks. Disengage as soon as you can. Message ends."

The parakeet squawked its acknowledgement and launched itself into the air.

With Burton navigating, Trounce steered the harvestman up the hill on the western side of the clearing. They travelled over sandy soil, thick with thorn bushes, and, after a succession of rolling hills, descended into rich parkland dotted with mangoes and other tall trees. The sun was climbing behind them. The morning steam evaporated and the air began to heat up.

A little later, Pox rejoined them.

They came to a swamp, and waded the harvestman through it, scattering hippopotami from their path.

"This would have sent Speke into a frenzy," Burton noted.

"What do you mean?"

"He's a huntsman through and through. He'll shoot at anything that moves and delights in killing. When we were out here in '57, he slaughtered more hippos than I could count."

The giant mechanised insect pitched and swayed as it struggled through the stinking sludge, then it finally emerged onto more solid ground and began to move with greater speed.

A few beehive huts came into view, and the inhabitants, upon seeing the gigantic spider approaching, bolted.

Burton and Trounce crossed cultivated land, passed the village of Kuingani, which emptied rapidly, and proceeded onto broad grasslands flecked with small forests and freestanding baobab trees possessed of bulbous trunks and wind-flattened branches. It was here that Trounce saw his first truly wide African vista and he was astonished at the seeming purity of the land. Giraffes were moving in the distance to his right; two herds of antelope were grazing far off to his left; eagles hung almost motionless high in the sky; and on the horizon, a long low chain of mountains stretched from north to south. This Eden should, perhaps, have been caressed by the freshest of breezes, but the atmosphere was heavy and stagnant and filled with aggressive insects. The back of Trounce's hands, his forearms, and his neck were covered in bumps from their bites.

After a further two hours of travel, Burton pointed and exclaimed: "Look! I see them!"

There was a village ahead, and around it, many people were gathered. Burton could tell by the loads he saw on the ground that it was his expedition.

"That little collection of huts is Bomani," he told Trounce.

The harvestman drew closer and the natives reacted as those before them had done and fled en masse.

"Well met!" Maneesh Krishnamurthy cried out as the harvestman came to a halt and squatted down with a blast of steam and a loud hiss. "They wanted all our tobacco in return for safe passage through their territory. You soon saw them off!"

"You've made good time," Burton noted, jumping to the ground.

"Saíd had us packed and moving well before sun up," Krishnamurthy revealed. "The man's a demon of efficiency."

Burton turned to the Arab: "Hail to thee Saíd bin Sálim el Lamki, el Hináwi, and the blessings of Allah the Almighty upon thee. Thou hast fulfilled thy duties well."

"Peace be upon thee, Captain Burton. By Allah's grace, our first steps have been favoured with good fortune. May it continue! Thou hast caught up with us earlier than anticipated."

"Our mission did not take the time I expected. The Daughters of Al-Manat were ferocious and the Prussians barely looked in our direction. We were able to recover our supplies quickly. Are we fit to continue?"

"Aye."

"Very well. Have the porters take up their loads."

The *ras kafilah* bowed and moved away to prepare the safari for the next stage of the journey.

Burton spoke to Miss Mayson. "Swap places with William, Isabella. We'll take shifts in the harvester. It's more agreeable than a mule."

The young woman smiled and shook her head. "To be honest, I'd rather stay with my flea-bitten animal. I'm better with beasts than with machines."

"You're not uncomfortable?"

"Not at all. I feel positively liberated!"

It was Thomas Honesty who took over from Trounce in the end, for Sister Raghavendra also refused to give up her mount, preferring to ride alongside Swinburne's litter. The poet was awake but weak.

"My hat, Richard!" he said, faintly. "Was that really Christopher Rigby? What in blue blazes happened to him?"

"Count Zeppelin. I think he carries some sort of venom in his claws. Either he didn't pump much of it into Peter Pimlico or his talons were less well grown when he strangled him. Rigby, by contrast, received the full treatment."

"And it turned him into a prickly bush?"

"Yes. It was a close call, Algy. What devils the Eugenicists have become!"

"Not just them," Swinburne said, glancing at the harvestman. "If you ask me, all the sciences are out of control. I think my Libertine friends were right all along. We need to give more attention to the development of the human spirit before we tamper with the natural world."

Herbert Spencer limped over to them. "Mr. Saíd says we're all set for the off."

"Tell him to get us moving then, please, Herbert."

"Rightio. Pardon me, Boss, but would you mind windin' me up first? Me spring is a little slack."

"Certainly. Fetch me your key."

The clockwork man shuffled off.

"How are you feeling, Algy?" Burton asked his friend.

"Tip top, Richard," Swinburne replied. "Do you think I might have a swig of gin, you know, to ward off malaria?"

"Ha! You're obviously on the mend! And, no."

When Spencer returned, he turned his back to Burton, and the king's agent, after first checking that the porters couldn't see what he was doing, felt around for the holes that had been cut in the back of the philosopher's many robes, and the polymethylene suit beneath them. He pushed a large metal key through and into the opening in the brass man's back, then turned it until the clockwork philosopher was fully wound.

Spencer thanked him and went to help get the safari back under way.

It took half an hour for the crowd of men and animals to open out into a long line, like a gigantic serpent, which then slowly made its way westward.

What a site that column was! At its head, Burton and Trounce rode along on mules, the explorer noting everything in his journal, assessing the geography and geology as Palmerston had ordered, while the Scotland Yard man scanned the route before them with the field glasses. A few yards to the left, Honesty drove the harvestman, while behind, Isabella Mayson and Sister Raghavendra, with dainty parasols held over their heads, rode their mounts side-saddle. Swinburne, in his stretcher, was carried by four of the Wasawahili, and behind him, the rest of the porters and pack mules followed, all heavily laden. Most of the men carried a single load balanced on their shoulder or head, while others shared heavier baggage tied to a pole and carried palanquin fashion. Each man also bore his private belongings upon his back—an earthen cooking pot, a water gourd, a sleeping mat, a three-legged stool, and other necessities.

The Wasawahili wore little; just rough cloth wound about their loins, and, when the rains came or the sun had set, a goatskin slung over their backs. Some had a strip of zebra's mane bound around their head; others preferred a stiffened ox-tail, which rose above their forehead like a unicorn's horn; while many decorated their craniums with bunches of ostrich, crane and jay feathers. Bulky ivory bracelets and bangles of brass and copper encircled their arms and ankles, and there were beads and circlets upon their necks. At least half of them had small bells strapped just below their knees, and the incessant tinkling blended with the heavier clang of the bells attached to the mules' collars. This, along with ceaseless chanting and singing and hooting and shouting and squabbling and drumming, made the procession a very noisy affair, though not unpleasantly so.

At the rear of the long line, Krishnamurthy and Spencer rode their mules and kept their eyes peeled for deserters, but it was Saíd bin Sálim and his eight Askari bully boys who were, by far, the most industrious members of the party. With illimitable energy, they ranged up and down the column, keeping it under tight control and driving the men on with loud shouts of "Hopa! Hopa! Go on! Go on!"

The expedition soon came upon one of Africa's many challenges: a forest, thick and dark and crawling with biting ants. They struggled through it, with low branches snagging at the loads the porters carried on their heads. Honesty had great difficulty in forcing the harvester through the unruly foliage.

They eventually broke free and descended a long gentle slope into a ragged and marshy valley. Here, the mules sank up to their knees and blundered and complained and had to be driven on by the energetic application of a *bakur*— the African cat o' nine tails. After a long delay, with the fiery sun beating down on them, they reached firmer ground and struggled up through thick luxuriant grass to higher terrain. From here, they could see the village of Mkwaju. Once again, the prospect of a gigantic spider approaching sent the villagers racing away.

"This is an advantage I hadn't anticipated," Burton told William Trounce. "They're too scared of the harvestman to hold us up with demands for *hongo*. Damnation! If only we had all our vehicles! Without the crabs to clear a route through the jungles, we'll soon reach a point where the harvester will be stymied and we'll be forced to abandon it."

Mkwaju was little more than a few hovels and a palaver house, but it was significant in that it was the last village under the jurisdiction of Bagamoyo. The expedition was now entering the Uzamaro district.

The sun was at its zenith, and the soporific heat drained the energy out of all of them, but they were determined to reach Nzasa before resting, so they plodded on, glassy eyed, the sweat dripping off them.

The loss of the harvestman came much sooner than Burton expected. Less than two hours after he'd expressed his concern to Trounce, they encountered a thick band of jungle too dense to chop a wide enough path through and too high for the vehicle to pick its way across. Honesty ran the spider along the edge of the barrier for a mile southwards, then back and for a mile to the north. He returned and shouted down from the cabin: "Stretches as far as the eye can see. No way through. Shall I go farther?"

"No," Burton called back. "It wouldn't do to get separated. I don't want to lose you! We'll have to leave it. We knew it was going to happen at some point. I suppose this is it. And at least the porters will be able to dump the coal supply."

Honesty turned off the machine's engine and climbed down a leg. "Should destroy it," he said. "Prussians might follow. Don't want them to have it."

Burton considered a moment then nodded. "You're right."

While the safari began to machete its way through the dense undergrowth, the king's agent and the detective tied a rope around the upper part of one of the harvestman's legs and used it to pull the vehicle over onto its side. Honesty drew his Adams police issue revolver and emptied its chamber into the machine's water tank. They picked up rocks and used them to batter one of the spider's leg joints until it broke.

"That'll do," Burton said. "Let's press on to Nzasa. The sooner we get there, the better. We're all tired and hungry!"

The band of jungle sloped down to a narrow river. Mosquitos swarmed over the water and crocodiles basked on its banks. The crossing was difficult, perilous, and uncomfortable, and by the time the expedition emerged from the tangle of vegetation on the other side, everyone was covered with mud, scratches, leeches, insect bites and stings.

They moved out onto cultivated land and trudged past scattered abodes concealed by high grass and clumps of trees.

They were seeing kraals now—large round huts or long sheds built from sticks woven through with grass. Around these, in a wide circle, thorny barriers had been erected. Constructed by slaver caravans, their presence indicated that the inhabitants of this region were hostile and didn't welcome strangers at their villages.

The trail broadened and the going became easier. They slogged up a hill then descended into the valley of the Kinganí River—called *Wady el Maut* and *Dar el Jua*; the Valley of Death and Home of Hunger—which they followed until they spotted Nzasa, which Burton knew was one of the rare friendly settlements in the area.

He and Saíd rode ahead. They were met by three *P'hazi*, or headmen, each with a patterned cotton sheet wrapped around his loins and slung over his shoulder, each sheltering under an opened umbrella. The Africans announced themselves as

Kizaya, Kuffakwema, and Kombe la Simba. The latter, in the Kiswahili language, greeted the two visitors with the words: "I am old and my beard is grey, yet never in all the days I have lived have I beheld a catastrophe like this; the *muzungo mbáyá* once again in the land of my people!"

Muzungo mbáyá translated as "the wicked white man."

"I understand thy dismay," Burton responded. "Thou remembers me not then, O Kombe?

The ancient chief frowned and asked, "I am known to thee?" He squinted at Burton, then his eyebrows shot up and he exclaimed: "Surely thou art not the *Murungwana Sana*?"

Burton bowed his head and murmured, "I am pleased that thou recollects me as such," for the words meant "real free man" and were the equivalent of being called a "gentleman."

Kombe suddenly gave a broad smile, his jet-black face folding into a thousand wrinkles, his mouth displaying teeth that had been filed to points. "Ah!" he cried. "Ah! Ah! Ah! I see all! Thou art hunting the *shetani*?"

"The Devil?"

"Aye! The *muzungo mbáyá* of the long soft beard and gun that never ceases!"

"Thou art speaking of my former companion, John Speke? Thou hast seen him of late?"

"No, but a man from the village of Ngome, which is far north of here, came to us this many—" he extended the word to indicate the time that had passed: *maaaannny*, "—days ago and told of a bad man with bad men who came to his village intent on bad things. They were led by the *muzungo mbáyá*, and when he was described to me, I remembered the one thou callest Speke, though now they say his head is half of metal"

Burton said: "So his expedition is taking the northern trail eastwards?"

"Aye, and killing and stealing as he goes. Dost thou mean to do the same?"

"Absolutely not! My people seek only to rest for a single night, and for this we shall pay with copper wire and cotton cloth and glass beads."

"And tobacco?"

"And tobacco."

"And drink that burns the throat in a pleasurable manner?"

"And drink that burns the throat in a pleasurable manner."

"I must consult with my brothers."

The three *P'hazi* stepped away and conversed out of Burton's earshot.

Saíd gave a snort of contempt and said, in a low voice: "They will come back and demand much *hongo* to allow us passage through their territory."

"Of course," Burton answered. "What else do they have to bargain with?"

Sure enough, Kombe returned with what amounted to an extravagant shopping list. Burton and Saíd, both experienced in such matters, bartered until an agreement was reached. The village would receive around two thirds of the specie demanded—which, in fact, was a much better deal than the elders had expected.

Kombe, well satisfied, allowed the expedition to set up camp beside Nzasa and announced that a feast would be held to honour the arrival of the *Murungwana Sana*.

Their first full day of African travel had exhausted them all. Isabella Mayson said to Burton: "I'm confused, Sir Richard. My body tells me we've travelled many miles, but my head says we've hardly progressed at all."

"Such is the nature of our task," he replied. "This was a good day. On a bad, a single step must be counted an achievement."

As the afternoon wore into evening, the tents were put up, the animals corralled, and the supplies secured.

The rains came.

There were no warning droplets or preliminary showers. One minute the sky was clear, the next it was a dark purple, then the *Msika* fell, a sheet of unbroken water. It hit the tents like an avalanche, and Burton, Saíd, Trounce, Honesty, Krishnamurthy, Spencer, Sister Raghavendra, and Miss Mayson—who'd all gathered in the biggest of the rowties— had to raise their voices, first against the sound of the deluge pummelling the canvas, then against the cacophonous thunder, which grumbled without a pause.

"Excuse my language, ladies," Trounce shouted. "But bloody hell!"

"Can the tent stand it?" asked Krishnamurthy. "I think the ocean is being emptied on top of us!"

Honesty pulled the entrance flap aside and peered out. "Can't see a thing!" he called. "Solid water."

"There'll be two hours of this," Burton announced. "So if Sadhvi and Isabella don't mind, I propose a brandy and a smoke."

"I don't mind at all," Isabella said.

"Nor I," added Sadhvi. "In fact, I'll take a tipple myself."

A reedy sigh of frustration came from within Herbert Spencer's many robes and scarves.

Pox, perched as usual on the clockwork philosopher's head, gave a loud musical whistle, then squawked: "Flubberty jibbets!"

"Hurrah!" Krishnamurthy cheered. "That's a new one!"

"The nonsensical insults are definitely the most entertaining," Isabella agreed.

"By Jove!" Trounce blurted. "That reminds me. I say, Richard, those horrible plant things we saw at Mzizima—"

"What about them?" Burton asked.

"I was wondering; what with Eugenicist creations, such as Pox, here—"

"Pig snuggler!" Pox sang.

"—always displaying a disadvantage in proportion to whatever talent the scientists have bred into them—"

"Yes?"

"Well, what might be the drawback to those vegetable vehicles, do you think?"

"That's a good question, William, and one I can't answer!"

Burton served brandies to them all, including the women, and the men lit their various cigars and pipes, with many a nervous glance at the tent roof, which was billowing violently under the onslaught of rain.

Sister Raghavendra distributed small vials of a clear liquid that she insisted they all add to their drinks. "It's a special recipe we use in the Sisterhood of Noble Benevolence to deal with fevers," she said. "Don't worry, it's quite tasteless."

"What's in it?" Honesty asked.

"A mix of quinine and various herbs," she answered. "It won't make you immune, but it will, at least, make the attacks shorter and less damaging."

The tent flap suddenly flew open and a drenched imp hopped in.

"Bounders!" it shrieked. "Cads! Fiends! Traitorous hounds! Taking a drink without me! Without *me*! Aaaiiii!"

The thing bounded to the table, and, with wildly rolling eyes, snatched up the brandy and took an extravagant swig from it. Banging the bottle back down, it wiped its mouth on its sleeve, uttered a satisfied sigh, belched, then keeled over like a toppled tree and landed flat on its back.

"Great heavens! Is that Algernon?" Herbert Spencer tooted.

Sister Raghavendra bent beside the sodden and bedraggled figure and put a hand to its forehead. "It is," she said. "And despite that display, he doesn't seem to be feverish at all."

Burton stepped over, lifted his assistant up, and carried him to a cot at the side of the tent. "Algy tends to operate, as a matter of course, at a level that most people would consider feverish," he said. "I think, on this occasion, he has simply overestimated his own strength."

"Indeed so," the nurse agreed. "Any man would require a week to recover from blood loss like Algernon experienced."

"In which case, Algy will probably need just a couple more days, for he is most certainly not *any* man!"

They dried their friend as best they could, made him comfortable, and let him sleep.

The rain eventually stopped as quickly as it had started, and the silence of another African night settled over them. They sat quietly, comfortable in each other's company, too exhausted for conversation.

A hyena cackled in the distance.

A shout came from the village.

One drumbeat sounded.

Then another.

All of a sudden, a deep, loud, rhythmic pulsation filled the air as many drums were pounded. A boy's voice hailed them from outside. Burton stepped out of the tent and a child, about ten years old, grinned up at him.

"O *Murungwana Sana*," he said. "The fire is lit and the meat is cooking and the women are restless and want to dance. The men desire news of the far off lands of the *Muzungu*—the white man. Wouldst thou attend us?"

Burton gave a bow. "We shall come with thee now."

So it was that the expedition's first day ended with a feast and a party, attended by all but the philosopher Herbert Spencer and the poet Algernon Swinburne.

In the tent, the brass man placed a stool beside the cot, sat on it, and leaned forward, bracing himself with his staff.

Deep in the shadow of his *keffiyeh*, his metal face seemed to gaze unwaveringly at Burton's assistant.

And Swinburne dreamed of war.

CHAPTER 7

Battle at Dut'humi

"To plunder, to slaughter, to steal, these things they misname empire; and where they make a wilderness, they call it peace."
—Tacitus

Warm rain hammered against Burton's tin helmet and poured from its brim down the back of his greatcoat. An explosion momentarily deafened him, knocked him to his hands and knees, and showered him with clods of mud and lumps of bloody flesh. The black water at the bottom of the flooded trench immediately sucked at his limbs, as if the earth was greedy for yet another corpse. A head floated to the surface. Half of its face was missing. He recoiled in shock, splashing back to his feet, and ducked as another pea burst just yards away. Men and women shrieked in agony, cried out for their mothers, spat the same profanity over and over and over.

A seed thudded into a soldier's face. Blood sprayed. His helmet went spinning. He slumped as if his bones had suddenly vanished, and slid into the mire.

Burton stumbled on, sloshing forward, peering at the troops who were lining the right side of the trench and firing their rifles over its lip. He eventually saw the man he was searching for—a big Askari with a patch covering his right eye. He climbed up beside him and shouted into his ear: "Are you Private Usaama?"

"What?"

"I'm looking for Private Usaama. I was told he knows Wells."

"I'm him. What wells?"

"Herbert Wells. The correspondent. I think he's with your company."

The man's answer was lost as a squadron of hornets swept overhead, flying low, buzzing furiously, their oval bodies painted with the Union Jack, their guns crackling.

"What did you say?" Burton hollered.

"I said if he hasn't bought it he'll be in the forward listening post. Keep on down the trench until you come to an opening on your right. It's there."

They both ducked as seeds howled past them and embedded themselves in the opposite wall of the trench. Rain-loosened dirt collapsed inward.

Burton jumped back down into the water and moved along, picking his way past the dead and the mutilated, whispering a Sufi meditation to keep himself sane.

A female Askari, who was propped against a pile of saturated sandbags, grabbed at his sleeve and said, in a pleading tone: "I've lost my boot. I've lost my boot. I've lost my boot."

He looked down and saw that the woman's left leg was a ragged mess beneath the knee. The foot was missing.

"I've lost my boot. I've lost my boot."

He nodded helplessly and yanked his arm from her grasp. Another explosion. More terrible screams.

The passage to the listening post, seen dimly through the downpour, was now just a few steps away. He waded towards it, the smell of cordite and rotting flesh and overflowing latrines thick in his nostrils.

Sirens wailed through the staccato gunfire and thumping detonations: "Ullah! Ullah! Ullah!"

He entered the narrow passage and pushed through the water to its end, which widened into a small square pit. Its sides were shored up with wood, its upper edges protected by sandbags. To his right, a mechanical contrivance rested on a table beneath a canvas hood. Nearby, a corpse lay half submerged, its eyes gazing sightlessly at the sky. Straight ahead, a short and plump man was standing on a box and peering northwards through a periscope. He had a bugle slung over his shoulder and his tin helmet was badly dented on one side.

"Bertie?"

The man turned. The left side of his face was badly disfigured by a burn scar. He was unshaven and smeared with dirt.

"Lieutenant Wells, if you don't mind," he shouted. "Who the devil are you?"

"It's me. Burton."

Wells squinted through the rain, then gave a sudden whoop of joy and jumped from the box. He splashed over to Burton and gripped him by the hand.

"It's true! It's true!" he yelled, his voice pitched even higher than usual. "By gum, Burton, it's been two years! I thought I'd imagined you! But look at you! Alive! In the flesh! The chronic argonaut himself!" Wells suddenly stepped back. "What happened to you? You look like a skeleton!"

"War has been happening to me, Bertie, and to you too, I see."

They both jerked down as something whistled overhead and exploded in the trenches behind them.

"This is the ugliest it's ever been," Wells shouted. "It's attrition warfare now. The Hun has abandoned all strategy but that of battering us into oblivion. Grab a periscope and join me. Ha! Just like when we first met! What happened to you after the Battle of the Bees?"

"The what?"

"Tanga, man!"

Burton took one of the viewing devices from the table and climbed onto the box beside Wells.

"I fell in with a group of guerrilla fighters. We spent eighteen months or so raiding Hun outposts around Kilimanjaro, before I suffered a fever and severe leg ulcerations that had me laid up in a field hospital for seven weeks. While I was there, the guerrillas were killed by A-Spores. During my final week in the hospital, I heard from—" They both crouched as three explosions tore up the battlefield nearby. "—from another patient that you were heading to Dut'humi, for the attack on the Tanganyika Railway, so I hooked up with a company that was heading this way."

"I can't tell you how good it is to see you again!" Wells exclaimed. "By heaven, Richard, your inexplicable presence is the one spark of magic in this endlessly turgid conflict! Is your memory restored? Do you know why you're here?"

Burton peered through the periscope. He saw coils of barbed wire forming a barrier across the landscape ahead. Beyond it there were German trenches, and behind them, the terrain rose to a ridge, thick with green trees. The Tanganyika railway line, he'd learned, was on the other side of that low range.

"I remember a few more things—mainly that there's something I have to do. The trouble is, I don't know what!"

From over to their left, a machine gun started to chatter. Four more explosions sounded in quick succession and lumps of mud rained down on them. Someone screeched, coughed, and died.

"Forgive the mundanity," Wells said, "but I don't suppose you've got biscuits or anything? I haven't eaten since yesterday!"

"Nothing," Burton replied. "Bertie, the forest—"

"What? Speak up!"

"The trees on the ridge. There's something wrong with them."

"I've noticed. A verdant forest—and one that wasn't there two days ago!"

"What? You mean the trees grew to maturity in just forty-eight hours?"

"They did. Eugenicist mischief, obviously."

"They aren't even native to Africa. *Acer pseudoplatanus*. The sycamore maple. It's a European species."

"For a man whose memory is shot through you know far too much latin. Down!"

They ducked and hugged the dirt wall as a pea thumped into the mud nearby and detonated.

Wells said something. Burton shook his head. He couldn't hear. His ears had filled with jangling bells. The war correspondent leaned closer and shouted: "The Hun have recently solved the problem with growing yellow pea artillery. The shrapnel from these projectiles is poisonous. If you're hit, pull the fragments out of your wound as fast as you can."

An enormously long thin leg swung over the listening post as a harvestman stepped across it. Burton looked up at the bottom of its small oval-shaped body and saw a trumpet-ended weapon swivelling back and forth. He straightened, wiped the rain from his eyes, and lifted the scope. A long line of the mechanised spiders was crossing the forward trenches and approaching the barbed wire barrier. There were at least twenty vehicles. Their weapons began to blast out long jets of flame.

All of a sudden, the downpour stopped, and in the absence of its pounding susurration, the loud clatter of the vehicles' steam engines and roar of their flamethrowers sounded oddly isolated.

A strong warm breeze gusted across the battlefield.

Burton was shaken by a sense of uneasiness. Wells obviously felt it too. "Now what?" he muttered.

A shell, fired from the German trenches, hit one of the harvestmen. "Ulla!" it screamed, and collapsed to the ground. Its driver spilled from the saddle, started to run, and was shredded by gunfire.

"Something's happening up on the ridge," Wells said.

Burton turned his attention back to the distant forest. He frowned and muttered, "Is there something wrong with my sense of perspective?"

"No," Wells answered. "Those trees are gigantic."

They were also thrashing about in the strengthening wind.

"This doesn't feel at all natural," Burton said.

"You're right. I think the Hun weathermen are at work. We'd better stand ready to report to HQ."

"HQ? Are you Army now, Bertie?"

"Aren't you? You're in uniform."

"My other clothes rotted off my back—"

Another pea burst nearby. A lump of it clanged off Burton's helmet.

"—and I was given these at the field hospital. No one has officially drummed me into service. I think they just assume I'm a soldier."

"Such is our state of disorganisation," Wells responded. "The fact is, Richard, everyone is a soldier now. That's how desperate things have become. There's no such thing as a British civilian in the entire world. And right now, I'm assigning you as my Number Two. The previous—Private Michaels—poked his head over the sandbags, the silly sod, and got hit by a sniper. Be sure you don't do the same. Get over to the wireless."

Burton glanced back at the apparatus on the table. "Wireless? I—er—I don't know how to use it."

"Two years here and you still can't operate a bloody radio?"

"I've been—"

He was interrupted by whistles sounding all along the front line trench.

"This is it!" Wells exclaimed. "The lads are going over!"

To the left and right of the listening post, Askari soldiers—with some white faces standing out among them—clambered out of the waterlogged trenches and began to move across the narrow strip of No Man's Land in the wake of the advancing Harvestmen. They were crouching low and holding bayoneted rifles. Seeds from the opposing trenches sizzled through the air. Men's heads were jerked backwards; their limbs were torn away; their stomachs and chests were rent open; they went down, and when they went down, others, moving up from behind, replaced them. Peas arced out of the sky and slapped into the mud among them. They exploded, ripping men apart and sending the pieces flying into the air. Still the British troops pressed on.

"Bismillah" Burton whispered, as the carnage raged around him.

"Look!" Wells yelled. He pointed up at the ridge. "What the hell is that?"

Burton adjusted his viewer and observed, through its lens, a thick green mass boiling up from the trees. Borne on the wind, it came rolling down the slope and passed high above the German trenches. As it approached, he saw that it was comprised of spinning sycamore seeds, and when one of them hit the leg of a harvestman, he realised they were of an enormous size—at least twelve feet across. The seed didn't merely hit the spider's leg, either—its wings sliced right through it; they were as solid and sharp as scimitars. He watched horrified as thousands upon thousands of the whirling seeds impacted against the lofty battle machines, shearing through the long thin legs, chopping into the oval bodies, decapitating the drivers. As the harvestmen buckled under the onslaught, the seeds span on towards the advancing troops.

"Take cover!" Wells bellowed.

Burton and the war correspondent dropped to their knees in filthy water and hugged the base of the observation pit's forward wall. Eight sycamore seeds whisked through the air above them and thudded into the back of the excavation. A ninth sliced Private Michael's corpse clean in half. A green cloud hurtled overhead and mowed into the front line trenches.

Its shadow passed. The wind stopped. Burton looked up at the sky. The rainclouds were now ragged tatters, fast disappearing, and the blistering sun shone between them down onto a scene of such slaughter that, when Burton stood, climbed back onto the box, and looked through his periscope, he thought he might lose his mind with the horror of what he saw. He squeezed his eyes shut. Ghastly moans and whimpers and shrieks of agony filled his ears. He clapped his palms over them. The stench of fresh blood invaded his nostrils.

He collapsed backwards and fell full length into the trench water. It closed over him and he wanted to stay there, but hands clutched at his clothing and hauled him out.

"Run!" Wells cried out, his voice pitched even higher than usual. "The Germans are coming!"

Burton staggered to his feet. His soaked trousers clung to his legs; filthy liquid streamed from his jacket and shirt.

"Move! Move!" Wells shouted. He grabbed Burton and pushed him toward the connecting passage. As they splashed through it, the little war correspondent lifted his bugle to his lips and sounded the retreat. With the urgent trumpeting in his ears, Burton blundered along and passed into the forward trench. It looked as if Hell itself had bubbled up out of the mud. The sycamore seeds were everywhere, their blades embedded in sandbags, in the earth, and in soldiers. The troops had been diced like meat on a butcher's slab; body parts were floating in rivers of blood; and in the midst of the carnage, limbless men and women lay twitching helplessly, their dying eyes wide with terror and shock.

As Burton and Wells raced from the foremost trench and made their way through the connecting ditches towards the rear, the smaller man blew the retreat with frantic desperation, while the taller, whenever he spotted a soldier still capable of moving, gathered wits enough to shout: "Withdraw! Withdraw!"

Eventually they came to the final trench, clambered out of it, their uniforms red with other men's gore, and began to run.

Burton glanced to either side and saw a straggling line of fleeing soldiers—so few!—then looked back and gasped: "What are they?"

Wells said something but it was lost as a barrage of explosive peas came whistling down, punched into the ground just behind them, and sent up huge spouts of mud.

The world slowed down, became utterly silent, and revolved majestically around Burton. The sky passed underneath. Men performed loose-limbed pirouettes through it. Some of the loose limbs weren't attached to the men.

I have to be somewhere.

The ground swung upwards to meet him.

Time resumed.

The earth smacked into his face.

He coughed, groaned, spat soil from his mouth, and lifted himself onto all fours.

Wells was spreadeagled nearby.

Burton crawled over to him. His friend was alive and conscious and his mouth was moving but there was no sound. There was no sound anywhere.

Wells pointed at the trenches.

Looking back, Burton saw the *Schutztruppen* approaching. One of the Germans was very near. He was dressed in a slate grey uniform and his helmet was spiked at its crown. He held in his hands, like a rifle, a long seedpod, with a vicious thorn dripping venom at its end.

The *Schutztruppen* weren't human.

Burton pushed himself backwards through the mud, kicking his feet, trying to get away. He couldn't take his eyes off the approaching soldier. Though a man in shape, the German's head was deformed—his jaws were pushed forward into a snout, and his slavering mouth was filled with long canines. He was a tawny yellow colour, and black spotted, and his golden eyes had vertical irises.

The name Laurence Oliphant jumped into Burton's mind, and in a flash, he recalled a duel, a clashing of swords, with a man half human and half white panther. The memory was hallucinogenic in its power. He reached for his sword, looked into the thing's feline eyes, and whispered: "Good lord! What have you done to yourself?"

When his hand came whipping up there was not a sword in it, but a pistol, and without even thinking, he pumped four bullets into the German.

He watched as the trooper staggered, dropped the seedpod, and teetered to one side. The creature—a leopard given human shape—flopped to the ground. There were more approaching. Some of them were similarly formed from lithe jungle cats; others were bulky rhinoceros men, or vicious hyena things. Hardly any were fully human.

Fingers closed over Burton's arm. He jerked free of them and scrabbled away before realising they belonged to Bertie

Wells. The war correspondent was on his feet. His mouth was working, and faintly, as if from a long way off, Burton heard: "Come on, man! We have to get out of here!"

A chunk of dirt was thrown up near his head. Something tugged violently at his wet sleeve and scored the skin beneath. It finally registered that he was being shot at.

He pushed himself to his feet and, with Wells, started to run as hard as he could.

They passed between two Scorpion tanks whose tail cannons were spewing fire at the oncoming enemy troops. A pea smashed square into one and the war machine flew apart, sending shards of splintered carapace skittering past the two men.

Burton's hearing returned with a clap, and the dissonances of battle assaulted his already overwhelmed senses.

He and Wells veered to the right, ducked behind the swollen carcass of a long-dead mega-dray horse, and bolted through a field of broken wagons and wrecked wooden shacks.

They ran and ran and eventually reached the base of the Dut'humi Hills.

Seven British hornets, flying extremely low, came buzzing from behind the higher ground. They swept down, over the two men, and raked the battlefield with bullets. One of the giant insects was struck mid-thorax by an enemy cannon. It hit the earth and tumbled, enveloped in flames.

At the edge of the undergrowth, Burton noticed a bright poppy—a red beacon amid the foliage.

"This way!" he shouted, and pulled Wells towards it. They threw themselves past the little flower and into thick purplish vegetation. Careless of thorns, they heaved themselves through bushes, climbed over twisted roots, ducked under looped lianas, and forced their way uphill until the frightful noise of conflict began to fade behind them.

Vegetation snagged at and tore their uniforms. Wet leaves dripped on them, though they were already soaked to the skin. Still, they kept going, passing over the brow of a jungly hill and down into a stinking swamp. They waded through it, thigh deep, careless of crocodiles, and emerged onto firmer land, where the terrain once again sloped upward. The vegetation was slightly less dense here, and they slowed to walking pace as they passed between tree boles, with a tightly packed canopy overhead.

Burton noticed another poppy off to his left. He steered his companion in that direction.

"There's a place I must go, Bertie."

"Where?"

"I wish I knew."

A prickly and malformed plant to Wells's right twitched spasmodically. Milky liquid spurted from it and hit the sleeve of the war correspondent's greatcoat. The material immediately started to smoulder.

Wells swore, ripped the garment open, and pulled it off, throwing it to the ground. He pushed Burton onwards, leaving the plant and the coat behind.

"Bloody Eugenicist creations are starting to sprout up all over the place," he growled. "And they're all acid spitting, blood-sucking, needle shooting, poison scent emitting atrocities! Look at those, for instance—" He nodded towards the base of a nearby tree. Burton looked and saw a clump of bulbous white fungi.

"Those are Destroying Angel mushrooms. The species they get the A-Spores from. Not native to Africa until the Eugenicists meddled with them. Now they're everywhere!"

They steered carefully past a nest of pismire ants. They were natural, but, nevertheless, dangerous. Burton knew from painful experience that their bite was like the jab of a red-hot needle.

For the next hour, the two men forced their way onwards. Twice more, Burton saw poppies and altered his direction in order to pass by them. He did not mention this to Wells.

Finally, with gasps of relief, they emerged into a small glade. It was carpeted with the bright red blossoms, and in its very centre, upon a mound, a profusion of multi-coloured flowers were thriving. A single beam of sunlight angled through tree branches and brightly illuminated the vivid reds, yellows, blues and purples. The air was filled with pollen, which shone like gold dust in the shaft of light. Butterflies danced over the flowers. Everything was glowing with an almost supernatural radiance.

"A patch of beauty, at last!" Wells cried. "My eyes can hardly bear it! And look—your favourite poppy is everywhere!"

The two men threw themselves down beside the mound. For thirty minutes or so, they sat in silence, each dealing in his own way with the atrocities they'd witnessed.

Eventually, Burton spoke: "What is it about you, Bertie, that attracts death from the sky? When I first met you it was the spores. Then it was bees. This time, sycamore seeds. What next? Boulder-sized hailstones? Acidic rain? Explosive bloody bird shit?"

"Whatever else I might have to say about them," Wells responded, "I can't deny that the Germans are damned creative."

"Unquestionably. What the hell were those *Schutztruppen*?"

"The Eugenicists are turning animals into soldiers," Wells replied. "Because they're running out of Africans."

Burton groaned. "So the loathsome treatment of this continent now extends even to its flora and fauna? I swear to you, I wish a plague would wipe mankind from the face of this world! How despicable we are!"

The smaller man shrugged. "I don't think a plague is required; we're doing a pretty good job of it ourselves. You know, there was a time in my life when I fancied that we could all work together as equals for the good of the species, when I thought that our true nationality was *Mankind*. Now I recognise that I vastly overestimated the human race. We disguise imperialism as the spread of higher civilisation, but it's blatantly animalistic in its nature. We are no better than carnivores or carrion eaters. Having beast-men fighting this dreadful war is wholly appropriate."

He took a canteen from his belt and drank from it.

Burton said: "I remember you saying that Palmerston was responsible."

"Yes."

"And now you say the imperialistic drive is an animal impulse. Yet I can think of no one more divorced from nature than Palmerston!"

"Pah!" Wells snorted. He handed the canteen to Burton. "Did it never strike you that in his efforts to conquer the natural in himself, he was merely signposting the trait of his that he felt most vulnerable to? All those Eugenics treatments he paid for, Richard—they were the mark of the beast!"

"Humph! I suppose."

"And where was nature better symbolised in your age than in Africa? No wonder this continent fell victim to his paranoia!"

Burton shook his head despairingly. "I don't know how you can endure it."

"Somehow, I still have hope," Wells answered, "or I could not live."

Burton took a gulp from the canteen. He coughed and spluttered as brandy burned its way down his throat.

"I was expecting water!" he croaked.

Wells watched two dragonflies flitting back and forth over the flowers. "It's ironic," he said, softly.

"What is?"

"That I'm fighting the Germans."

"Really?"

"Yes, for in some respects, since he seized power, Nietzsche has expanded upon the beliefs I held as a younger man, and I feel strongly drawn to his philosophy." Wells looked at Burton. "You were right, by the way: Nietzsche did seize power in 1914 and Rasputin did die. According to our Intelligence agents, he suffered a brain haemorrhage. It happened in St. Petersburg, so your claim that you were responsible doesn't hold up, unless, that is, you possess extraordinary mediumistic powers, in which case I should deliver you to Colonel Crowley at the soonest possible moment."

Burton shook his head. "I have no such abilities, Bertie. So what is Nietzsche's philosophy?"

Wells sighed and was silent for a moment. Then he said: "He proposes an entirely new strain of human being. One that transcends the bestial urges."

A memory squirmed uncomfortably at the back of Burton's mind. He reached out, picked a flower from the mound, and held it in front of his face, examining its petals. They did nothing to aid his powers of recollection.

"The Greek *Hyperanthropos*?" he asked.

"Similar. The term he uses is *Übermensch*. A man free from the artificial limitations of moral codes." Wells snorted contemptuously. "Moral codes! Ha! As much as we invoke God with our exclamations and curses, we all know that he's dead. Your Darwin killed him outright, and the concept of supernaturally defined morals should have died with the deity!"

Burton held up an objecting hand and blew out a breath. "Please!" he exclaimed. "He was never my Darwin!"

"He was a man of your time. Anyway, without a God to impose ideas of right and wrong, mankind is left with a moral vacuum to fill. Nietzsche's *Übermensch* populates it according to an inner inclination that is entirely divorced from social, cultural, or religious influences. What blossoms within him is therefore utterly authentic. Such an individual will, according to Nietzsche, transcend his animal instincts. Furthermore, from amid all these singular standards of behaviour, certain common values will emerge, and they will be so completely in tune with the zeitgeist that human evolution will accelerate. God left a vacancy. We shall fill it."

Burton considered this for a moment, then said: "If I understand you correctly, the implication is that the zeitgeist, time itself, has some sort of beneficial purpose."

"Yes. Nietzsche posits that, through living as we do, we have impeded our proper relationship with time. We misunderstand it. We see only one aspect of it and we allow that to dominate us. It keeps us bound to the natural world. Only by becoming an *Übermensch*, can an individual grow beyond it."

The sky suddenly grew darker. The sun was beginning to set.

Wells said: "You don't happen to be an *Übermensch*, I suppose? You have, after all, somehow managed to defy the normal limitations of time."

Burton gave a wry smile. "I very much doubt that I'm anything Nietzsche might aspire to."

He reached among the flowers, and brushed idly at a flat moss-covered stone. "Beresford. That's who I've been trying to remember. Henry—um—Henry de La Poer Beresford. Yes! The Mad Marquess! Bismillah! Bertie! This *Übermensch* business is remarkably similar to something the creator of the Libertine and Rake movements came up with. He was obsessed with the idea of what he termed the *trans-natural man*, and he was inspired in that by—by—bloody hell!"

"What is it?" Wells asked, puzzled.

"By Spring Heeled Jack!"

"By folklore?"

"By Edward Oxford!"

"Are you referring to the man who assassinated Queen Victoria?"

"Yes—and no."

"You're not making any sense, Richard!"

"I'm—I'm trying to remember!"

Burton scrubbed furiously at the stone, as if cleaning it of moss might also clear his foggy memory.

"The Libertines," Wells said. "I believe they opposed the Technologists for a period but pretty much died out during the 1870s or 80s."

Burton didn't answer. He was leaning forward and frowning. Wells looked at him curiously then moved to his side. He reached out, pushed flowers out of the way, and, in the dwindling light, peered at the flat stone.

"Are those letters on it?" he asked.

"Yes," Burton murmured. "There's some sort of inscription."

Wells reached into his pocket and pulled out a dagger. "Here, use this."

Burton took it and used the blade to scrape the moss away. Words were revealed. They read:

THOMAS MANFRED HONESTY
1816-1863
LOST HIS LIFE WHILE
LIBERATING THE ENSLAVED.
R.I.P.

§

On the morning the expedition departed Nzasa, Sir Richard Francis Burton sent Pox to Isabel to report his position. When the parakeet returned, it squawked: "Message from Isabel Arundell. We are still harassing the stinky-mouthed enemy. I have so far lost eighteen of my women to them. They are preparing a moronic party to follow you. We will try to hold them back. Grubby pants. Message ends."

With the threat of pursuit, Burton tried to establish a greater sense of urgency among his porters, but, already, his safari was assailed by problems. Upon packing to leave the village, it was discovered that two boxes of equipment were missing and three of the Wasawahili had deserted; one of the mules appeared to be dying; and water had found its way into three sacks of flour, rendering them unusable.

The explorer, who from previous experience had resigned himself to such misfortunes, put a bullet through the mule's head, discarded the flour, redistributed the loads, and got his people moving.

The second day saw them trek from Nzasa to Tumba Ihere. The route led over gently undulating grasslands and through miry valleys, past a bone-strewn burial ground where witches and other practitioners of *uchàwi*—black magic—had been burned at the stake, and across a fast flowing stream where they lost another mule after it slipped and broke a leg.

They rested for an hour.

Swinburne abandoned his stretcher.

"I'm fine and dandy! In the pink! Fit as a fiddle!" he announced. "How far to the next village?"

"At least four hours march," Burton replied. "You can't possibly be in full bloom. You had half your blood sucked out a couple of days ago."

"Pah! I'm perfectly all right. Confound it! I was hoping the village would be closer."

"Why?"

"Because I want to try that *pombe* African beer you once told me about!"

They started moving again, crossing a plain that seethed with wildlife, and for half an hour, Swinburne, who was now riding a mule while holding an umbrella over his head, amused himself by shouting the names of every species he spotted: "Zebra! Koodoo! Giraffe! Guinea-fowl! Lion! Quail! Four-legged thingummy!"

He then fell off his mount, having fainted.

They put him back onto the stretcher.

After wrestling their way through a long stretch of sticky red soil and onto firmer, hilly ground, they were met by men from the village of Kiranga-Ranga. These Wazamaro warriors each bore three long puckered scars extending across both cheeks from the ear lobes to the corners of the mouth. Their hair was plastered down with ochre coloured mud and twisted into a double row of knobs that circled the head. They wore loincloths of unbleached cotton, and had strings of beads looped around their necks, which were also fitted with tightly beaded bands, known as *mgoweko* collars. A solid ring of brass circled their wrists. They carried muskets, spears, bows with poisoned arrows, and long knives.

They were not friendly.

Tribute was demanded, haggled over, and finally paid in the form of two *doti* of cloth and some much-prized *sami-sami* beads.

The safari continued, meandering past fertile fields of rice, maize and manioc before coming up against a snarled and riotous jungle, which they were still hacking through when the rains started. They eventually stumbled out of it, soaked to the skin and covered with ticks, and found themselves amid fetid vegetation from which misshapen dwarf mango trees grew, and in this unlikely spot—Tumba Ihere—they were forced to establish their camp.

That evening, in the main rowtie, Isabella Mayson announced that she was feeling out of sorts. By the morning she was trembling with ague and hallucinating that ravenous birds were trying to peck out her eyes. Swinburne gave up his stretcher for her.

"I have developed a horror of the horizontal!" he declared.

"Sit on your mule," Burton instructed, "and don't overexert yourself."

The explorer ordered the commencement of the next march.

"Kwecha! Kwecha!" Saíd bin Sálim and his Askaris yelled. "Pakia! Hopa! Hopa!" Collect! Pack! Set out! Safari! A journey! A journey today!

So began the third day of their hike.

Pox made the daily flight eastwards and back again. The report was not good. A ship had delivered two thousand Prussian reinforcements to Mzizima. The Daughters of Al-Manat had divided into two groups of ninety women; one continuing to wage a guerrilla campaign against the burgeoning town; the other harassing a contingent of men that had set off in pursuit of Burton's expedition.

"We have to move faster," the king's agent told Saíd.

"I will do all I can, Mr. Burton," the *ras kafilah* promised in his habitually polite manner. "And the rest is as Allah wills it."

They tramped through alternating bands of richly cultivated land and matted flora, with Saíd's Askaris forcing the porters to a brisk pace wherever possible, until they eventually found themselves in a large forest of copal trees that oozed resin and filled the air with a cloying perfume. Horseflies attacked them. Thomas Honesty was stung below the left eye by a bee and the side of his face swelled up like a balloon. Trounce started to feel a stiffness in his limbs. For an hour a strange whistling noise assaulted their ears. They never discovered its source.

They kept going

About noon, Burton—who'd succumbed to the turgid heat and was gazing uncomprehendingly at the back of his mule's head—was roused by Swinburne, who, in his piping voice, suddenly announced:

"The dense hard passage is blind and stifled
That crawls by a track none turn to climb
To the strait waste place that the years have rifled
Of all but the thorns that are touched not of time.
The thorns he spares when the rose is taken;
The rocks are left when he wastes the plain.
The wind that wanders, the weeds wind-shaken,
These remain."

"What?" Burton mumbled.

"Police pottery," Swinburne replied. "Do you remember Matthew Keller in Leeds? Seems like a long time ago, durn't it?"

"I'm losing track," Burton replied. "Since we left the *Orpheus*, I've been forgetting to record the date in my journal. I don't know why. It's out of character."

He squinted against the glaring light and for the first time realised that the forest had been left behind; they were now traversing broad grain fields. He recognised the place—he'd passed through it during his previous expedition.

"We're approaching the village of Muhogwe. Its people have a reputation for violence but last time I was here they settled for mockery."

William Trounce cleared his throat and said: "My apologies, Richard." He slipped to the ground.

It was another case of seasoning fever.

"We're succumbing considerably sooner than I expected," Burton said to Sister Raghavendra, as they lowered the police detective onto a litter.

"Don't worry," she replied. "There's usually a fairly long incubation period with this sort of affliction but the medicine I've been feeding you negates it. The stuff brings on the fever more rapidly, makes it burn more fiercely, and it's all over and done with in a matter of hours instead of weeks."

Burton raised his eyebrows. "I should have liked that during my previous expedition!"

They came to Muhogwe. It was abandoned.

"Either the slavers have taken the entire population, or the entire population has upped and moved to avoid the slavers," Burton observed.

"The latter, I hope," Swinburne responded.

Beyond the village it was all jungle and forest again, then a quagmire where they had to fire their rifles into the air to scare away a herd of hippopotami.

A slope led up to a plateau, and here they found a *boma*—a fenced kraal—and decided to set up camp. No sooner had they erected the last tent than the clouds gathered and the rain fell.

They ate and rested, except for Burton who braved the downpour to take stock of the supplies. He found that two more porters had run away and three bundles of specie were missing.

Night came. They tried to settle but the air smelled of putrefying vegetation, the mosquitos were remorseless, and they all felt, to one degree or another, ill and out of sorts.

Hyenas cackled, screamed and whined from dusk until dawn.

And so it went. The days passed and the safari crept along, seemingly at a snail's pace, and wound its way over the malarious plain of the Kinganí River toward the low peaks of the Usagara highlands. Each in turn, they came down with fever then made an astonishingly rapid recovery. Burton was in no doubt that Sister Raghavendra was a miracle worker, for there could be no greater contrast than that between his first expedition, during which he and John Speke had been permanently stricken with an uncountable number of ailments, and this, his second, where illness was the exception rather than the rule.

Isabel's reports came every morning. A force of four hundred men was now following in the expedition's tracks. The Daughters of Al-Manat were making daily attacks against them but nine more of her followers had been killed and the distance was closing between the two groups.

"If we can just make it to Kazeh before they catch up," Burton told his friends. "The Arabians there are well-disposed towards me. They would loan us men and weapons."

They trudged on.

Plains. Hills. Forests. Swamps. Jungle. The land challenged their every step.

Sagesera. Tunda. Dege la Mhora. Madege Madogo. Kidunda. Mgeta. The villages passed one after the other, each demanding *hongo*, each whittling away at their supplies.

Desertions. Theft. Accidents. Fatigue. The safari became ever more frayed and difficult to control.

One night, they heard distant gunshots.

They were camped at Kiruru, a small and semi-derelict village located deep in a plantation of holcus, whose tall, stiff canes almost completely hid the ragged beehive huts and slumping *bandani*.

Herbert Spencer, freshly wound up, had been explaining to them some of his *First Principles of Philosophy* when the crackle and pops of rifle fire echoed faintly through the air.

They looked at each other.

"How far away?" Thomas Honesty asked.

"Not far enough," Maneesh Krishnamurthy grunted.

"It's from somewhere ahead of us, not behind," Burton noted.

"Lardy flab!" Pox added.

"Sleep with your weapons beside you," the explorer ordered. "Herbert, I want you to patrol the camp tonight."

"Actually, Boss, I patrol the camp every blinkin' night," the philosopher answered.

"Well, with extra vigilance tonight, please, and I think Tom, William, Maneesh, Algy and I will stand shifts with you."

Burton turned to Saíd. "Wilt thou see to it that we are packed and on the move well before sunrise?"

Saíd bowed an acknowledgement.

The night passed without incident but the march the following morning was one of the worst they'd so far experienced.

They found themselves fighting through thick razor-edged grass, which towered over their heads and dripped dew onto them. The black earth was greasy and slippery and interlaced with roots that caught at their feet. The mules brayed in distress, refused to be ridden, and had to be forced along with swipes of the *bakur*, not moving until the cat had raised welts on their hindquarters.

Pox, who'd been sent to Isabel earlier, returned and shrieked: "Message from Isabel Big Nose Arundell. We have reduced their cretinous number by a quarter but they are less than a day behind you. Move faster, Dick. Message bleeding well ends."

"We're moving as fast as we bleeding well can!" Burton grumbled.

The grass gave way to a multitude of distorted palms, then to a savannah which promised easier going but immediately disappointed by blocking their progress with a sequence of steep *nullahs*—watercourses whose near vertical banks dropped into stinking morasses that sucked them in right up to their thighs.

"I suspect this plain is always water laden," Burton panted, as he and Krishnamurthy tried to haul one of the mules through the mire. "The water runs down from Usagara and this area is like a basin; there's no way for it to quickly drain. Were we not in such a confounded hurry, I would have gone around it. The ridge to the north is the best route, but it would've taken too long to get there. Bismillah! I hope they don't catch us here. This is a bad place for armed conflict!"

Krishnamurthy pointed ahead, westward, at plum-coloured hills. "Higher ground there," he said. "Hopefully it'll be easier going. The height would give us an advantage, too."

Burton nodded an agreement, and said: "Those are the hills of Dut'humi."

§

They finally reached the slopes.

Burton guided his expedition along a well-trodden path, up through thick vegetation, over a summit, and down the other side. They waded through a swamp that sent up noxious bubbles of hydrogen sulphide with their every step. The rotting carcass of a rhinoceros lay at the far edge of the morass, and beyond it a long sparsely forested incline led them to an area of tightly packed foliage. Monkeys and parrots squabbled and hooted in the branches around them.

They forced their way along the overgrown trail until they suddenly came to a clearing, where seven elderly warriors stood, each holding a bow with a trembling arrow levelled at them. The old men were plainly terrified and tears were streaming down their cheeks. They were no threat and they knew it.

Saíd called for the porters to halt, then stepped forward to speak to the old men, but one suddenly let loose a cry of surprise, dropped his weapon, pushed the Arab aside, and ran over to Burton.

"*Wewe! Wewe!* Thou art *Murungwana Sana* of Many Tongues!" he cried. "Thou wert here long long days ago, and helped our people to fight the *p'hazi* whose name is Manda, who had plundered our village!"

"I remember thee, *Mwene Goha*," Burton said, giving the man his title. "Thy name is Máví ya Gnombe. Manda was of a neighbouring district, and we punished him right and good, did we not? Surely he has not been raiding thy village again?"

"No, not him! The slavers have come!" The man loosed a wail of despair. "They have taken all but the old!"

"When did this happen?"

"In the night. It is Tippu Tip, and he is still here, camped beyond the trees, in our fields."

A murmur of consternation rose from the nearest of the porters and rippled away down the line. Burton turned to Saíd. "See to the men. Bring them into this clearing. Do not allow them to flee."

The *ras kafilah* signalled to his bully boys and they started to herd the porters into the glade.

The king's agent instructed Trounce, Honesty, Krishnamurthy, Spencer, Isabella Mayson and Sister Raghavendra to help the Arab guard the men and supplies. He gestured for Swinburne to join him, then addressed Máví ya Gnombe: "*Mwene Goha*, I wouldst look upon the slavers' camp, but I do not wish the slavers to see me."

"Follow, I shall show thee," the elder said. He and his companions, who'd put away their arrows, led Burton and Swinburne to the far side of the clearing, where the path continued.

Between the glade and the cultivated fields beyond, there was a thick band of forest. The trail led halfway through this, then veered sharply to the left. The African stopped at the bend and pointed down the path.

"It is the way to the village," he said.

"I remember," Burton replied. "The houses and *bandani* are in another clearing some way along. I had arranged for a forward party of Wanyamwezi porters to meet us at thy village with supplies, but the plan went awry."

"Had they come, they would now be slaves. So it is good the plan did not work. *Murungwana Sana*, this is one of three paths from the village clearing. Another leads from it down to the plain and is better trodden than this."

"I was wondering why this one is so overgrown," said Burton. "The last time I was here, it was the main route."

"We changed it after Manda attacked us."

"And the third path?"

"Goes from the village, through the forest, to the fields. All these paths are now guarded by old men, as this one was. But let us not follow this way. Instead, we shall go through the trees here, and we will come to the fields at a place where the slavers would not expect to see a man, and will therefore not be looking. My brothers will meanwhile return to the village, for the grandmothers of those taken are sorely afraid."

"Very well."

Máví ya Gnombe nodded to his companions, who turned and continued down the trail, then he pushed through a sticky-leafed bush and disappeared into the undergrowth. Burton followed, and Swinburne stepped after him, muttering about leeches and ticks and fleas and "assorted creepy crawlies."

They struggled on for five minutes, then the trees thinned, and the men ducked low and proceeded as quietly as possible. They came to a bush, pushed aside its leaves, and looked out over cultivated fields, upon which was camped a large slave caravan.

There were, Burton estimated, about four hundred slaves, men and women, mostly kneeling, huddled together and chained by the neck in groups of twelve. Arabian traders moved among and around them—about seventy, though there were undoubtedly more in the large tents that had been erected on the southern side of the camp.

A little to the north, a great many pack mules were corralled, along with a few ill-looking horses.

Swinburne started to twitch with fury. "This is diabolical, Richard!" he hissed. "There must be something we can do!"

"We're vastly outnumbered, Algy," Burton said. "And we have the Prussians breathing down our necks. But—"

"But what?"

"Perhaps there's a way we can kill two birds with one stone. Let's get back to the others."

They retraced their steps through the foliage until they emerged once again onto the path. Burton addressed the elderly African: "Máví ya Gnombe, go thou to thy village and bring all who remain there to the glade where we encountered thee. Do not allow a single one to remain behind."

The old man looked puzzled, but turned and paced away to do as commanded.

Burton and Swinburne returned to the clearing, where they found the porters restless and unhappy. The king's agent walked over to the bundle of robes that hid Herbert Spencer and reached up to the parakeet that squatted atop it. Pox jumped onto his outstretched hand, and Burton took the bird away from his companions and quietly gave it a message to deliver to Isabel. He included a description of their location, outlined a plan of action, and finished: "Report the enemy's numbers and position. Message ends."

Pox disappeared into the green canopy overhead.

As if turned on by a switch, the day's rainfall began. Everyone moved to the more sheltered edges of the glade.

Burton called his companions over and told them what he intended.

"You've got to be bloody joking!" Trounce exclaimed.

"Chancy!" Thomas Honesty snapped.

"Perilous!" Krishnamurthy grunted.

"Inspired!" Swinburne enthused.

"I see no other way," Burton said.

They ate a hurried meal while awaiting the parakeet's return.

The villagers arrived, pitifully few in number, and all elderly. Burton described to them what was soon to happen, and drilled into them that their silence would be essential. They huddled together, wet, miserable and scared.

The expedition members took rifles and pistols from the supplies and began to clean and load them.

"You'll remain with the porters," Burton told the two women.

Isabella Mayson picked up a revolver, flicked open its chamber, and started to push bullets into it. "Absolutely not," she said.

Sister Raghavendra hefted a rifle. "Do you consider us too frail, Richard?"

"On the contrary, you have proven yourselves—"

"—equal to any man?" the Sister interrupted. "Good. Then we shall do what needs to be done and fight at your side, and don't you dare attempt to persuade us otherwise."

Burton gave a curt nod.

Forty minutes later, Pox returned.

"Message from Isabel Arundell. We are ready. Estimate a hundred and fifty thumb-sucking men fast approaching your position. You have an hour at most, chamberpot lover. Be prepared."

"You all understand what you must do?" he asked his friends.

They gave their grim assent, pushed pistols into their belts, slung rifles over their shoulders, and divided into two teams of four: Trounce, Swinburne, Krishnamurthy and Mayson; and Burton, Honesty, Spencer and Raghavendra. Pox huddled on the explorer's shoulder.

Burton addressed Saíd: "To thee falls responsibility for the porters and villagers. It is vital that they neither flee nor make a sound."

"I understand."

The king's agent and his companions moved out of the glade and along the path. The rain hammered against the leaves around them, hissing loudly, soaking through their clothing, making the ground squelch beneath their feet.

They followed the trail as it veered to the right, and traipsed on until they eventually reached the abandoned village, which was some considerable distance from the original clearing.

The second glade was much bigger. There were twenty or so beehive huts in it, and a well-built palaver house. A massive fig tree spread over the central space.

"The first shot is yours," Burton said to Trounce. "Judge it well. Don't be too eager."

"Understood."

Trounce led his team to the eastern edge of the village and they disappeared into the vegetation, following the path down the hill towards the marshy ground where the rhinoceros carcass lay. Burton and the rest went in the opposite direction, cautiously proceeding along the trail towards the fields. Halfway along it, they left the path and pushed into the bushes and plants that crowed around the boles of the trees. Struggling through the roots and vines and thorns and branches, they made their way to the edge of the forest until, through the dripping verdure, they saw the cultivated land and the slave encampment.

The sun was low in the sky by now, and turned the fringes of the passing clouds a radiant gold.

The rain stopped.

"It won't be long," Burton said, softly. "Spread out. Don't shoot until I do. And, remember, keep moving."

Honesty, Spencer and Sadhvi Raghavendra slipped away.

Burton lay flat on his stomach and levelled his rifle, aiming at the slavers who were moving around their tents and captives.

He flicked a beetle from his cheek and crushed a leech that had attached to the back of his left hand.

Pox hopped from his shoulder to his head and mumbled, "Odious pig."

The shadows lengthened.

A seemingly endless line of ants marched over the mulch just in front of him. They were carrying leaf fragments, dead wasps, and caterpillars.

He heard Honesty sneeze close by.

A rifle cracked in the near distance.

All of a sudden, gunfire erupted and echoed through the trees, the sound rising up from the base of the hill on the other side of the village. Burton knew what it meant; the Prussians were very close, and Trounce and his team had opened fire on them.

Sheltered behind the roots of trees, the police detective's team could take pot-shots at the hundred and fifty Prussians with impunity. Not only were they concealed but they were also on higher ground, while the pursuing party had to struggle through the marsh before ascending a slope that, while forested, was considerably more open than the uppermost part of the hill.

Trounce, Swinburne, Krishnamurthy and Isabella Mayson would be silently and invisibly moving backwards as they picked off the enemy, drawing the Prussians towards the village and away from the other clearing.

The noise of battle had reached the Arabs. Burton watched as they grabbed rifles and gestured at the forest. A large group of them started running toward where he and the others were hidden.

He took aim at a particularly large and ferocious-looking slaver and shot him through the heart.

Immediately, rifles banged loudly as Honesty, Spencer and Raghavendra opened fire.

Burton downed two more of the slavers, then, as the other Arabs started shooting blindly into the undergrowth, he crawled backwards and repositioned himself behind a tangle of mangrove roots from where he could see the beginning of the path to the village.

Bullets tore through the foliage but none came close to him. He put his rifle aside and pulled two six-shooters from his belt. Four Arabs ran into view. He mowed them down with well-placed shots then crawled away to reposition himself once again.

Slowly, in this fashion, Burton and his friends retreated towards the village.

The slavers followed, and though they sent bullet after bullet crashing into the trees, they didn't once find a target.

On the other side of the empty settlement, Trounce and his companions were performing exactly the same manoeuvre. They had slightly less luck—a bullet had ploughed through Krishnamurthy's forearm and another had scored the skin of Isabella Mayson's right cheek and taken off her ear lobe—but the effect was the same; the Prussians were advancing toward the village.

After some minutes, Burton came closer to the end of the path where it opened into the clearing. He fired off three shots and wormed his way under a tamarind tree whose branches slumped all the way to the ground forming an enclosed space around the trunk, and here he found Herbert Spencer collapsed and motionless in the dirt.

A rifle cracked, tamarind leaves parted, and Thomas Honesty crawled in. He saw the bundle of Arabian robes and whispered: "Herbert! Dead?"

"He can't die," Burton replied in a low voice. "He's clockwork. Fool that I am, I forgot to wind him up this morning—and the key is back with the supplies!"

"Manage without him. Almost there!"

"Let's get into position," Burton said. "Stay low—things are about to get a lot hotter around here!"

He dropped onto his belly and—followed by the Scotland Yard man—wriggled out from beneath the tamarind, through thorny scrub, and into the shelter of a matted clump of tall grass. Using his elbows, he propelled himself forward until he reached the edge of the village clearing. Honesty crawled to his side. They watched the action from behind a small acacia bush. The police detective glanced at it and murmured: "Needs pruning, hard against the stem."

Guns were discharging all around them, and they immediately saw that the thing they'd hoped for had come to pass. The slavers had entered the village from the west; Trounce and his team had lured the Prussians into it from the east; and now the two groups, convinced that the other was the enemy, were blazing away at each other.

"Now we just lie low and wait it out," Burton said.

Four of the plant vehicles he'd seen at Mzizima were slithering into view, and cries of horror went up from the Arabs, who aimed their matchlocks at the creatures and showered them with bullets. Burton plainly saw the men sitting in the blooms hit over and over, but they seemed unaffected, apart from one who took a shot to the forehead. He went limp, and his plant thrashed wildly before flopping into a quivering heap.

Over the course of the next few minutes, the two forces battled ferociously while the king's agent and his friends looked on from their hiding places in the surrounding vegetation. Then a slight lull in the hostilities occurred and a voice shouted from among the slavers: "We shall not submit to bandits!"

A Prussian, in the Arabic language, yelled back: "We are not bandits!"

"Then why attack us?"

"It was *you* who attacked *us*!"

"You lie!"

"Wait! Hold your fire! I would parley!"

"Damn it!" Burton said under his breath. "We can't let this happen, but if any of us shoots now, they'll realise a third party is present."

"Is this trickery, son of Allah?" the Prussian shouted.

"Nay!"

"Then tell me, what do you want?"

"We want nothing but to be left alone. We are en route to Zanzibar."

355 Expedition to the Mountains of the Moon

"Why, then, did you set upon us?"

"I tell you, we did not."

Burton saw the Prussian turn to some of his men. They talked among themselves, holding their weapons at the ready and not taking their eyes from the Arabs, some of who were crowded around the end of the westernmost path, while others crouched behind the native huts.

Moments later, the Prussian called: "Prove to us that you are speaking the truth. Lay down your weapons!"

"And allow you to slaughter us?"

"I told you. We are not the aggressor!"

"Then you lay down your guns and withdraw those—those—plant abominations!"

Again, the Prussian consulted with his men.

He turned back to the slavers. "I will only concede to—"

Suddenly, one of the slavers—swathed in his robes and with his head wrapped in a *keffiyeh*—ran out from among his fellows, raised two pistols, and started blasting at the Prussians.

Immediately, they jerked up their rifles and sent a hail of bullets into the man. He was knocked off his feet, sent twisting through the air, and hit the ground, where he rolled then lay still.

The battle exploded back into life, and, on both sides, man after man went down.

A stray bullet ripped into the tall grass, narrowly missing Burton. He turned to make sure Honesty was unharmed but the Scotland Yard man had, at some point, silently moved away.

"Message to Isabel Arundell," Burton said to Pox. "Your company is requested. Message ends."

As the parakeet flew off, one of the plant vehicles writhed past Burton's position and lay into a group of slavers. Its spine-covered tendrils whipped out, yanked men off their feet, and ripped them apart. Some tried to flee but were shot down as the Prussians began to gain control of the clearing. One group of about twenty Arabs had secured itself behind a large stack of firewood in the *bandani*, and it wasn't long before they were the last remaining men of the slave caravan's force. The Prussians, by contrast, had about fifty soldiers left, plus the three moving plants. Individuals in both groups were drawing swords, as ammunition ran out; wicked-looking scimitars on the Arabian side; straight rapiers on the Prussian.

Pox returned: "Message from Isabel Arundell. We had problems getting the buttock wobbling horses through the bloody swamp but are now regrouping at the bottom of the hill. We'll be with you in a stench filled moment. Message ends."

One of the mobile plants crashed into the barrier behind which the slavers were sheltering and lashed out at them, tearing their clothes and flaying their skin. Screaming with terror, they hacked at it with their scimitars, which, in fact, turned out to be a more efficient way to tackle the monster than shooting.

An Arab climbed onto the woodpile and jumped from it into the centre of the bloom, bringing his blade swinging down onto the head of the man sitting there. The plant shuddered and lay still.

The cavalry arrived.

The Daughters of Al-Manat, eighty strong and all mounted, came thundering into the village, emerging in single file from the eastern path. With matchlocks cracking, they attacked the remaining Prussians. Spears were thrust into the plant vehicles and burning brands thrown onto them.

Those few slavers who remained alive took the opportunity to flee, and plunged away down the path, disappearing into dark shadow, for now the sky was a deep purple and the sun had almost set.

The last Prussian fell with a bullet in his throat.

The Daughters of Al-Manat had been savage—ruthless in their massacre of the enemy who, at Mzizima, had killed thirty or so of their number. Now, they reined in their horses and waited while Sir Richard Francis Burton and the others emerged from the vegetation.

Krishnamurthy was holding his forearm tightly and blood was dribbling between his fingers. Isabella Mayson's right ear had bled profusely and her clothes were stained red. Swinburne, Trounce, and Sister Raghavendra were uninjured. They were all wet through and covered with dirt and insects.

"Well done," Burton told them.

"Where's Tom?" Trounce asked.

"Probably dragging Herbert out of the bushes. His spring wound down. Sadhvi, would you see to Isabella and Maneesh's wounds?"

While the nurse got to work, Burton indicated to Trounce the area where Spencer had been left, then paced over to Isabel Arundell, who was sitting on her horse quietly conversing with her Amazons.

"That was brutal," he observed.

She looked down at him. "I lost a lot of good women at Mzizima and on the way here. Revenge seemed … appropriate."

He regarded her, moistened his lips, and said: "You're not the Isabel I met twelve years ago."

"Time changes people, Dick."

"Hardens them?"

"Perhaps that is necessary in some cases. Are we to philosophise while slaves remain in shackles or shall we go and liberate them?"

"Wait here a moment."

He left her and approached Swinburne.

"Algy, I want you and Maneesh to leg it along to the other clearing. Bring the villagers, Saíd, and our porters back here. They can help move the bodies out to the fields. They'll need to start work digging a pit for a mass grave."

He returned to Isabel. She indicated a riderless horse, which he mounted. Holding burning brands to light the way, they led a party of ten of the Daughters out of the glade and along the path to the fields. Burton felt sickened by the slaughter he'd witnessed but he knew it was the only option. On the one hand, the Prussians would certainly have killed him and his party, but on the other, he couldn't allow the villagers to fall into the hands of Tippu Tip.

They rode out of the forest and approached the caravan. Five Arabs were guarding it.

"He who raises a weapon shall be shot instantly!" Burton called.

One of the guards bent and placed his matchlock on the ground. The others saw him do it and followed suit.

Burton and Isabel stopped, dismounted, and walked over to them.

"Where is el Murgebi, the man they call Tippu Tip?" Burton asked, in Arabic.

One of the men pointed to a nearby tent. Burton turned to Isabel's Amazons and said: "Take these men and make a chain gang of them. Then get to work liberating the slaves."

The women looked for confirmation from Isabel. She gave them a nod, then she and Burton strode over to the tent, pushed aside its flap, and stepped in.

By the light of three oil lamps, they saw colourful rugs on the ground, a low table holding platters of food, and piles of cushions upon which sat a small half-African, half-Arabian individual. His teeth were gold, and though he appeared less than thirty years old, his beard was white. He raised his turbaned head and they noted that a milky film covered his eyes. He was blind.

"Who enters?" he asked in a reedy voice.

"Thy enemy," Burton replied.

"Ah. Wilt thou take a sweet mint tea with me? I have been listening to the noise of battle. An exhausting business, is it not? Refreshment would be welcome, I expect."

"No, Tippu Tip, I will not drink with thee. Stand up, please."

"Am I to be executed?"

"No. There has been enough death this night."

"Then what?"

"Come."

Burton stepped forward, took the trader by the elbow, and marched him out of the tent and over to the chained up slaves. Isabel followed and said nothing. Her women were busily releasing the four hundred captives, who, in a long line, were making their way towards the village.

As Burton had ordered, the five guards were now tethered together, with short chains running from iron collar to iron collar, and from ankle manacle to ankle manacle. Their hands were tied behind their backs. The king's agent positioned Tippu Tip at the front of the line and locked him in fetters, joining him to the chain gang but leaving his hands unbound. He then pulled the prisoners along, away from the crowd of slaves and out into the open field.

"What are you doing?" Isabel whispered.

"Administering justice," he replied, and brought them to a halt. "Aim your matchlock at Tippu Tip, please, Isabel."

"Am I to be a firing squad of one?"

"Only if he attempts to point this at us," the king's agent responded, holding up a revolver. He placed it in the Arabian's hand and stepped away. The slaver's face bore an expression of bafflement.

"Listen carefully," Burton said, addressing the prisoners. "You are facing east, towards Zanzibar. However, if you walk straight ahead, you will find yourselves among the villagers and slaves we have just liberated and they will surely tear you limb from limb. You should therefore turn to your left and walk some miles north before then turning again eastward. In the morning, the sun will guide you, but now it is night, a dangerous time to travel, for the lions hunt and the terrain is treacherous in the dark. I can do nothing to make the ground even, but I can at least give you some protection against predators. Thus, your leader holds a pistol loaded with six bullets. Unfortunately, he is blind, so you must advise him where to point it and when to pull the trigger to ward off anything that might threaten you, but be cautious, for those six bullets are the only ones you have. Perhaps if walking all the way to Zanzibar is too challenging a prospect for you— well, there are six bullets and there are six of you. Need I say more?"

"Surely thou cannot expect us to walk all the way to the coast in chains?" Tippu Tip protested.

"Didst thou not expect just that of thy captives?" Burton asked.

"But they are slaves!"

"They are men and women and children. Now, begin your journey, you have far to go."

"Allah have mercy!" one of the men cried.

"Perhaps he will," Burton said. "But I won't."

The man at the back of the line wailed: "What shall we do, el Murgebi?"

"Walk, fool!" the slave trader barked.

The chain gang stumbled into motion and slowly moved away.

"Tippu Tip!" Burton called after it. "Beware of Abdullah the Dervish, for if I set mine eyes on thee again, I shall surely kill thee!"

S

No one slept that night.

The liberated slaves carried the dead Arabs and Prussians along the path and into the fields, leaving them in a distant corner, intending to dig a mass grave when daylight returned. A number of Isabel's women stood guard over the corpses to prevent scavengers getting to them. The Africans were too afraid to do the job, believing that vengeful spirits would rise up and attack them.

Of the four hundred slaves, most had been taken from villages much farther to the west. This turned out to be a blessing, for Burton's porters had been so terrified by the sounds of battle and proximity of slavers that they'd overpowered Saíd and his men and had melted away into the night. No doubt they were fleeing back the way the expedition had come. Fortunately, their fear had outweighed their avariciousness and they'd departed without stealing supplies. The released slaves agreed to replace the porters on the understanding that each man, as he neared his native village, would abandon the safari in order to return home. Burton calculated that this would at least cover the marches from Dut'humi to distant Ugogi.

The Arab camp was stripped of its supplies, which were added to Burton's own and stored in the village's *bandani*. Tippu Tip's mules were also appropriated.

A large fire was built and the plant vehicles were chopped up and thrown into the flames.

The Daughters of Al-Manat corralled their hundred and eight horses.

"We're starting to lose them to tsetse bites," Isabel informed Burton. "Twelve, so far. These animals were bred in dry desert air. This climate is not good for them. It drains their resistance. Soon we'll be fighting on foot."

"Fighting whom?"

"The Prussians won't give up, Dick. And remember, John Speke almost certainly has a detachment of them travelling with him."

"Hmm. Led by Count Zeppelin," Burton muttered.

"He may be taking a different trail to us," Isabel observed, "but at some point we're bound to clash."

Swinburne bounded over, still overexcited and moving as if he'd come down with a chronic case of St. Vitus' dance.

"My hat, Richard! I can't stop marvelling at it! We were outnumbered on both sides yet came out of it without a scratch, unless you count the five thousand three hundred and twenty six that were inflicted by thorns and hungry insects!"

"You've counted them?" Isabel asked.

"My dear Al-Manat, it's a well-educated guess. I say, Richard, where the devil has Tom Honesty got to?"

Burton frowned. "He's not been seen?"

"Not by me, at least."

"Algy, unpack some oil lamps, gather a few villagers, and search the vegetation over there—" He pointed to where he'd last seen the Scotland Yard man. "I hope I'm wrong, but he may have been hit."

Swinburne raced off to organise the search party. Burton left Isabel and joined Trounce at the *bandani*. The detective was rummaging in a crate and pulling from it items of food, such as beef jerky and corn biscuits.

"I'm trying to find something decent for us to chow on," he said. "I don't think the villagers will manage to feed everybody. I put Herbert over there. He still needs winding."

Burton looked to where Trounce indicated and saw the clockwork man lying stiffly in the shadow of the woodpile. The king's agent suddenly reached out and gripped his friend's arm. "William! Who found him?"

"I did. He was in a hollow under a tree."

"Like that?"

"Yes. What do you mean?"

"Look at him, man! He had Arabian robes covering his polymethylene suit. Where are they?"

"Perhaps they hindered his movement, so he took them off. Why is it important?"

Burton's jaw worked. For a moment, he found it impossible to speak. His legs felt as if they couldn't hold him, and he collapsed down onto a roll of cloth, sitting with one arm outstretched, still clutching Trounce.

"Bismillah! The bloody fool!" he whispered and looked up at his friend.

Trounce was shocked to see that the explorer's normally sullen eyes were filled with pain.

"What's happened?" he asked.

"Tom was next to me when the Prussians and Arabs started to powwow," Burton explained, huskily. "We were near Herbert; just a little way past him. The parley threatened to ruin our entire plan. The Arab who lost patience with the conflab and ran out shooting saved the day for us. Except—"

"Oh no!" Trounce gasped, as the truth dawned.

"I think Tom may have crawled back to Herbert, taken his robes, put them on, and—"

"No!" Trounce repeated.

They gazed at each other, frozen in a moment of anguish, then Burton stood and said: "I'm going to check the bodies."

"I'm coming with you."

They borrowed a couple of horses from Isabel and, by the light of brands, guided their mounts along the path to the fields then galloped across the cultivated ground to where the dead had been laid out. Dismounting, they walked up and down the rows, examining the corpses. The Prussians were ignored, but each time either man came to a slaver, he bent and pulled back the cloth that covered the corpse's face.

"William," Burton said, quietly.

Trounce looked up from the man he'd just inspected and saw the explorer standing over a body. Burton's shoulders were hunched and his arms hung loosely.

Something like a sob escaped from the Scotland Yard man, and the world seemed to whirl dizzyingly around him as he staggered over to his friend's side and looked down at Thomas Manfred Honesty.

His fellow detective was wrapped in the robes—ragged and blood-stained—that he'd borrowed from Spencer. He'd been riddled with bullets and must have died instantly, but it was no consolation to Trounce, for the little man, who'd mocked him for nearly two decades over his belief in Spring Heeled Jack, had, in the past couple of years, become one of his best friends.

"He sacrificed himself to save us," Burton whispered.

Trounce couldn't reply.

§

They buried Thomas Honesty the next morning, in the little glade to the north of the village.

Burton spoke of his friend's bravery, determination, and heroism.

Trounce talked hoarsely of Honesty's many years of police service, his exemplary record, his wife, and his fondness for gardening.

Krishnamurthy told of the respect the detective inspector had earned from the lower ranks in the force.

Swinburne stepped forward, placed a wreath of jungle flowers on the grave, and said:

"For thee, O now a silent soul, my brother,
Take at my hands this garland, and farewell."

Sister Raghavendra softly sang *Abide With Me*, then they filed back along the trail to the village, a subdued and saddened group.

For most of the rest of the day, Burton and his fellows caught up with lost sleep. Not so William Trounce. He'd found a large flat stone on the slope beneath the village, and, borrowing a chisel-like tool from one of the locals, he set about carving an inscription into it, sitting alone, far enough away from the huts that his chipping and scraping wouldn't disturb his slumbering companions. It took him the better part of the day to complete it, and when it was done, he took it to the glade, placed it on the grave, and sat on the grass.

"I'm not sure I really understand it, old chap," he murmured, "but apparently the whole Spring Heeled Jack business sent us all off in a different direction. None of us is doing what we were supposed to be doing, although I rather think I would have carried on as policemen no matter what."

He rested a hand on the stone.

"Captain Burton says this history we're in isn't the only one, and, in any of the others, meddlers like Edward Oxford might be at work, and whenever they tamper with events, they cause new histories. Can you imagine that? All those different variations of you and me? The thing of it is, my friend, I hope—I really hope—that, somewhere, a Tom Honesty will be tending his garden well into old age."

He sat for a few minutes more, then bent over and kissed the stone, stood, sighed, and walked away.

The tear he left behind trickled into the inscription, ran down the tail of the letter "y," and settled around a seed in Swinburne's wreath.

CHAPTER 8

To Kazeh

Omne solum forti patria
(Every region is a strong man's home)
—Sir Richard Francis Burton's motto

The clangour of the parade bell sounded and voices hollered: "Alle aufstehen! Alle aufstehen!"

In Barrack 5, Compound B, of Stalag IV at Ugogi, Sir Richard Francis Burton and his fellow prisoners of war dragged themselves wearily out of their bunks, quickly put on their grey uniforms, and tumbled out onto the dusty parade ground, which was baking in the afternoon heat.

Obeying shouted orders, they arranged themselves into three rows, facing forward, blinking and screwing up their faces as the glare of the white sky burned the sleep out of their eyes.

"What now?" the man to Burton's right grumbled. "Surely they can't be sending us back to the pass already?"

"They'll work us to death as long as they get the blasted road built," another man growled.

They were referring to the passage the prisoners had been carving through the Usagara Mountains. Burton and his fellows had originally been incarcerated at Stalag III, near Zungomero, on the other side of the range. From there, they'd been escorted out daily, in a chain gang, to work on the road. When the halfway point had been reached, three months ago, they'd been marched to this new P.O.W. Camp, at Ugogi, to commence the second half of the route.

Standing midway down the second row, Burton looked up at the guard towers. The man-things in them, standing with their mounted seedpods trained on the prisoners, appeared rather more alert than usual.

Over to the left, the gates in the high barbed wire fence surrounding the compound were swinging shut, and inside, a large plant had just drawn to a halt, squatting down on its roots. A group of German officers stepped out of the vehicle.

"Bloody hell!" a man gasped. "That's Lettow-Vorbeck!"

"Which?" Burton asked.

"The small bloke with the wide-brimmed hat. What the hell is he doing here?"

Burton watched as the officer, with a swagger stick under his right arm and a leather briefcase in his left hand, met with Oberstleutnant Maximilian Metzger, the camp commandant. They conversed for a few minutes then marched over to the lined up prisoners and started walking from one end of the first row to the other. They gave each man a cursory glance, reached the end of the line, then proceeded down the second row.

When they reached Burton, they stopped, and Metzger said: "Hier, Generalmajor! Das ist der gesuchte Mann!"

Loettow-Vorbeck examined Burton's face. He pulled a photograph from his pocket, looked at it, and nodded.

"Sehr schön! Bringen Sie ihn her!"

Metzger signalled to two rhino guards. They stamped over, took Burton by the elbows, and dragged him out of the line. He was taken across the parade ground, into the commandant's office, and pushed into a chair opposite a heavy desk. The guards stood to attention to either side of him.

Loettow-Vorbeck entered and barked: "Lassen Sie uns alleine!"

The guards clicked their heels and thudded out.

There was a clockwork fan revolving on the ceiling. Burton leaned his head back, closed his eyes, and allowed the air to wash over his face. He was weary to the bone

"Do you know who I am?" Loettow-Vorbeck said, in strongly accented English.

Without opening his eyes, Burton replied: "Generalmajor Paul Emil von Lettow-Vorbeck. You command the German forces in East Africa."

"That is correct. Sehr gut. So."

Burton heard a chair scrape on the floor and creak as the other man sat down. There was a soft thump—the briefcase being swung up onto the desk—and a click as it was opened.

"I have here a file in which you feature with some considerable prominence."

Burton didn't respond. He was hungry and thirsty but most of all, he needed to sleep.

"Private Frank Baker, captured on the western slopes of the Dut'humi hills two years ago. You were alone—a refugee from the failed British assault on the Tanganyika railway."

There was a long moment of silence. Burton had still not opened his eyes. He thought about Bertie Wells and the night they'd slept in the open, beside Thomas Honesty's grave. The temperature had plummeted after sunset, and, during the hours of darkness, both of them developed a fever. Burton's dreams had been filled with violence; with scenes of Prussians and Arabians slaughtering each other—and he'd woken up soaked with dew, filled with memories, and cursing himself. How could he have forgotten there was a village nearby? Just along the trail!

Wells was in the grip of hallucinations, which—to judge from his babbling monologues—involved insects crawling out of the moon, invisible madmen, and three-legged harvestmen. With what little strength remained to him, Burton had hauled the war correspondent to his feet and dragged him along an overgrown trail that eventually opened into another clearing where a decrepit village stood. Its menfolk were long gone—conscripted—and the remaining villagers were elderly and half-starved. Burton left Wells with them while he went to hunt game.

He'd become the prey. Three lurchers had blundered out of the undergrowth and pursued him across boggy ground and into thick jungle. It was peculiar; he felt certain they could have caught him, but instead they seemed to be herding him along.

One of them sprouted poppies as it floundered after him.

By the time he'd eluded them, he was lost and in the grip of malaria.

The Germans found him unconscious at the side of a trail. Since then, he'd spent nearly two years in the Stalag III P.O.W. camp before his recent transference to Ugogi.

Large parts of his memory had returned. He knew he was the king's agent. He was aware that Algernon Swinburne, William Trounce, Thomas Honesty, Maneesh Krishnamurthy, Herbert Spencer, Sister Raghavendra, Isabella Mayson, and Isabel Arundell had travelled to Africa with him. But he didn't know why, what had become of them, or how he'd been transported into the future.

He'd been here for five years. Five years!

Why? For what purpose?

"Why?" Lettow-Vorbeck said.

Burton opened his eyes and met those of the generalmajor. Behind the officer's head, pencil thin shafts of light shone through the slats of the window shutter. Motes of dust entered them, blazed, then vanished into the shade. Against this illumination, Lettow-Vorbeck's features were very dark— almost silhouetted—but, by some quirk, his eyes shone with an almost feral intensity.

"Why what?"

"Why are you British so destructive? Do you not believe in evolution?"

"Evolution? What do you mean?"

The officer drummed the fingers of his right hand.

"The Greater German Empire seeks to advance the human species. We wish to liberate every man and every woman from slavery so that each can fulfil his or her greatest potential. So each can become an *Übermensch*. Perhaps this translates as 'Over Man,' ja?"

Burton gave a snort of disdain. "I don't think your Askaris feel particularly liberated."

"Nein. Nein. And it is the fault of your people. We are forced to employ the Africans to oppose British assaults on the infrastructure we are building here. Were it not for your people, Africa would have atmospheric railways and well-developed cities by now. And Europe would be a paradise, where trivial jobs and the necessities of survival are taken care of by plant life, leaving the human species free to explore its best potentials. Instead, we must assign our resources on both continents to resisting your vandalism."

Burton's breath whistled from between his teeth. "It's always the same," he said. "A madman creates a plan for the future of humanity, and, in unleashing it, causes untold suffering. Generalmajor, do I really need to point out that your vegetation is proliferating without check, or that, while many individuals may be capable of advancing themselves, most are content to be well-fed and sheltered and wish for little more?"

Lettow-Vorbeck nodded thoughtfully. "Es trifft zu, dass, what you say of our plants. But that situation will be corrected once hostilities cease. As for your suggestion that the populace is not willing or able to evolve; I cannot agree. It is typical British thinking, for you built your empire on the premise that an educated and privileged minority should benefit from the labours of a downtrodden majority."

Lettow-Vorbeck suddenly slapped his hand down on the thick dossier that lay before him. "So! Lassen Sie uns auf den Punkt kommen! No more—what is the expression?—beating around the bush?"

He put his elbows on the desk and steepled his fingers in front of his face. "Ich kenne die Wahrheit. Your name is not Frank Baker. You are Sir Richard Francis Burton. You were born in the year 1821. You died in the year 1890. And you were sent to the year 1914 from the year 1863. Es ist ein außerordentlicher Umstand! Unglaublich!"

Burton sat bolt upright. His exhaustion fell away.

Lettow-Vorbeck gave a slight smile, his teeth white in the shadow of his face. "Sehr gut. Sehr gut, Herr Burton. I have your full attention now. You will listen to me, ja? I have a story to tell you. But first a question: do you possess die telepathische Fähigkeiten?"

"Mediumistic abilities? No."

"Nor I. Hah! It is a misfortune! I should like them! You are aware, ja, that many people do? In increasing numbers, it seems. Your Colonel Crowley has his people—and they are strong—while we Germans have our weathermen, and, of course, the Kaiser himself, who is the greatest Psychisch of them all."

Burton's right eyebrow rose slightly. "Nietzsche styles himself emperor now, does he?"

"Es ist angebracht."

A large fly buzzed lazily around Lettow-Vorbeck's head and landed on the desk. The German picked up the dossier and whacked it down onto the insect. He flicked the flattened corpse onto the floor, and resumed his former position.

"And in Russland, there was Grigori Rasputin, also a great Psychisch, who, as you may know, died of—how do you say *Gehirn-Blutung*?"

"Brain haemorrhage," Burton answered.

"So. Ja. Thank you. He died of that two years ago. It is him my story concerns."

Burton remained silent.

Lettow-Vorbeck pointed a finger down at the report lying in front of him.

"This dossier was entrusted to me by Kaiser Nietzsche himself. It contains information that no other man is aware of—just he and I—and now I will tell you."

Still, Burton said nothing.

"Thirteen years ago, after we were forced to destroy your nation's capital city, our troops discovered a number of black diamonds beneath the rubble of the Tower of London. They were the seven fragments of the Cambodian Eye of Nāga, and the seven of the African Eye. We know this because documents concerning them were also found, and, in these documents, another Eye—from South America, and also in seven pieces—was described. Of it, though, there was no sign. You know of what I speak, ja?"

"I'm aware of the Eyes of Nāga, Generalmajor," Burton said. "But I can't help you. I don't know where the South American stones are."

"That is not why you are here. We have already located them; our people have sensed their presence in Tabora—your last stronghold. We will recover them when we drive you from that place."

"So far, I believe, you've not been very successful in that endeavour."

"Ich kann es nicht verleugnen! The South American stones are being used to protect the city, Herr Burton, but the Heereswaffenamt—our Army Ordnance people—have a solution to that. A final solution! It will be put into operation soon and Tabora will be destroyed. But let us not stray from the subject—we must talk of the other Eyes, ja? For many decades, even before the Great War commenced, your people committed mediumistic acts of sabotage against German industry. When it was discovered that the diamonds were the tools your Psychischen had used to perpetrate their crimes, Bismarck passed them to Nietzsche, that he might employ them to—what is the word?—*accentuate* the talents of our own people. Nietzsche kept the Cambodian stones but sent the African ones to Rasputin, and the two men used the power of the Eyes to secure an alliance between Germany and Russland. Then, in 1914, Nietzsche overthrew Bismarck and Rasputin deposed the Tsar."

"Two traitors betraying their leaders," Burton said, scornfully.

"Two visionaries," Lettow-Vorbeck countered, "committed to creating a better world."

Shouts penetrated the office from outside. The prisoners were being rounded up and marched out of the camp, on their way into the Usagara Mountains to continue work on the road.

Burton asked: "What has any of this to do with me?"

"We shall come to that. Nietzsche took control of the Greater German Empire, but before Rasputin could do similar in Russland, he died of the Gehirn-Blutung. German agents retrieved the African stones and returned them to Nietzsche. Now we come to the interesting part of the story, for our emperor had spent considerable time probing the Cambodian fragments and he'd detected in them a remnant intelligence."

"Yes. The Nāga," Burton muttered.

"The mythical reptiles? Nein, das ist falsch."

Burton looked surprised. "Then what?"

"A man. A philosopher named Herbert Spencer. It was little more than an echo, but some information could be gleaned from it; specifically that Spencer died in 1862 yet his intelligence somehow survived for a further year, before finally being extinguished in a temple filled with jewels."

"A temple? Where?"

"Somewhere here in Africa. Fascinating, ja? So now Nietzsche probed the African stones, also, and in them, too, he found the remains of a man—the residual memories—and, in these, the temple was also present, but in greater detail, and Nietzsche saw that this mysterious place, encrusted with gems of unsurpassed value, was a vast device designed to channel enormous energy."

"To what purpose?"

"To transcend the boundaries of time, Herr Burton. And it was also recorded in the remnant memories that you, mein Freund, were sent through the device. It is how you came to 1914 from 1863."

"I was? Why?"

"You ask me that! Es ist meine Frage!"

Burton examined his blistered hands and frowned with frustration. "I don't remember. These past five years, I've been slowly piecing together what happened to me prior to my arrival in 1914, but there are still gaps."

"Ah. I am pleased. You admit who you are. And do you remember this temple?"

"No."

"That is unfortunate. The Kaiser knows only that it is located somewhere in the Ruwenzori Range, deep inside the Blutdschungel."

"The Blood Jungle? This Ruwenzori Range, was it—?"

"—once known as the Mountains of the Moon? Ja. That is the case. An area of Africa most important to you, I think!"

The German fell silent for a moment and considered Burton, who warily watched the other man's glittering eyes.

Paul Emil von Lettow-Vorbeck, the explorer decided, was as dangerous as a venomous snake.

"Well," the generalmajor said. "We have attempted to burn away the Blutdschungel but it grows back so fast! It is impenetrable, it covers the mountains, and it is spreading. All these years we have made no progress into the region, but that, perhaps, is because we do not know where in it we should be going. So, we have a plan."

"And your plan involves me?"

"Ja. That is correct. As I have said, the Kaiser saw in the diamonds that the temple sent you to 1914. He therefore ordered me to find you. It has taken a long time. Africa is big! But, finally, here you are. A man from the past."

"So?"

"So you will locate the temple for us. You somehow found your way out of it and through the Blutdschungel, so obviously there is a route."

"But, I told you, I don't remember."

"I think this—" The German raised a hand and tapped his forefinger against the side of his head. "—will return to you."

Burton sighed. "So what now?"

"Now we shall escort you all the way to your Mountains of the Moon and you shall show us the way to this fabulous temple. With it, the Kaiser can send agents back in time to prevent the interference that has so delayed the expansion of the Greater German Empire! British interference, Herr Burton!"

Lettow-Vorbeck stood and slipped the dossier back into his briefcase.

He barked "Wache!" and the two rhino guards returned. "Ab mit ihm zum Transport!"

They hoisted Burton to his feet.

"Wait! Wait!" he urged.

Lettow-Vorbeck looked at him and asked: "Haben Sie eine Frage?"

"Yes," Burton replied. "Yes, I have a question. The memories imprinted in the African stones. Whose are they?"

"Ah," Lettow-Vorbeck said. "Ja. Ja. This you should know! They belonged to a man named William Trounce."

§

"I'm dead!" Trounce announced. He waved a large earthenware jar in the air. "Not a drop left!"

"All is not lost!" Swinburne declared. He held up a second container, and the *pombe* in it sloshed invitingly. "I must say, though, Pouncer: while there may be life left in my jar, the invincible languor and oppression of this climate has sucked the very last drop of it from yours truly."

"But not the poetry," Trounce growled. "Invincible languor, my foot! Why can't you just say, the weather in Africa is as hot as Hell, like any normal person would? Pass the beer."

After taking an immoderate swig from it, Swinburne handed the container to Trounce, who poured an extravagant amount of its contents into his mouth, swallowed, hiccupped, then said: "We've been on the blasted continent for so long that I'm even beginning to enjoy this foul brew."

He received a belched response.

The two men, dressed in light khaki suits, were relaxing beneath a calabash tree in the centre of Ugogi, a village that lay slightly more than halfway along their route to Kazeh. It had taken two weeks to reach here from Dut'humi, passing first through cultivated lands, then following the marshy bank of the Mgazi River, before chopping their way through thick dripping jungle of the most obstinately difficult kind, and crossing a quagmire, two miles wide, where a mule had sunk completely out of sight in the stinking, sulphurous mud.

Arriving at Zungomero, in the head of the Khutu Valley, they'd at last begun the climb onto higher terrain, escaping the dreadful and diseased swamps that had made the first stage of their safari so miserable. The foothills of the Usagara Mountains, which now rose all around, were densely forested and resplendent with jungle flowers and fruits; the air was laden with the scent of jasmine, sage, and mimosa blossoms; and fresh springs jumped and tinkled across the sloping land.

It had been the only pleasant stage of the trek. All too soon, the ascents and descents became so steep that the mules had to be relieved of their loads before attempting them, and the watercourses in the valleys grew deeper and stronger and more perilous to cross.

The climate changed, too. As they gained altitude, the temperature swung from one extreme to the other. The nights were raw, the days bright and hot. But it was the damp mornings that had the most impact, for thick mist bubbled out of the mountains and drowned the valleys around them in a milky sea, out of which peaks rose like islands. Visually, it was stunning, but it chilled them to the bone.

While passing through this region, Trounce developed severe ulcerations on his legs; so painful that he couldn't walk or sit on a mule without suffering. So they carried him on a litter and Sister Raghavendra collected wild herbs and experimented with them until she found a combination that, when applied as a poultice, eased the pain and hastened the healing process.

There were other troubles.

The people of the region, the Wasagara, were recalcitrant and, on one occasion, hostile. Fortunately, despite shouting loudly and shooting arrows, they lacked courage and were bad marksmen. Rifle fire, aimed over their heads, was enough to discourage them.

As always, the terrain did far more damage than its inhabitants. Four mules and five horses died, one porter broke his leg, and another fell to his death.

Equipment was damaged by mildew and rust. Food and clothes rotted.

And, of course, there were insects: biting, stinging, scratching, wriggling, tickling, burrowing and bloodsucking insects. The travellers felt they were being eaten alive.

They struggled through it, crossed the mountains, and arrived at Ugogi on the other side.

The village, being the first port of call after the Usagara range and the last before the dry lands, was a favourite stopping point for caravans, and had thus developed into a prosperous trading centre, which the slavers left untouched. 2,750 feet above sea level, it enjoyed a comfortable heat and refreshing breezes, and its surrounding hills were rich in cattle, and its plains in grain.

Ugogi's people welcomed the expedition. Partridge and guinea fowl were pushed into cooking pots and a feast was prepared. There was drumming and dancing and laughter. There was *pombe*.

Burton announced that they would rest in the village for three days before embarking on the four-day march across the western wilderness.

That first evening, with distended bellies and befuddled senses, everyone stumbled to their beds apart from Swinburne and Trounce, who decided to lie beneath the calabash, share a couple more jars of *pombe*, and gaze at the Milky Way—and Herbert Spencer, whose belly couldn't distend, much to his evident disappointment, and whose senses were powered by clockwork.

The brass man returned to his tent to work on the final chapters of his *First Principles of Philosophy*. His parting words were: "I'm feeling a little bilious, anyway, gents."

An oil lamp hung from a branch above Swinburne and Trounce. Mosquitos danced around the light and big ugly moths regularly threw themselves violently into the glass.

"I bloody hate Africa!" Trounce proclaimed, with the trace of a slur. "Except for Ugogi. I bloody love Ugogi. What's your opinion, Algernon?"

"My opinion, my dear Detective Inspector William Ernest Pouncer Trounce, is that you are drinking far more than your fair share. Pass that jar back at once or I shall report to the witch doctor that you covet his wife!"

"Has he got a wife?"

"I don't know."

"Is there even a witch doctor?"

"Confound your deductive abilities! Give me the beer!"

Trounce handed over the jar.

Swinburne drank deeply, gave a satisfied sigh, and looked up at the branches.

"How did so many stars get tangled up in the tree, I wonder?"

"They're not stars, you ass. They're glow worms."

"I absolutely refuse to believe your perfectly logical explanation. Mine is far more poetical and therefore speaks of a greater truth."

Trounce grunted. "The greater truth being that you're three sheets to the wind, lad."

Swinburne blew a raspberry.

They lapsed into silence for a few minutes. A mongoose chirruped somewhere in the near distance. Farther away, something hooted mournfully. Swinburne hooted back at it.

"Seventeen," Trounce said.

"Seventeen what?"

"Mosquito bites on my right forearm."

"Ah, but look at this," Swinburne replied. He stuck his left leg into the air and pulled back the trouser leg. His ankle was swollen and the skin was dark and puckered around two small puncture marks.

"Snake," he said. "Poisonous, too. That had Sadhvi going, I can tell you! She flapped about like a goose down a chimney before settling on the appropriate miracle cure!"

"Humph!" Trounce responded. He sat up, shifted until his back was to the poet, then yanked up his shirt. There was what appeared to be a bullet hole just above the small of his back.

"How about that, then? Hornet sting. Got infected. Worse than being stabbed with a stiletto."

Swinburne unbuttoned his own shirt and displayed his left armpit. Just below it, a cluster of nasty-looking swellings decorated his ribs.

"Boils," he revealed. "I shan't elaborate."

Trounce winced, then said: "You'll not beat this." He reached up, pressed his right nostril closed, and blew a hard breath out through the left. One of his ears emitted a startlingly loud whistle.

The unidentified animal hooted a reply from the darkness.

"My hat!" Swinburne exclaimed. "What's caused that?"

"I haven't a notion. It did it when I blew my nose a few days ago, and it's been doing it ever since!"

The poet lifted the jar and gulped more beer. "Very well," he said, and wobbled to his feet. He stood swaying for a moment, then undid his belt, dropped his trousers, and showed the Scotland Yard man his pale white buttocks, which shone in the lamplight like the full moon. They appeared to be zebra-striped.

"Ye gods!" Trounce gasped.

"Three days ago," Swinburne slurred. "My mule was getting obstinate in one of the swamps. Saíd took a mighty swipe at it with that *bakur* of his, but, just as he lashed out, the blessed animal's hind legs suddenly sank about three feet down. I was sent sliding backwards and received the cat myself!"

"Ouch! Did it hurt?"

"Deliciously!"

"You," said Trounce, reaching for the *pombe*, "are a very curious young man, Algernon."

"Thank you."

A few more minutes of quiet were suddenly broken by a loud gurgling rumble, which echoed across the village.

"Elephant," Trounce murmured.

"Thank goodness," Swinburne replied. "I thought it was you."

Trounce responded with a snore, which, as it happened, was a fair challenge to the nearby pachyderm.

Swinburne lay back down and considered the heavens. He reached into his jacket and pulled out Apollo's gold-tipped arrow of Eros, which he'd carried with him ever since the death of Thomas Bendyshe. He pointed it at the stars.

"I'm coming for you, Count Zeppelin," he whispered.

About half an hour later, he clambered to his feet and stretched. He looked down at his sleeping companion and decided to leave him there beneath the tree. Pouncer would be fine. Even a predator brave enough to enter the village would shy away from such volcanic rumblings and snorts. Besides, the Yard man would receive a rude awakening soon enough, when the nightly rain arrived.

The stars to the east were already being obscured by cloud. The downpours were coming later and later, and were far shorter in duration. Soon the rainy season would end.

"Herbert," Swinburne whispered. "I'll go and have a little chinwag with old tin head."

He staggered away, stopped when his trousers slipped to his ankles, hauled them up, fastened his belt, and continued on until he came to the philosopher's tent.

He pushed through the flap.

"I say, Herbert, I'm not in the slightest bit sleepy. Shall we—"

He stumbled to a halt. The clockwork philosopher was sitting at a makeshift table and was completely motionless. Wrapped in robes, he looked somewhat akin to a bundle of laundry.

"Herbert?"

There was no response.

Swinburne stepped over to his friend, put a hand on his shoulder, and gave him a shove.

Herbert didn't budge.

He'd wound down.

The poet sighed and turned to leave, but as he did so, a book on the table caught his eye. It was a large notepad, on the cover of which was written the legend: *First Principles of Philosophy*.

Curious to see how far along Herbert had got with his project, Swinburne reached for the book, slid it towards himself, and opened the first page. He read:

Only equivalence can lead to destruction or a final transcendence.
Only equivalence can lead to destruction or a final transcendence.
Only equivalence can lead to destruction or a final transcendence.
Only equivalence can lead to destruction or a final transcendence.

The poet frowned and flipped the pages to the middle of the book.

Only equivalence can lead to destruction or a final transcendence.
Only equivalence can lead to destruction or a final transcendence.

He kept turning until he came to the last page upon which anything was written.

Only equivalence can lead to destruction or a final transcendence.
Only equivalence can lead to destruction or a final transcendence.
Only equivalence can lead to destruction or a final transcendence.

"My aunt Agatha's blue feather hat!" he exclaimed.

S

The next day, William Trounce complained of a thumping headache, Maneesh Krishnamurthy collapsed with malarial fever, and a messenger arrived in Ugogi. The latter had run all the way from Mzizima with a dispatch for Isabel from those Daughters of Al-Manat who'd remained behind at the fast-expanding Prussian settlement. His first words to her, in Kiswahili, and translated by Burton, were: "You will pay me very well, I should think, for I have run far and far and far!"

Burton assured him that he'd be generously rewarded.

The man closed his eyes and recounted the message in a sing-song voice. He spoke in Arabic, though he obviously didn't understand the language and was merely recounting what he'd been told, parrot fashion. He said: "O Al-Manat, peace and mercy and blessings of Allah upon thee, and upon those who follow thy lead, and upon those who travel with thee. May he grant safety, speed and good fortune to this messenger, who, regrettably, must deliver to thee bad tidings, for a great many Prussians continue to arrive in Mzizima and they are now too strong for us to fight without thy wise counsel. A force of perhaps a thousand has departed the camp and is travelling westward. We follow and are striking them at intervals, in the manner thou taught us, though we are far fewer in number. May Allah protect us and you and give us all strength to endure."

Burton instructed Saíd to issue the man with a *doti* of richly patterned cloth, a box of *sami-sami* beads, and three coils of brass wire. The messenger, much pleased, joined the villagers to rest, drink beer, swap news, and boast of his newfound wealth.

"It sounds like an invasion force," Isabel said to Burton. "What is Bismarck up to, sending so many troops to Africa?"

"Palmerston thinks he's trying to establish a German empire, and that he intends to use Africa's vast natural—and human—resources to fuel it."

"So the Prussians are here to stake a claim?"

"It would seem so."

"Then we must stop them"

"I don't see how we can. Besides which, that's not what we're here for."

"But surely this is a challenge to the British Empire, Richard? Is it not our duty to do something about it?"

"What do you suggest?"

"We fight!"

Burton held his hands out wide in a gesture of disbelief. "Look at us, Isabel! We're nothing but a ragtag expedition! The clothes are half rotted off us! We look positively skeletal! We're exhausted and ill!"

"Will Palmerston send troops?"

"I consider that highly probable."

"Then, once your mission is done, Richard, I shall lead my women against the Prussians until the British Army arrives."

The king's agent blew out a breath and shook his head. "I can't stop you, of course. You're the most obstinate woman I've ever met. You infuriate me—and it's why I fell in love with you. Just don't take unnecessary risks, please."

"We shall do what we do best: hit them and run. Then wait, and, when they least expect it, we'll hit them again and we'll run again."

The expedition spent the rest of the day resting, writing journal entries, checking equipment, and socialising with their generous hosts.

Before sun up the following morning, much recovered, the travellers set forth across the Marenga M'khali, a stretch of desert that took four days to traverse. The ground was hard and cracked, the scrub thorny, and the horizon lumpy with low, quivering and blurring hills.

Close up, the terrain was a rusty brown shade, strewn over with rocks and rubble and tufts of brittle white grass. As it receded into the distance, it grew paler, bleaching to a soft yellow that eventually blended hazily into the washed out blue sky, which deepened in colour overhead.

The sun was like fire upon their necks in the mornings, and blinded them in the afternoons.

Burton, Swinburne, and Trounce were mounted on mules. Sister Raghavendra and Miss Mayson were riding with the Daughters of Al-Manat. Krishnamurthy was being born along on a litter.

Saíd bin Sálim and his eight Askaris kept the liberated slaves moving despite their inclination to laze until sundown.

Burton by now considered his *ras kafilah* a marvel of efficiency and industriousness. Between Saíd and Sister Raghavendra, the expedition had progressed with a minimum of annoyances and illnesses.

Herbert Spencer limped along at the back of the column of men.

Algernon Swinburne had said nothing to anyone about what he'd seen in the clockwork man's book. He didn't know why he kept it quiet—he simply felt no need to raise the subject. At one point, on the third day, when they were climbing onto higher ground and passing huge blocks of weathered granite, he had a sudden urge to speak to Herbert about the *First Principles of Philosophy*, but when he'd approached him, he heard Pox—on the philosopher's head—mutter "Sweet cheeks," and changed his mind. Herbert was the only individual the parakeet ever complimented, and for some reason, hearing the messenger bird was enough to make the poet change his mind. Swinburne dropped the subject. He knew it was wrong to do so; he knew it made no sense; but he dropped it anyway.

The expedition did not cross the desert alone. Antelope and buffalo, giraffe and rhinoceros, elephants and zebra, in herds and alone, they all plodded along wearily, making their way towards the nearest watering holes. Burton watched and envied them their uncomplicated instincts. He wished his own possessed such clarity, and wondered whether he'd made the right choice in accepting the king's commission.

Marry the bitch, Burton. Settle down. Become Consul in Fernando Po, Brazil, Damascus, and wherever the fuck else they send you. Write your damned books!

Those had been the words of Spring Heeled Jack, the man from the future. The "bitch" referred to was Isabel Arundell, and the speech had been a clue to the life he would have led had history not changed—perhaps the life he was *meant* to lead. In rejecting it, it now seemed that he'd he inadvertently placed himself at the centre of a maelstrom that would shape the future of the world.

Why must it rest on my shoulders?

He watched the animals moving through the heat.

A horrible sense of inevitability settled over him.

The long slog continued.

Eventually, the desert became a featureless grassy plain, which disappeared into a tough, tightly packed jungle, and beyond it they reached the village of Ziwa, where they were received with war cries and a shower of poison-tipped arrows.

Five porters were killed and three mules went down before Saíd managed, through much shouting, to communicate the fact that the long line of men was not an invading army but a peaceful safari.

The headman argued that all *muzungo mbáyá* came to kill and steal. "Go!" he hollered. "Turn around and go all the way back to your own lands and remain in them! This place is our home and if you try to cross it we shall kill you with our arrows and then we shall take our spears and use them to kill you a second time!"

One of the lead porters lay down the bundle of cloth he'd been carrying on his head and stepped forward. "Goha!" he cried. "Do you not recognise me? It is Kidogo, who was stolen from this village by slavers some days and days and days ago!"

The *p'hazi* moved his head left and right as he examined the man. "H'nn! Yes, you are the son of Maguru-Mafupi, who was the son of Kibuya, who had pain in his joints and was the son of a man whose name I cannot remember but he had big ears. So now you, who were taken from us, are the slave of these white devils?"

"No! It was the one named Tippu Tip who put me in chains, but these men came and set me free. They set all these others free, too. And now I have come home, and I see my mother!"

Before the *p'hazi* could react, a caterwauling arose from behind the gathered warriors and a woman shoved her way through them and ran to the porter, throwing herself upon him.

"It is Kidogo, my son!" she wailed, and gave forth a loud ululation, which was quickly taken up by all the women of the village.

Goha threw down his bow and jumped up and down on it in a fit of temper. He yelled at Kidogo: "See what noise you have caused by coming home after being stolen from us? Now the women will expect a feast and drumming and dancing and we will have to dress in our finest cottons! Is there no end to the troubles and inconveniences caused by the *muzungo mbáyâ*?"

Burton stepped forward and spoke in the man's language: "Perhaps, O *p'hazi*, if we provided the food?"

"And alcohol?"

"Yes. We have beer and gin and—"

Swinburne, who understood nothing except the words "beer" and "gin," whispered urgently: "Don't give him the brandy!"

"—and gifts."

"You will pay *hongo*?"

"We will pay."

Goha scratched his stomach and looked at Burton with interest. He shouted: "Kidogo! Tell your mother to be quiet! I can't think with all her clucking and twittering!"

The liberated slave nodded and guided his parent into the village. The ululations quietened. The headman huddled into a group with his warriors and they murmured and argued and complained, with many a glance at the white men. After a few minutes, Goha turned back to Burton. He bent and picked up his bow.

"See," he said. "You have been here but a little time and already you have broken my bow, which I have treasured my entire life, and which I made just yesterday. You people have skin like ghosts and cause destruction and misery and problems wherever you put your feet."

"We shall replace your weapon."

"Whatever you give me will not be as good. Is it true that you eat your dead and use their bones to make the roofs on your huts?"

"No, that is not true."

"Is it true that *Uzungu*—the White Land—is far across the water and in it bright beads grow underground and the men have more wives even than I?"

"How many wives do you have?"

"Eight."

"No, that, also, is not true, though my land is far across the water."

"I meant five."

"It is still not true."

"And the beads?"

"They do not grow underground."

"Is it true that the flowers and plants obey your will?"

"They will not obey my people but there are white men from a different land who possess some such control. They are my enemy. Have you seen them?"

"Yes. They came at night and took our cattle for meat and killed two of our women for no reason except that they like killing. They were angry because their porters kept running away and they tried to take the men of this village to replace them but we prevented that from happening, for we are fierce warriors."

"How did you prevent it?"

"By running fast and hiding in the jungle. Sit and eat and sing and dance with us and I will tell you more of them after you have given me some beer and a better bow than this excellent one, which you broke."

In this long-winded manner, Burton was invited to set up camp at the village, and while his friends and the porters enjoyed what turned out to be fine hospitality, Burton sat in conference with Goha and the other elders and learned that the whole region was aware that two expeditions were travelling towards the interior, and that one of them did not respect the customs of the people, while the other one did.

Of Speke's expedition, he was informed that it was perhaps three times the size of his own and comprised mainly of Prussians, with just a few African guides and maybe seventy porters. There were eight of the plant vehicles with it, and these, just as Burton's harvestman had done on the first day of the safari, caused great fear wherever they were seen.

Despite this, Speke's people were in complete disarray.

Confident that he could forge ahead by brute force alone, Burton's former travelling companion had opted not to carry specie and was refusing to pay *hongo*. As a result, his path through East Africa, which had thus far followed a route parallel to and some fifty miles north of Burton's own, had been made extremely hazardous by villagers, who'd run ahead to warn of his approach. Traps and obstructions had been set: the thorns of bushes to either side of the trail were smeared with poison; sharp spines were pushed point upwards into the mud of countless *nullahs*; and arrows and spears were launched from the undergrowth.

As it struggled through this, Speke's column of men had become ever more ragged. His porters were not paid, like Burton's, but were slaves, and they took every opportunity to slip away, often carrying equipment off with them. As for the Prussian soldiers, not being accompanied by a Sister of Noble Benevolence, they had succumbed again and again to fevers and infections.

Just as Burton had suspected it would be, Speke's long head start had been eaten away, and, frustrated, the traitor had recently attempted to solve his problems by leaving the northern trail to join the southern one, which the king's agent was following. The question was: how far in front was he?

As usual, establishing a realistic sense of time was a hopeless endeavour. When asked how long ago Speke had passed, Burton received the reply: "Days and days and days and days and days and days."

"How many?"

"This—" And Goha stretched out his arms to indicate a distance.

It was impossible to understand what he meant, and despite Burton's experience, and no matter how many different ways he asked the question, he didn't receive a comprehensible answer.

Later, he said to Swinburne: "Time is not the same in Africa as it is in Europe. The people here have an entirely different conception of it."

"Perhaps they are rather more poetical," Swinburne replied.

"What do you mean?"

"Maybe they measure time not by the beat of a second or minute or hour, but by the intensity of their reactions to a thing. If they feel very disgruntled by Speke's expedition, that means it was here not long ago. If they feel mildly irritated, but they remember that they were more annoyed before, then a greater amount of time must have passed. And if they feel fine, but recall once being upset, then obviously the reason for it occurred long ago."

"I never considered it that way," Burton confessed. "I think you might be on to something."

"Not that it helps much," his assistant noted. "We still can't establish when Speke was here. How much easier it would be if old Goha could tell us 'five o'clock last Sunday afternoon!'" He looked puzzled, and continued: "I say, Richard! What's the confounded day, anyway? I haven't a giddy clue!"

Burton shrugged. "Nor have I. I've haven't noted the date in my journal since—" He paused, then stretched out his arms. "—this long ago."

§

They left Ziwa, trudged across broad rolling savannahs, and climbed onto the tableland of the Ugogo region. From here, they could see in the distance to their rear, crowned with mist and cut through by streaks of purple, the pale azure mountains of Usagara. In front, in the west, the terrain sank into a wide tract of brown bush land, dotted with grotesquely twisted calabash trees through which herds of elephants roamed, then rose to a range of rough hills. South and northward, verdure-crowned rocks thrust up from an uneven plain.

The villages they encountered, as they traversed this country, were inhabited by the Wagogo people, who, not having suffered as much the decimating attentions of slavers, demonstrated less timidity and a greater degree of curiosity. They turned out of their settlements in droves to watch the *wakongo*—the travellers—passing by, and cried out: "Wow! Wow! These must be the good men who are chasing the bad ones! Catch them, *Murungwana Sana* of Many Tongues, for they killed our cattle and chased us from our homes!"

However, while the people in general seemed to regard Burton's safari as a force bent on vengeance for the crimes committed by Speke's, the village elders with whom the explorer spoke proved rather more suspicious. "What will happen to us," they asked, "when your people take the land?"

To this question, Burton had no reply, but it caused him more and more to think of Palmerston.

They will be accorded the rights given to all of our citizens.

The explorer felt increasingly uneasy.

They stopped for a day at a settlement called Kifukuru, the first where the Kinyamwezi language was spoken, rather than Kiswahili.

Swinburne entertained its inhabitants with a poetry reading. They didn't understand a word of it, of course, but they laughed uproariously at his odd twitches and hops, his jerky gestures and exaggerated facial expressions, and, for some obscure reason, they attached themselves to a stanza from *A Marching Song*, and demanded that he repeat it over and over:

> *Whither we know, and whence,*
> *And dare not care wherethrough.*
> *Desires that urge the sense,*
> *Fears changing old with new,*
> *Perils and pains beset the ways we press into.*

Something about the first line of this caused the audience great merriment—perhaps its rhythm, or the sound of the words—and throughout the rest of the day, the diminutive poet was followed everywhere by hordes of children, who chanted: "Widdawenow! Anwense! Andah! Notkah! Wedru!"

"My hat, Richard!" he exclaimed. "I feel like the blessed Pied Piper of Hamlin! Aren't these little scamps marvellous though?"

"They're the future, Algy!" Burton replied, and was instantly stricken by an incomprehensible sadness.

The next morning, the expedition took up its baggage and moved on, and Burton carried with him a growing depression and irritability. It was obvious to the others that he was lost in thought. He sat on his mule with his dark eyes smouldering, and his jaw, hidden behind a long bushy beard, set hard.

The rainy season had ended now and the plain, clothed in long ossifying grass, was already a mosaic of deep cracks. It took them two days to cross it, during which time Burton spoke little, then they chopped their way through a jungle and emerged into a ten-mile wide clearing. Here, a powerful Wagogo chief named Magomba, who'd caused problems for Burton in '57, did so again by demanding that *hongo* be paid not just for the explorer's expedition but also for Speke's, which had forced its way with violence through the area. Reparation was also demanded for seven men killed by the Prussian forces.

Magomba was jet black in colour and his skin was criss-crossed with thousands of fine wrinkles. From the back and sides of his half-bald head, a few straggly corkscrews of grey hair depended; the whites of his eyes were actually yellow; and his filed teeth were brown. Brass rings dragged his earlobes down to his shoulders.

He squatted, all bones and joints, on a stool in his village's *bandani*, chewed constantly at a quid of tobacco, and expectorated without mercy.

Burton and Saíd bin Salím sat cross-legged before him.

"There was *uchawi*—black magic," Magomba said. "And I will not have *uchawi* in my land."

"What happened, O Magomba?" Burton asked. "Explain to me."

"One of thy people—"

"Not mine!" Burton interrupted. "They are the enemy of my people!"

"—one of thy people took a man by the neck and shook him until he dropped to the ground. The next morning, the man had turned into a tree. We had to cut off his head and burn him. Now, listen carefully, whilst I tell thee of the tax thou must pay in order to pass through my domain."

Magomba's demands were extortionate. Burton and Saíd spent the entire afternoon haggling, and eventually paid ten patterned cloths, six coils of brass wire, seven blue cottons, a pocket watch, twenty-five brass buttons, four boxes of beads, a quarter of tobacco, and a bottle of port.

"Good," Magomba said. "Now I shall order a calf killed so that thy people may eat. It is good to see thee again, *Murungwana Sana*. Ever hast thou been my favourite of all the foul devils that plague this unhappy land."

The next morning, as the expedition prepared for departure, the old chief confronted Burton and said: "I have had the blue cottons counted. There are only seven rolls."

"It is what we agreed."

"No. Thou promised nine."

"You are mistaken. We said seven, and seven it is."

"I will accept eight, providing thou swears an oath."

"What oath?"

"Thou must give thy word not to strike my land with drought, nor with disease, nor with misfortune."

"Eight it is, then. And I swear."

Burton's porters hacked a route through the bordering jungle and the explorer led his people out of the clearing and, eventually, up into the hills and onto the glaring white plains of the Kanyenye region. Though the going was easier here, the heat was hellish, and pertinacious gadflies assailed them all. The Daughters of Al-Manat had trouble controlling their horses, which constantly shied under the onslaught, and the pack mules bucked and kicked and shed their loads. As the ground gradually rose and became rockier, the expedition also suffered from a want of water, having used up their supply more rapidly than usual.

They started across rolling, very uneven ground, congested with gorse-like bushes and deeply pocked with holes and crevices.

Burton's calf muscles kept cramping, causing him such agony that he could barely keep from screaming.

Swinburne was thrown from his steed and landed among long, viciously sharp thorns. He emerged with his clothes in tatters and his body scratched and bleeding from head to toe. He announced, with much satisfaction, that it would sting for the rest of the day.

William Trounce slipped on stony ground and twisted his ankle.

Maneesh Krishnamurthy, who'd recovered from his malarial attack, was stung in his right ear. It became infected, and his sense of balance was so badly disturbed that he suffered severe dizziness and spent a whole day vomiting until he lapsed into unconsciousness. Once again, he had to be carried on a stretcher.

Isabella Mayson was prostrated by a gastric complaint that caused embarrassingly unladylike symptoms.

Isabel Arundell's horse collapsed and died beneath her, sending her crashing to the ground where she lay stunned until they revived her with smelling salts and a dash of brandy.

Herbert Spencer declared that he was experiencing shooting pains along his limbs, which was impossible, of course, but they'd all concluded that his hypochondriacal tendencies really did cause him discomfort.

Sister Raghavendra developed ophthalmia and could see nothing but blurred shapes and moving colours.

Two of Saíd bin Sálim's Askaris collapsed with fever, and the *ras kafilah* himself was stricken with an indefinable ague.

Nearly half of the Daughters of Al-Manat were beset by illness and infections.

Two more horses and three mules died.

Pox the parakeet flew away and didn't return.

As the sun was setting, they arrived in the district of K'hok'ho and wearily set up camp on open ground. No sooner had they lit a fire than angry warriors from the two nearby villages surrounded them and demanded that they move on. No amount of arguing would convince them that the expedition was anything other than an invading force, like the one before it. Tempers flared. A warrior stepped forward and thrust a spear into William Trounce's upper arm. Burton fought to control the Askaris, who stepped forward with scimitars drawn. "Stand down! We are going!" he shouted. "Kwecha! Kwecha! Pakia! Hopa! Hopa! Collect! Pack! Set out!"

Hurriedly, they struck camp and picked their way across the moonlit ground with the warriors escorting them on either side, mocking and jeering and threatening.

Sister Raghavendra, by touch alone, bandaged Trounce's arm.

"I'll need to stitch the wound, William, but we'll have to wait until we're safely away from these ruffians. Are you in pain?"

"By Jove, Sadhvi! Between this and the ankle, I'm having a fine day of it! I feel absolutely splendid! In fact, I thought I might top things off by repeatedly banging my head against a rock! What do you think?"

"I think you'd better chew on this." She handed him a knob of a tobacco-like substance. "These herbs have strong pain relieving properties."

"What do they taste like?"

"Chocolate."

Trounce threw the herbs into his mouth and started chewing. He gave a snort of appreciation. His ear whistled.

The warriors yelled a few final insults and withdrew.

Burton, at the front of the column, crested the brow of a hill, looked down onto a small plain, and saw the stars reflected in a number of ponds and small lakes.

"We'll rest there," he said. "And let's hope that water is fresh."

§

The division between the days became ever more nebulous and confusing.

Consciousness and unconsciousness merged into a single blur, for when they slept, they dreamed of passing terrain, and when they were awake, they were so often somnambulistic that they might well have been dreaming.

From K'hok'ho into the land of Uyanzi, from village to village, through an ugly and desiccated jungle and over baked earth; then into the sandy desert of Mgunda Mk'hali, where lines of elephants marched in stately fashion, trunk to tail, past petrified trees filled with waiting vultures.

Mdaburu to Jiwe la Mkoa; Jiwe la Mkoa to Kirurumo; Kirurumo to Mgongo Thembo; Mgongo Thembo to Tura.

Days and days and days.

This long.

As they approached Tura, Burton said to Swinburne: "I keep seeing animal carcasses."

"Funny," the poet murmured. "I keep seeing a pint of frothy English Ale. Do you recall The Tremors in Battersea? I liked that tavern. We should go back there some day."

The two men were walking. So many of the freed slaves had left them now—gratefully returning to their home villages—that all the animals were required to help carry the supplies, and there were no more spare horses.

Burton looked down at his assistant. The roots of Swinburne's hair were bright scarlet. The rest of it was bleached an orangey straw colour all the way to its white tips. It fell in a thick mass to below his narrow, sloping shoulders. His skin had long ago gone from lobster red to a deep dark brown, which made his pale green eyes more vivid than ever.

He had a thin and straggly beard. His clothes were hanging off him in ribbons and he was painfully thin and marked all over by bites and scratches.

"I'm sorry, Algy. I should never have put you through all this."

"Are you joking? I'm having the time of my life! By golly, in a poetical sense, this is where my roots are! Africa is *real*. It's *authentic*! It's *primal*! Africa is the very *essence* of poetry! I could happily live here forever! Besides—" He looked up at Burton. "—There is a matter of vengeance to be addressed."

After a pause, Burton replied: "In that, you may not have to wait much longer. The dead animals I've been seeing; I think they were killed by a bloodthirsty hunter of our acquaintance."

"Speke!"

"Yes."

They came to Tura, the easternmost settlement of Unyamwezi, the Land of the Moon. Burton remembered the village as being nestled amid low rolling hills and cultivated lands; that it was attractive to the eye and a balm to wearied spirits after so many days of monotonous aridity. But when his expedition emerged from the mouth of a valley and looked upon it, they saw a scene of appalling destruction. Most of Tura's dwellings had been burned to the ground, and corpses and body parts were strewn everywhere. There were only fifty-four survivors—women and children—many wounded, all of them dehydrated and starving. Sister Raghavendra and Isabella Mayson—both recovering from their afflictions—

treated them as best they could but two died within an hour of the expedition's arrival and during the course of the following night they lost eight more.

The camp was set up, and Burton gathered those women whose injuries were slightest. For a while they refused to speak and flinched away from him, but his generosity with food and drink, plus the presence of so many women in his party, especially Isabel Arundell, whom they took to almost straight away, eventually quelled their fears, and they explained that the village had been ravaged by "many white devils accompanied by demons who sat inside plants." This terror had descended upon them without warning or mercy, had killed the men, and made away with grain and cattle and other supplies.

The sun, Burton was informed, had risen two times since the attack.

He gathered his friends in the village's half collapsed *bandani.*

"Speke and the Prussians have not respected the customs of Africa at all," he observed, "but this degree of savagery is new."

"What prompted it?" Isabel Arundell asked. "John is a schemer but not a barbarian."

"Count Zeppelin is behind this carnage, I'm sure," Swinburne opined.

"Aye, lad," Trounce muttered. "I agree. They went through this place like a plague of locusts. Looks to me as if they badly needed supplies and hadn't the patience or wherewithal to trade."

"We're about a week away from Kazeh," Burton said. "It's an Arabic town, a trading centre, and it marks the end of our eastward march. It's where we'll restock with food, hire new porters, and buy new animals, before heading north to the Ukerewe lake and the Mountains of the Moon. Speke will be following the same route and no doubt intended to obtain fresh provisions there too, but perhaps he couldn't make it. I'd lay money on him having squandered all his supplies between Mzizima and here."

"So Tura bore the brunt of his ineptitude," Krishnamurthy growled.

Some of the Daughters of Al-Manat were patrolling the outskirts of the village. One of them now reported that a body of men were approaching from the west. They were carrying guns, in addition to the usual spears and bows.

Burton hurried over to where the women of Tura were sitting together and addressed them in their own language: "Men are coming; perhaps Wanyamwezi. If they've heard what has happened here, they will assume my people are responsible and they will attack us."

One of the women stood and said: "I will go to meet them. I will tell them of the white devils who killed our men and I will say that you are not the same sort of devil and that even though you are white you have been good to us."

"Thank you," Burton replied, somewhat ruefully.

As he'd predicted, the new arrivals were Wanyamwezi. They stamped into Tura—two hundred or so in number—and levelled their weapons at the strangers. They were mostly very young men and boys, though there were a few oldsters, too. All were armed with matchlock rifles; all bore patterned scars on their faces and chests; all frowned at Burton and his associates; and all bared their teeth, showing that their bottom front two incisors had been removed.

From among them, a man stepped forward. He was tall, gaunt and angular, but powerfully built, with long wiry pigtails hanging from his head. There were rings in his nose and ears and a profusion of copper bangles on his wrists and ankles.

"I am Mtyela Kasanda," he said. "They call me Mirambo."

It meant *corpses*.

"I am Burton," the king's agent responded. "They call me *Murungwana Sana* of Many Tongues."

"Dost thou see mine eyes?" Mirambo asked.

"I do."

"They have looked upon thee and they have judged."

"And what did they find?"

Mirambo sneered. He checked that there was priming powder in the pan of his matchlock. He tested the sharpness of his spear with a fingertip. He examined his arrow points. He cast an eye over his warriors. "Mine eyes see that thou art *muzungo mbáyá*, and therefore bad."

"My people are the enemy of those who destroyed this village. We found the women injured, and we helped them."

"Did doing so darken thy skin?"

"No, it did not."

"Then thou art still *muzungo mbáyá*."

"That is true, but, nevertheless, we remain the enemy of those who did this deed." Burton held his hands open, palms upward. "We have come to help thee."

"I will not be friends with any *muzungo mbáyá*."

Burton sighed. "I have learned a proverb from thy people. It is this: *By the time the fool has learned the game, the players have dispersed*."

Mirambo turned his head a little, chewed his lip, and regarded Burton from the corner of his eyes. He coughed and spat, then said: "I understand thy meaning. If I do not choose, I will have no say in the outcome."

"That is probably correct."

There was a sudden commotion among the gathered warriors, and a small man pushed his way to the front of them. He was wearing a long white robe and a white skullcap, had a matchlock rifle slung over his shoulder, and a machete affixed to his belt. At the sight of him, Burton felt a thrill of recognition.

"Wow! I know this scar-faced man, O Mirambo," the newcomer announced. "I have travelled far and far with him. He is ugly and white, it is true, but he is not as those who passed before. He is fierce and loyal and good, though filled with crazy thoughts. I speak only the truth."

The Wanyamwezi chief pondered this for a few moments, then said to the man: "Give me *pombe*, Sidi Bombay."

The small man took a goatskin flask from one of his companions and handed it to the chief. Mirambo drank from it then passed it to Burton, who did the same.

"Now," Mirambo said. "Tell me of our foe."

§

The season of implacable heat arrived, and each morning they struck camp at 4 a.m., walked for seven hours, then stopped and did their best to shelter from it. It meant slow progress, but Burton knew Speke wouldn't be able to move any faster.

Their first three days from Tura saw them trekking over cultivated plains. The sky was so bright it hurt their eyes, despite that they wore *keffiyehs* wrapped around their faces.

The Daughters of Al-Manat, now supplemented by the women and children of Tura, rode and walked to the right of the porters.

Mirambo and his men marched on the other side of the column, keeping their distance, holding their matchlocks at the ready and their heads at an aloof angle. Sidi Bombay, though, walked along next to Burton's mule, for he knew the explorer of old, and they were firm friends.

A one-time slave, who'd been taken to India then emancipated upon his owner's death, Bombay spoke English, Hindustani, and a great many African languages and dialects. He'd been Burton's guide during the explorer's first expedition to the Lake Regions, in '57, and had then accompanied Speke on his subsequent trek in '60. Burton now learned that he'd also accompanied Henry Morton Stanley, last year.

As they pushed on across a seemingly unchanging landscape, Bombay cast light on some of the mysteries surrounding the latter two expeditions.

Burton already knew that, after discovering the location of the African Eye of Nāga in '57, but failing to recover the jewel, Speke had returned to Africa with a young Technologist named James Grant. They'd flown towards Kazeh in kites dragged behind giant swans, but, en route, had lost the birds to lions. He now learned that when they'd arrived at the town on foot, they'd hired Bombay to guide them north to the Ukerewe lake, then west to the Mountains of the Moon.

"Mr. Speke, he led us into a narrow place of rocks. Wow! We were attacked by Chwezi warriors."

"Impossible, Bombay!" Burton exclaimed. "The Chwezi people are spoken of all over East Africa and all agree that they are long extinct. Their legendary empire died out in the 16th century."

"But perhaps no one has told them, for some have forgotten to die, and live in hidden places. They guard the Temple of the Eye."

"A temple? Did you see it?"

"No, Mr. Burton. It is under the ground, and I chose not to go there, for I met my fourth wife in an ill-lit hut and I have never since forgotten that bad things happen in darkness. So I remained with the porters and we held back the Chwezi with our guns while Mr. Speke and Mr. Grant went on alone. Only Mr. Speke came back, and when he did—wow!—he was like a man taken by a witch, for he was very crazy, even for a white man, and we fled with him out of the mountains and all the way back to Zanzibar. On the way, he became a little like he was before, but he was not the same. I think what he saw under the ground must have been very bad."

Stanley's expedition had also ended in disaster. The American newspaper reporter's team—five men from the Royal Geographical Society—had employed porters to carry rotorchairs from Zanzibar to Kazeh, then flew them north to locate the source of the Nile. They'd returned a few days later, on foot. Their flying machines had stopped working.

Bombay, who at that time was still living in Kazeh, was commissioned as a guide. He led Stanley to the Ukerewe, and the expedition started to circumvent it in a clockwise direction. But at the westernmost shore, Stanley became distracted by the sight of the far off mountains and decided to explore them.

"I told him no, it is a bad place," Bombay said, "but—wow!—he was like a lion that has the musk of a gazelle in its nostrils and can think of nothing else. I was frightened to go there again, so I ran away, and he and his people went without me. They have not been seen again. This proves that I am a very good guide."

"How so?"

"Because I was right."

The safari trudged on.

The cultivated lands had fallen behind them. Now there was nothing but shallow, dry, rippling hills that went on and on and on.

"The same!" Swinburne wailed, throwing his arms out to embrace the wide vista. "The same! The same! Won't it ever change? Are we not moving at all?"

During the nights, swarms of pismire ants crawled out of the ground and set upon the camp. They chewed through tent ropes, infested the food supplies, shredded clothes, and inflicted bites that felt like branding irons.

On the fourth day, the safari left the region behind with heartfelt expressions of relief and entered the Kigwa forest, a wide strip of gum trees and mimosas spread over uneven, sloping land. The boles were widely spaced but the sparse canopy nevertheless provided a little shade and for the first time in many weeks they weren't bothered by mosquitos or flies.

They camped among the trees, dappled by shafts of pollen-thick light, with butterflies flitting around them and birds whistling and gabbling overhead. The scent of herbs filled their nostrils.

"We've travelled almost six hundred miles," Burton said. He was sitting on a stool in front of the main rowtie, massaging his left calf, which felt bruised after his bout of cramps. Trounce was on chair at a folding table. The Scotland Yard man's beard reached halfway to his chest, and he'd had enough of it. He was attempting to crop it close to his chin with a pair of blunt scissors. "But how long has it taken us?" he asked.

"That's the question. It took me a hundred and thirty-four days to reach this spot during my previous expedition. I feel we've been considerably faster but I couldn't tell you by how much. It's very peculiar. All of us appear to have lost track of time. Do you want a hand with that, William? You appear to be struggling."

"If you wouldn't mind," the other man answered. "It's my bloody arm. The spear wound still hurts like blazes when I move it. So are you suggesting that something is having an adverse influence on us?"

Trounce stuck out his chin. Burton stood, took the scissors, and attacked his friend's facial hair.

"Perhaps. But the Mountains of the Moon are still at least two hundred miles away, so if the Eye of Nāga is responsible, then its emanations are reaching a damned long way."

"If it didn't affect your timekeeping back in '56," Trounce said, "Then why would it be doing so now?"

"The only explanation I can think of is that there's an intelligence directing it."

"Which knows we're here? I don't like the sound of that."

"Nor I."

A few minutes later, Burton finished his hacking and held up a small round mirror so Trounce could examine the results.

"By Jove!" the detective exclaimed. "It's made no difference at all! I still look like a confounded Robinson Crusoe!"

Burton smiled, turned away, and watched as the Daughters of Al-Manat rolled out their prayer mats and began to praise Allah. He looked at Mirambo's warriors, sitting in a group on small portable stools, sharpening their weapons and cleaning their matchlocks. He observed Saíd redistributing the baggage among the remaining porters. He examined the horses and mules and saw that many were covered in tsetse bites. They wouldn't survive much longer.

A commotion over to his left attracted his attention. It was Swinburne, leaping around like a possessed forest sprite.

"Look! Look!" the poet cried, jabbing his finger in Herbert Spencer's direction.

Burton turned his eyes towards the robe-wrapped clockwork philosopher and saw that he was approaching with Isabella Mayson at his side. He had a colourful parakeet on each shoulder.

"Pox is back!" Swinburne cheered.

"Slippery sewer sniffer!" Pox cawed.

"And he's been courting!"

"*She's* been courting," Isabella corrected.

Swinburne gave a screech: "What? What? You mean Pox is—is—?"

"Is a girl, yes. She always has been. I believe I pointed that out when I first introduced you to her."

Swinburne looked flummoxed. "I—I—I suppose the bad language caused me to assume the reverse."

"Danglies clutcher!" Pox added.

The other bird let loose a piercing squawk.

"Parakeets usually mate for life," Isabella told Burton. "So perhaps you'd like to give a name to the new member of your family."

The king's agent groaned. "You don't mean to say I'll have to accommodate two of the beastly things when we return to London?"

Spencer piped: "At least only one of 'em will insult you, Boss."

"Sheep-squeezing degenerate!" Pox crowed.

"Monkey cuddler!" her mate added.

"Oh no!" Burton moaned.

"My mistake," Spencer admitted.

"Hah!" Swinburne cried out. "Malady is learning!"

They all looked at him.

"It's the perfect name," he said. "Don't you think Pox and Malady sound like they belong together?"

There was a pause, then William Trounce threw his head back and let loose a roar of laughter. "On the button, Algernon!" he guffawed. "On the blessed button! Oh my word! What more fitting remembrance of this endeavour could you have, Richard, than to leave Africa with a Pox and a Malady? Ha ha ha!"

Burton shook his head despairingly.

"Cheer up!" Swinburne grinned. "If I remember rightly, when you were a young soldier returning from India and its whorehouses, you brought back similar!"

Trounce doubled over and bellowed his mirth.

"Algy, there are ladies present," Burton said, glowering at his assistant.

Isabella gave a dismissive gesture. "I rather think Africa has stripped me of all the social niceties, Richard. Try as any of you might, you'll not induce a fit of moral outrage in me!"

"I say! Could we make an attempt anyway?" Swinburne enthused.

"Certainly not."

Krishnamurthy came running over. "Shhh!" he urged. "Stop making such a confounded racket! Listen!"

They did so, and heard gunfire snapping and popping faintly in the far distance.

"Speke," Swinburne whispered.

"How far?" Trounce asked.

"It's difficult to say," Burton responded. "But we'd better stay on our toes."

The next morning, they proceeded with caution and with four Wanyamwezi scouting a little way ahead. Gunfire continued to crackle faintly from the west. It sounded like a battle was being fought. Burton unpacked all the spare rifles and distributed them among Mirambo's warriors, replacing the ancient matchlocks. He and the rest of his expedition kept their own guns cleaned, oiled, and loaded.

The forest was fairly easy going. Its canopy was high and the undergrowth light. Nevertheless, it required two more marches to traverse. When they finally emerged from it, they found themselves in a long valley through which sweet water bubbled in a wide stream. The hills to either side were swathed in bright yellow grain, blazing so brightly that the travellers were forced to walk through it with eyes slitted. In the furnace-like heat, it was, Herbert Spencer commented, "like walkin' on the surface of the bloomin' sun itself!"

The terrain gradually opened onto a flat plain, empty but for stunted trees. On the horizon ahead, low forested hills could be seen, though they folded and jumped in the distorting atmosphere. From the other side of them, the noise of battle raged on. The sound was carrying a long way.

They walked and walked and seemed to make no progress.

"I can't judge the distance," Trounce muttered. "Those hills are like the mirages we saw back in Arabia. One minute they spring up right in front of us, the next they're not there at all."

"They're fairly close," Burton advised.

"And so is one heck of a scrap by the sound of it!"

"Wow! It is from Kazeh!" Sidi Bombay noted.

Burton walked back along the line of porters and mules to where Swinburne was striding along. The poet had a rifle slung over his shoulder and was holding an umbrella over his head.

"I'm going to gallop ahead to take a peek over those hills, Algy. Will you join me? Can you bear it during the hottest part of the day?"

"Rather! Anything to break the monotony of this flatland."

They stopped and waited for Isabel Arundell, who was riding near the middle of the column, to catch them up.

"I need two of your fittest horses," Burton said as she drew abreast of them. "Algy and I are going to reconnoitre."

"Very well, but I'm coming with you. If we're joining a battle, I want to see for myself how best to deploy my women."

"Very well."

Mounts were selected, supplies were packed into saddlebags, and the threesome rode back to the head of the safari.

Burton took the field glasses from Trounce and informed him of their intentions. "You're in charge while we're gone. Keep going until the heat gets too much. You'll not make Kazeh in a single march, or even the base of the hills, so stop when you must but don't erect the tents. Get what rest you can."

They kicked their heels into the sides of their mounts and raced away, leaving a cloud of dust rolling in their wake.

It took them an hour to catch up with one of Mirambo's scouts. They stopped to greet him and offer water but he ignored them, as if by doing so he could make the *muzungo mbáyá* cease to exist.

The entire afternoon was spent pushing the horses to their limits until, with the sun swelling and melting in front of their faces, they arrived at the edge of the plain and threw themselves down beside a narrow stream. They drank deeply and washed the dust from their faces, splashed their steeds to cool them, then left them reined to trees but with enough slack to be able to reach the water.

Gunfire stammered and echoed around them.

"They've been fighting for three days, at least," Isabel noted.

"We'll take a look at the combatants presently," Burton said. "First, eat, rest, and attend to your weapons."

This was duly done, and slightly under an hour later, they climbed the hill, passing through the trees, descended the other side, scrambled up the next slope, and crawled onto its summit. They looked out over the twilit plain on the other side. The sun had just set and the western horizon was blood red, the sky above it deep purple and flecked with bright stars.

The land beneath was considerable more verdant than the ground they'd just crossed; large tracts had obviously been irrigated; there were grain fields and many trees, the latter casting very long shadows.

A little to the north, a monolithic verdure-topped outcrop of rock dominated the otherwise flat landscape, and just to the south of it, right in front of them, there was a small town, little more than a wide scattering of wooden houses and shacks, with a few larger residences at its centre.

Lights flashed all along its eastern and northern borders and the noise of gunfire punctured the African night.

Burton whispered: "The Prussians have Kazeh under siege!"

CHAPTER 9

A Parting of Ways

We do not see things as they are. We see them as we are.
—The Talmud

The plant was roughly the shape of a boat. It moved on thick white roots that grew in tangled bunches beneath its squat, flattened and elongated stem. From this, ten white flowers grew in pairs, aligned in a row. Their petals were curled around the men who sat in them, forming extremely comfortable seats. Sir Richard Francis Burton was in one of the middle blooms. Generalmajor Paul Emil von Lettow-Vorbeck was sitting beside him. *Schutztruppen* occupied the others. The driver's head was pierced just above the ears by thorny tendrils through which he controlled the conveyance. The soldier beside him was positioned behind a seedpod, which, to Burton, looked exactly like a mounted gun. From the rear of the vehicle, three long leaves curved upward and forward like a canopy, protecting the passengers from the sun.

It was a bizarre conveyance. It was also a very fast one.

They'd left Stalag IV at Ugogi yesterday and were travelling along a well-defined trail—almost a road—in a westerly direction.

As the landscape unfolded around them, another unfolded inside Burton. His lost memories were returning, and each one inserted itself into his conscious mind with a violent stab that made his eyes water and caused a curious sensation in his sinuses, as if he'd accidentally snorted gunpowder instead of snuff.

The vehicle scuttled over the Marenga M'khali desert, and he recognised it. A grassy plain, a jungle, and rolling savannahs—he'd seen them all before. He was familiar with every hill, every *nullah*. He'd walked this route.

He remembered his companions and felt the hollow grief of untimely deaths. He knew who Al-Manat had been.

Isabel. Whatever became of you?

As if reading his thoughts, Lettow-Vorbeck said: "This road, it is built on the old trail that you followed so many years ago, ja?"

"Yes, I think so."

"And the other trail, the one parallel to it, to the north, that is now our Tanganyika railway line, which the Greater German Empire employs to bring civilisation to Africa, and which your people attack and sabotage with such tedious frequency."

Burton shrugged. He was sick of this war. He'd had more than enough of the 20th century.

The plant raced across dusty ground and climbed into the Ugogo region.

"Nearly two hundred miles westwards," the generalmajor informed him, "then we shall steer north to avoid Tabora. An inconvenience, but one that we'll not have to put up with for much longer."

"The 'final solution' you spoke of before?"

"Ja. It is on its way, even now, Herr Burton. We have a great flying ship, the *L.59 Zeppelin*, following inland the river that so obsesses you. I speak of the Nile, of course."

Another missing shard of Burton's memory slammed into place, causing him to catch his breath and stifle a groan.

Lettow-Vorbeck continued: "The name *Zeppelin* is a very suitable one for das Afrika Schiff, I think. For it is widely held that a Zeppelin was present at the start of the war, and now a Zeppelin will be present at its end!"

The generalmajor suddenly frowned and peered inquisitively at his prisoner. "Ja, ja," he said, thoughtfully. "You, also, were in Africa when all this began. Perhaps you met the Ferdinand Graf von Zeppelin of whom I speak? Maybe you can enlighten our historians and tell us how and where he died, for this is a great mystery."

Burton shook his head. "No, sir, I didn't and I cannot."

"Hmm, so you say, aber ich denke dass Sie mehr wissen, nein?"

"No. I know nothing more."

The road bisected a rolling plain then ran through a chaotic jungle that had been burned back from the thoroughfare and was held at bay by tall wire fences.

Lettow-Vorbeck pointed. "You see there, the unkontrollierbare Anlagen!"

The "uncontrollable plants" were lurchers. There were many hundreds of them writhing against the barrier.

"We will see more as we approach the Lake Regions, for they are much more numerous near der Blutdschungel. What a nuisance they are!"

The hot air blew against Burton's face as the vehicle raced along, then the sun set and he fell asleep. When he awoke, it was early morning, and they were leaving the Uyanzi region and entering another blistering desert.

He stretched and yawned and said: "Generalmajor, where is all the wildlife? I haven't seen an elephant for years!"

"Elephants are extinct, mein Freund. As for the other creatures, our Eugenicists have adapted a great many for frontline warfare, and the rest have sought refuge in less battle torn areas of the country; the South, primarily, where you British have no presence and where civilisation prospers in harmony with nature."

"No presence? South Africa was part of the British Empire in my day."

"That is so, and the Boers and the Zulus were not happy about it. My people offered them full independent rule, and, with our military assistance, they overthrew you. It took less than a year to drive the British out. After that, it was simply a case of establishing strong trade and industrial relations, and, before many years had passed, the South was very willingly incorporated into the Greater German Empire."

They soon left the desert and the road began to snake between small domed hills. It emerged from a valley into a wide basin. The ground was torn up and dried into grotesque configurations; the trees were nothing but stumps; burnt wreckage was strewn about; but there was something in this old battlefield that Burton recognised—its contours told him that this was where the village of Tura had stood. There was no sign of the settlement.

The driver shouted something.

"Ah," Lettow-Vorbeck said. "Now we leave the road and travel north. Later we shall go west again. You are hungry?"

"Yes."

The generalmajor snapped an order, and the man sitting in front of Burton lifted a hamper onto his lap, opened it, and started to pass back packets of sliced meat, a loaf of bread, fruit, and other comestibles. With a shock, Burton noticed that the soldier's face was covered in short bristly fur and that his jaws extended forward into a blunt muzzle. His mouth was stretched into a permanent and nasty smile. A hyena.

They sped out of the hills onto a wide expanse of flatland broken only by a long ridge that ran along to the north of them.

The sun was high in the sky. The scenery around them jiggled in and out of focus as if struggling to maintain its reality.

"How will the *L.59 Zeppelin* destroy Tabora?" Burton asked.

Lettow-Vorbeck gave a peal of laughter and slapped his thigh. "Hah! I was wondering how long it would take before you asked me that!"

"I assumed you'd inform me that it's top secret."

"So warum bitten Sie jetzt?"

"Why do I ask now? Because this journey is interminable, Generalmajor, and I'm bored. Besides, it occurs to me that since I'm your prisoner, and I don't even know where Tabora is, and the attack is imminent, there can be little harm in you telling me."

"Ja, das ist zutreffend. Very well. In forty-eight hours, the *L.59 Zeppelin* will drop an A-Bomb on the city."

"And what is that?"

"You are aware of the A-Spores, ja?"

"An obscene weapon."

"Quite so. Quite so. But very effective. The bomb will deliver, from a very high altitude, a concentrated dose of the spores to the entire city. The Destroying Angel mushroom is among the most toxic species of fungus in the world, Herr Burton. Its spores kill instantly when they are breathed, but they are easily resisted with a gas mask. Not so the ones in the bomb, for they have been specially bred to such microscopic size that they will penetrate the pores of a person's skin. No one will escape."

"Barbaric!"

"Hardly so. It is a very sophisticated weapon."

"And still you claim the Greater German Empire is a superior civilisation?"

"It is you British who have driven us to such extremes."

"I hardly think that—"

The plant suddenly lurched to the left, and the driver screamed: "Gott im Himmel! Was ist das? Was ist das?"

Burton looked to the right. The most incredible machine he'd ever seen was mounting the ridge. It was completely spherical; a gigantic metal ball about two hundred feet in diameter and painted a dark jungle green. A wide studded track was spinning at high speed vertically around it, providing the motive force. Burton guessed that the same gyroscopic technology that kept penny farthings upright in his time was here employed to prevent the sphere from rolling to its left or right.

Four long multi-jointed arms extended from the sides of it. The upper pair ended in lobster-like claws; the lower in spinning circular saw blades. These were obviously used to tear through whatever vegetation couldn't be simply rolled over.

Three rows of portholes and cannon ports ran horizontally around the orb, and four curved chimneys pumped steam into the air from just below its apex.

A puff of smoke erupted from its hull. A loud bang followed, and another, even louder, as an explosion threw up the earth ahead of the German transport.

"Warning shot!" Burton shouted. "You have to stop! You'll never outrun it!"

"Halt! Halt!" Lettow-Vorbeck yelled.

The plant jerked to a standstill. The generalmajor stood, drew his pistol, pushed the barrel into the side of Burton's head, and waited as the sphere drew closer.

"I am sorry, Herr Burton, I will kill you rather then allow you back into British hands, but let us first see what they have to say."

There was a hard thud.

Lettow-Vorbeck looked down at the hole that had just appeared in the middle of his chest and muttered "Himmelherrgott! Just that?"

He collapsed backwards out of the plant.

Thud. Thud. Thud.

One after the other, in quick succession, the *Schutztruppen* slumped in their seats.

The rolling sphere drew to a stop, casting its shadow over the German vehicle. Burton watched as a thin wedge opened from it, angling down to form a sloping platform with a door at the top. There was a figure framed in the portal.

"Don't just sit there, you chump!" Bertie Wells called. "Come aboard!"

§

It was named the S. S. *Britannia*, and was captained by Commander Aitken himself—the director of all British military operations in East Africa—whom Burton remembered from the bombing of Dar es Salaam back in 1914.

"It's good to see you again, Bertie!" the famous explorer enthused, as Wells and three British Tommies led him through the ship towards the bridge. "What happened to you? And how did you end up aboard this behemoth?"

"Adventures and perils too numerous to recount happened to me, Richard, but eventually I made my way to Tabora like everyone else. Practically every free Britisher in Africa—perhaps in the entire world—is there now."

"Bismillah!" Burton swore, grabbing at his friend's arm. "Praise to Allah that you rescued me now and not two minutes earlier!"

"What do you mean?"

"First, answer me this: how were my captors shot with that kind of precision at such a distance? I've never seen anything like it!"

"Marksmen with the new Lee-Enfield sniper rifles. A remarkable weapon—the most accurate long-range rifle ever manufactured."

"And these marksmen, would they have recognised the men they were shooting?"

"As Germans? Of course! The uniform is unmistakable."

They passed through a room lined with gun racks then rounded a corner into a corridor along which many men were moving.

"You should have examined the bodies, Bertie, instead of just leaving them there."

"Why so?"

"Because one of them was Generalmajor Paul Emil von Lettow-Vorbeck."

Wells stumbled to a halt, his mouth hanging open, eyes wide. His three companions stopped, too, but instinctively retreated a few paces, displaying a typically British sensitivity to Wells and Burton's need for a moment of privacy. Nevertheless, having heard the pronouncement, they gaped.

"Wha—what?" Wells stuttered, then his voice rose to a squeal: "We just killed Lettow-Vorbeck? We killed him? Are you sure?"

"He was holding a pistol to my head when he took a bullet through the heart."

Wells smacked a fist into his palm and let loose a whoop of triumph. "Bloody hell! This could change everything!"

"No, Bertie, it's too late."

"Too late? What do you mean, it's too late?"

Very quietly, Burton said: "In forty-eight hours, a German flying ship is going to drop a bomb on Tabora."

"That's nothing new. The plants fly over, we shoot 'em down."

"This one will be at a high altitude, and it's carrying an A-Bomb."

"A what?"

In a whisper, Burton explained, and as he did so, his friend's burn-scarred and sun-browned face turned white. Wells looked to the right and left, gestured to the three guards, indicating that they should wait, then pulled Burton back along the passage and into the gunroom. He spoke quietly and urgently: "We have to tell Aitken, but don't give away too much about yourself. Keep your true identity under wraps, for starters. The situation is complicated, and there's no time to fill you in right now. Suffice to say, your impossible presence in Africa has been detected. Colonel Crowley himself sent us to rescue you—"

"Your so-called wizard of wizards?"

"Yes. Apparently he's been aware of an anomaly on the continent since 1914 and has been trying to identify it ever since. He finally traced it to the Ugogi Stalag, then honed in on you as you were being transported. He sent the *Britannia* to intercept the vehicle and retrieve you."

"But he doesn't know who I am?"

One of the Tommies appeared in the doorway, cleared his throat, and jerked his head to suggest that they should move on. Wells gave a slight nod. He guided Burton back into the corridor and they followed a few steps behind the three soldiers. They came to a staircase and started up it.

"All Crowley knows is that you don't belong in 1919," Wells whispered. "I think, through you, he's hoping to unlock the secrets of time travel."

"Lettow-Vorbeck had the same idea."

"Listen, this is important. My old editor, the man who used to run *The Tabora Times* before it folded, needs to see you. I don't know the full story, but there are moves being made, and we can't allow you to fall under the wizard's spell."

"What does that mean?"

"Crowley is a tremendously powerful mesmerist. Once pierced by those fiendish eyes of his, you'll have no willpower of your own."

"I'm no mean mesmerist myself," Burton pointed out.

Wells grunted. "I remember reading that. You're no match for our chief medium, though. But my editor has connections. He pulled a few strings and arranged that these men—" he gestured towards the three soldiers, "—and myself be aboard the *Britannia*. We're going to kidnap you."

"Kidnap?"

They reached the top of the stairs and started down a short passage.

"Just trust me, Richard."

The Tommies stopped at a door. One of them opened it, and Wells led Burton through onto the bridge.

The explorer found himself in a chamber filled with consoles and levers, wheels, pipes and gauges. There were twelve crew members at various stations, but Burton's attention immediately centred on a tall man standing before a wide curved window.

"Private Frank Baker, sir," Wells announced.

The man turned. He was slim, with sad eyes, unevenly arranged features, and a clipped moustache, wearing a dark uniform with a double row of silver buttons and a peaked cap. He looked Burton up and down.

"You've attracted the attention of men in high places, Baker," he said. His voice was sharp and precise, with a nasal twang. "Why?"

Burton saluted. He staggered.

"It's all right," Aitken said. "Steady yourself. We're going over some hills."

"I didn't realise we were moving," Burton answered.

"The only time you'll feel it is on rough terrain, and even then not much. It's like being on an ocean liner. Answer the question."

"I honestly haven't the vaguest idea why there's any interest in me at all, sir. I've been in a P.O.W. camp for two years."

"And before that?"

"Civilian Observer Corp at Dar es Salaam and Tanga, then a guerrilla fighter until I was captured at Dut'humi."

"Where were they taking you?"

"To the Lake Regions, but they didn't tell me why."

"Sir," Wells interjected. "Apparently one of the men we just shot dead was Lettow-Vorbeck."

Burton watched as the major general's Adam's apple bobbed reflexively. All the crew members turned. Aitken cleared his throat, looked around, and snapped: "Attend your stations!"

"There's something else, sir," Wells added. "I think you might prefer to hear it in private."

Aitken gazed at the little war correspondent for a moment, gave a brusque nod, then turned away and issued a sequence of orders concerning the velocity and course of the ship to the bridge crew. He returned his attention to Burton and Wells, jabbed a finger at them, and said: "You and you; follow me."

They did so, trailing after him back out into the corridor and through a door into the Captain's office.

Aitken positioned himself behind a desk but remained standing with his hands held behind his back.

"What do you have to tell me, Wells?"

"I think it best that Baker explains, sir."

"I don't give two bloody hoots who does the talking, just get on with it!"

Speaking slowly and clearly, Burton told him about Lettow-Vorbeck's A-Bomb.

Moments later, Aitken collapsed into his chair.

§

Burton was confined to a cabin with Bertie Wells as his guard. He'd washed, thrown away his prison uniform, and dressed in clean tick-free battle fatigues. A cup of tea and a plate of sandwiches had been provided.

"They've radioed ahead," Wells told him. "And so have I."

"And the city's being evacuated?"

"Evacuated? To where? There's no place to go. Tabora has been under siege for half a century, and all the rest of Africa is under German control. My guess is they'll try to get as many people as possible into underground bunkers. Whether that'll save them or not remains to be seen. If the spore cloud is dense enough, I don't suppose there'll be anywhere safe."

"Yet we're going back?"

"To rescue the top brass."

"And take them to—?"

"Your guess is as good as mine. I suppose it's possible there's another British enclave somewhere; a place only the bigwigs know about. Or maybe we'll head into one of Africa's wildernesses and lay low while Crowley experiments on you."

"I don't like the sound of that." Burton took a bite out of a sandwich and frowned thoughtfully while he chewed and swallowed. "Who did you radio?"

"I sent a coded message to my editor; told him about the A-Bomb."

"Will he be able to get to safety?"

"Probably not. As I say, the city is surrounded."

"Then how do we get in? How does the *Britannia* come and go?"

"We manage to keep a passage—we call it Hell's Run—open through the besieging German forces to the east of the city. The most ghastly fighting occurs along its borders, but Crowley and our mediums focus their efforts there and have so far prevented the Germans from closing the route."

A siren started to blare.

"That's the call to battle stations!"

The door opened and an Askari stepped in. "You're both ordered to the bridge," he said. "Tabora just radioed a message that's put the wind up Aitken. We're approaching the city now."

"What message?" Wells asked, as they followed the African out of the room.

"I don't know the details, Lieutenant."

They passed along corridors and up stairs, with men rushing around them and the siren howling continuously. The moment they entered the bridge, Aitken rounded on

Burton and snapped: "Baker, did Lettow-Vorbeck tell you anything about lurchers? Have the Germans regained control of them?"

"He pointed out a crowd of the plants," Burton replied. "And said they're most numerous up near the Blood Jungle, but control? No, quite the opposite."

"Well, that's damned strange. Tabora reports that thousands of them are approaching the city from the north."

Burton and Wells looked at each other. The explorer gave a shake of his head and shrugged, baffled.

"We're currently racing straight down the middle of Hell's Run, well away from German pea shooters," Aitken said. "When was the last time you were here, Baker?"

"I've never been to Tabora, sir."

"You haven't? Well take a peek out of the window. We're almost there."

Burton and Wells stepped over to the glass and looked out over the African landscape. The *Britannia* was travelling at a tremendous speed over flat ground. To the north and south of her, black clouds humped up into the blue sky. Lightning flickered inside them. Puffs of smoke rose from the ground beneath. There were flashes. Tiny dots could be seen flying through the air.

"Those are the edges of Hell's Run," Wells murmured. "As you can see, the Hun weathermen are at work. The storms are more or less constant, as is the fighting beneath them. Tabora is behind the hills you see ahead of us."

As he examined the terrain, Burton was overcome by a sense of *déjà vu*. He struggled for breath and clutched at Wells' arm.

The *Britannia* shot up a slope, over the crest of a hill, sank into the valley beyond, navigated up the next slope, and reached the second summit. Burton saw a wide plain stretched out below. Much of it was obscured by a blanket of dirty steam, which was particularly dark and opaque straight ahead, where, from out of the pall, there rose a tall rock, topped with green vegetation.

"Kazeh!" Burton croaked. "Tabora is Kazeh!"

§

"Kazeh is under siege!"

Sir Richard Francis Burton, Algernon Swinburne, and Isabel Arundell had ridden back through the night to where Trounce and the expedition were bivouacked. All three of them were coated with dust and thoroughly exhausted, but there was no time to rest.

Burton fired his rifle into the air to rouse the camp and yelled: "Hopa! Hopa! Pakia!"

Trounce responded to the announcement with: "By the Prussians? Are there that many of them?"

"There's enough! We have to get moving! If they take the town, we won't be able to resupply for the next leg of the safari."

"But what the blazes are they up to?"

"It's the key to central East Africa, William. Whoever controls Kazeh, controls the region all the way from Lake Tanganyika to Zanzibar, and up to the Mountains of the Moon. My guess is they mean to drive the Arabs out and make of it a Prussian base of operations."

Burton ordered Saíd bin Sálim to have the porters take up their loads. Mirambo silently appeared beside him and asked: "Will the coming day be that in which we fight?"

"Yes. I bid thee prepare thy warriors, O Marimbo."

"We are always prepared, *muzungo mbáyá*. It is wise to be so when devils such as thee walk the land."

The African stalked away.

Krishnamurthy, Spencer, Isabella Mayson, Sister Raghavendra, and Sidi Bombay gathered around the king's agent. He described to them the scene he'd witnessed.

Krishnamurthy asked: "Can we get into the town from the west?"

"Yes," Burton replied. "If we follow the hills south, remaining on this side of them, then cross when—"

"No. We can't enter the town at all," Isabel Arundell interrupted.

They all looked at her, surprised.

"It would be suicidal. I have a hundred and twenty fighters and another ninety or so on the way. Mirambo has two hundred boys. The Prussians already greatly outnumber us and there are a thousand more fast approaching. If we're in the town when they arrive, we'll be pinned down and we'll likely never get out again."

Burton nodded his head thoughtfully. "You're the expert in guerrilla tactics," he said. "And I'll bow to your expertise. What do you recommend?"

Isabel positioned herself directly in front of him and placed her hands on his shoulders. "The king made you his agent, Dick, and you have your orders. What is the distance from here to the Mountains of the Moon?"

"Something under two hundred miles."

"Then go. Forget about resupplying in the town. You and your people take two horses each and the bare essentials in supplies. No porters. Nothing but what you can carry. Travel as fast as you can. It's a race, remember? I have no doubt that John Speke is already on his way."

"And you?" Burton asked.

"Mirambo and I will lead our forces against the Prussians."

William Trounce interjected: "But why, Isabel? If we're going to bypass the town, why risk yourselves in battle at all?"

Isabel stepped back and pulled the *keffiyeh* from her head. The sickle moon had just risen over the horizon and its pale light illuminated her long blonde hair.

"Because despite these robes, I'm British, William. If what we saw at Mzizima, and what we are witnessing here at Kazeh, are the first skirmishes in a clash of empires, then it's my duty to defend that to which I belong—besides which, if we don't keep the Prussians occupied here, they'll be able to rapidly establish outposts all the way to the Mountains of the Moon, making it almost impossible for you to get there."

For a long moment, no one spoke.

Isabella Mayson cleared her throat. "Richard," she said. "If you don't mind, I think I would like to stay and join the Daughters of Al-Manat."

"And I," added Sister Raghavendra. "Besides, you'll probably travel more quickly as a smaller group."

The explorer looked from one woman to the other, then his gaze went past Isabel and his eyes locked with Swinburne's, and even in the dim light, the poet could see in them a great depth of despair.

"I'm afraid Isabel is right," the poet said, quietly. "We can't allow Speke to reach the Eye of Nāga before us. Equally, we can't let Kazeh fall to the Prussians. The only option is to split the expedition."

Burton leaned his head back and considered the stars. Then he closed his eyes and said: "And you, William?"

Trounce stepped forward and spoke in a low, gruff voice: "Am I supposed to run off and leave women to fight?"

Isabella Mayson whirled around to face him: "Sir! The fact that I wrote a book about cookery and household management doesn't mean I'm incapable of putting a bullet through a man's head! Have you forgotten this—" She pulled back her hair to reveal the notch in her right ear. "I fought by your side at Dut'humi. Was I any less effective than you? Did I scream? Did I faint? Did I start knitting a shawl?"

"No, of course not! You're as brave as they come. But—"

"No buts! No medieval nonsense about honour and chivalry! There isn't time for such indulgence! We have a job to do! Yours is to accompany Sir Richard and to retrieve that diamond!"

"Well said!" Isabel Arundell put in.

They all looked at Burton, who was standing stock-still.

Gunfire rattled from the town.

The cough of a lion sounded from afar.

Pox, on Herbert Spencer's head, muttered something unintelligible, and Malady responded with a click of his beak.

"All right! Enough!" Burton snapped, opening his eyes. "Sadhvi, will you prepare for us a pack of remedies and treatments?"

"Yes, certainly."

"Take Algy with you and instruct him in their use. Maneesh—"

Krishnamurthy moved closer. "Yes?"

"I'm sorry but I have to give you a very difficult mission. Sidi Bombay says an aggressive tribe called the Chwezi live among the Mountains of the Moon, so there's every chance that we won't make it out. It's imperative that the government learns what is happening here. For that reason, I'm going to entrust you with my journals and reports. I want you and Saíd and his men to trek all the way back to Zanzibar. I'm going to pay our remaining porters to accompany you as far as Ugogi. There, you can hire more. Once you reach the island, catch the first ship home and report to Palmerston."

Krishnamurthy straightened his back and squared his shoulders. "You can rely on me, sir."

"I don't doubt it, my friend."

Burton next addressed Trounce and Bombay: "You two, Algy, Herbert, and I, will depart at sun up. Work with Isabella to get everything prepared. I'll join you presently. First though—" He took Isabel Arundell by the arm and steered her away. "—you and I need to talk."

They walked a short distance away, then stopped and stood, listening to the battle, and watching dark shapes moving across the plain near the horizon.

"Elephants," Isabel murmured.

"Yes."

"You don't have to say anything, Dick. I'm familiar with your hopelessness when it comes to goodbyes."

He took her hand. "Did you know that, had history never changed, this is the year we'd be celebrating our honeymoon?"

"How do you know that?"

"Countess Sabina. Palmerston's medium."

"I ought to slap your face for reminding me that you broke our engagement."

"I'm sorry."

"I know. Do you think we'd have been happily married?"

"Yes."

He was silent a moment, then: "Isabel, I—I—"

She waited patiently while he struggled to express himself.

"I'm filled with such regret I can barely stand it," he said, his voice breaking. "I've done everything wrong. Everything!

I should never have accepted the king's commission. I panicked. Speke had ruined my career and reputation. Then he put a bullet into his head and people said it was my fault!"

"Which is when Palmerston threw you a lifeline."

"He did, but even with the situation as it was, I'm not certain I'd have accepted his offer had Spring Heeled Jack not assaulted me the night before."

"There you have it, Dick. You regret a decision you made, but how much can you blame yourself when you were under the influence of such extraordinary circumstances? We all like to fool ourselves that we are independent and that our minds are our own, but the truth is we're always swayed by events."

Burton smacked his right fist into his left palm. "Yes! That's exactly it! My decisions were made according to context. But have I ever properly understood it? Since the advent of Spring Heeled Jack, I feel like I've not had a firm grip on events at all. It's all slipped away from me. It feels to me as though things that should have occurred over a long stretch of history are all piling up at once—and it's too much! It's too confusing! Bismillah! I can sense time swirling through and around me like some sort of discordant noise. But—"

Burton paused and raised his hands to his head, pushing his fingertips into his scalp and massaging it through the hair, as if to somehow loosen blocked thoughts.

"What is it?"

"I have this feeling that time is—is—like a language! Damn it, Isabel! I have mastered more than thirty tongues.

Why does this one elude me? Why can't I make any sense of it?"

Burton's eyes momentarily reflected the moonlight and Isabel saw in them the same torment Swinburne had spotted minutes ago.

He continued: "Tom Bendyshe, Shyamji Bhatti, Thomas Honesty—all dead; and we—we have pushed through pain and fever and discomfort to the point of utter exhaustion. That is the context by which I have to now judge my decisions, but I don't comprehend the significance of it! Surely there has to be one! Why can't I translate the language of these events?"

"I have never before known a man with your depth of intellect, Dick, but you're demanding too much of yourself. You haven't slept. You're overwrought. You're trying to do what no man—or woman—can do. The workings of time are obscure to us all. Your Countess Sabina, who has insight into so much more than the rest of us; does she understand it?"

"No. If anything, the more of it she observes, the more confused she gets."

"Perhaps then, it cannot be deciphered by the living, which is why meaning is assigned retrospectively, by those who inhabit the future. By historians."

"Who weren't even a part of the events! Are future historians better placed to interpret the life of Al-Manat than you are? Of course not! But will their reading of your life make more sense than anything you can tell me now—or at any other point while you're alive? Yes, almost certainly."

"Are you afraid of how history will judge you?"

"No. I'm afraid of how I'm judging history!"

Isabel gave a throaty chuckle.

Burton looked at her in surprise, and asked: "What's so funny about that?"

"Oh, nothing, Dick—except, I imagined that perhaps you took me aside to tell me that you love me. How silly of me! Why on Earth didn't I realise it was for nothing more than a philosophical discussion!"

Burton looked at her, then looked down and directed a derisive snort at himself.

"I'm an idiot! Of course I love you, Isabel. From the moment I first laid eyes on you. And it gives me a strange kind of comfort to know that there's another history, and in it we are together, and not parted by—" He gestured around them. "—this."

"I always thought that if anything was going to come between us it would be Africa," she said.

"But it wasn't," Burton replied. "It was the Spring Heeled Jack business."

"Yes." Isabel sighed. "But I suspect that, somehow, those events, just like the River Nile, have their source here."

§

The freshly risen sun turned the plain the colour of blood. From the summit of a hill, Burton, Swinburne, Trounce, Spencer and Sidi Bombay looked down upon it and watched as the expedition divided into three. One group, led by Maneesh Krishnamurthy, was heading back in the direction they'd all come; another—the Daughters of Al-Manat—was riding away, along the base of the hills, intending to set up camp among the trees to the southeast of Kazeh; while the third—Marimbo and his men—was moving into the forest directly east of the town.

Burton, with a savage scowl on his face, muttered, "Come on," pulled his horse around, and started along a trail that led northwards. There were two horses, lightly loaded with baggage, roped behind his mount. Trounce had two more behind his. Swinburne's horse led the eighth animal, upon which Herbert Spencer was rather awkwardly propped, and the ninth horse was tethered behind that. The clockwork man wasn't heavy—his mount could easily carry him—but he'd only thus far ridden a mule side-saddle, and wasn't used to the bigger beast.

Sidi Bombay's horse led no others, for the African frequently rode ahead to scout the route.

Traversing a long valley, they moved through the trees and, thanks to the scarcity of undergrowth and the canopy sheltering them from the sun, made rapid progress. They didn't stop to rest—nor did they speak—until they reached the edge of a savannah midway through the afternoon; and when they sat and shared unleavened bread and plantains, the conversation was desultory. Each man was preoccupied, listening to the distant gunfire, dwelling on those from whom they'd parted. Even the three screechers, Pox, Malady, and Swinburne, were subdued.

"We'll endure the heat and keep going," Burton muttered.

They resumed their journey, shading themselves beneath umbrellas, guiding their horses over hard, dusty ground, watching as herds of impala and zebras scattered at their approach.

The rest of the day passed sluggishly, with the interminable landscape hardly changing. The climate had all three men so stupefied that they frequently slipped into a light sleep, only to be awakened by Spencer shouting: "The bloomin' horses are stoppin' again, Boss!"

Shortly before sunset, they set up their one small tent beside a stony outcrop, ate, then crawled under the canvas to sleep. Sidi Bombay wrapped himself in a blanket and slumbered under the stars. Spencer, having had his key inserted and wound, kept guard.

In the few seconds before exhaustion took him, Swinburne remembered the clockwork philosopher's book, and the phrase: *Only equivalence can lead to destruction or a final transcendence.*

He wondered how he'd come to forget about it; why he hadn't mentioned it to anyone; then he forgot about it again and went to sleep.

Sir Richard Francis Burton dreamed that he was slumbering alone, in the open, with unfamiliar stars wheeling above him. There was a slight scuffing to his left. He opened his eyes and turned his head and saw a tiny man, less than twelve inches high, with delicate lace-like wings growing from his shoulder blades. His forehead was decorated with an Indian *bindi*.

"I don't believe in fairies," the explorer said. "And I've already looked upon your true form, K'k'thyima."

He sat up, and blinked, and suddenly the fairy was much larger, and reptilian, and it had one or five or seven heads.

"Thou art possessed of a remarkable mind, O human. It perceives truth. It is adaptable. That is why we chose thee."

Burton was suddenly shaken by a horribly familiar sensation; an awareness that his identity was divided, that there were two of him, ever at odds with each other. For the first time, though, he also sensed that some sort of physical truth lay between these opposing forces.

"Good!" the Nāga hissed. "Still we sing, but soon it will end, and already thou hears the echo of our song."

"What are you suggesting? That I'm sensing the future?"

The priest didn't answer. His head was singular. His head was multiple.

Burton tried to focus on the strange presence, but couldn't.

"I dreamed of you before," he said. "You were in Kumari Kandam. This, though, is Africa, where the Nāga are known as the *Chitahuri* or the *Shayturáy*."

"I am K'k'thyima. I am here, I am in other places. I am nowhere, soft skin, for my people were made extinct by thine."

"Yet the essence of you was imprinted on one of the Eyes; you lived on in that black diamond until it was shattered."

Again, the Nāga chose not to respond.

A flash drew Burton's eyes upward. He saw a shooting star; the brightest he'd ever witnessed. It blazed a trail across the sky, then suddenly divided into three streaks of light. They flew apart and faded. When he looked down, the Nāga priest was gone.

He lay back and woke up.

"It's dawn, Boss. I can still hear shots from Kazeh."

Herbert Spencer's head was poking through the entrance to the tent. It was wrapped in a *keffiyeh* but the scarf was pulled open at the front and the polymethylene suit beneath was visible, as were the three round openings that formed the philosopher's "face." Through the glass of the uppermost one, Burton could see tiny cogs revolving. Spencer was otherwise motionless.

A moment passed.

"Was there something else, Herbert?"

"No, Boss. I'll help Mr. Bombay to load the horses."

The philosopher withdrew.

Swinburne sat up. "I think I shall take lunch at the Athenaeum Club today, Richard, followed by a tipple at the Black Toad."

"Are you awake, Algy?"

The poet peered around at the inside of the tent.

"Oh bugger it," he said. "I am."

Burton shook Trounce into consciousness and the three of them crawled into the open, ate a hasty breakfast, packed, and mounted their horses.

Burton groaned. "I'm running a fever."

"I have some of Sadhvi's medicine," Swinburne said.

"I'll take it when we next stop. Let's see how far we can get today. Keep your weapons close to hand; we don't know when we might run into Speke."

They moved off.

Most of the day was spent crossing the savannah.

Vultures circled overhead.

The far-off sounds of battle faded behind them.

They entered a lush valley. Clusters of granite pushed through its slopes, and the grass grew so high that it brushed against the riders' legs.

"Wow! This is the place called Usagari," Bombay advised. "Soon we will see villages."

"Everyone move quietly," Burton ordered. "We have to slip past as many as we can, else the few boxes of beads and coils of wire we're carrying will be gone in an instant."

After fording a *nullah*, they rode up onto higher ground and saw plantations laid out on a gentle slope. Bombay led them along the edges of the cultivated fields, through forests and thick vegetation, and thus managed to pass four villages without being spotted. Then their luck ran out, and they were confronted by warriors who leaped about, brandishing their spears and striking grotesque poses that were designed to frighten but which sent Swinburne into fits of giggles.

After much whooping and shouting, Bombay finally established peaceful communication. The Britishers paid three boxes of beads and were given permission to stay at the village overnight. It was called Usenda, and its inhabitants proved much more friendly than their initial greeting had suggested. They shared their food and, to Swinburne's delight, a highly alcoholic beverage made from bananas, and gave over a dwelling for the explorers' use. It was a poor thing constructed of grass, infested with insects, and already claimed by a family of rats. Trounce was too exhausted to care, Swinburne was too drunk to notice, and Burton was so feverish by now that he passed out the moment he set foot in it. They all slept deeply, while Spencer stood sentry duty, and Bombay stayed up late gossiping with the village elders.

When they departed the next day, the king's agent was slumped semi-aware in his saddle, so Trounce took the lead. He successfully steered them past seven villages and out of the farmed region onto uninhabited flatlands where gingerbread palms grew in abundance. It was easy going but took two days to traverse, during which time Burton swam in and out of consciousness. His companions, meanwhile, grew thoroughly sick of the unchanging scenery, which offered nothing to suggest that they might be making any progress.

At last, they came to the edge of a jungle and began to work their way through it, with Trounce and Spencer leading the way while Swinburne and Bombay guided the horses behind them. Burton remained mounted and insensible.

For what seemed like hours, they fought with the undergrowth, until Spencer pushed a tangle of lianas out of their path and they suddenly found themselves face to face with a rhinoceros. It kicked the ground, snorted, and moved its head from side to side, squinting at them from its small, watery eyes.

They raised their rifles.

"Absolute silence, please, gentlemen," Trounce whispered. "The slightest noise or movement could cause it to charge us."

"Up your sooty funnel!" Pox screamed.

"Pig jobber!" Malady squawked. "Cross-eyed slack-bellied stink trumpet!"

The rhino gave a prodigious belch, turned, and trotted away.

"My hat!" Swinburne exclaimed. "Malady has been learning fast!"

"Humph!" Trounce responded. "Next time we're confronted by a wild beast, I won't bother to unsling my rifle. I'll just throw parakeets."

It was close to nightfall by the time they broke free of the mess of vegetation and found a place to camp. Burton recovered his wits while the others slept, and he sat with Spencer, listening to the rasping utterances of lions and the chuckles and squeals of hyenas.

"How're you feelin?" the philosopher asked.

"Weak. How about you?"

"Phew! I'll be glad when all this walkin' an' ridin' is over an' done with. It's playin' merry havoc with me gammy leg."

"Your leg is just dented, Herbert."

"Aye, but it aches somethin' terrible."

"That's not possible."

"Aye. Do you think, Boss, that I've lost some qualities that a man possesses only 'cos he's flesh?"

"What sort of qualities?"

"A conscience, for example; a self-generated moral standard by which a man judges his own actions. Old Darwin said it's the most important distinction between humankind an' other species."

"And you think it's a characteristic of corporeality?"

"Aye, an evolution of a creature's instinct to preserve its own species. Compare us to the lower animals. What happens when a sow has a runt in her litter? She eats it. What happens if a bird hatches deformed? It's bloomin' well pecked to death. What do gazelles do with a lame member of the herd? They leave it to die, don't they? Humans are the dominant species 'cos we're heterogeneous, but to support all our individual specialisations, we have to suppress the natural desire to allow the weak an' inferior to fall by the wayside, as it were, 'cos how can we evaluate each other when, from every individual, reality demands somethin' different? A manual labourer might consider a bank clerk too physically weak; does that mean he should kill the blighter? The clerk might think the labourer to unintelligent; is that reason enough to deny him the means to live? In the wild, such judgements apply, but not in human society, so we have conscience to intercede, to inhibit the baser aspects of natural evolution an' raise it to a more sophisticated level. As I suggested to you once before, Boss, where mankind is concerned, survival of the fittest refers not to physical strength, but to the ability to adapt oneself to circumstances. The process wouldn't function were it not for conscience."

Burton considered this, and there was silence between them for a good few minutes.

Spencer picked up a stone and threw it at a shadowy form—a hyena that had wandered too close.

"You're suggesting," Burton finally said, "that conscience has evolved to suppress in us the instinct that drives animals to kill or abandon the defective, because each of us is only weak or strong depending on who's judging us and the criteria they employ?"

"Precisely. Without conscience we'd end up killin' each other willy nilly until the whole species was gone."

"So you associate it with the flesh because it ensures our species' physical survival?"

"Aye. It's an adaptation of an instinct what's inherent in the body."

"And you suspect that your transference into this brass mechanism might have robbed you of your conscience?"

"I don't know whether it has or hasn't, Boss. I just wonder. I need to test it."

They sat a little longer, then Burton was overcome by weariness and retired to the tent.

Travel the following morning proved the easiest since their arrival in Africa. The ground was firm, trees—baobabs—were widely spaced, and undergrowth was thinly distributed. Small flowers grew in abundance.

As they entered this district, Pox and Malady launched themselves from Spencer's shoulders and flew from tree to tree, rubbing their beaks together and insulting each other rapturously.

"It's love," Swinburne declared.

Almost before they realised it, they found cultivated land underfoot and a village just ahead. It was too close to avoid, so *hongo* was paid and, in return, a hut was assigned for their use.

They rested and took stock.

Sadhvi's medicine was driving the fever out of Burton. He ached all over but his temperature had stabilised and his strength began to seep back into his limbs.

Trounce, though, was suffering. The spear wound in his arm had become slightly infected, and his legs were ulcerating again.

"I shall be crippled at this rate," he complained. He sat on a stool and allowed Swinburne to roll up his trouser legs.

"Yuck!" the poet exclaimed. "What hideous pins you have, Pouncer!"

"You're not seeing them at their best, lad."

"Nor would I want to! Now then, it just so happens that I'm the sole purveyor of Sister Raghavendra's Revitalising Remedies. Incredible Cures and Terrific Tonics, all yours for a coil of wire and three shiny beads! What do you say?"

"I say, stop clowning and apply the poultice or I'll apply the flat of my hand to the back of your head."

Swinburne got to work.

"Shame you can't do nothin' for mine," Spencer piped.

Burton, who, with Bombay, had been parlaying with the village elders, walked over and plonked himself on the ground beside the Yard man.

"We need to navigate a little more in a north-easterly direction," he said. "It will save us from having to pass through a densely populated region."

They departed before sun up the next morning, descended into a deep and miry watercourse, struggled through bullrushes, then climbed to the peak of a hill just as the sun threw its rays over the horizon. The next few hours were spent crossing uneven ground cut through with marshy rivulets, each filled with tall, tough reeds. There were cairns dotted over the land for as far as the eye could see, as well as stubby malformed trees in which hundreds of black vultures sat in sinister contemplation.

"Yea, though I walk through the valley of Death," Swinburne announced.

"Spongy brained measles rash!" Pox added.

A steep incline led them up onto firmer ground and into a forest. The two parakeets once again left Spencer's shoulders and travelled overhead, with Pox teaching Malady new insults.

Burton rode onto a fairly well defined trail.

"This is the path I think Speke is following," he said.

"Wow!" Bombay answered. "It is the one he took before, when I was with him."

"Then we should proceed with caution."

They stopped to eat, then rode on at a brisk pace until they emerged from the trees at the head of a shadowed valley. Its sides were thickly wooded and a clear stream ran through its middle with reasonably open ground to either side. There were pandana palms in profusion, rich groves of plantains, and thistles of extraordinary size. In the distance, the land rolled in high undulations to grassy hills, which Burton identified as the districts of Karague and Kishakka.

Late in the afternoon, they approached a village and were surprised when the inhabitants, upon sighting them, ran away.

"By Jove! That hasn't happened since we had the harvestman," Trounce observed.

Riding among the huts, they noticed that the usual stocks of food were missing. There were also a couple of ominous-looking stains on the ground in the central clearing.

"It looks like they received some non-too-friendly visitors," the king's agent said. He unpacked two boxes of beads from one of the horses and placed them at the entrance to the chief's dwelling. "Let's leave them a gift, if for no other reason than to demonstrate that not all *muzungo mbáyá* are bad."

The remainder of the day was spent travelling through the rest of the valley before crossing fine, rising meadowlands to a stratified sandstone cliff, beneath which they rested for the night.

Another early start. Hilly country. Herds of cattle. Forests of acacias.

All around them, the trees were alive with a profusion of small birds, whistling and chirping with such vigour that, for the entire day, the men had to raise their voices to be heard above the din.

They left the boisterous tree-dwellers behind as the sun was riding low in the sky, and drew to a halt on a summit, looking across a broad, jungle-thick basin. On the far side, they spotted movement on the brow of a hummock. Trounce lifted the field glasses, clipped them onto his head, and adjusted the focusing wheels.

"About twenty men," he reported. "On foot. And one of those plant vehicle things."

"Let me see," Burton said.

His friend passed the magnifying device and Burton looked through it, watching the distant group as it disappeared from view.

"Speke," he said.

They decided to stop where they were, quickly set up the camp, and without bothering to eat first, immediately fell into an exhausted sleep.

Herbert Spencer stood outside the tent, leaning on his staff. His shadow lengthened, turned a deep shade of purple, then dissipated into the gathering gloom. When they awoke in the morning, he was still there. Burton wound him up.

"I say, Herbert, is your mind still active when your spring is slack?" Swinburne asked, as he prepared their breakfast.

"Yus, lad," the mechanical man tapped a gloved finger to his scarf-enshrouded head. "The babbage in here interprets the electrical field held in the diamonds an' translates its fluctuations as speech an' movement. In the other direction, it channels sensory information about the environment from this brass body to the gemstones, which the field interprets as sound an' sight. When the babbage has no bloomin' power, I have no idea what's happenin' around me, but I can still think."

"It must feel like you're trapped. I should probably go mad under such circumstances."

"You're already mad," Trounce put in.

One of the horses had died during the night. They redistributed its load, then, after eating, began the trek down the slope to the edge of the jungle. When they reached it, they found the verdure to be extravagantly abundant and chaotic, pressing in to either side of the narrow trail. Speke's party had passed this way recently, but there was very little evidence to suggest it, and guiding the horses past the thorny bushes and dangling, ant-covered lianas proved extremely difficult.

"I'll set to with me machete, Boss," Spencer announced, limping to the front of the party.

He unsheathed his blade and began to swipe at the undergrowth. A man would have been exhausted by this very quickly but the clockwork philosopher's mechanical arm hacked without pause, widening the path, until four hours later they emerged onto a huge flat rock, as big as a tennis court, surrounded on all sides by lush green vegetation.

Spencer moved onto it, stumbling slightly, then lay down his blade, pulled a 54-bore Beaumont-Adams revolver from his waistband, and said: "Shall we stop here awhile?"

Burton glanced at Trounce and said: "Yes, I think William's ulcers are paining him. We'll lay up until the day's heat abates a little."

"I'm fine," the Scotland Yard man protested.

"Wow! It is a good place to rest, Mr. Trounce," said Sidi Bombay.

Pox and Malady, who'd been snuggled together on Spencer's head, suddenly squawked and flew into the trees.

"Yes, William," the brass man said in his hooting voice. "You should take the weight off your feet."

He lifted his gun, aimed carefully between Trounce's eyes, and pulled the trigger.

THE THIRD PART

Time

Oh glory, that we wrestle
So valiantly with Time!
—Richard Monckton Milnes

CHAPTER 10

To the Mountains of the Moon

"Death must be so beautiful. To lie in the soft brown earth, with the grasses waving above one's head, and listen to silence. To have no yesterday, and no tomorrow. To forget time, to forgive life, to be at peace.
—Oscar Wilde

Eighteen-year-old PC53 William Trounce had failed to make his first arrest.

He always timed his beat so he'd reach Constitution Hill in time for Queen Victoria's spin around Green Park. He thought the young monarch—who was just three years into her reign—was taking a needless risk with these daily excursions. He understood her need to escape for a few precious moments from the stuffy formality of Buckingham Palace, but there were many who still thought her a puppet of the unpopular prime minister, Lord Melbourne, and they often took the opportunity to jeer and boo as she rode through the park in her open-topped carriage. Trounce considered it one of his essential duties to be there in time to move the naysayers along.

Today he was going to be late, and it was Dennis the Dip's fault. He'd spotted the notorious East End pickpocket on the

Mall. The crook was, as usual, dressed as a gentleman and looked entirely at home among the well-heeled crowd that sauntered back and forth along the ceremonial avenue. He scrubbed up well, did Dennis, and easily passed muster as a gent so long as he kept his mouth shut. Were any of his fellow perambulators to hear him speak, though, they would have instantly recognised the harsh accent and mangled grammar of the Cauldron and would most certainly have given him a very wide berth indeed.

As it was, Dennis mingled with his potential victims with nary a glance of suspicion cast his way. No glances—but there was one unwavering gaze, and that belonged to PC53 Trounce.

It would have been a very satisfying first feather in his cap for the young constable if he'd ended the career of this particular villain today, but alas it was not to be. Dennis's eyes flicked from handbag to handbag, pocket to pocket, but his long restless fingers remained in plain view the whole time, and Trounce had to settle for warning the man away.

"Oh bleedin' 'eck, I ain't up to nuffink, am I?" Dennis had whined. "Jest givin' me Sunday best an airing, that's all!"

"It's Wednesday, Dennis," Trounce pointed out.

The thief objected and wriggled on the spot a little more before finally scurrying off, and Trounce resumed his beat, a mite disappointed that he'd still not "christened his badge" after two weeks on the beat.

At the end of the Mall he passed Buckingham Palace and turned right into the park. He preferred to walk along on the grass rather than on the Constitution Hill path itself; it was better to position himself behind the crowds that often gathered along Victoria's route, for the troublemakers nearly always hid at the back, where they could more easily take to their heels should anyone object to their catcalls.

He saw that Her Majesty's carriage, drawn by four horses—the front left ridden by a postilion—was already trundling along a little way ahead of him. He increased his pace to catch up, striding down a gentle slope, with an excellent view of the scene. Despite the mild weather, the crowd was sparse today. There were no protests and few hurrahs.

He jumped at the sound of a gunshot.

What the hell?

Breaking into a run, he peered ahead and noticed a man wearing a top hat, blue frock-coat and white breeches walking beside the slow-moving carriage. He was throwing down a smoking flintlock and drawing, with his left hand, a second gun from his coat.

In an instant, horror sucked the heat from Trounce's body and time slowed to a crawl.

His legs pumped; his boots thudded into the grass; he heard himself shout: "No!"

He saw heads turning towards the man.

His breath thundered in his ears.

The man's left arm came up.

The queen stood, raising her hands to the white lace around her throat.

Her husband reached for her.

A second man leaped forward and grabbed the gunman. "No, Edward!" came a faint yell.

The scene seemed to freeze; the two men entwined; their faces, even from this distance, so similar, like brothers; each person in the crowd poised in mid-motion, some stepping forward, some stepping back; the queen upright in the carriage, wearing a cream-coloured dress and bonnet; her consort, in a top hat and red jacket, reaching for her; the four outriders turning their horses.

Christ! thought Trounce. *Christ, no! Please, no!*

A freakish creature suddenly flew past.

Tall, loose-limbed, bouncing on what seemed to be spring-loaded stilts, it skidded to a halt in front of him. Trounce stumbled and fell to his knees.

"Stop, Edward!" the weird apparition bellowed.

A bolt of lightning crackled from its side into the ground and the lean figure staggered, groaning and clutching at itself. Below, the two struggling men turned and looked up.

A second shot echoed across the park.

§

Mist-enshrouded Tabora was dirty and crowded and filled with oppressively monolithic buildings and bustling, noisy streets. Its many vehicles reminded Sir Richard Francis Burton of hansom cabs, except their steam horses had been incorporated into the body of the cabin, so the things rumbled along on four wheels with no visible means of locomotion. Bertie Wells referred to them as "motor-carriages."

The two men were in one now, along with the three Tommies from the *Britannia*, one of whom was driving the contraption by means of a wheel and foot pedals. Burton watched him and thought the operation looked exceedingly complicated.

Upon the rolling sphere's arrival in the besieged city, the king's agent had been hustled out of the ship and marched straight to a rather more luxurious motor-carriage than the one in which he was currently sitting. He'd waited in it for a while before being joined by Wells, Major General Aitken, and a driver. The latter started the engine, steered the vehicle onto a broad street, and sent it rattling along until they reached the centre of the city. A second conveyance—the one Burton was now in—had followed behind.

He was escorted into a large square building that, from the outside, reminded him of London's Athenaeum Club but which, on the inside, proved far less opulent. Here, he was presented to twelve generals who, along with Aitken, acted in lieu of an elected government. They ordered him to explain how he'd come to be in the Ugogi P.O.W. camp and why he was being moved. He answered the first part of the question truthfully. To the second part he said simply: "I don't know."

The men then requested a full description of Paul Emil von Lettow-Vorbeck and demanded that Burton recount everything the German had said to him. He told them as much as he could without revealing his identity.

Finally, they questioned him about the approaching *L.59 Zeppelin* and its payload, the A-bomb.

When he'd finished explaining, he was summarily dismissed.

Bertie Wells had taken him back outside and to the second car, in which the Tommies were waiting.

They were now on their way to a secret destination.

"We're supposed to be escorting you to Colonel Crowley," Wells said. "But we're disobeying orders. When he finds out, if we're lucky, we'll be court marshalled and executed by firing squad."

Burton looked at his companion and asked: "And if you're unlucky?"

"He'll use his mediumistic powers on us. I dread to think how that might turn out. One way or the other, though, this is a suicide mission."

"Bloody hell!" Burton exclaimed. "Why didn't you tell me that before? I'd rather face this Crowley character than have you sacrifice yourself!"

"Which is exactly the reason I kept it quiet. I'm only telling you now so you'll realise the importance of what we're doing. I trust my editor implicitly, despite his eccentricities, and if he says the future depends on him meeting you, then I'm willing to bet my life that it does. Here, strap on this pistol, you shouldn't be without a weapon."

Burton clipped the holster to his belt. He watched, amazed, as three smaller versions of the *Britannia* suddenly sped out of the billowing mist and swept past the motor-carriage. They were about eight feet in diameter and lacked the jungle-slicing arms of the bigger ship.

"What are those things?"

"Steam spheres. I suppose the nearest equivalent you had in your time was the velocipede."

Burton shook his head in wonder, then said: "Eccentricities?"

Wells smiled. "The old man has a rather unconventional sense of style and his, um, 'living arrangements' tend to raise eyebrows."

"Why so?"

"The gentleman he lodges with is, er, rather more than a friend, if you know what I mean."

Burton threw up his hands in exasperation. "Good grief! It's 1919 and that's still considered unconventional? Has the human race not evolved at all since my time?"

The driver swung the motor-carriage into a narrow side street and accelerated down to the end of it, drawing to a stop outside a plain metal door.

Bertie stepped out of the vehicle. Burton and the Tommies followed. The explorer wiped perspiration from his eyes and muttered an imprecation. Tabora possessed the atmosphere of a Turkish bath.

"Keep alert," the war correspondent said to the three soldiers. They nodded, drew pistols from their holsters, and stood guard at the door while Wells ushered Burton through it.

"Up the stairs, please, Richard."

The king's agent passed an opening on his left and ascended. There was an oil lamp hanging from the upper landing's ceiling, and by its light, he saw that the walls were painted a pale lilac and were decorated with colourful theatre posters, most of them dating from the 1880s. He reached the top and stopped outside a wooden door with a glowing fanlight above it. Wells reached past him and rapped his knuckles against the portal: *knock. Knock-knock-knock. Knock-knock.*

"Code?" Burton asked.

"Open sesame," Wells replied.

Algernon Swinburne's face flashed before the explorer's mind's eye.

"Come," a voice called from the room beyond.

They pushed the door open and stepped through into a large chamber. It was lit by four wall lamps and reminded Burton of his study in Montagu Place, for it was lined with bookshelves, had two large desks, and was decorated with all manner of ornaments and pictures and nicknacks.

A crimson rug lay between four leather armchairs in the centre of the room. A heavyset man was standing on it, and, immediately, Burton felt that he'd seen him somewhere before. He was tall, rather fat, and appeared to be in his mid-sixties. His brown hair—which had obviously been dyed, for its roots were grey—was long and fell in waves to his shoulders. It framed a jowly face, with creases and wrinkles around the grey, indolent eyes, and full-lipped mouth. He was wearing a black velvet smoking jacket, inky blue slacks, and leather button-up boots. There was a long cigarette holder held between the pudgy, ringed fingers of his left hand.

After a long pause, spent staring fixedly at the king's agent, the man drawled: "The tragedy of old age is not that one is old, but that one is young."

His voice was deep and mellow and lazy. It possessed an Irish lilt.

Burton almost collapsed.

"Quips!" he cried out. "Bismillah! It's Quips!"

Oscar Fingal O'Flahertie Wills Wilde grinned, displaying crooked teeth, threw his cigarette holder onto a table, rushed forward, and took Burton by both hands.

"Captain Burton!" he exclaimed. "You're alive and young again! By heavens! How have you done it? I demand to know the secret! To get back my youth I would do anything in the world, except take exercise, get up early, or be respectable!"

Burton gave a bark of laughter. "Still the rapier sharp wit! The war hasn't blunted that I see, and praise be to Allah for it! It's good to see you, lad! It's bloody good to see you!"

"Sure and begorra, he's calling me lad now! And here's me a quarter of a century his senior by the looks of it!"

Wilde caught Burton as the explorer suddenly sagged. "Hey now, you're trembling all over! Come and sit down. Bertie, in the drinks cabinet—there's a decanter of brandy. Fetch it over would you? Sit, Captain. Sit here. Are you feeling faint?"

"I'm all right," Burton croaked, but, to his horror, he suddenly found himself weeping.

"It's the shock, so it is," Wilde said. "A dash of brandy will put you right. Pour generously, Bertie, the Captain probably hasn't tasted the good stuff for a long while."

"I haven't—I haven't tasted it at all since—since Dut'humi," Burton said, his voice weak and quavering.

Wells passed him a glass but Burton's hand was shaking so violently that Wilde had to put his own around it and guide the drink to the explorer's mouth. Burton gulped, coughed, took a deep shuddering breath, and sat back.

"Quips," he said. "It's really you."

"It is, too, Captain. Are you feeling a little more steady now?"

"Yes. My apologies. I think—I never—I never expected to find a little piece of home in this hellish world."

Wilde chuckled and looked down at himself. "Not so little any more, I fear." He addressed Herbert Wells: "Bertie, you'd best be getting off. We don't have much time. The Devil himself will be snapping at our heels soon enough, so he will."

Wells nodded. "Richard," he said, "I'm going to prepare our escape. All being well, I'll see you within a couple of hours."

"Escape?"

Wilde said: "Are you fit to take a walk? I'll explain as we go."

"Yes." Burton drained his glass and stood up. "By 'the Devil himself,' I assume you mean Crowley."

The three men moved to the door and started down the stairs.

"That I do, Captain."

They reached the lower landing. Wells opened the street door and peered out. The three Tommies were waiting by the car. The little war correspondent nodded to Burton and Wilde and slipped out into the mist, closing the portal behind him.

Wilde gestured to the opening in the side wall. "Into the basement, if you please, Captain."

Burton stepped through and started down the wooden stairs he found beyond. "I don't understand Crowley and all this mediumistic business, Quips. The only evidence I've seen of it is the Germans occasionally manipulating the weather."

"When the Hun destroyed London, they killed most of our best mediums, which is horribly ironic, do you not think? Here we are. Wait a moment."

The stairs had ended in a large basement, which was filled with old furniture and tea chests. Wilde crossed to a heavy armoire standing against the far wall.

"Ironic?" Burton asked.

"Yes, because our clairvoyants didn't predict it! As a matter of fact, we now think their opposite numbers, on the German side, may have perfected some sort of mediumistic blanket that can render things undetectable."

"The approaching A-Bomb, for instance?"

"Unfortunately, yes. Ah ha! That's got it!"

Wilde had been fiddling with something behind the big wooden unit. Now the whole thing slid smoothly aside, revealing the entrance to a passage. He turned and grinned at Burton. "Do y'know, I became the captain of a rotorship thanks to you? Do you remember old Nathaniel Lawless? A fine gentleman!"

"I remember him very clearly, and I agree."

"After you wangled me the job on the poor old *Orpheus*, Lawless would never settle for another cabin boy. He sponsored my training, helped me rise through the ranks, and, before you know it, I was given captaincy of HMA *Audacious*. A lovely vessel, so she was, but the war had broken out by then and she was put to fiendish use. I soon found that I was losing myself in the mesmeric brutality of battle. As long as war is regarded as wicked, it will always have its fascination. When it's looked upon as vulgar, it will cease to be popular. It took me a few years, I must confess, to realise that vulgarity."

He indicated that Burton should follow and disappeared into the secret passage.

"So I had myself drummed out of the Airforce."

"How did you manage that?"

"Through what they call 'conduct unbecoming to an officer and a gentleman.' I inspired the wrath of a certain Colonel Queensbury, and he rather gleefully put his proverbial boot to my backside. It caused a bit of a stir at the time, I can tell you."

"And afterwards you became a newspaper man?"

"Aye, I did that—going back to my roots, as you might say—and I wound up in Tabora."

The passage made a sharp turn to the right. As they continued on, Burton looked at the small lights that, strung along a long wire, gave illumination. "How do these work?" he asked, pointing at one.

"Electricity."

"Ah! Like I saw on the *Britannia*! Was it Isambard who mastered the technique?"

"Good Lord!" Wilde cried out. "Brunel! I haven't thought of him in years! What a genius he was!"

"And for all his faults, loved by the public," Burton noted.

"To be sure! To be sure! Ah, what a delight it must be to be a Technologist! So much more romantic than being the editor of a newspaper! I can assure you that popularity is the one insult I have never suffered. But to answer your question; yes, he mastered electricity; in 1863, as it happens."

They hurried on, with Wilde panting and puffing as he propelled his bulk forward.

"Where are we going, Quips?"

"All in good time, Captain."

Burton began to wonder if the tunnel spanned the entire city.

"So the mediums," he said. "They were killed when London fell?"

"So they were. And we had no more of them until 1907, when Crowley came to the fore. In recent years he's focused his talents on defending this city, which is why the Germans have never managed to conquer it."

"Surely, then, he should be regarded as a hero? Why is it that no one seems to have a good word to say of him?"

Wilde shrugged. "That's a difficult one. There's just something about him. He's sinister. People suspect that he has some sort of hidden agenda. Here we are."

They'd reached a door. Wilde knocked on it; the same arrhythmic sequence Wells had used earlier. It was opened by a seven-foot tall Askari—obviously of the Masai race—who whispered: "You'll have to be quick. There's some sort of flap on. They're going to move the prisoner."

Wilde muttered an acknowledgement. He and Burton stepped into what appeared to be a records room, followed the soldier out of it into a brightly lit corridor, and ran a short distance along until they came to a cell door. However, when it was unlocked and opened, the room behind it proved not a cell at all but a very large and luxurious chamber, decorated in the English style, with Jacobean furniture, and paintings on its papered walls.

In its middle, there was a metal frame with a wizened little man—naked but for a cloth wrapped around his loins—suspended upright inside it. He was held in place by thin metal cables that appeared to have been bolted straight through his parchment-like skin into the bones beneath. His flesh was a network of long surgical scars and he was horribly contorted; his arms and legs twisted out of shape, their joints swollen and gnarled, and his spine curved unnaturally to one side. His finger and toenails were more than two feet long and had grown into irregular spirals. Bizarrely, they were varnished black.

Large glass bulbs also hung from the frame, and were connected to the figure by tubes through which pink liquid was pumping. Each one held an organ: a throbbing heart, pulsating lungs, things that quivered and twitched.

Burton saw all this in a single glance, then his eyes rested on the man's face and he couldn't look away.

It was Palmerston.

Henry John Temple, 3rd Viscount Palmerston, was bald, and the skin of his face was stretched so tightly that it rendered him almost featureless. But despite the eyes being mere slits, the nose a jagged hole, and the mouth a horribly wide frog-like gash; despite that the ears had been replaced by two brass forward-pointing hearing trumpets, riveted directly into the sides of his skull; despite all this, it was plainly Palmerston.

The old man's eyes glittered as he watched his visitors enter.

Wilde closed the door and stepped to one side of it. He gently pushed Burton forward. The king's agent approached and stopped in front of the man who'd once been prime minister. He tried to think of something to say, but all that came out was: "Hello."

Just above Palmerston's head, an accordion-like apparatus suddenly jerked then expanded with a wheeze. It gave a number of rapid clicks, expelled a puff of steam, then contracted and emitted a sound like a gurgling drain. Words bubbled out of it.

"You filthy traitorous bastard!"

Burton recoiled in shock. "What?"

"You backstabbing quisling!"

The explorer turned to Wilde: "Did you bring me here to be maligned?"

"Please allow him a moment to get it out of his system, Captain. It's been pent up for half a century."

"Prussian spy! Treasonous snake! You dirty collaborator!"

"I have no idea what he's talking about. Is he sane?"

"In a manner of speaking."

"How old is he?

"A hundred and thirty-five."

"You never bloody told me!" Palmerston gurgled.

"Have you finally run out of insults, Pam?" Burton asked.

"*Lord Palmerston*, you insolent cur! You never told me!"

"Told you what?"

The misshapen figure squirmed and stretched spasmodically.

Wilde said: "Calm yourself, please, Lord Palmerston. We don't have time for tantrums."

The ex-prime minister went limp. He glared at Burton with sulphurous hatred. The accordion-thing shook and rattled and groaned, expanded, blew out more steam, and squeezed shut.

"I sent you to Africa to find the Eye of Nāga. You succeeded in your mission but you neglected to report that, in the course of retrieving it, you'd visited the future!"

"Sir," Burton replied. "You must understand; you're berating me for something that, from my point of view, I haven't done yet."

"You saw this damned war. You saw that the Germans were running rampant over the entire globe. You saw that the British Empire had been reduced to this one small enclave. Yet you purposely kept it from me! You were working for the Prussians all along!"

"No, I was not."

"Then why?"

"How can I possibly account for decisions I haven't yet made?"

"Traitor!"

Burton looked at Oscar Wilde and gave a helpless shrug.

Wilde stepped forward. "Gentlemen, let us get straight to the point. Captain, if I might explain; Lord Palmerston is blamed by the majority of Britishers for the woeful position we find ourselves in."

"Yes, Bertie Wells expressed such a sentiment."

"Indeed. Fortunately, Bertie has acted counter to his views on the matter out of loyalty to me, for I, along with a few others, am of the opinion that Lord Palmerston only ever had the best interests of the Empire in mind when he made the decisions that led to this war."

Burton looked at the monstrosity hanging in the frame and murmured: "I don't disagree."

"However, those 'best interests' were envisioned according to the influences at play; the political landscape; the perceived shape of society and culture; the advice of his ministers; and so forth."

The king's agent nodded his understanding.

Wilde said: "You have just learned that you will return to the past, which, I'm sure, is very welcome news indeed. Bertie is currently making arrangements to ensure that you get out of Tabora, to enable you to follow whatever sequence of events lead to that return."

Burton was suddenly filled with longing. How he missed Mrs. Angell, his comfortable old saddlebag armchair, his library, even Mr. Grub, the street vendor, whose pitch was on the corner of Montagu Place!

"Captain," Wilde said. "Just as Lord Palmerston made his decisions according to how he gauged the state of affairs, so will you. In 1863, you will determine—you *did* determine—not to reveal that you had survived for a number of years in a war torn future where you witnessed the death of the British Empire. Our history books, such as they are, don't reveal anything that casts light on why you took this course of action. Biographies written about you don't even mention that you were the king's agent, for that was a state secret. They say the second half of your life was lived quietly, indulging in scholarly pursuits. This is only partially true. What really happened is that you exiled yourself to Trieste, on the northeastern coast of Italy, from there to watch the seeds of war sprouting. You died in that city in 1890, ten years before the Greater German Empire invaded its neighbouring countries."

Sir Richard Francis Burton moistened his lips with his tongue. He raised his hand and put his fingertips to the deep and jagged scar on his left cheek, the one made by a Somali spear back in '55.

"Am I to take it that you're blaming me for the war?" he asked, huskily.

"Yes!" Palmerston gurgled.

"No, not at all," Wilde corrected. "People are wrong to condemn Lord Palmerston, and Lord Palmerston is wrong to condemn you. You do not represent the evils of this world, Captain Burton—you represent hope."

"Because you think I can alter history?"

"Indeed so. Lord Palmerston and I were already aware that Crowley had, in 1914, detected an aberrant presence in Africa. When Bertie Wells told me—about eighteen months ago—that he'd met you, we realised what that aberration was and how it—you—could be employed to change everything."

"So whatever the circumstances I find when I return to 1863, you want me to ignore what will obviously be my better judgement, and—" He turned to face Palmerston, "—and tell you everything I've seen here during the past five years?"

"Tell me *everything*, Burton!"

"Should I even describe your present—um—condition?"

"I insist upon it. I would like the opportunity to die naturally, with a little grace, at a much earlier time."

Burton sighed. "I'm sorry. It won't work."

"Why not?" Wilde asked.

"I will most assuredly do as you suggest, and I might succeed in creating a history in which this war never happens. If so, I'll have the good fortune to live in it. But you won't.

Here, nothing will change. You won't wink out of existence and wake up in a new world. Instead, a new history will branch off from the moment I change my actions, and it will run parallel to this one."

"Is there then no hope for us?"

"If I understand the workings of time correctly, the only way to alter the circumstances in which you exist, as opposed to the future that lies ahead, would be to somehow change the past without leaving the present—like sitting on a tree branch and sawing it through behind you, at the trunk."

"Isn't that what we're doing by making this request?"

"Asking a a person to perform an action, is not the same as performing that action yourself."

"Captain, you're implying that time and history are entirely subjective."

"Yes, I rather think I am."

There came a knock at the door. It opened and the Masai guard poked his head into the room. "You have to get out of here," he said. "They're on their way. They're going to move Lord Palmerston onto the *Britannia*."

Wilde nodded and the guard withdrew.

"Don't allow them to move me!"

"The city is about to be destroyed, sir," Wilde said. "A select few will attempt to escape in the sphere. It seems you'll be among them."

Palmerston was silent for a moment, then: "Burton, do as we say. If it won't change this world, it will, at least, create another, better one, and Mr. Wilde and I can die knowing that somewhere, other versions of us lived better lives."

Burton looked at Wilde, who nodded, and said: "We have to go."

"Wait!" Palmerston ordered. "Burton, I don't trust you. You have to demonstrate your loyalty."

"How?"

"Obey my final order. Without question!"

"What is it?"

"I have received so many Eugenicist treatments that I cannot die a natural death. That fiend Crowley has been feeding off my mental energy like a damned vampire to supplement his mediumistic powers. I cannot stand it any more. Take out your pistol right this minute and shoot me through the head."

Without hesitation, Burton drew his revolver, raised the weapon, looked Palmerston in the eyes, and pulled the trigger.

"They probably heard that!" Wilde exclaimed. "We'd better leg it!"

They left the cell and raced down the corridor. The Masai ushered them into the records room. Burton saw that the tunnel entrance was normally concealed behind a tall filing cabinet.

"Go through and I'll slide it back," the guard said. "Then I'll hold them at bay until I'm dead or out of ammo."

"You're a good fellow, so you are," Wilde said as he stepped through the opening.

"The word is out," the Masai replied. "It was announced on the wireless minutes ago. Everyone knows what's coming. It's the end. I might as well go out with a bang!" He vanished from view as he slid the filing cabinet into place.

"The fool!" Burton hissed. "Why doesn't he come with us?"

"Whenever a man does a thoroughly stupid thing, it's always from the noblest motives," Wilde replied. "Come on! Let's not make his death in vain!"

It took them maybe fifteen minutes to reach the other end of the passage. They stepped out into Wilde's basement, and the ex-editor panted: "I'm pooped!"

"You never abandoned your diet of gobstoppers and butterscotch, I take it?" Burton ventured.

"I never expected to be running along secret corridors at the age of sixty-five!" Wilde replied. "Up the stairs with you!"

They ascended, stopped at the front door, and Wilde opened it a crack and peeked out.

"Good!" he exclaimed. "Your motor-carriage is still there. The guards will take you to Bertie."

"You'll come too, of course!"

Wilde took Burton's hand and shook it. "No, old friend. This is where we must say goodbye. I'm too old to go hurrying out into the depths of Africa."

"But Quips! You'll be killed!"

"Yes. But thanks to the help you gave me when I was a boy, I have lived, Captain, and to live is the rarest thing in the world. Most people exist, that is all."

"But—"

"I want to spend my last hours with the man I love."

Burton put a hand to his friend's shoulder. "I'm glad you found happiness in this ugly world. What's his name?"

"Paul. He was a shopkeeper in his younger days—what people call a very ordinary man, but it happened that he brought to me extraordinary peace of mind and contentment."

Burton smiled, and his eyes filled with tears. "I fear I may weep in front of you again, Quips."

"The clock is ticking. Be off with you, man!"

Burton loosed an unsteady breath, opened the door, and stepped out into the hot mist of the Taboran night. He crossed to the motor-carriage where the three guards waited. One of them opened its door and gestured for him to enter.

"Captain!" Oscar Wilde called from the doorway.

The explorer turned.

"If the processes of time and history truly are subjective, do not be afraid of the past. If people tell you that it is irrevocable, do not believe them. The past, the present and the future are but one moment. Time and space, succession and extension, are merely accidental conditions of thought. The imagination can transcend them."

Oscar Wilde smiled and closed the door.

§

Dawn wasn't far off. Tabora was enveloped in steam. A great crowd of people milled through it, moving alongside the motor-carriage in an easterly direction.

"Are they trying to leave the city?" Burton asked.

"I suppose so," one of the Tommies replied. "But to make it through Hell's Run, you either have to be in a very fast vehicle or crawling along on your own, keeping low and out of sight. A mob like this will never make it. They'll be slaughtered!"

"It's certain death if they stay," one of the other men noted. "So it's worth taking the risk. I'm going to chance it, for sure."

Burton watched in horror as shadowy forms occasionally emerged from the pall; people with fear in their eyes, carrying bags and bundles and children, looking hunted and desperate.

"Bismillah!" he muttered. "Nowhere to go, and very little chance of getting there. This is ghastly."

With delays and diversions, the vehicle made slow progress, and the three soldiers became increasingly nervous.

"I'm sorry, sir. We didn't count on this."

Screams and shouts came out of the cloud.

A line of steam spheres shot past.

Burton heard a gunshot.

The motor-carriage moved on.

Finally, they drew to a stop and the Tommies disembarked. The king's agent followed and was escorted to a door in the side of a warehouse. Stepping through, he entered into a very spacious and well-lit space.

"Good! You made it!" Bertie Wells called.

The little war correspondent was standing beside one of two big harvestman machines. They were of the variety Burton had become familiar with here in the future—with a saddle on top of the carapace rather than a seat inside it—but they were slung rather lower to the ground than he'd seen in other models, with the middle joints of the legs rising high to either side of the body.

"Built for speed!" Wells announced.

"I assume we're to escape the city on these things?"

"Yes. We have to set off now while fortune favours us."

"In what manner is it doing that?"

Wells grinned. "The lurchers are attacking the Germans! Hell's Run is clear!"

"The lurchers? Why?"

"No one knows!"

Burton turned to his escort: "You men heard that?"

They nodded.

"So get going! Get out of the city. Africa's a big continent. Find a quiet valley, build a village, live off the land, stay out of trouble."

"And learn to speak German," one of the men said.

"Yes, that might be advisable."

They saluted and hastily departed.

Burton joined his friend by the giant insects. There were bulging pannier bags hanging against their sides. Wells reached up and patted one. "Food and supplies to keep us going for at least a couple of weeks." He touched a long leather sheath. "And Lee-Enfield sniper rifles. I'll start the engines. You go and open up." He indicated large double doors. Burton strode over and, with some difficulty, slid them apart. It was lighter outside; dawn was breaking. Mist rolled in around him as he returned to the now chugging harvestmen. Wells was already mounted on one. Burton reached up to the other's stirrup and hauled himself into its saddle. He took hold of the two control levers.

"Follow me!" Wells called.

The two spiders clanked out of the warehouse and onto a wide thoroughfare. For half a mile, the machines scuttled along the road, weaving in and out between other vehicles, with crowds surging along to either side of them. Then they passed the last outlying building and Wells led the way off the road and onto the dusty savannah, leaving the fleeing Taborans behind. He stopped his vehicle and Burton drew his own to a halt beside him. The mist was thinning and, through it, the huge orange globe of the sun was visible ahead of them.

"We'll go eastwards across country," Wells said. "If we stay a little north of the exodus, we'll be closer to the German forces but free of the crowds."

"What's your destination, Bertie?"

"My only objective is to get past the end of Hell's Run. After that, I don't know. Where do we have to go to get you home to 1863?"

"To the Mountains of the Moon."

Wells shook his head. "We'll not get through the Blood Jungle. It's impassible."

"Nevertheless."

The war correspondent lifted his shoulders and let them drop. "Whatever you say. Onwards!"

"Wait!" Burton snapped. He pointed to Wells's left, at the ground.

His friend looked down. "What the hell?" he uttered, in astonishment.

A line of poppies was sprouting out of the hard earth.

Wells looked at Burton, a baffled expression on his face.

"It keeps happening," the king's agent said. "They bloom right in front of me, in an instant."

"It's impossible, Richard. How can they grow so fast? Have the Eugenicists made them?"

"*How* is one thing, Bertie, but I'm more interested in *why!*"

They watched as the flowers opened, a long line of them, snaking unevenly into the haze.

"North," Burton muttered. "Bertie, I want to follow them."

"It will take us straight into the German trenches. If the Hun doesn't do for us, the lurchers will."

"Maybe."

Wells reached down and unclipped the sheath containing his rifle. He took his pistol from its holster, checked that it was fully loaded, then slipped it back into place. He looked at Burton, smiled, and, in his high-pitched squeaky voice, said: "Well then: in for a penny, in for a pound!"

The two harvestmen scurried northwards, following the line of red flowers, and disappeared into the mist.

§

"What the devil are you playing at?" William Trounce roared.

"You nearly gave me a bloody heart attack!"

Herbert Spencer lowered the pistol, which, when he'd pulled the trigger, had done nothing.

"Herbert! Explain yourself!" Burton demanded.

"I'm sorry, William," Spencer said. "I didn't mean to scare you."

"How in blue blazes can shooting at a man's head not scare him, you tin headed dolt?"

"But I didn't shoot, an' that's the point."

"Not for want of trying! I clearly saw you squeeze the trigger!"

"So did I," Swinburne added. He'd drawn his own weapon and was pointing it uncertainly at the philosopher.

"Yus, an'—as I expected—nothin' bloomin' well happened, did it!"

Burton paced forward and snatched the gun out of Spencer's hand. "As you expected? What are you talking about?"

"When we stepped onto this rock, Boss, I felt every spring in me body go slack. We've entered the Eye of Nāga's area of influence. None o' the guns will work now. Nor will any other mechanical device. Henry Morton Stanley couldn't fly his rotorchairs any farther than this. You'll remember they was found by Arabs, an' they weren't functionin' at all."

Swinburne directed his gun at the sky and squeezed the trigger. It felt loose under his finger. The weapon didn't fire.

Trounce scowled. "Firstly, Spencer, there was no need for a bloody demonstration, especially one that involved me! You've been fitted with voice apparatus—ruddy well use it! Secondly, why are you still standing?"

Burton answered before Spencer could. "We encountered this same emanation when we went after the South American Eye. The fact that Herbert's mind is embedded in the Cambodian stones gives him the ability to neutralise it."

"I say, Herbert!" Swinburne exclaimed. "If you radiate an opposing force, could you cast it wide enough to make our guns work? It would give us one up on the Prussians!"

"Perhaps a gun I was holdin' meself," Spencer replied.

"By thunder!" Trounce yelled furiously. "You see! What if your magic rays, or whatever they are, had worked on the pistol in your hand? You'd have blown my bloody head off!"

"All right, all right," Burton growled impatiently. "Let's leave it be. But if you ever pull a stunt like that again, Herbert, I'll throw your key into the middle of the Ukerewe lake."

"I'm sorry, Boss."

Leading the horses, they moved to the edge of the rock, which the jungle overhung, and settled in the shade. The trees around them were crowded with blue monkeys that had fallen silent when the men appeared but which now took up their distinctive and piercing cries again—*Pee-oww!*

Pee-oww!—and began to pelt the group with fruit and sticks. Sidi Bombay shouted and waved his arms but the tormentors took no notice.

"Confound the little monsters!" Trounce grumbled. "We'll not get any peace here!"

Swinburne removed the dressings from the detective's legs and applied fresh poultices. He checked the wound on his friend's arm. It was red and puckered but the infection had disappeared.

They abandoned the clearing and plunged back into the jungle, the men trailing behind Spencer as he swiped his machete back and forth, clearing the route. Pox and Malady had elected to sit on one of the horse's saddles, rather than in their habitual position on the clockwork philosopher's head, causing Swinburne to wonder whether Spencer had fallen out of favour with the two parakeets.

The poet struggled with his thoughts. Hadn't he noticed something about the brass man's philosophical treatise back in Ugogi? Something unusual? What was it? Why couldn't he remember? Why was a part of him feeling ambivalent about Spencer? It didn't make sense—Herbert was a fine fellow!

Moving to Burton's side, he opened his mouth to ask if the explorer shared his misgivings. Instead, he found himself saying: "It's awfully humid, just like in the coast regions."

"Humph!" Burton replied, by way of agreement.

It was near sundown by the time they stumbled wearily out of the vegetation. They were at the base of a hill, with a wide, clear and shallow stream crossing their path.

The horses drank greedily. One of them collapsed.

"It's done for, poor thing," Trounce said. "I'd put a bullet through its brain if I could. It's the proper thing to do."

"If our guns worked," Burton responded, "that would alert Speke to our presence."

"Allow me," said Spencer, limping over to the stricken animal. He bent, took its head in his hands, and twisted it with all his mechanical might. The horse's neck popped. It kicked and died.

They moved half a mile upstream, washed, ate, and set up camp.

Burton spoke to Pox: "Message for Isabel Arundell. Please report. Message ends. Go."

Pox blew a raspberry, took to the air, and disappeared over the jungle.

"Weasel thief!" Malady screeched, and flew after his mate.

The men sat quietly for a little while then entered the tent and almost immediately fell into a deep slumber.

Dawn came, and so did a warning from their clockwork sentry: "Rouse yourselves, gents! Twenty men approachin' an' they don't look very cheerful!"

Burton, Swinburne and Trounce crawled into the open and rubbed the sleep from their eyes. They found Spencer and Bombay watching a gang of men, some way off, marching towards them. Their hair was fashioned into multiple spikes and held in place with red mud, their faces striped with ridged scars, their noses adorned with copper rings, and their shadows stretched across the golden hillside. They were armed with spears and held long oval shields.

"Wow! They are Wanyambo," Sidi Bombay advised. "A peaceful people."

"Not if their expressions are anything to go by," Burton observed. "Do you speak their language, Bombay?"

"Yes. I shall talk with them." The African set off to greet the newcomers, braving their scowls and brandished weapons. Burton and his friends watched as an argument commenced, gradually cooled to a heated debate, then settled into a passionate discussion, and, finally, became a long conversation.

Bombay returned. "Wow! These fine warriors are from the village of Kisaho. They say the *muzungo mbáyá* arrived at Kufro, which is nearby, and took all the food and weapons from the people. Wow! The jungle moved among them and killed nine men."

"The Prussian plant vehicle!" Burton murmured.

"And a mighty wizard took the chief by the neck and turned him into a tree which killed three more villagers by sucking out their blood. The men had to burn it to kill it." Bombay gestured back towards the Wanyambo. "These from Kisaho came to fight you but I told them that, although you are ugly and strange, you are an enemy of the wizard and you have come to punish the wicked white men. They will help."

"Tell them we will be honoured if they join us. Ask them to send a man running ahead to inform the villages that we are approaching, and that we are here to avenge the dead."

This was done, and the Britishers packed their tent and set off up the hill, following the warriors over its brow and down into the forested valley beyond.

They passed along a dirt path bordered by fruit-bearing trees and fragrant flowery shrubs, then stepped out into cultivated fields where peas grew in profusion. While they were crossing these, Pox and Malady returned.

"Message from Isabel Arundell. The Arabs are holding stinking cesspit Kazeh. My witless reinforcements from Mzizima have arrived but Prussian numbers are building steadily. We're keeping them occupied. Isabella and Sadhvi are safe. Mucous bag Mirambo is injured but will recover. When you get home, tell Palmerston to send troops as a matter of urgency. May Allah guide and protect you. Bettawfeeq!"

"That means 'good luck,'" Burton explained in response to a puzzled look from Trounce.

"Are you going to send the bird to Maneesh?" the police detective asked.

"No. I fear it's too great a distance by now."

The whole day was spent crossing valleys and hills. On the next, they trekked over an alluvial plain until they reached the Kitangule Kagera; a river that, according to Speke's account of his earlier expeditions, flowed into the Ukerewe lake. Crossing it proved so awkward that their supplies got soaked and another of the horses died.

The swelling terrain on the other side was alive with antelope, which scattered as the twenty Wanyambo led the Britishers up to the crest of a hill. From there, they saw, stretching for miles and miles to their right, a rich, well-wooded, swampy plain, containing large open patches of water.

A band of light blazed across the horizon.

Burton waved a fly away from his face and shaded his eyes. "Bismillah!" he exclaimed. "Look at the size of it!"

"Is it a mirage?" Swinburne asked, squinting.

"No, Algy. That's it. That's the lake!"

"Ukerewe? Are you sure? It looks like the sea! Perhaps we've walked right across Africa—or we've wandered in an enormous circle!"

Burton cast his eyes around the landscape, taking in every topographical detail, making rapid mental calculations, adding it to his knowledge of the country to the southwest, around Lake Tanganyika.

"I think he was right all along," he murmured. "I think Speke got it. Ukerewe has to be the source!"

"But I don't want him to be right!" Swinburne objected. "He doesn't deserve it!"

They continued west.

The ground rose and fell, rose and fell, and rolled away to the hazy horizon. Through the moisture-heavy air, distant peaks faded into view, dark green at their base, blanching up to such a pale blue that they merged with the sky. Hovering above, as if floating, their jagged peaks were white.

"It's wonderful!" Swinburne enthused, jerking and waving his arms. "Snow in the middle of Africa! No one will believe it!"

"Our destination!" Burton announced. "The Mountains of the Moon!"

"Wow! I do not want to go there again," Sidi Bombay said softly. "But I shall because I am with you, and I am certain you will pay me very well indeed."

Yet another horse succumbed. The men were all on foot now. The baggage was divided between the remaining animals. There wasn't much of it. Burton had no idea how they were going to make it back to Zanzibar.

As they progressed, villagers turned out to greet them and to press food and weapons into their hands. Word had spread like wildfire across the lands between the lake and the mountains, and now the air throbbed with drums—a deep thunderous booming, ominous and threatening and incessant.

"I don't think we'll be taking Speke by surprise," Swinburne commented.

In one settlement, the *p'hazi* led them into a hut where four men lay groaning. Their skin was lacerated, in some places to the bone, and none were likely to live.

Bombay translated: "Warriors attacked Mr. Speke's people but the jungle thing killed many. Wow! Five died in this village, and the *p'hazi* says that in the next, Karagu, you will discover all the men gone, for there was a very big battle there."

"How far behind Speke are we?" Burton asked.

"He says the wicked *muzungo mbáyá* are four or five villages ahead."

"We're too done in to catch up with him today. Ask if we can stay here overnight."

Permission was granted, and the Britishers slept with drums pounding through their dreams.

In the morning, the women intoned a warlike chant as the expedition set off again. Burton, Swinburne, Trounce, Spencer, Bombay, and the twenty Wanyambo marched out of the village and onto marshy plains studded with rounded knolls, each topped by an umbrella cactus. They pushed through tall grasses where buffaloes were numerous and mosquitos were legion.

At noon, they arrived at Karagu, which was nestled against a strip of jungle, and found it half wrecked and filled with keening women. The men, as the *p'hazi* had stated, were all dead.

On Burton's behalf, Bombay promised the women that vengeance would soon fall upon those responsible.

The expedition rested and ate a light meal, then prepared to move on.

"Kwecha!" Burton called. "Pakia! Hopa! Hopa!"

The Wanyambo gathered at the edge of the jungle. One of them shouldered through a screen of vegetation to the path beyond. He suddenly howled and came flying back out, cartwheeling over the heads of his fellows, spraying blood onto them. He thudded to the ground and lay still.

"What the—" Trounce began, then tottered back as the Prussian plant vehicle burst out of the undergrowth and plunged into the warriors. He cried out in horror as the thing's spine covered tendrils lashed like whips, opening skin, sending blood splashing. The Wanyambo yelled in agony as their flesh was sliced and torn. Sidi Bombay was hoisted into the air and flung into the trees. The village women screamed and raced away. Trounce instinctively drew his pistol, aimed at the plant, and pulled the trigger. Nothing happened. He threw the weapon down in disgust and swore at himself.

"Stop it!" Swinburne shouted. He hefted a spear and charged forward, plunging the shaft into the centre of the repulsive bloom. Its point sank into the driver's stomach but had little effect. A thorny appendage slashed across the poet's forehead and sent him spinning away, with red droplets showering around him. He crashed into the side of a wrecked hut, which collapsed under the impact, burying the poet beneath sticks and dried mud.

The Wanyambo fought desperately, dodging and ducking, lunging in then backing away. They fell over one another and became wet with each other's blood. They went down and struggled up again. They threw and jabbed their spears until the huge weed-like thing was bristling with shafts. But despite their efforts, the plant continued to lurch back and forth, with the Prussian cradled in its bloom screeching furiously in incomprehensible German.

Burton looked this way and that, hoping to see fire somewhere in the village; sticks burning beneath a cooking pot; anything that he might fling at the plant to set it alight; but there was nothing. He snatched a spear from the ground, and started to circle the monstrosity, looking for an opening that would allow him to leap in and drive the weapon through the Prussian's head. He got too close; a thick ropey limb smacked against his torso and ripped upward, shredding his shirt and flaying a long strip of skin from his chest. He stumbled and dropped to his knees.

"Stay back, Boss!" a voice piped.

A bundled mass of robes dived past Burton and launched itself into the writhing vegetation. Herbert Spencer landed on top of the driver and was immediately entwined by creepers. His robes and polymethylene suit were ripped apart as he fought with the frenzied, flailing appendages. A thick coil whipped around him, its thorns gouging deep scratches into his brass body.

The philosopher groped downward and forced his right hand into the fleshy petals. His three brass fingers slid over the driver's face. The man hollered and the plant shook and bucked as two of Spencer's digits found his eyes. The philosopher put his full weight on his arm and drove his fingers through the back of the Prussian's eye sockets and into the brain behind. The vehicle convulsed. Burton ran over and thrust his spear through the man's neck, severing the spine. The plant's tendrils flopped down, a tremor ran through it, then it was still.

Spencer fell backwards and clanged onto the ground.

"Oof!" he piped.

The Wanyambo—those who weren't dead, unconscious, or in too much pain to notice—stared at him in astonishment. A metal man!

Burton tottered away from the Eugenicist creation, pulled what remained of his shirt off, and pressed the material against the deep laceration that angle up over his chest onto his left shoulder. He groaned with the pain of it, but, upon looking at the African warriors, saw that many had suffered much worse injuries.

He made his way over to Swinburne, who was crawling out from beneath the collapsed hut. Blood was streaming down the poet's face, dripping onto his clothing.

The king's agent called to Trounce, who was standing dazed. "William, are you hurt?"

"What? Huh, no."

"Come and bandage Algy, would you?"

The Scotland Yard man dragged a hand over his face as if to clear his mind, nodded, then ran over to the horses, which were being held on the far side of the village by a woman who'd had the foresight and courage to stop them from stampeding away. Pox and Malady were huddled on the saddle of one. The parakeets had slept through the entire drama.

Trounce retrieved the medical kit and returned to the poet.

Burton, meanwhile, spoke to Spencer: "Are you all right, Herbert?"

"Battered, Boss. Dented an' scratched all over—but tickin' an' serviceable."

Burton saw that the able-bodied among the Wanyambo had drawn together and were talking quietly, with many a gesture in Spencer's direction.

"I don't think our friends consider you a leper any more," he said.

Sidi Bombay crawled out of the undergrowth. "Wow! Mr. Spencer is like the thing called *pocket watch*, which you gave me long and long ago and which one of my six wives stole!"

"Yes, he is, Bombay," Burton agreed. "Can you explain that to the Wanyambo?"

"I shall try, though none of them have met my wives."

While Bombay joined the surviving warriors, Burton checked the injuries of the fallen. Eight were dead. Five were probably going to die. Six were too seriously hurt to continue on to the Mountains of the Moon. That left twelve—which meant his forces and Speke's were about even.

Bombay rejoined him and explained: "Wow! I told them that, just as the bad *muzungo mbáyá* has bad magic, so the good *muzungo mbáyá* has good magic. And Mr. Spencer is good magic."

"And they believed you?"

"Not at all. But they will continue with us to the mountains, anyway."

"Good."

"They will not go into them, though, for the Wanyambo are afraid of the Chwezi, who you say don't exist."

"Very well. Help me with these injured, then we'll regroup and go after Speke. It's high time he and I brought our feud to an end—whatever it takes to do so."

§

Sidi Bombay stood motionless and gazed up at the mountains. He made clicking noises with his tongue.

Burton watched him, then stepped to his side and asked: "You are sure this is the route Speke took?"

Without moving, his eyes remaining glued to the scene ahead, Bombay answered: "Oh yes, this is it. Wow! It is an evil place. There is a bad feeling in the air, like when my wives stop speaking to me because I have come home drunk."

"It's certainly quiet," Burton replied. "An oppressive silence."

"There are no birds in the trees."

"There are two. We're having the devil of a time getting Pox and Malady down. Algy is climbing up to them."

"Your friend is like a little monkey."

"I'll be sure to tell him."

"I do not like these mountains, Mr. Burton. The Chwezi live here. The Chwezi who don't exist, and who serve the Batembuzi."

"And who are the Batembuzi?"

"They are the children of the gods who once ruled these lands. Long and long ago they disappeared into the underworld."

"We have no choice but to go on, Bombay," Burton said. "But you aren't obliged to accompany us. Do you want to remain here in the camp with the Wanyambo?"

"Wow! I want to, but I will not, because I have five wives and I expect you will pay me much more if I accompany you."

"I thought you had six wives?"

"I am trying to forget number four."

It was early in the morning. Two days had passed since the plant vehicle had attacked them. In that time they'd trekked across sodden and difficult terrain, and had at last reached the base of the Mountains of the Moon. They were now camped at the tree line.

A steep ravine lay ahead of them. Tall pointed rocks of a blueish hue stood like gateposts at the foot of the slope leading into it. According to Bombay, this was the path to the Temple of the Eye.

"I found them!" Swinburne announced as he shinned down the trunk of the Red Stinkwood tree into which the parakeets had vanished the night before. "They've nested in a hollow—and Pox has laid an egg!"

"By Jove!" Trounce exclaimed. "And what did the happy parents-to-be have to say on the matter?"

Swinburne jumped to the ground. "Pox called me a fumbling toad gobbler, and Malady told me to sod off."

Burton moved away from Bombay and over to his friends. "It looks like this expedition has had a happy ending for one of our little family, anyway," he said. "Come on, let's leave them to it and get ourselves moving."

"I've divided what's left of the supplies into light packs," Trounce advised. "And what equipment remains, we'll have to leave here."

Swinburne, looking up into the branches he'd just vacated, shook his head. "Why would they want to live in a place like this?" he asked. "There are no other birds."

"P'raps they likes their privacy," Herbert Spencer suggested.

"Maybe they need the space so they can begin a dynasty," Trounce offered.

The poet sighed. "I shall miss the foul-mouthed little blighters."

They hefted their bags, took up their spears, and started to scrabble up steep loose shale, sending rivulets of stone clattering down behind them.

Sir Richard Francis Burton, Algernon Swinburne, William Trounce, Herbert Spencer—with his discoloured, scratched and dented body unencumbered by robes or polymethylene—and Sidi Bombay, entered the Mountains of the Moon, and more than one of them had a question on his mind.

How many of us will come back?

CHAPTER 11

The Temple

"—the sombre range
Virginal, ne'er by foot of man profaned,
Where rise Nile's fountains, if such fountains be."
—José Basilio da Gama, O Uruguay, Canto V

Burton and Wells drew their harvestmen to a halt at the top of an incline and turned the vehicles to face the way they'd come. Beneath the mechanised spiders' feet, poppies grew in abundance. The red flowers weaved away in an irregular line, disappearing into the hazy distance, back towards the dirty grey smudge that marked the position of Tabora.

High overhead, looking enormous, even though it was flying at a very high altitude, the *L.59 Zeppelin* drifted closer to the city.

It was a remarkable craft—a vegetable thing, like a gargantuan pointed cigar with ruffled seams on its sides. All along this join, oval bean-like growths swelled outward, and even from afar, it was apparent that they'd been hollowed out and fitted with portholes.

A giant purple flower grew from the rear of the vessel, similar in appearance to a tulip. Its petals were opening and closing, throbbing like a pulsing heart, driving the ship through the air.

"It's magnificent," Wells said. "And utterly horrible."

"Horrible because we know what its carrying," Burton replied. "I wonder how big an area the A-Bomb will destroy? Surely the spores will drift?"

"Perhaps they're potent for only a few minutes," Wells mused. "But even if the effects are of short duration and confined to the city, thousands of people are going to die. There simply hasn't been time for everyone to get out. Look! Those dots rising up from Tabora! That's a squadron of hornets!"

"We need a rotorship."

"There are none. Our last was brought down more than a year ago."

The hornets—twelve of them—raced across the shrinking distance between the city and the German vessel. As they neared the bomb carrier, they exploded one after the other and fell to the earth trailing smoke behind them.

"No!" Wells shrilled. "What the hell happened?"

"There!" Burton pointed. "See the trails of vapour curving out from the *Zeppelin*? The Germans must have some sort of manoeuvrable shells."

"By heavens, Richard. Has it reached Tabora already? I can't tell."

"Any time now," Burton replied. "Be prepared to—"

Without warning, the sun erupted from the ground beneath the city. A blinding light blazed outward, and though Burton squeezed his eyes shut in an instant and clapped his hands over them, still he could see it. He heard Wells scream.

"Bertie, are you all right?" he yelled.

Wells groaned. "Yes. I think—I think it's passed."

Burton, realising that his friend was right, lowered his hands and opened his eyes. Wherever he looked, he saw a ball of fire.

"The damned after-image has blinded me," he said.

"Me too."

They sat with hands held to faces, waiting for their retinas to recover.

A strong wind hit them.

"Shockwave!" Wells exclaimed.

"No! It's going in the wrong direction," Burton noted, puzzled.

They looked up, blinking, vision returning.

A dense yellow mass of Destroying Angel spores was bubbling up from where the city stood—and as the two men watched, the billowing substance slowly revolved, as if around a central axis.

"The wind!" Wells said. "It's the blasted Hun weathermen! They're keeping that damned mushroom cloud in check, concentrating it in the city, preventing it from drifting!"

Burton moaned: "Quips! Poor Quips! Bismillah, Bertie! How many have just died?"

"Tens of thousands," Wells said, and his voice was suddenly deep and oily and unpleasant. "But I am not one of them."

Burton looked at the little war correspondent and was shocked to see that every visible part of his eyes had turned entirely black. There was a terrible menacing quality about them, and Burton couldn't tear his own away.

Wells gestured at the dying city.

"The generals are eager to locate a safe haven," he said, "so, regrettably, the S. S. *Britannia* is rolling in an easterly direction and will soon turn south, whereas you, I see, are heading north. Why is that, Private Frank Baker? Hah! No! That won't do! That won't do at all! Let us call you by another name. Let us call you Sir—Richard—Francis—Burton." He enunciated Burton's name slowly, emphasising each syllable, as if to drive home the point that he knew the explorer's true identity.

"Bertie?" Burton asked, uncertainly.

"Obviously not! Tell me, how did you do it?"

"How did I do what? Who are you?"

"Control the lurchers—make them open up a route through the besieging German forces?"

"Crowley?"

"Yes, yes! Now answer the question!"

"I didn't."

"What? You didn't control them? Then who, or what, did?"

"I have no idea. What do you want, Colonel?"

"I have seven black diamonds, Sir Richard; the fragments of the South American Eye of Nāga. There is much about them I do not understand." The black eyes glittered. The king's agent felt them penetrating his soul. "For example, you, sir, who should be three decades dead—your metaphorical fingerprints are all over them. Are they somehow responsible for transporting you from your time to mine?"

Again, Burton didn't respond.

Wells—Crowley—regarded him silently.

The wind gusted past them.

"I shall tell you a secret, Sir Richard Francis Burton—something that, were it known by the generals aboard this ship, would prompt my immediate execution."

"What?"

"I am in contact with Kaiser Nietzsche."

"You're a collaborator?"

"Not in the sense you mean it. The German emperor and myself share a talent for clairvoyance. We've both detected through the diamonds that other realities exist, and that other versions of ourselves inhabit them. We want to know more. Your presence here seems to have some bearing on the matter." Wells gave an elaborate shrug and his oleaginous voice took on a carefree airiness. "But, here we are: you fleeing in one direction and me fleeing in the other. Very inconvenient! I really should do away with this Wells fellow. He acted against me. But I shall allow him to live, for I sense that he's a vital ingredient in the shape of things to come."

"Crowley," Burton said. "Nietzsche dropped a bomb on you."

Wells emitted a thick chuckle.

"Ah! So you doubt his commitment to me? Do not concern yourself. He gave me fair warning, and it was preordained that I would get away."

"You knew Tabora would be destroyed? You allowed all those people to die? Your countrymen?"

"Ordinary morality is only for ordinary people. The end of the British Empire was long overdue. I merely bowed to the inevitable."

"In the name of Allah, what kind of man are you?"

"Allah? Don't be ridiculous. And as for what I am, perhaps the embodiment of the Rakes, who, if I remember rightly, prospered in your age."

"You're an abomination!"

"I'm an individual who shares with Nietzsche the desire to create a superior species of man."

For the first time since he'd taken possession of Wells, Crowley took his eyes from Burton. He looked at the yellow cloud enveloping Tabora.

"Multiple futures," he said. "Different histories. Maybe some of them don't end like this. I should like to visit them."

He returned his dreadful gaze to the explorer.

"Perhaps we'll get it right in one of them, hey?"

He made Wells stretch and groan.

"Ho hum, Sir Richard! Ho hum! I've been here long enough. It's not comfortable. Has he told you how his leg is perpetually paining him? I don't know how he can bear it. Anyway, I'll say farewell. We shall meet again, sir; in this world or another version of it; maybe in your time, maybe in mine, maybe in another. But we shall meet again. And when we do—"

Wells smiled wickedly. The expression lingered, then the black faded from his eyes, they slipped up into his head, and he fell sideways from his saddle to the ground.

Burton hurriedly dismounted and threw himself down beside his friend.

"Bertie! Bertie!"

The war correspondent rolled onto his side and vomited. He curled into a foetal position and moaned. "He was in my head. The filth, Richard! The filth of the man! He's the Beast personified!"

"Has he gone? Is he watching us?"

"He's gone. But he's going to come after you. Wherever— whenever—you are; he's coming after you!"

Burton helped Wells to sit up. The smaller man wiped his mouth and looked at the far off mushroom cloud, and the flying machine shrinking to the south.

"It's finished," he said. "The Germans probably think they've won, but they're wrong. Everything is ending. This world is done for."

Burton could think of nothing to say, except: "I'm sorry, Bertie."

Wells stood, swayed slightly, and reached up to the stirrup of his harvestman.

"Let's get back on the trail. I want to know where these poppies are leading us."

They clambered back onto their saddles and turned their vehicles, sending them scuttling over the savannah.

S

For two days, they steered their harvestmen over what, to Burton, was eerily familiar territory.

He felt detached. All the connections to this world, formed over the past five years, were unfastening. Change was coming to him, of that he was certain, but he didn't know how.

Change, or, perhaps, restoration.

The Mountains of the Moon.

His destiny lay there.

Maybe it always had.

The trail of poppies led to those peaks, that was obvious even before the snow capped summits rose over the horizon. He saw them, jagged and white, seeming to hover in the air above the blood red base of the mountains.

"Red!" he exclaimed. "I remember this view—but the mountains were green!"

"That might have been true in the 1860s," Wells replied, "but the Blood Jungle has grown since then."

They raced over the empty landscape. Where there had once been villages, there were none. Were there had once been herds of antelope and zebras, there was nothing. Where fields had been cultivated, there was now rampant undergrowth.

Increasingly, they saw lurchers. The ungainly plants were shuffling over the hills and through the valleys with an unnerving air of sentience that prompted Wells to ask: "What are the damned things up to, Richard?"

"I know what you mean," the explorer replied. "They seem to be purposeful, don't they? Do you remember the one that attacked us at Tanga? See how differently they move now! The mindless thrashing has been replaced by shudders and ticks, as if they're operating under some sort of restraint."

With so much of his memory restored, Burton recognised that the lurchers were the same species of plant as the vehicles the Prussians had used back in 1863—the same but horribly different, for there were no men enfolded in their fleshy petals—which meant, if there was something still controlling them, it wasn't necessarily human.

As they drew closer to the mountains, the vegetation grew thicker and wilder. Its flowers and fruits took on a reddish hue, deepening the farther they travelled, until blood-coloured blooms and berries and globular dew-dripping swellings of indiscriminate form surrounded them. The poppies guided the steam-driven spiders straight into the humid tangle, and, astonishingly, the chaotic verdure parted in front of them to allow their passage.

Shafts of light angled through the trees. Lianas drooped and looped and dangled. The air was heavy with scent, one minute perfumed, the next pungent with the stench of maggoty meat, then delightful again. Fat bees droned lazily through it. Dragonflies and butterflies flitted hither and thither. Seeds floated past on feathery wings. And in the canopy overhead, thousands upon thousands of parakeets squawked and screeched and cackled and whistled and cursed and insulted.

Burton started to laugh and couldn't stop.

Wells, who was at that point leading the way, looked back, raised his eyebrows, and asked: "What the heck has got into you?"

"Pox!" Burton cried out. "Pox and Malady! Ye gods! How many eggs did that confounded bird lay? Hah!" He raised his face to the sky and bellowed: "Pox! Pox! Pox!" then bent forward and was suddenly wracked by violent sobs, for too many memories were returning, and he knew for sure that he was going back, and he recalled what to.

Wells reined in his harvestman until it was beside the explorer's. "What is it, man? Are you all right?"

"I can't bear it," Burton whispered. "I can't bear it. It would be too much for any man. I have to find a way to change everything, Bertie. *Everything.*"

"Let's rest here," the war correspondent suggested. "There's some grub left in one of the packs. We'll eat and grab forty winks."

They turned off their vehicles' engines and dismounted. Beside them, a thick mass of crimson foliage suddenly rustled and parted like a pair of curtains, unveiling a short pathway to a beautiful poppy-filled glade.

"By golly! An invitation, if ever I saw one!" Wells exclaimed. "Whatever's behind your poppies obviously has power over this jungle, too!"

They walked into the open space and sat down. Wells had carried one of the panniers with him, and now opened it and pulled out a loaf of bread and a wedge of cheese. The two men ate.

Burton seemed lost in himself. His dark eyes were haunted, his cheeks sunken. Wells, feeling concerned, was watching him from the corner of his eye when something else caught his attention. At the edge of the clearing, a tree, heavy with large pear-shaped gourds, was moving. One of its branches, with creaks and snaps, was extending outward, into the open space. Burton, upon hearing it, turned his head and watched as the limb manoeuvred a gourd above them, then lowered it until it hung between the two men.

"A gift?" Wells asked.

Burton reached up to the red, pumpkin-sized fruit. It snapped loose from the branch—which swung back out of the way—with ease, and as he lowered it, a small split opened in its top and an amber coloured liquid sloshed out. He sniffed it, looked surprised, tasted it, and smacked his lips.

"You'll not believed this!" he said, took a swig, and passed the gourd to the war correspondent.

Wells tried it.

"It's—it's—it's brandy!"

They drank, they ate, they were insulted by parakeets.

Night came. They slept.

At dawn, the two men returned to their vehicles and continued along the trail of poppies.

"Either I'm riding a giant steam-powered spider through a benevolent living jungle with a man from the past," Wells pondered, "or I'm dreaming."

"Or stark staring mad," Burton added.

At noon, they came to a steep incline, bracketed on either side by tall pointed outcrops of blueish rock. Burton stopped his harvestman and peered through the branches at the mountains that towered ahead of them. He slid down from his saddle, bent, and examined the ground. The slope was comprised of shale bound together by a network of threadlike roots.

"This is it, Bertie."

"What?"

"This is the path that leads to the Temple of the Eye."

"Then onwards and upwards, I say!"

Burton remounted and steered his vehicle up the incline and into the mouth of a narrow crevasse. Thickly knotted vines grew against the rocky walls to either side, and the ground was deep in mulch, from which poppies and other flowers grew in profusion.

As the walls rose and the shadows deepened, swarms of fireflies appeared, bathing the two travellers in a weird, fluctuating glow.

They'd travelled for about a mile through this when the harvestmen passed a small mound of rocks—quite obviously a grave—and Burton, remembering who was buried there, was stricken with misery.

They went on, through thick foliage that parted as they approached, under hanging lianas that rose to allow them passage, over tangled roots that burrowed into the mulch so as not to trip the big machines.

And even in this place, so sheltered from the sunlight, parakeets ran riot through the vegetation, enthusiastically delivering their insults, which, as Wells noted, were invariably in English, despite that they were deep in the heart of German East Africa.

On, up, and the fissure opened onto a broad forested summit. Through the thick canopy, the men glimpsed distant snow-topped mountain peaks chopping at the sky.

"The Blood Jungle covers the whole range," Wells noted. "And has been gradually expanding beyond it for the past couple of decades."

The terrain angled downward, and the trail of poppies eventually led them into the mouth of a second crevasse, this one narrower and deeper than the previous. As they entered it, the verdure closed around them like a tunnel. Strange vermillion fruits hung from its branches, spherical and glowing with a ghostly radiance.

"I've never seen anything like it," Wells muttered. "I have the distinct impression that this is all one single plant. I feel as if we're inside a gigantic living thing."

Now the parakeets became less numerous, and a deep hush settled over them, broken only by the quiet chugging of the vehicles' steam engines and the buzzing of insects.

"We're being watched," Burton announced.

"What? By whom? Where?"

Burton pointed to a gap in the leaves up to his right. Wells squinted into the gloom and saw, vaguely illuminated by the red light, a naked man squatting on a branch. His skin was black and seemed reptilian. There was a bow in his hands.

"Chwezi," Burton said. "The Children of the Eye. They won't harm us."

"How can you be sure?"

"I'm sure, Bertie."

They spotted more of the silent, motionless observers as they drove on, deeper and deeper into the gorge.

All of a sudden, there was daylight.

They'd emerged into a wide natural amphitheatre. Sunshine filtered through leaves and branches and slanted across such an unruly mass of vegetation that both men cried out in wonder. Branches and leaves and creepers and vines and lianas and stalks and stems and fruits and flowers were all jumbled together, all red, all climbing the surrounding cliffs, carpeting the ground, and drooping from overhead.

A colossal trunk rose from the centre of it all, and, high above them, it divided into many limbs from which big fleshy leaves grew, and among which bizarre vermillion flowers blossomed. One of the branches was moving down towards them, with much groaning and screeching as its wood bent and stretched. It manoeuvred a giant flower, a thing with spiny teeth in its petals and odd bladder-like protuberances at its base, until it hung just in front of Burton.

The bladders inflated. The petals curled open to reveal a tightly closed bud-like knot. The bladders contracted. Air blew from between the lips of the bud, making a high-pitched squeal, like a child's balloon being deflated. The lips moved and shaped the squeal into words.

The plant spoke.

"My hat, Richard! You took your giddy time! What the blazes have you been up to?"

§

From the deep indigo of the African sky, a thin line descended.

It wobbled and wavered through the hot compressed air, arcing down into the crevasse.

Sidi Bombay shouted "Spear!" an instant before it emerged from the heat haze and thudded into his chest, knocking him backwards. He sat on the rocky ground, looked at the vibrating shaft, looked at the sky, then looked at Burton.

"Wow!" he said, "Mr. Burton. Please send a message to my fourth wife. Tell her—"

He fell backwards and the shaft swung up into a vertical position.

Blood gurgled out of his mouth. His eyes reflected the azure heavens and glazed over.

"Ambuscade!" Burton bellowed. "Take cover!"

The Englishmen dropped their packs and dived into the shadow of an overhanging rock. Spears rained down, clacking against the rocky ground.

From behind a boulder, Burton peered up at the opposite lip of the gorge. Figures were silhouetted there. A spear thwacked against the stone inches from his face. He ducked back.

Spencer was beside him. "Are you all right, Herbert?" Burton asked.

"Yus, Boss."

"William!" the explorer shouted. "Are you fit?"

"As a fiddle! But I'd feel a lot better if our bloody rifles worked!" came the response from behind an outcrop some hundred and eighty feet away.

"Algy?" Burton called.

Swinburne—who'd thrown himself behind a rock off to Burton's right—leaped back into the open. He looked up and waved his arms like a lunatic. "Hi!" he hollered at the shadowy figures overhead. "Hi there! You Prussians! Why don't you do us a favour and bloody well bugger off out of here?"

His voice bounced off the high walls. Spears descended and clattered around him.

"Algy!" Burton yelled. "Get under cover, you addle-brained dolt!"

Swinburne walked casually over to Burton and joined him behind the boulder.

"I'm trying to make them throw more of the bally things," he said. "They don't have an infinite supply."

"Actually, that's not too bad an idea," Burton muttered, "but poorly executed. Try to remember the difference between fearless and foolhardy."

He examined the rock-strewn fissure. The expedition's packs lay scattered, with multiple spear shafts rising out of them.

"There's not going to be much left that's usable in that lot; least of all the water bottles!" he grumbled.

Trounce's voice echoed: "How many bloody spears have they got up there?"

"Far fewer than before!" returned Burton. "Algy had it right; the more they waste, the better."

"Perhaps not such a waste," Swinburne said. "They're purposely trying to keep us pinned down, which suggests to me that some of them have gone on ahead."

Burton called: "William! Can you make it over here?"

"Watch me!" came the response.

Trounce leaped into view and sprinted across the intervening space, weaving from side to side as spears started to rain around him. He swept up three of the packs as he passed them, dragging them along, then, batting a falling shaft aside, hit the ground, and slid into shelter in a cloud of dust.

"Phew! Am I in one piece?"

"Not a single perforation as far as I can see. How do you fancy a little bit more of that?"

The Scotland Yard man handed over the packs for Swinburne to check. "I don't much. My legs are still afire with damned sores. What's the plan?"

"We'll dart from cover to cover and keep moving. Don't so much as pause for breath in the open or you'll end up a pin cushion!"

"Right you are."

The king's agent looked over at Sidi Bombay's body. Another death. Another friend lost. Another part of his world ripped out of him.

He wondered how much more of it he could take.

There was no option but to leave the African where he lay. Perhaps there'd be an opportunity to bury him later, if animals didn't get to the corpse first.

Trounce watched Swinburne reorganising the contents of the three bags, fitting it all into one pack. "What do we have?" he asked.

"Not a lot!" the poet replied. "One intact water bottle, a dented sextant, Herbert's key, an oil lamp, a box of lucifers, the field glasses from the *Orpheus*, and a small stock of food that looks as if it's been trampled by a herd of elephants."

"What took a hundred and twenty men to carry at the start of the expedition now takes one!" Burton muttered. "Throw away the sextant, and let's get on with it."

He took the bag, slung it over his shoulder, and pointed at fallen rocks farther up and to either side of the faint trail that wound through the middle of the crevasse. "William, you leg it to the base of the cliff, there. Algy, you dive beneath the overhang, there. And Herbert, you make for that boulder, there. I'm going to try for the rock at the bend in the trail—do you see it? From there, I'll survey the next stretch and call instructions to you. All ready? Good. Get set! Go!"

The three men—and one clockwork device—burst out of cover and dashed towards the locations the explorer had indicated. Spears started to fall, their points shattering as they landed.

Swinburne dived into cover first.

Burton was next, though his allotted position was farthest away.

Trounce stumbled when a rebounding shaft cracked painfully against the side of his face but made it without any more serious injury.

Herbert Spencer fared less well. Hampered by his damaged leg, his run was more of a fast shuffle, and three spears hit him. The first bounced from his shoulder with a loud chime.

"Ow! Bleedin' heck!" he piped

The second ploughed a furrow down his back.

"Aagh! They've got me!"

The third sliced through his left ankle, leaving his foot dragging behind him, attached by a single thin cable.

"Cripes! That's agony!" he hooted, falling into the shadow of the large boulder Burton had assigned to him.

"Ouch! Ouch! Ouch!" he said, and, reaching down, he tore the foot off completely and held it up so the others could see it.

"Look at this!" he cried. "Me bloomin' foot's been chopped off!"

"Can you still walk, Herbert?" Burton called.

"Yus, after a fashion. But that ain't the point, is it?"

"What is the point?" Swinburne asked from his nearby position.

"That me bleedin' foot's come off, lad!"

"I'm sure Brunel will have you polished and repaired in no time at all after we get back to Blighty," Swinburne responded. "There's no need to worry."

"You're still missin' the point. Me foot's come off. It hurts!"

Burton, who'd identified points of cover among the rocks ahead, shouted instructions back to them.

They ran.

Herbert Spencer hobbled along, scraping his stump over the hard ground. A spear clunked into his hip and stuck there.

"Yow!" he cried. He yanked it out and threw it aside.

Another clanged off his head.

"Bloody hell! Bloody hell!"

He reached the side wall, where it bulged outwards, and collapsed into its shadow. He lay, groaning.

"Herbert," Swinburne called. "For the umpteenth time: it's all in your mind! You can't feel pain!"

"Ready for more dodging?" Burton called.

"Wait a moment!" Trounce shouted. A spear tip had scooped a furrow across his thigh and blood was flowing freely. He tore off one of his shirtsleeves and used it to bind the wound.

"All set!"

Another mad dash, more spears—but far fewer this time—and they reached the space beneath a leaning slab without further injury.

"They must have stolen every spear from every village they pillaged," Swinburne noted. "Either that or they have a portable pointy stick factory with them."

A wailing scream suddenly echoed and a body thumped into the gorge near to where they squatted. It was a white man, blonde haired and blue eyed and dead. An arrow, striped red and black, was sticking out of his chest.

Shouts and screams sounded from above.

"They're being attacked!" Burton exclaimed.

"Who by?" Swinburne asked.

"Let's not dally to ponder that! Come on!"

They dashed out of their hiding place—the king's agent giving support to Trounce, and Swinburne to Spencer—and hurried along the cleft, leaving the embattled Prussians behind.

After they'd traversed perhaps two miles, the ground angled steeply upward. It was tough going.

Burton's stomach rumbled. Sweat dripped from the end of his nose.

He tried to remember what it felt like to sit in his old saddlebag armchair by the fire in his study.

"We're gettin' close, Boss," Spencer announced. "I can feel the Eye's presence."

The group struggled on through the fissure. By mid-afternoon, its walls had opened out and they emerged onto a low summit. The temperature plummeted, and suddenly they were shivering. The low mountains and hills they'd trekked through humped away to the rear; to either side, a long ridge zig-zagged away to rising snow-covered peaks, which jaggedly heaped into the distance; and ahead, a long slope of crumpled strata plunged steeply downwards and was split by a second shadowy crevasse.

Footing became precarious now; the ground was very uneven, with patches of loose slate-like rock that slipped from beneath their feet and rattled away down the incline.

They reached the fracture in the mountain's side and entered into it. Darkness closed around them. Sheer rock faces soared up to the left and right, reaching such a height that the sky was reduced to nothing but a thin line of serrated blue.

They stopped for a moment while Burton rummaged in the pack for the oil lamp. Its glass was broken but it was functional. He struck a lucifer, put it to the wick, and moved on, illuminating the cracks and irregularities in their path.

"That's rummy!" Swinburne muttered. "No echoes!"

It was true: their footsteps and voices; the knocks and scrapes of displaced stones; it was all sucked into an overwhelming silence.

The eerie atmosphere increased as the party moved ever deeper into the gloom.

"If Speke went on ahead while the Prussians tried to stick us with spears, then surely we must be hot on his heels by now," Trounce whispered.

Burton clenched his jaw and fists.

After a while, they found themselves catching swift movements from the corners of their eyes—indistinct things flitting through the shadows—but when they looked, there was nothing.

The thread of sky was so far away that the darkness was almost complete. Burton raised his lamp. It illuminated men, naked but for loincloths and necklaces of human finger bones, standing dark and motionless against the cliffs to either side. Their faces were scored by a network of scars, making their skin resemble the segmented hide of reptiles; they were holding bows fitted with red and black striped arrows, and their eyes were fixed on Herbert Spencer.

"How many?" Swinburne hissed.

"Hard to tell. A lot," Burton replied "Chwezi. It was obviously they who attacked the Prussians."

"Look at the way they're all a-gogglin' at me," Spencer said.

"I'm not surprised," Swinburne responded. "With all those dents and scratches, you're quite a sight!"

"Thank you, lad. But it ain't that. I reckons they can feel the diamonds what's in me head."

"They're closing in to the rear," Trounce warned.

The others looked back and saw a number of the Chwezi slowly moving towards them.

"But they've left the way ahead open," Swinburne observed. "Seems to me like they're here to escort us. Or do I mean herd us?"

"To the Eye?" Burton asked.

"It's in this direction, Boss," Spencer confirmed. "The emanations are very strong now."

"Then I suggest we allow ourselves to be guided."

The king's agent continued on along the narrow path, and Swinburne, Trounce and Spencer trailed after him. The Chwezi stood in eerie silence, not moving until the Britishers had passed, then falling in behind.

Untouched by the sun, the mountain air grew increasingly frigid, and the men's breath clouded in front of their faces. Snow, piled at the sides of the crevasse, reflected the light of Burton's lamp, stark white in the black shadows, and ice glittered on the walls.

"This fault line," Swinburne said. "We climbed up through it on the other side of the mountain, and now we're descending through it on this. It's as if the whole peak has been split down its centre. What unimaginable energy must have caused that?"

"Not volcanic," Burton mumbled, distractedly. "This is metamorphic rock. You can see from the angle of the strata how subterranean pressures have pushed it upward." He frowned and looked up at the thin strip of blue sky high overhead. "You're right, though, Algy. There are very powerful geological forces at work here!"

Maybe half a mile farther on, the chasm suddenly opened out, to form a broad, bowl-shaped arena into which the sun shone, warming the air dramatically.

"Look!" Trounce said softly, and pointed ahead.

Across the space, the high wall was cut through, as the great crack in the mountain's side continued. The mouth of it was blocked by more of the silent Chwezi. Burton looked around. He and his companions were surrounded.

"There's a cave," Spencer announced. He pointed to the right, at a gap in the ranks of encircling warriors, where a shadow in the rock concealed a blacker patch of darkness.

"Bombay said the temple was underground and accessible through a cave. I suppose that's it," Burton said. "And our escort obviously wants us to go down there."

He moved warily to the opening and extended his lamp into it, illuminating a deep hollow at the back of which he saw a narrow opening.

"Come on," he called, and ushered the others in with a wave of his hand. They filed past and he followed, stepping through the aperture in the rear wall while watching to see if the Chwezi were going to come in after them. They didn't.

He turned and saw a smooth rocky passage.

"Wait," he instructed. His friends stopped and he squeezed past them until he was in point position.

They moved on, following the irregular tunnel. It descended, bending to the right and to the left.

There were no sounds of pursuit.

After a while, the detective became aware of something peculiar. He ordered a halt and blew out his lamp's flame. By degrees, a faint bluish luminescence became apparent.

"What's that?" came Swinburne's whisper.

"Some sort of phosphorescent fungus or lichen by the looks of it. Let's proceed without the lamp. Our eyes will adjust."

Gingerly, measuring every step as the passage inclined more steeply, they inched onwards. As they did so, the glowing fungus became more prevalent until, a few yards farther on, it covered the walls entirely, lighting the way with a weird, otherworldly radiance.

The crooked corridor veered sharply to the left and plunged downwards at a severe angle. They struggled to maintain their footing, slipping and stumbling until they were moving faster than they could help. Almost running, they plunged down and out onto the level floor of a fantastical chamber—a large domed grotto—so filled with ambient blue light that its every feature stood out in sharp focus.

They gasped, astonished at the spectacle.

Stalagmites, ranging from tiny to huge, rose from the floor, stretching towards stalactites of similar proportions, which hung from the high roof. Many of them had met and melded together to form massive asymmetrical pillars, giving the chamber the appearance of a gigantic organic cathedral.

Veins of glittering quartz were embedded in the walls, and serrated clumps of the crystal rose from the floor. On the far side of the chamber, a small fountain of clear water tinkled as it bubbled up from its underground source, spreading into a pool, roughly oval in shape and about twenty feet across at its widest point. Draining from it, a narrow stream had cut a channel through the stone floor to the centre of the cavern, where the kidney-shaped forty-foot wide mouth of a sinkhole opened in the floor. The stream plunged into the darkness of this cavity, disappearing back into the depths of the Earth.

A number of tall wooden posts, with roughly spherical masses stuck at their tops, stood around the hole.

At the base of the walls, mushrooms—probably white but appearing pale blue in the light—stood clustered in groups; mushrooms of wildly exaggerated proportions, many of them more than twelve feet tall.

Trounce gasped: "Somebody pinch me!"

"Incredible!" Swinburne spluttered. "If an emissary of the fairy nation stepped forward and, on behalf of his monarch, welcomed us to his kingdom, I wouldn't be a bit surprised!"

They moved farther into the grotto and peered into the well. Trounce picked up a rock and dropped it in. They waited, expecting to hear a crack or splash echoing up from the darkness. Neither came.

"A bottomless pit," the Scotland Yard man muttered.

The men stepped over to the pool. Burton knelt and lifted a handful of water to his lips.

"Wonderfully pure," he said. "Thank heavens!"

They slaked their thirst.

"Boss," Spencer said.

Burton looked at the philosopher and saw that he was pointing at the nearest of the upright poles. The king's agent examined it and let out a gasp of horror.

The lump at its top was a desiccated human head. Though wrinkled and shrunken, it was unmistakably that of a European.

There were seven poles and seven heads. Burton examined them all. He recognised one. It was was Henry Morton Stanley.

"These others must be the five men who travelled with him," he said. "Which leaves one extra."

A harsh voice rang out: "Ja, mein Freund! It is the head of poor James Grant!"

They whirled around.

Count Zeppelin stepped into view from behind a thick stalagmite. He was a tall and portly man, with a completely bald head and a big white walrus moustache. His hands were gripped tightly around the neck of a second individual. It was John Hanning Speke. The vicious-looking claws at the end of Zeppelin's fingers were pressing against, but not yet piercing, the skin of the Britisher's throat.

"Es ist sehr gut!" said the Count, enthusiastically. "We have reached the end of our journey, at last!"

§

"Bastard!" Swinburne hissed. "You have the blood of Tom Bendyshe and Shyamji Bhatti on your hands!"

"I do not know those people," Zeppelin answered. "And I do not care."

Burton whispered to Spencer: "Herbert, if you can make your revolver work, now is the time. On my command, draw it and shoot him."

"Rightio, Boss."

"And what is the death of one man," Zeppelin was saying, "or two, or even a hundred, when we—how do you say it, Herr Burton?—wenn wir mit der Welt spielen?"

"When we are gambling with the world. I would say the death of one man might make all the difference, Count Zeppelin. Hello, John. Your erstwhile ally seems to have you at a disadvantage."

Bedraggled, and skinny to the point of emaciation, with his beard grown almost to his waist, Speke's pale blue right eye was wide with fear. The left was a glass lens—part of the brass clockwork apparatus that had been grafted to his head, replacing the left hemisphere of his brain. It was a prototype constructed by Charles Babbage, designed to process the electrical fields stored in two fragments of the Cambodian Eye of Nāga. Those diamonds had been stolen before the scientist could properly experiment with them, so he'd passed the device over to a cabal of Technologists and Rakes, and they'd fitted it to Speke in order to gain control of him. Later, Babbage had constructed a much more sophisticated version of the device, and that now sat in Herbert Spencer's head, along with all seven of the Cambodian stones.

"Dick!" Speke gasped. "It wasn't me! It wasn't me! I didn't do any of it!"

"I know, John. You've been the greatest victim of them all."

"Please! We have to get out of here! They'll come for us!"

Zeppelin grinned. "He believes there are monsters in this place."

"I see only one," Swinburne snarled, stepping forward with his fists raised.

"Remain where you are, kleiner Mann," Zeppelin growled.

Burton said: "Let's not waste any more time. Now, Herbert."

The clockwork philosopher drew his revolver, aimed it at Zeppelin's head, and did nothing.

Burton sighed. He turned to William Trounce and asked, in an exasperated tone: "Have you noticed how he winds down at the most inconvenient of times?"

"I have!" The Yard man grumbled.

Count Zeppelin laughed nastily. "Your clockwork toy seems to have become a statue. Sehr gut! Now, let us get to business. I want your little assistant to go around the rock behind me. He will find there a pack, and in it some lengths of rope. Have him fetch them, if you please."

"Up yours, you murdering git!" Swinburne spat.

"It would be more convenient for me to keep the Lieutenant alive for a while longer, Herr Burton, but I am prepared to inject him with venom now, if necessary. It will cause him to transform in a most painful fashion. He is your enemy, ja? But he was once your friend. Are you prepared to watch him die?"

The count applied pressure to Speke's neck. The Englishman started to choke.

"Stop!" Burton barked. "Algy, fetch the ropes."

"But, Richard—"

"Just do it, please."

Swinburne hesitated, then stamped past Zeppelin and his captive, found the pack, retrieved the coils of rope, and returned to his former position.

"Don't—" Speke began, but was cut off and shaken hard.

"You will be quiet!" the Count said. He looked at Trounce and demanded: "You there! Who are you?"

Trounce scowled. "I'm Detective Inspector William Trounce of Scotland Yard."

"Ha ha! A policeman in Africa! Most amusing! You will kneel down and the little man will bind your wrists."

"I'll not kneel for you!"

"You are of no consequence to me, Detective Inspector. If you allow yourself to be tied, I give you my word that I will leave you here alive. Perhaps you will manage to free yourself and make your way out of this cavern, ja? But if you resist, I shall most certainly kill you like a dog." Zeppelin transferred his attention to Burton. "Do not doubt that I can defeat all three of you, Herr Burton!" He took his right hand from Speke's neck, held it up, and flexed his fingers. His claws gleamed in the phosphorescent light. "It takes but one scratch!"

"William," Burton said, quietly. "Do as he says, please."

Trounce looked shocked. "We can overpower him!" he hissed.

"The risk is too great. As he says: one scratch. I would prefer to keep you alive while this affair plays itself out."

"Kneel with your back to me, Herr Policeman. I wish to see that the rope is made tight."

Trounce slowly obeyed, his face livid with anger.

Burton said: "Go ahead, Algy."

The poet, whose eyes were also blazing with fury, squatted behind Trounce and began to tie his wrists.

"Nein! Nein" Zeppelin shouted. "Das ist ein slipknot! Ich bin kein Narr! Do not try to deceive me! Do it properly!"

Swinburne cursed under his breath and started again.

When he'd finished, the Count ordered the poet to rejoin Burton. He then dragged Speke forward, still holding him by the neck with just his left hand, and inspected the handiwork.

"Das ist besser!" he exclaimed.

He pulled a revolver from his belt and pointed it at the back of Trounce's neck.

"No!" Swinburne shrieked.

Burton looked on, his face mask-like.

Zeppelin noticed the explorer's expression and grinned at him. "You think perhaps that my pistol is useless, ja?"

He received no response.

"You are wrong, Herr Burton. Observe!"

The Prussian sliced the weapon upward into the bony side of Speke's head. The lieutenant slumped, and the count let him slip senselessly to the ground.

"Effective, do you not think?"

Zeppelin reversed the weapon and held it in his left hand like a club. He stepped closer to Trounce, pressed his knee between the detective's shoulder blades, and, with his right hand, reached down over the Yard man's face. He curled his fingers under the bearded chin and levered Trounce's head back until his spine was agonisingly arched and the Prussian's claws were pressed dangerously into the skin of his neck.

"Now, Herr Burton, you too will kneel and your assistant will tie you. If you do not do this, I will break this man's back."

"You gave your word!" Swinburne shrilled.

"I gave my word that I would leave him here alive. I did not say anything about the condition of his spine."

"Damn the man!" Burton muttered. He knelt, facing away from Zeppelin.

"As before, little assistant. None of your tricks!"

Swinburne bent over Burton and began to bind his wrists.

"What's the plan then, Richard?" he whispered eagerly.

"I was hoping you'd tell me, Algy."

"Be quiet!" Zeppelin commanded.

Swinburne finished the job and stood back.

The count released Trounce. "Das war einfach!" he said. "It is more convenient to kill a man when he is on his knees, nein?"

He raised the clubbed revolver over Trounce, looked at Swinburne, and asked: "Do you wish to say goodbye to your friends?"

The poet's mouth fell open.

"Your word, Zeppelin!" Burton yelled.

The count laughed. "Who heard it except the men who will die here today? I will leave this place, by myself, with the Eye of Nāga in my hand and my honour intact! I will be a hero to the Germanic people!"

He swung the pistol up and back.

Swinburne let loose a scream of rage and flung himself forward. The Prussian turned and swiped at him, but the poet, with astonishing speed, ducked and rolled through Zeppelin's widespread legs. Snatching up a lump of quartz, he bounded to his feet and threw it with all his might into the side of his opponent's head.

Zeppelin staggered and groaned. He turned and hit out, blindly. Swinburne was already scampering clear and scooping up a fist-sized stone. He threw it and it cracked off the bigger man's kneecap, causing him to scream with pain.

"Bravo, lad!" Trounce cheered.

"Your aim is improving, Algy!" Burton called.

"I was trying to hit his nose!"

"Oh!"

"Come here!" Zeppelin roared, hopping on one leg.

"Not bloody likely!" Swinburne answered. Maintaining his distance, he picked up more crystals and rocks and started pelting the count with them.

"Gott im Himmel!" Zeppelin cried out. He backed away, coming perilously close to the lip of the sinkhole.

"Send him over the edge, lad!" Trounce urged.

In desperation, the Prussian hurled his revolver at Swinburne. It flew wide of the mark.

"Ha!" the poet squealed. He aimed at Zeppelin's uninjured knee, and, putting all his strength behind it, launched another stone. It caught the count in the middle of his forehead. The big man groaned and sat down hard, his eyes glazing over. Blood poured down his face.

Swinburne bent and lifted a large serrated lump of amethyst, heaved it over his head, and staggered towards the Prussian, intending to crack it down onto the man's skull.

"Algy!" Burton yelled. "Stay away from him!"

His assistant, oblivious to all but revenge, ignored the command and reached his opponent's side. He swung the amethyst higher.

Zeppelin's fist lashed out and caught him in the stomach. The crystal shattered on the rocky ground as Swinburne dropped it and doubled over. The count grabbed him by the neck and dug his claws in. He pushed himself to his feet and, standing behind the poet, yanked him around to face Burton and lifted him into the air.

Swinburne's eyes bulged. His face began to turn blue. He jerked and kicked in Zeppelin's grip. Black lines of venom crawled under his skin as the talons sank in.

"Don't!" Burton screamed.

"He is very irritating to me, Herr Burton!" Zeppelin explained, shaking his victim.

Swinburne's tongue protruded. His eyes started to roll up into his head.

"Let him go!" Trounce bellowed.

"I will be certain to do so, Herr Policeman—when he is dead! But, see! He has a little life left in him still! How he kicks!"

With his last vestiges of strength, the poet reached into his jacket and pulled from it Apollo's gold-tipped arrow of Eros. He jerked it upwards and backwards over his shoulder. The point sank into Zeppelin's right eye.

With an agonised shriek, the Prussian reeled backwards, teetered on the edge of the sinkhole, and plunged into it, dragging Swinburne with him.

Suddenly: silence.

Burton and Trounce knelt, staring, unable to comprehend that their companion was gone. An incalculable interval passed; perhaps a moment, maybe an hour; to the two men, it seemed that time wasn't moving at all; then John Speke moaned and shifted and everything snapped back into focus.

"I say, chaps!" came Swinburne's voice. "Culver Cliff!"

Burton loosed a bark of laughter. On a previous occasion, when his assistant had been dangling over a precipice and holding on by his fingertips, he'd referred to that youthful escapade of his, when he'd climbed Culver Cliff on the Isle of Wight. It had become a symbol of his seeming indestructibility.

"Hold on!" Burton called. He struggled to his feet, his wrists still bound behind him, paced over to the lip of the well, and knelt beside it. Swinburne was just below, hanging on to a narrow shelf with both hands. His neck was bruised purple, and blood flowed from the puncture marks in it.

"William!" Burton snapped. "Get over here, put your back to me, and untie these confounded knots. Can you hang on there for a little longer, Algy?"

"Yes, Richard. But I feel jolly peculiar."

It was no wonder; the capillaries of the poet's face were black and appeared to be writhing beneath the skin. Small white buds were pushing through at the corners of his nose, and, even as Burton watched, leaves started to open amid his friend's long hair, like a laurel wreathe.

"Hurry, William!" he hissed, as he felt Trounce's fingers getting to work.

The whites of Swinburne's eyes suddenly turned green.

"I'm thirsty," he said.

"Almost there!" Trounce grunted.

"And my arms are aching," the poet added.

"Got it!" the Scotland Yard man announced, and Burton felt the ropes loosen. He yanked his wrists free, threw himself on his stomach, and reached down to his assistant.

"Grab hold!"

Hanging on to the ledge with just his left hand, Swinburne stretched the right up towards Burton.

"My hat!" he exclaimed, and drew his hand back a little, for a bright red flower had suddenly bloomed from the back of it. "It's—it's a poppy, Richard!"

His fingers slipped from their hold.

Swinburne dropped into darkness.

"Have you got him?" Trounce asked.

Burton didn't reply.

"Richard?"

The Yard man crawled around on his knees.

"Richard? Richard? Do you have him?"

The king's agent remained still, his tears dripping into the void beneath his face.

"Oh no," Trounce whispered huskily. "Oh no."

§

Burton untied Trounce.

John Speke stirred and sat up.

"Dick," he groaned. "I'm so sorry. I'm so sorry for everything." He touched the babbage embedded in his skull. "It was this damned thing. Every time I wound it up, it forced decisions upon me. I've been like an opium addict with it. Unable to stop!"

"But now?" Burton asked, dully. He felt remote. Disengaged. Broken.

"It was all about coming here," Speke responded. "The wretched thing was designed to make me fetch the black diamond for the Technologist and Rake alliance. When you killed the madmen behind that scheme, the compulsion to come here remained, but I had no sponsor, so it forced me to find one."

"The Prussian government."

"Yes. I guided Zeppelin here, and as soon as I set foot in the place, the device, having realised its purpose, stopped working."

An expression of sheer torment passed over his face.

"I still have the addiction, Dick. I'm on fire with the urge to wind it up again! But Babbage booby-trapped it. If I use it even once more, a timing mechanism will activate and it will explode!"

Herbert Spencer broke his pose and stepped forward. He spoke in an uncharacteristically precise voice: "The man you refer to was rather precious about his contraptions, wasn't he? I understand he booby-trapped them all to prevent others from discovering the secret of their construction." He aimed his pistol at the king's agent. "This revolver will operate perfectly well while it's in my grasp, Sir Richard. Don't you think it rather regretful that destructive forces must so often be employed to achieve one's ends?"

Burton gasped and clutched at Trounce's arm for support.

Spencer made a piping noise that may have been a chuckle. "Pretending to have lost motive energy is by no means an original trick but it is an effective one. As you can see, I have power in my mainspring."

"What—what are you playing at, Herbert?" Burton stammered. "Why didn't you help us?"

"The song must be sung in the proper manner."

"Song? What are you talking about?"

"The Song of the Nāga. Let us not stand here discussing it. A demonstration will be far more effective. If you would all please step over to that outcrop of blue crystal—" The brass man gestured with his revolver towards the wall of the cavern where a tall formation of amethyst hunched up from the floor. They moved to it. There was a low opening in the wall behind; a big enough space for a man to crawl into.

Spencer said: "Go in first, please, Mr. Speke; then you, William; and you last, Sir Richard."

One by one, they entered what proved to be little more than a winding tube. Patches of phosphorescence illuminated its length.

Burton fought to quell his rising panic. He had an irrational fear of enclosed spaces. The passage into the grotto had been bad enough, but this was far worse.

As they inched along, flat on their stomachs, the clockwork man explained: "The fact of the matter is that I'm not Herbert Spencer and never have been. When he died in close proximity to the Cambodian diamonds, his mind was imprinted onto them, just as you thought, but it never had the power to motivate this mechanical body. It was I who did so, using his personality as a bridge—or a filter, if you will—through which to interact with you. Spencer is, I'm afraid to say, thoroughly suppressed. The poor man! I can feel his frustration, his eagerness to help you!"

"Then who are you?" the king's agent asked, fighting to keep his voice steady.

"I am K'k'thyima, high priest of the Nāga."

Burton, whose mind had barely functioned since the loss of Swinburne, struggled to make sense of this revelation.

"I dreamed of you. You sounded different."

"As I said, I employ the mind of Herbert Spencer in order to communicate. I could chinwag more like what he bloomin' well does, if'n it'll make you feel more comfy, like."

"I'd prefer it if you didn't."

"A little farther, gentlemen. We're almost there."

Moments later, the three men wormed their way out of the tunnel and got to their feet. They stood paralysed, with hearts hammering and eyes popping.

What confronted them was virtually incomprehensible.

They were standing on a ledge, hundreds of feet above the floor of a vast cavern, which was ablaze with the strange azure radiance; and if the previous vault had seemed magical, then this one appeared miraculous!

A megalithic temple rose from the centre of the massive space. Its soaring walls, spires and columns were decorated with complex geometrical designs and friezes. The men gazed in awe at its sweeping arches and curving arcades; at the many gargoyles and representations of lions and oxen and other, extinct, animals; and at the thick round central tower that rose to the distant ceiling and merged with it.

The entire temple complex—for there were many outbuildings squatting around the base of the edifice—was hewn from solid rock, and for many minutes, Burton, Trounce and Speke stood silent and confounded, wondering what manner of tools had been employed to achieve this eighth—and foremost!—wonder of the world.

As the brass man scraped out of the tunnel behind them, Speke whispered: "I never knew! I never got this far! Both times, when I reached the grotto, the things came and dragged me out of it."

"Then when did you see the Eye?" Burton asked.

"I didn't. Not physically. But I had a clear vision of it."

"*What*? All this we've been through began with nothing but a *vision*?"

"I planted it in Mr. Speke's mind," K'k'thyima said.

"Things?" Trounce interrupted. "You said *things* dragged you out, Speke?"

"Yes. They were—they were—"

"They were the Batembuzi," the brass figure interjected. "Long ago, they served the Nāga and had an empire that covered all of the Lake Regions, but now this—" He swept out his arm to indicate the temple. "—is their home." He gestured to their right with his revolver. "The ledge goes down here and slopes around the wall to the floor. Follow it, please."

They walked slowly, as necessitated by the condition of the clockwork man's left leg.

The ledge narrowed for a stretch, and they had to press themselves against the cavern wall to navigate along it.

"Allow me to tell you a little of the Nāga," K'k'thyima said. "Long, long ago, we lived where the three Eyes had fallen; here, and in South America, and on the continent of Kumari Kandam—and though our colonies were separated, we bonded in a Great Fusion through means of the diamonds."

"Until Brahmin Kaundinya came along," Burton murmured.

"Ah, of course, you have studied the legend. Yes, your spy, Kaundinya, broke the Kumari Kandam Eye into seven fragments, causing the physical death of all the Nāga on that continent. Their essence lived on in the stones, of course, but now they were isolated, for the other two Eyes were whole, whereas theirs was shattered."

"Your Great Fusion requires the three Eyes to be in the same state?"

"It does."

The group was now about halfway down the path. Speke led the way, self-absorbed and tormented; Trounce followed, listening to what he considered a fairy tale; Burton was third in the line; and the clockwork man hauled himself along behind, holding his pistol aimed steadily at the back of the explorer's head.

K'k'thyima continued: "When a Nāga completes its lifespan, the Great Fusion offers the choice of true death—which many prefer—or a transcendence. Kaundinya's act of betrayal denied us all these options, and condemned us to eternity and eventual madness. Obviously, this is a situation that has to be corrected."

"Only equivalence can lead to destruction or a final transcendence," Burton said. "You can't put a broken diamond together again, so you have to shatter the other two stones to achieve equivalence."

"And restore the Great Fusion, yes. Incidentally, your friend Spencer is a very determined man. He is not happy that I borrowed his personality. He tried to leave a clue for the unfortunate Mr. Swinburne in *First Principles of Philosophy*. It was all I could do to stop the poet from telling you about it."

"How did you do that?"

"I've been radiating a mesmeric influence to make you all consider me harmless and friendly."

They reached the cavern floor, and K'k'thyima directed them along a well-worn path towards the buildings at the foot of the temple.

"So we were at an impasse. We couldn't shatter the other two Eyes while our South American and African colonies still lived, for it would have physically killed them. Nor could we stand to exist in a state of disconnection. We thus lost the will to survive in the material realm, and allowed you soft skins to hunt us to extinction."

"But the essence of you continued to dwell in the Eyes?" Burton asked.

"Yes, and now we had to wait for your species to discover the diamonds."

"Why?"

"So that we might use you to bring equivalence. As high priest, I was the only one of my people whose essence spanned all of the stones, and I was able to channel the mesmeric abilities of my species through any of them. I was thus able to manipulate you soft skins. Ah, look! Here come the Batembuzi!"

Up ahead, figures were slouching out of doorways and sliding out of glassless windows. A large crowd of them gathered and loped forward to meet the approaching party. They were small and ape-like, with skin of a dull white hue, and their eyes were strange and large and greyish-red. Shaggy flaxen hair descending to their shoulders and grew down their backs, and they moved with their arms held low, sometimes resorting to all fours. Thoroughly nightmarish in aspect, they proved too much for Speke. With a wail of terror, he threw himself backwards.

"Hold him!" K'k'thyima ordered.

Burton and Trounce grabbed the lieutenant. He fought them, emitting animalistic whines of fear.

"They aren't going to harm you!" the priest said. "They'll just escort us into the temple,"

Speke finally quietened down when the hideous troglodytes, rather than attacking, simply fell into position beside the group.

As they entered among the squat buildings, the brass man instructed the Britishers to walk straight ahead to the central thoroughfare, then turn right and proceed along it. They followed his instructions and saw, some way ahead, the tall double doors of the temple entrance.

"Everything!" Burton suddenly exclaimed. "Bismillah! You orchestrated *everything*! You planted in Edward Oxford an irrational obsession about his ancestor, so he'd travel back in time and cause all of the Eyes to be discovered! You manipulated Rasputin, so you could occupy that clockwork body, commandeer Herbert Spencer's mind, and shatter the South American Eye! And you caused that damned babbage to be grafted onto Speke's brain so he'd lead me here!"

"That has been my song," K'k'thyima confessed. "And now we shall shatter the last of the Eyes and the Nāga will be free."

Passing blocky, unadorned buildings, they came to the foot of a broad set of steps leading up to the temple's imposing arched entrance. They ascended, and a group of Batembuzi put their shoulders to the doors and pushed. As the portals swung slowly inwards, Burton asked: "But what of the fragments Oxford cut from the South American Eye for his time suit? Surely they unbalance the equivalence you seek?"

"Soon, Sir Richard, you will discover the beauty and elegance of paradox. Those shards were cut in a future where the stone was complete. I changed that future when, earlier in the same diamond's history, I broke it into seven. Thus the pieces could not be cut from it."

"I don't understand any of this," Trounce grumbled.

The clockwork man gave a soft hoot. "Do not be embarrassed, William. Non-linear time and multiplying histories are concepts that most soft skins struggle with. For your kind, it is virtually impossible to escape the imprisoning chains of narrative structure. We have come here to address that deficiency."

"Oh. How comforting."

They entered a prodigious and opulent chamber. Its floor was chequered with alternating gold and black hexagonal tiles. The walls were carved into bas reliefs, inset with thousands of precious gemstones, and the ceiling was a solid blanket of scintillating phosphorescence from which hung censers forged from precious metals and decorated with diamonds.

Oddly, though, the chamber reminded Burton and Trounce less of a temple and more of Battersea Power Station, for there were strange structures arrayed around the floor and walls; things that appeared to be half mineral formation and half machine, with, dominating the centre of the space, a thick floor-to-ceiling column made up of alternating layers of crystalline and metallic materials.

Despite the abundance of precious stones on display, there was an air of abandonment about the place. As they passed through the chamber and started up a winding stairwell, Burton noted that many of the gems had fallen from their housings in the patterned walls and were lying scattered around the floor. There were cracks and crumblings in evidence everywhere, and at one point they had to step over a wide hole where the stone steps had collapsed and fallen away.

"Straight ahead, please, gentlemen."

"My bloody legs!" Trounce groaned, as they climbed higher and higher.

The stairs led up to a long, wide hall, with gold panelled double doors at its far end. Fourteen statues stood against the walls, seven to each side. They depicted Nāga, squatting on short plinths, some with one head, some with five, some with seven.

At K'k'thyima's command, the three men approached the doors. The brass man clanked past, holding his gun levelled at Burton's face, took hold of a handle with his free hand, and pulled one of the portals open far enough for the men to pass through it.

"Enter, please, gents."

They stepped into what turned out to be a medium-sized room. It was square and the walls were panelled with oblongs of phosphorescence. The tall ceiling was shaped like an upside-down pyramid, with an enormous black diamond, the size of a goose egg, fitted into an ornate bracket at its tip.

"The last unbroken Eye of Nāga!" K'k'thyima announced.

A stone altar was laid out beneath the gemstone. Metal manacles were fitted to it, and there were stains on its surface that Burton didn't want to examine too closely. Gold chalices, containing heaps of black diamond dust, stood to either side. The explorer noted nasty looking instruments, like something one might find in a surgery, arranged on a nearby block, and there were other things around the room that, again, seemed somehow more machine than architecture or decoration.

"William, Mr. Speke, if you would move over there—" K'k'thyima gestured to one side of the chamber, "—and, Sir Richard, I'd be much obliged if you'd climb onto the altar and lie down."

"Do you intend to sacrifice me, Nāga?"

The clockwork man gave his soft hooting chuckle. "Rest assured, you'll leave here alive. On you get, please, or—" He moved the pistol, aiming it at Trounce, "—or do I have to shoot William in the leg before you'll comply?"

Scowling ferociously, Burton sat on the altar, swung his legs up, and lay down. Immediately, he felt an energy, like static electricity, crawling over his skin.

With one hand, K'k'thyima closed the manacles around the explorer's wrists and ankles.

Speke, who'd been detached and withdrawn since they'd entered the temple, suddenly spoke up: "Wait! Whatever you're going to do, do it to me instead!"

"I'm afraid that wouldn't be at all satisfactory," K'k'thyima responded. "Only this man is suitable for the task."

Speke fell to his knees and held his hands out imploringly. "Please!"

"Quite impossible. Stand up, Mr. Speke, and be quiet. The song will not require you again until the final verse."

"Task?" Burton asked.

K'k'thyima picked up a wicked looking knife from among the instruments on the nearby block.

Trounce stepped forward.

"Back, William! I intend no harm to your friend! See, I'm putting down the pistol now—" He placed his revolver next to Burton's head, "—but I'll slice his throat if you come any closer."

Trounce bit his lip and gave a curt nod. He returned to his former position

The brass man took hold of Burton's hair and, working quickly, began to slice it off.

"You have a most remarkable mind, Sir Richard," he said. "When you wandered into this diamond's range of influence during your first expedition, we immediately recognised that you were the soft skin we'd been waiting for."

Burton winced as the blade scraped across his scalp.

The priest continued: "The one with an open and inquiring intellect; the observer; sufficiently separated from his own culture as to be able to easily absorb the ways of others; one who isn't disorientated by the unusual or unfamiliar."

"Why is that of any significance?"

K'k'thyima removed the last few strands of hair from the explorer's head, and said: "William, Mr. Speke, I have to perform a delicate operation now. Do not interfere. If you try anything, he'll die, and so will you. Is that understood?"

Both men nodded.

The clockwork man put down the knife and took up a small bowl. It was filled with a sticky paste.

"Excellent!" he exclaimed. "The Batembuzi prepared everything well!"

He scooped the bowl into a chalice, filling it with black diamond dust, then used a small instrument to work the dust into the paste. Limping to the head of the altar, he employed the same instrument to paint an intricate hieroglyph on Burton's naked scalp.

"It is of significance, Sir Richard, because it gives you the wherewithal to remain sane while experiencing history beyond the boundaries of your natural lifespan."

"Beyond the—" Burton began. He stopped and his eyes widened. "You surely don't intend to send me through time!"

"I intend exactly that."

The Nāga priest finished painting, put the bowl aside, and reversed the instrument he was holding. Its other end was needle sharp.

"This will hurt," he said, and started to jab the point over and over into Burton's skin, working at such speed that his hand became a blur.

Burton groaned and writhed in pain.

"Time, Sir Richard. Time. Time. Time. You soft skins have such a limited sense of it. You think it's the beat of a heart, that its pulses are regular, that it marches from A to B to C. But there's much more to time than mere rhythm and sequence. There's a melody. There are refrains that arise and fade and arise again. Time can change pitch and timbre and texture. Time has harmonies. It has volume. It has accents and pauses. It has verses and choruses. Your understanding of it is tediously horizontal, but it has all these vertical aspects, too."

William Trounce snorted. "Even if all that gobbledegook is true," he growled, "so bloody well what?"

"Just this, Detective Inspector: when the ripples of consequence spread out from an action taken, they go in all directions, not just forward, as you soft skins would have it. All directions."

"Ruddy nonsense!"

K'k'thyima straightened up from his task and said: "Do you happen to have a handkerchief?"

Trounce shook his head, but Speke reached into his pocket, pulled out a square of cotton, and passed it to the clockwork priest. K'k'thyima used it to wipe the blood and excess paste from the explorer's freshly etched tattoo.

"All done," he announced. He picked up his revolver. "We shall now send our friend Sir Richard Francis Burton into the future, where he'll witness the music of time in all its glory. It is a gift from the Nāga to the race that destroyed us."

Burton said: "Why?"

"Because you have to learn! If you don't, this world is doomed! It is in your hands now, soft skin; teach the lesson you learn today."

"Hogwash!" Trounce spat.

"It's a terrible shame," K'k'thyima said. "And I'm truly sorry, but, as has ever been the case, the Eye requires a sacrifice to activate it. The essence of you will, however, be imprinted on the stone, if that's any consolation, William."

He raised the pistol and shot Trounce through the head.

Burton screamed.

There was a blinding white flash.

CHAPTER 12

Escape From Africa

"In despair are many hopes."
—Arabic proverb

The prodigious plant quivered, and the huge red flower swung upwards into a sunbeam and unfurled its outer layer of spiny petals to soak in the light and heat. The air bladders at the top of its stalk expanded like balloons, then contracted, and the resultant squeak seemed oddly dreamy in tone.

"One, who is not, we see; but one, whom we see not, is;
Surely this is not that; but that is assuredly this.

"What, and wherefore, and whence? for under is over and under;
If thunder could be without lightning, lightning could be without thunder."

The bloom shifted again, with a woody creak, and seemed to look back down at the two men, who sat on their harvestmen and gaped at it in utter astonishment.

Bertie Wells whispered the obvious: "It's a talking plant. A talking bloody plant!"

Two long narrow leaves, positioned a little way below the petals, stretched and curled in a gesture that resembled a man throwing out his hands. "So explain yourself, you rotter! Why did you ignore me for so long? Wasn't it obvious that I was calling you back? The poppies, Richard! The poppies!"

Burton turned off his harvestman's steam engine, toppled from his saddle, thumped onto the ground, and lay still.

Behind him, Wells hurriedly stopped his own machine, dismounted, and ran over to kneel at his friend's side.

"I say!" the flower exclaimed. "Who are you? What's wrong with Richard?"

"I'm Bertie Wells, and I think he's fainted. Probably out of sheer disbelief!"

"Ah," said the bloom, and added:

"Doubt is faith in the main; but faith, on the whole, is doubt;

We cannot believe by proof; but could we believe without?

"Why, and whither, and how? for barley and rye are not clover;

Neither are straight lines curves; yet over is under and over.

"Two and two may be four; but four and four are not eight;

Fate and God may be twain; but God is the same as fate."

"God is a proven fallacy," Wells muttered distractedly as he took a flask from his belt and splashed water onto Burton's face.

"Indeed he is," the plant agreed. "Darwin drove the sword home and left us with a void. What now, hey? What now? I say we should fill it with a higher sort of pantheism. What do you think, Mr. Wells?"

Without considering the fact that he'd somehow become engaged in a theological discussion with oversized vegetation—for he felt that to do so would lead to the inevitable conclusion that he'd gone completely barmy—Wells replied: "I feel Man would be wise to work at correcting his own mistakes instead of waiting for intervention from on high, and should replace faith in an unknowable divine plan with a well thought out scheme of his own."

"I say! Bravo! Bravo!" the plant cheered.

"Ask a man what he thinks, and get from a man what he feels;

God, once caught in the fact, shows you a fair pair of heels."

Burton blinked, sneezed, lay still for a moment, then scrambled to his feet, swayed, and grabbed at one of his harvestman's legs for support.

He looked up at the flower.

It angled itself downward, and squealed: "I didn't think you were the fainting type, Richard! A hangover, I suspect! Did you drink too much of my brandy? I exude it like sap, you know! A very ingenious process, even if I do say so myself!"

Very slowly, Burton replied: "You, Algernon, have *got* to be bloody joking."

"What? What? Why?"

"A *flower*?"

"Oh! Ha ha! Not just a flower—a whole bally jungle! What a wheeze, hey?"

"But is it—is it really you?"

The blossom twisted slightly, a gesture like a man angling his head to one side in contemplation. It refilled its air bladders and squeaked:

"Body and spirit are twins; God only knows which is which;

The soul squats down in the flesh, like a tinker drunk in a ditch.

"More is the whole than a part; but half is more than the whole;

Clearly, the soul is the body; but is not the body the soul?"

With a sudden jerk, the flower dropped until it was just inches from Burton's face.

"Is there something wrong with your memory, old horse?"

"Yes. There's a lot wrong. I've spent the past five years trying to piece it together while being pursued, shot at and bombed."

"And I suppose you've forgotten the poppy that sprouted from my hand?"

Burton flinched and put a hand to his head as an image flashed into his mind, bringing with it an overwhelming sense of loss. "Bismillah! I had! But I—wait! I think—I think— Culver Cliff!"

Swinburne shivered and rustled. "Unfortunately so."

With watering eyes, Burton squinted at the surrounding cliffs.

"I know this place. There's—"

He looked to his right, to where one of the plant's thick limbs crossed the ground and dug into the surrounding cliff. There was a dark opening in the root-like growth, and he could see that it was hollow.

Disparate recollections slotted together.

"There's a cave," he said, hoarsely. "It's there! I remember now. A grotto! You killed Count Zeppelin!"

"Yes! The golden arrow of Eros straight into his eyeball! Good old Tom Bendyshe avenged! But the Prussian injected me with that horrible venom of his and the next thing I knew I was falling. It took me an age to grow back out of that pit and into daylight, I can tell you! Lucky for me that Zeppelin fell into it, too. He made very good fertilizer!"

A black pit.

Algernon Swinburne hanging by his fingertips.

A green shoot emerging from the back of the poet's hand. Petals unfurling. A red poppy.

"The poppies," Burton whispered. "Now I understand."

"Bloody typical!" the poet trumpeted. "I stretched myself to the absolute giddy limit to signpost the way back here, and you didn't even recognise what the confounded signs meant!"

"I'm sorry, Algy. Something happened to me in that cave—in Lettow-Vorbeck's temple! Yes, I remember now! It's in there, beyond the grotto!"

"Lettow-Vorbeck?" Swinburne asked.

Wells answered: "A German general, Mr. Swinburne. Apparently he's been trying to burn his way through your jungle to find this place."

"The swine! I felt it, too! Very unpleasant!"

Burton murmured: "I lost my memory in that temple. The shock of your death was part of it, Algy, but there was more. And it ended with me being projected through time."

Swinburne inflated his bladders, fluttered his petals, and said: "I know. You can imagine my surprise when, after having had nothing but Pox and Malady's foul-mouthed descendants for company for decade after decade, I suddenly saw you come stumbling into this clearing! You were ranting and raving like a Bedlam inmate! I tried to speak to you but you legged it through the gorge and out of the mountains like a man with the devil himself at his heels. By the way, what year is this?"

"I arrived in 1914. It's now 1919."

"My hat! Really?"

The flower angled upwards as if regarding the sky.

"One and two are not one; but one and nothing is two;
Truth can hardly be false, if falsehood cannot be true."

It turned back to the two men.

"I find it rather difficult to measure time, these days. I've had such a different sense of it since I—er—took root, so to speak. It's not at all the way I used to think of it. Can you conceive of time as a thing filled with paradoxes and echoes? What a magnificent poem it would make!

"Once the mastodon was; pterodactyls were common as cocks;
Then the mammoth was God; now is He a prize ox.

"Parallels all things are; yet many of these are askew;
You are certainly I; but certainly I am not you.

"Springs the rock from the plain, shoots the stream from the rock;
Cocks exist for the hen; but hens exist for the cock.

"God, whom we see not, is; and God, who is not, we see;

Fiddle, we know, is diddle, and diddle, we take it, is dee."

Swinburne arched his thick stalk and shook with a peal of high-pitched laughter. Leaves drifted down from his higher branches.

Wells leaned close to Burton and whispered: "I'm of the opinion that your friend, the giant plant, is rip-roaringly drunk!"

The explorer seemed not to hear the little war correspondent. "Vertical as well as horizontal qualities," he mumbled to himself. "Who else spoke to me about the nature of time?"

Swinburne loosed a sound that resembled a belch, and directed his petals back at Burton.

"But for all my newfound perception," he said, "upon your appearance, I instantly recognised that you weren't where—or, rather, *when*—you belong; and I certainly didn't relish the thought of you being out there, beyond the mountains, among the savages."

"Actually, there aren't many left," Wells put in. "Most of those that remain are Askaris, now."

Swinburne gave a scornful hiss. "I'm not referring to the Africans, Mr. Wells. I mean the Europeans!"

"Ah. Quite so."

"The barbarities that have been committed on this continent in the name of one ideology or another, this social policy or that; quite dreadful! And I mean to put an end to it. I shall soon have the strength to make the German vegetation—the red weed and the venomous plants—whither and die. Already, I've gained influence over those horrible things the Prussians once employed as vehicles—"

Wells cried out: "Then it was you! You took control of the lurchers! You cleared the route out of Tabora for us!"

"Is that what you call them? Yes, of course it was me. Now I shall use them to rid this land of its armies. My influence is growing, Mr. Wells. My roots will one day reach from coast to coast. And when they do, I shall make a Utopia of Africa!"

"Utopia!" Wells's eyes glistened with hope.

"For as long as this version of history exists, Africa will be an Eden."

The flower bobbed low, until it was level with their faces.

"But," it squeaked, "this history should *not* exist. You have to go back, Richard, and you have to put an end to all such divergences."

Bertie Wells frowned and looked from the vermillion blossom to Burton and back again. "Mr. Swinburne," he said. "Richard has explained the phenomenon of alternate histories to me. Why can they not exist concurrently?"

"Time is a complex thing. It is like music. In addition to its rhythm, there is—"

"A melody," Burton interjected. "Refrains, pitch, timbre and texture. Time has harmonies, volume, accents and pauses. It has verses and—Bismillah! I've heard this before—from—from Herbert Spencer!" He looked confused. "But not Herbert Spencer."

"Good old tin head!" Swinburne exclaimed. "I wonder what became of him?"

Burton pointed to where Swinburne's hollow root blocked the cave mouth. "He's in there!"

"I say! Is he? Was he then involved in your transportation here?"

The explorer struggled for an answer. Something felt very wrong. The clockwork philosopher had been a friend and ally, yet, for reasons he couldn't determine, when he thought of him now, he felt threatened and distrustful. "He was," he said, and immediately felt he'd uttered an untruth.

"Then you must go to him," Swinburne said. "And he must return you to 1863. For, to answer Mr. Wells's question, these alternate histories are proliferating and turning time into a cacophony. Imagine ten orchestras playing different tunes in the same theatre. The musicians would lose their way. Some would play the wrong melody by mistake. Musical expressions would be misplaced and mixed up. There'd be pandemonium. And that is what's happening. If this situation is allowed to continue unchecked, the borders between each version of reality will be breached. Diverse technologies will become horribly intermingled. People's personalities will be bent entirely out of shape. Events will develop in increasingly eccentric directions."

"But how can I reverse the damage?" Burton asked.

"I haven't a clue! I'm just a poet! But you'll find a way."

The king's agent looked at the opening in Swinburne's root. He didn't want to enter the cave; didn't want to see the grotto or the temple; and, especially, he didn't want to see Herbert Spencer.

He noticed a flower-strewn mound. It looked like a grave. The back of his mind seemed to flex, as if to divulge a secret, but the information didn't come—only deep sadness.

He addressed Wells: "Algy is right, Bertie. And that means I have to leave you now. I have to enter the temple."

"I'm coming with you."

"There's no need, and it might be dangerous."

"I've seen this thing through with you from the start. I need to be there at the finish."

Burton considered a moment, then nodded.

"Algy," he said, turning back to the vermillion blossom. "I'm sorry this happened to you."

"Sorry?" the poet responded. "Don't be sorry! This is everything I could have hoped for! My senses are *alive*, Richard! And *what* senses! I've never felt so engaged with life! So intoxicated by it! Finally, I feel the inexpressible poetry of sheer *being*! It's wondrous!"

Burton reached up and placed a hand on the side of the flower. "Then I'm happy for you, my friend."

Swinburne's petals squeezed into a pucker, and the flower slid forward and placed a dewy kiss on the explorer's forehead.

Drawing away, Swinburne said: "Off you go."

Burton reached up to his vehicle's saddle and lifted down his rifle. Seeing this, Wells stepped back to his harvestman and did the same. They walked together across the glade to the opening in the plant's root.

The king's agent looked back. The huge red flower had risen up, back into the sunbeam. Its petals were open. A trio of butterflies danced around it. He smiled and moved into the hollow limb.

Swinburne whispered:

"A wider soul than the world was wide,
Whose praise made love of him one with pride,
What part has death or has time in him,
Who rode life's lists as a god might ride?"

§

Sir Richard Francis Burton and Herbert George Wells walked through the hollow root and down into the grotto. They stepped out of an opening in the limb, crossed the chamber, and wriggled through the narrow tube in its wall to the shelf overlooking the vast cavern. After following the path down, they were met by the Batembuzi, who shepherded them to the Temple of the Eye.

The war correspondent gazed in disbelief at the monolithic edifice. "By gum" he said. "It dwarfs even the pyramids!"

He glanced nervously at their escorts. "It's funny, though; I always imagined that it'd be the workers who ended up as troglodytes, rather than the priests."

"Historically, priests have probably lived underground more often than any other segment of the world's population," Burton commented.

Wells gave a dismissive grunt. "The power of faith over rationality."

"I used to think they were the opposite ends of a spectrum," Burton answered. "Now I'm not so certain."

"Surely you're not resurrecting God, Richard?"

"No. But perhaps I'm resurrecting myself."

"Ah. Faith in oneself. When confronting the unknown, perhaps that's the only thing one can truly hope for."

"I certainly have nothing else."

"You have my friendship."

Burton looked at Wells, reached out, and patted his shoulder.

"Yes. I do."

They trudged along the central thoroughfare, reached the steps to the temple entrance, climbed them, and passed through the tall double doors. The Batembuzi ushered them to the foot of the staircase then slunk away and were absorbed into the shadows.

"Are they even men?" Wells asked.

"I have no idea, but, according to legend, the Nāga managed to breech the natural divide between species to produce half-human offspring."

They ascended to the hall, walked between its statues, and stopped at the gold panelled doors.

Burton gripped a handle and said: "The last of my lost memories are in here, Bertie. Do you really want to face them with me?"

"Most assuredly!"

The king's agent swung the door open and they entered the chamber beyond.

He recognised it instantly. Everything was as it had been fifty-six years ago, except: "The Eye has gone!" Burton pointed to the empty bracket at the tip of the upside-down pyramid.

"That's the guarantee that you'll return to 1863," Wells replied. "For obviously you removed the diamond and took it to London."

Burton added: "Where it was recovered by the Germans after the destruction of the city. I go back knowing that will happen, so why do I allow it?"

"You'll find out! I say! This must be your Mr. Spencer!" He pointed to the floor.

The clockwork man was lying beside the altar. His brass body was battered, scratched and discoloured, its left leg bent out of shape and footless. What passed for his face was disfigured by a big indentation on the left side. The speaking apparatus had been removed from his head and was sitting on the nearby block, among the various instruments.

Burton pointed out the exposed babbage to Wells.

"Do you see the seven apertures? They're where the Cambodian diamonds were fitted. They contained Spencer's mind and—and—"

"What is it, Richard?" Wells asked, noticing his friend's pained expression.

"K'k'thyima! I was wrong, Bertie; it wasn't ever Spencer! It was a Nāga priest named K'k'thyima. He used the power of the diamonds to send me into the future—but I don't understand; the diamonds are gone, so how can I return?"

Wells pointed to something on the altar.

"Perhaps that holds the answer."

Burton looked and recognised the key that wound the clockwork man. He picked it up.

"Help me turn this thing onto its stomach," he said, squatting beside the brass machine.

Wells did so, then watched as Burton inserted the key into a slot in the device's back and twisted it through a number of revolutions.

The two men stood back.

A ticking came from the figure on the floor. A click and a whir and a jerk of the footless leg, then it rolled over, sat up, and struggled upright. It looked at Sir Richard Francis Burton, saluted, and pointed at the altar.

A tremor ran through Burton's body. "Of course. I have black diamond dust tattooed into my scalp. It must be connected through time to the Eye in '63."

He hesitated. "I'm torn, Bertie. My instincts object, but have I any other choice but to go through with this?"

"All the evidence tells us that you did, and therefore will. Hmm. I wonder. Does Fate eliminate paradox? Could Fate be a function of the human organism?"

Burton climbed onto the altar and lay down. He rested his sniper rifle between his body and left arm. "If it is, then perhaps these multiple histories are disrupting it, making us prone to paradox after paradox."

"Then you know what you have to do, Richard."

"What?"

"You have to seal your own fate."

Wells stood back as the clockwork man circled the altar, closing the manacles around Burton's wrists and ankles.

The explorer began: "Whatever the case, I—" then stopped with a strangled gasp as, without warning, the last missing fragment of memory returned to him.

"Oh no!" he hissed. "No no no!" He looked at Wells and bellowed: "Get the hell out of here, Bertie! Run! Run!"

"What—?"

"Run for your life! Get out!" Burton screamed, his voice near hysterical.

The clockwork man suddenly lunged at the war correspondent, grabbed his head with both hands, and twisted it violently. Bone cracked. Wells slumped to the floor.

"No!" Burton howled.

A bright flash.

§

The blinding light lingered in John Speke's one functional eye.

The gunshot left bells clanging in his ears.

The noise was gradually superseded by the sound of a man howling in pain and distress.

William Trounce fell against him and thudded onto the floor.

Speke blinked rapidly.

Vision returned.

Burton was on the altar. His head was thrown back and he was screaming hysterically. He'd undergone a shocking transformation. Where, seconds ago, his head had been shaved, tattooed, and smeared with blood, now it was covered by long snowy white hair. Where his face had been gaunt and savage and strong, now it was frail and lined and brutalised, as if the explorer had aged, and suffered intolerably.

His clothes were different. He was terribly emaciated. There was a rifle beside him.

K'k'thyima stepped back and placed the revolver on the block with the various instruments.

"Most satisfactory," he said. "A sacrifice was made and our intrepid traveller has returned. Mr. Speke, would you calm him down, please."

Speke breathed a shuddery exhalation and stepped to the altar. He took Burton by the shoulders and shook him slightly.

"Dick! Dick! It's all right, man! It's all right! Stop!"

Burton's eyes were wild. His lips were drawn back over his teeth. His screams gave way to words: "Bertie! Get out! Get out!"

"It's me, Dick! It's John! John Speke!"

"Get out. Get out. Get out."

Speke slapped him hard.

"Dick! Look at me! It's John!"

Burton's eyes fixed on him, focused, and sanity gradually bled back into them.

"Is it you, John?" he croaked. "John Speke?"

"Yes, it's me. We're in the Nāga temple. Do you remember?"

"I remember death. So much death."

Tears flowed freely and a sob shook the king's agent. "I have lost my mind. I can't take any more of it. Algy was—was—then William, and Bertie!" Burton looked over to K'k'thyima and suddenly screamed: "Get me out of these shackles you damned murdering lizard!"

"Welcome back, Sir Richard," the Nāga priest said. He limped to the explorer's side and clicked open the manacles on Burton's left wrist and ankle, then moved around the altar, leaned past Speke, and liberated the other two limbs.

Burton sat, swung around, pushed himself to his feet, and sent a vicious right hook clanging into the side of the brass man's head. He stifled a groan as pain lanced through his hand, but was satisfied to see that he'd just created the big dent he'd noticed in the clockwork man's face in 1919.

"You bastard!" he hissed. "I'm going to tear you apart!"

"I wouldn't recommend it, soft skin. Don't forget where you are. This is 1863. You need me to remain here, in this room and in one piece, for fifty-six years, else how can I return you from 1919?"

"You damned well know it doesn't work like that! I'm here, now, and I won't disappear if I rip your bloody cogs out!"

"Perhaps not, but even if you had the strength to overpower me—which I assure you, you don't—do you really want to create yet another history; one that denies a path home to that alternate you, condemning him to exile in Africa of 1919?"

Burton swayed. Speke, looking bemused, steadied him. "What happened to you, Dick? You didn't go anywhere but your appearance is—is—"

Burton looked down at William Trounce's body. His face twisted into an expression of fury, then of utter despair.

"I have been five years in the future, John," he said. "And now I must prevent that future from occurring." He turned back to K'k'thyima. "How?"

The high priest shuffled back to the other side of the altar. He reached up and began to work the Eye out of its housing.

"That's the question, isn't? How will you ever know whether what you're doing is, from the perspective of the time you just visited, any different from what you did?"

The black diamond came loose. K'k'thyima stepped back and held it up.

"You are on your own, Sir Richard. The Nāga are finally departing this world. We leave you to sing the final verse of our song."

The phosphorescence around the walls suddenly dimmed, its blue light seemed to concentrate around the diamond, and small crackles and snaps sounded, increasing in volume. Bolts of energy started to sizzle over the stone's many facets, then flared out, dancing across its surface and down K'k'thyima's arm. The Eye hummed, the sound rapidly deepening, causing

Burton and Speke's ears to pop before it passed below the range of human hearing.

Tiny fractures zigzagged across the Eye, and as each appeared, with a faint *tink!*, a small entity was expelled. To Speke's astonishment, they appeared to be tiny people with the wings of butterflies and dragonflies—fairies!—but Burton knew it was an illusion; that they appeared this way because the human mind wasn't able to process the things' true appearance, and so replaced it with a marvel from mythology. To him, the ejected forms were sparks of reptilian consciousness, sensed rather than seen. He'd witnessed the same dance around the South American stone when it had shattered.

The energy built to a storm-like frenzy, banging and clapping and sending out streaks of blue lightning that sputtered up the walls and across the floor and ceiling.

Speke cried out in fear: "What's happening, Dick?"

The king's agent yelled: "He's breaking the stone!"

Moments later, with a loud detonation, the enormous black diamond cracked and fell apart, dropping out of the brass man's hand and falling to the floor in seven equally sized pieces.

The room became still.

The bolts of energy vanished.

The smell of ozone hung in the air.

K'k'thyima bent and retrieved the stones.

"Equivalence! Though one or two or even all of the Eyes remain whole in some versions of history, in this one they are all divided into seven, thus, across all the realities, the Nāga can now transcend or die." He directed his misshapen face at Burton. "Our gratitude, Sir Richard. The Nāga thank you for the role you've played in our release."

"Oh just bugger off, why don't you?" the king's agent growled. He suddenly staggered, made a grab at Speke, missed, and fell to the floor, where he sat with his eyes open but glazed. Speke squatted beside him and felt his forehead.

"Feverish," he muttered. "And exhausted beyond endurance, by the looks of it."

"I don't know what to do," Burton mumbled. "How do I seal my own fate, Bertie?"

"Who's this Bertie he keeps mentioning?" Speke asked K'k'thyima.

"I don't know, Mr. Speke. Let's get him up." The brass man bent and hooked a metal hand through Burton's arm. Speke took the cue and supported the explorer on the other side. They pulled him upright and sat him on the altar.

"You had better be off, gentlemen," K'k'thyima said. "Our work here is done, at least for the next fifty-six years."

He opened Burton's shirt pocket and slipped the seven pieces of the African Eye into it. "You need to unscrew my speaking apparatus to expose the babbage. Remove the seven Cambodian stones and take them with you back to London. Leave my winding key on the altar, please. The babbage will have one function left to perform, which it'll fulfil in 1919, as you have seen."

"Damn you to hell," Burton whispered.

"On the contrary, I have chosen to transcend. Goodbye, Sir Richard Francis Burton."

K'k'thyima became silent.

For a few moments, the king's agent sat and did nothing, while Speke watched and fidgeted nervously; then the explorer stood and detached the clockwork man's speaking device. He pulled seven black diamonds out of the exposed babbage and put them into his pocket.

The brass device walked to the other side of the altar, saluted, and stopped moving.

Burton picked up his rifle and said to Speke: "Help me carry William outside. I want to bury him in the open.

$\mathcal{S}$

It was night when they emerged into the cliff-ringed arena. To Burton, it seemed strangely empty. He remembered where he'd seen flowers growing on a mound and lay Trounce there, piling rocks onto him by the starlight.

Chwezi warriors stepped out of the shadows. Silently, they escorted the two men through the gorges on either side of the mountain, leading them each by the arm in utter darkness.

When they reached the spot where Sidi Bombay had fallen, Burton found his friend's corpse undisturbed, and a second burial mound was built before they continued on.

The king's agent, asleep on his feet, lost all awareness of the environment and his own actions until, suddenly, they emerged from the Mountains of the Moon and found the Wanyambo sitting around a small crackling fire. The warriors stared in superstitious dread at the Chwezi and backed away. The mountain tribe broke its silence. Words of reassurance were spoken. An oath was sworn. Obedience was demanded. Agreement was reached. The groups banded together— thirty men in all—and continued on eastwards towards the Ukerewe lake.

It was mid-morning by the time they reached the first village. Its inhabitants, fearing the Chwezi, immediately offered shelter and sustenance. Burton, not knowing what he was doing, crawled into a beehive hut and slept.

When he awoke, he was being born along on a litter with Speke walking at his side. The lieutenant looked down and said: "You've been in a fever for three days. How are you feeling?"

"Weak. Thirsty. Hungry. Where's my rifle?"

"One of the Africans is carrying it."

"Get it. Don't take it from me again."

Another day. Another village. They stopped. They ate and drank.

Later, the king's agent sat with Speke in the settlement's *bandani* and watched the sun oozing into the horizon.

"Where are we, John?"

"I'm not certain. About a day's march from the northwestern shore of the lake, I hope. I didn't know what to do. Without this damned thing to help me—" he tapped the babbage embedded in the left side of his skull "—I find it almost impossible to make decisions, so I'm following what it had originally intended me to do upon gaining the diamond, which is to circumnavigate the water to its northernmost point, then march northwards. I think the Chwezi understood my intentions, though I've only been able to communicate through sign language."

Burton checked his pockets. The fourteen stones were still there.

"It seems as good a plan as any," he said. "As long as the Chwezi remain with us, the locals will supply what we need and we'll avoid demands for *hongo*."

Speke nodded and glanced at the other man. There was a disturbing lifelessness to Burton's voice, as if a large part of him had simply switched off.

The next afternoon, after mindlessly slogging over hill after hill, they caught sight of the great lake, stretching all the way to the horizon.

In a voice still devoid of emotion, Burton said: "I apologise, John. Had I seen this with my own eyes during our initial expedition, I would never have doubted your claims."

"It was my fault you didn't see it," Speke answered. "I became obsessed with the idea that my name alone should be forever associated with the solving of the Nile problem."

"The diamond influenced your judgement as soon as we were within range of it."

"Perhaps. Do you think we'll make it home?"

Burton looked down at himself. His tick-infested 1919 army fatigues were torn and rotting. His boots were cracked.

"I have reason to believe we will."

"And what then?"

Burton shook his head and shrugged.

Just before sunrise, they set out again. For a short time, Burton walked, then his legs gave way, and he collapsed onto the litter. He drifted in and out of consciousness. Fever raged through him like a forest fire.

Sometimes he opened his eyes and there was blue sky; other times, the Milky Way. On one occasion, he rolled his head to the right and saw a mirror-smooth expanse of water covered by thousands of pelicans.

For a long time, he saw nothing.

A hand shook his shoulder.

"Isabel," he muttered.

"Dick! Wake up! Wake up!"

He opened his eyes and looked upon John Speke's lined, heavily bearded features, and his own reflected in the other's black, brass-ringed left eye lens. He pushed himself up, and found that a little strength had returned to him.

"What is it?"

"Listen!"

Burton looked around. They were on a slope. It concealed the landscape ahead and to the right, but on the left jungled hills rolled away before climbing to far away mountains.

In front, from beyond the crest of the incline, mist was clouding into the sky.

A constant roar filled his ears.

"That sounds like—"

"Falling water!" Speke enthused. "Can you walk?"

"Yes."

The lieutenant took Burton's arm and helped him to his feet. With a gesture to the Chwezi and Wanyambo warriors, he indicated that they should stay put.

The two Britishers walked slowly towards the summit, Burton leaning heavily on his companion. The sun burned their faces. Mosquitos darted around them. The air was heavy and humid.

They reached the top.

Below them, the earth was cut by a wide and deep rift into which, from the edge of the Ukerewe, a great mass of water hurtled. Thundering beneath billowing vapour, it crashed and splashed and frothed over rounded rocks, and cascaded through the arch of a permanent rainbow. Fish leaped from it, flashing in the sunlight, and birds darted in and out of the rolling cloud.

There could be no doubt.

It was the source of the River Nile.

Burton thought: *Here it begins. Here it ends. Not the source, but just another part of a circle.*

They stood silently for a long while, deafened by the sound of the falling water, then Speke roused himself, leaned close to Burton, put his mouth to the explorer's ear, and shouted: "We've done it, Dick! We've discovered it at last!" He clutched his companion's elbow. "And we did it together!"

Burton tore himself away, and Speke took a step back, shocked by the ferocious expression on the other man's face.

"You can have it! I want nothing more to do with it! It's yours, Speke! The whole damned thing is yours!"

$\mathcal{S}$

Over the next few days, they followed the river north, struggled through an extensive quagmire, pushed through thickets of water hyacinth, and found themselves on the shore of a second lake, smaller and much shallower than the Ukerewe. It was completely covered in water lilies and smelled of rotting vegetation.

"What shall we name it?" Speke asked.

"Why name it at all?" Burton growled. "It is what it is. A bloody lake."

The lieutenant shook his head despairingly and walked away. He couldn't understand the other's mood at all. Burton had hardly spoken since their discovery of the falls. He wasn't even bothering to acquire the Chwezi language, which was entirely out of character, for in Speke's experience, Burton was driven by a mania to conquer every foreign tongue he encountered.

The Wanyambo warriors, now far from home and unwilling to go any farther, left them.

Over the next three days, the Chwezi guided the two Britishers around the southern shores of the lake to where, at its western tip, the river flowed out of it.

They followed the waterway. The land was boggy and swarming with snakes. Foul smelling gasses bubbled out of the ground.

The sun rose and set and rose and set, and they lost count of the days. Mosquitoes bit every inch of their exposed skin. Their clothes fell to pieces and had to be replaced with cotton robes, donated by villagers. They wound rough cloth around their now bootless feet and walked with staffs, looking like a couple of heavily bearded skeletons, burned almost black, too exhausted to communicate, or even to think.

One of their guides, who'd been scouting ahead, returned and spoke quietly to his colleagues. He approached Burton and Speke and jabbed his finger first at one, then at the other, then towards a ridge that lay just to the south of the river, a couple of miles to the west.

He rejoined the other Chwezi and, as a man, they disappeared into the undergrowth.

Suddenly, the Britishers were alone.

"Well then," Speke said, shading his one functioning eye and peering at the nearby high land. "I suppose we're meant to go up there."

They set off through sucking mud and shouldered past stiff bullrushes, until the terrain sloped upward, became firmer underfoot, and they climbed to the top of the ridge. On the other side of it, the Nile flowed into another vast lake, and on the near shore, just half a mile away, an air vessel was hovering about forty feet from the ground. It was a gargantuan cigar-shaped balloon, with a long cabin affixed beneath it and pylons, with rotor wings at their ends, extending out horizontally from its sides. The ship, which must have been close to a thousand feet in length, was painted with a Union Jack and bore on its side the name HMA *Dauntless*.

A large camp of rowtie tents lay in the shadow of the vessel.

Burton suddenly spoke: "John, I have to make a request of you."

"What is it?"

"Tell them nothing. Not now, and not when we return to London. Don't let on anything of what we've experienced here. The future may depend on it."

"Dick, I—"

"I need your word on it."

"Very well. You have it."

Burton took Speke's hand and shook it.

They stumbled down toward the camp and had crossed half the distance when they were spotted. A shout went up, men started running towards them, came close, and gathered around. One of them stepped forward.

"By James!" he exclaimed. "Is that you, Sir Richard?"

Burton's vision was swimming. The man in front of him blurred in and out of focus. Slowly, recognition dawned.

"Hello," the king's agent whispered. "I'm very happy to see that you've recovered from your injuries, Captain Lawless."

Everything toppled over and darkness rushed in.

CHAPTER 13

The Source

"We are each our own devil, and we make this world our hell."
—Oscar Wilde

While Sir Richard Francis Burton was in Africa, electricity came to London. Now, in early 1864, thick cables were clinging to the walls of the city's buildings, looping and drooping over its streets, dripping in the fog, and quietly sizzling as they conveyed energy from Battersea Power Station across the nation's capital.

Street lamps blazed. House and office windows blazed. Shop fronts blazed. The permanent murk effortlessly swallowed the light and reduced it to smudged globes, which hung in the impenetrable atmosphere like exotic fruits.

In the gloomy gullies between, pedestrians struggled through an unyielding tangle of almost immobile vehicles. The legs of steam-driven insects were caught in the spokes of wheels, panicky horses were jammed against chugging machinery, crankshafts were hammering against wood and metal and flesh.

Animalistic howls and screams and curses sounded from amid the mess.

And to this, Burton had returned aboard His Majesty's Airship *Dauntless*.

The vessel was the first of her type, the result of Isambard Kingdom Brunel's solving of the gas-filled dirigible problem. Design faults had been corrected and unstable flammable gasses replaced. The *Dauntless* was a triumph.

A slow but long-range vessel, she was propelled by electric engines, which, lacking springs, should have been impervious to the deleterious influence that had so far prevented any machine from piercing Africa's heart.

Unfortunately, this had proved not to be the case.

Following the Nile upstream, the ship had reached the northern outskirts of the Lake Regions. Her engines had then failed. However, the wind was behind her, so Captain Lawless allowed the vessel to be borne along, powerless, until the air current changed direction, at which point he'd ordered her landing on the shore of a great lake.

The crew set up camp.

There were two passengers on board: John Petherick and Samuel Baker, both experienced explorers from the Royal Geographical Society. They prepared an expedition, intending to head south to search for Burton. The day prior to their planned departure, he and Speke had come stumbling into the camp.

Lawless and his engineers had taken it for granted that the engines were still dysfunctional. Burton, though, knew that the Nāga were no longer present in the black diamonds, so their influence should have vanished.

He was correct. The engines functioned perfectly. The *Dauntless* flew home and landed at an airfield some miles to the south east of London. Damien Burke and Gregory Hare, Palmerston's odd-job men, were there to greet it. They took possession of the fourteen black diamonds—the seven fragments of the Cambodian Eye and the seven of the African.

"All the Nāga stones are in British hands now, Captain Burton," Burke said. "You've done excellent work for the Empire, isn't that so, Mr. Hare?"

"It most certainly is, Mr. Burke!" Hare agreed.

John Speke was taken into custody.

"He's a traitor," Burke observed. "The irony of it is that he'll no doubt be incarcerated in our chambers beneath the Tower of London, which is where the Eyes will go, too. One of the most disreputable men in the country held in the same place as what might well be our most precious resource. Such is the way of things."

Burton was taken to Penfold Private Sanatorium in London's St. John's Wood, where, for three weeks, the Sisterhood of Noble Benevolence fussed over him.

As his strength increased, so, too, did his anxiety. He had a terrible decision to make. By telling Palmerston about the future, and revealing to him his fate, he might persuade him to abandon plans to use the Eyes of Nāga as a means for mediumistic espionage against Prussia; might convince him that sending troops to Africa would lead to disaster. But if he succeeded in this, it would mean no reinforcements for the Daughters of Al-Manat. Bertie Wells had told him that the female guerrilla fighters survived at least into the 1870s. In changing history, Burton would almost certainly condemn Isabel Arundell, Isabella Mayson and Sadhvi Raghavendra to much earlier deaths.

Obviously, the future he'd visited had occurred because he'd favoured Al-Manat's survival over the 130-year-old Palmerston's direct order. As much as he loved Isabel, he had no idea why he might have done such a thing, for, in anyone's estimation, could three lives—even *those* three—be worth the savagery and destruction of the Great War?

He wrote much about this in his personal journal, examining the problem from every angle he could think of, but though he produced pages and pages of cramped handwriting, he could find no answer.

The solution finally came with a visit from Palmerston himself.

Two weeks into his treatment, Burton was sitting up in bed reading a newspaper when the door opened and the prime minister stepped in, announcing: "I'd have come earlier. You know how it is. Affairs of state. Complex times, Captain Burton. Complex times."

He took off his hat and overcoat—revealing a Mandarin-collared black suit and pale blue cravat—and placed them on a chair. He didn't remove his calfskin gloves.

Standing at the end of the patient's bed, he said: "You look bloody awful. Your hair is white!"

The king's agent didn't reply. He gazed dispassionately at his visitor's face.

Palmerston's most recent treatments had made his nose almost entirely flat. The nostrils were horizontal slits, as wide as the gash-like mouth beneath. A dimple had been added to the centre of his chin. His eyebrows were painted on, high above the oriental-looking eyes.

"You'll be pleased to hear, Captain, that not only do I fully endorse your recommendations, but I have acted upon them even in the face of virulent opposition led by no less than Disraeli himself," he announced.

Burton looked puzzled. "My recommendations, Prime Minister?"

"Yes. Your reports confirmed my every suspicion concerning Bismarck's intentions. Obviously, we cannot allow him to gain a foothold in East Africa. So British troops have already been conveyed there by rotorship, and I have more on the way. It's by no means a declaration of war on my part, but I do intend that they offer resistance to any efforts made by Prussia to claim territories."

Burton's fingers dug into the bedsheets beneath him. "My—my reports?" he whispered hoarsely.

"As delivered to us by Commander Krishnamurthy. A very courageous young man, Burton. He will be given due honours, of that you can be certain. And I look forward to receiving the remainder of your observations—those made between Kazeh and the Mountains of the Moon. Do you have them here?"

"N-no," Burton stammered. "I'll—I'll see that they're delivered to you." He thought: *Bismillah! Krishnamurthy!*

"Post-haste, please, Captain."

Burton struggled for words. "I— I wrote those reports before I had—before I had properly assessed the situation, Prime Minister. You have to—to withdraw our forces at once. Their presence in Africa will escalate hostilities between the British Empire and Prussia to an unprecedented degree."

"What? Surely you don't expect me to allow Bismarck free rein?"

"You have to, sir."

"Have to? Why?"

"Your actions will—will precipitate the Great War; the one that Countess Sabina has predicted."

Palmerston shook his head. "The Countess is working with us to prevent exactly that. She and a team of mediums have already employed the Nāga diamonds to great effect." He pointed at Burton's newspaper. "No doubt you've read that a second Schleswig conflict has broken out between Prussia, Austria and Denmark. We precipitated that, my dear fellow, by means of undetected mediumistic manipulations. I intend to tangle Bismarck up in so many minor difficulties that he'll never have the strength to challenge us in Africa, let alone establish his united Germany!"

Burton squeezed his eyes shut and raised his hands to his head in frustration. It was too late. The circumstances that would lead to all-out war had already been set into motion!

He thought rapidly. Now he understood the 130-year-old Palmerston's claim that he—Burton—had never revealed his visit to the future. The king's agent knew the way the prime minister's mind worked. Having already outmanoeuvred Benjamin Disraeli—a formidable political force—and got his way, Palmerston wouldn't under any circumstances backtrack, not even on his own advice! So what would he do instead? The answer was obvious: the prime minister would attempt to outguess his future self by ordering a preemptive strike; he'd throw every resource he could muster into defeating Bismarck before Prussia could properly mobilise its military might; and in doing that, in Burton's opinion, he was much more likely to incite the war at an earlier date than to prevent it.

Burton felt ensnared by inevitability.

"What's the matter?" Palmerston asked. "Should I call a nurse?"

The explorer took his hands from his head, feeling the ridges of his tattoo sliding beneath his fingertips.

"No, Prime Minister. I have a headache, that's all."

"Then I won't disturb you any further, Captain." Palmerston picked up his coat, shrugged it back on, took up his top hat, and said: "We've blown hot and cold, you and I, but I want you to know that I have renewed faith in you. You've done a splendid job. Absolutely splendid! Thanks to your actions, the Empire is secured."

He turned and departed.

Burton sat and stared into space.

A week later he was released from hospital and returned to his home at 14 Montagu Place.

Mrs. Angell, his housekeeper, was horrified at his appearance. He looked, she said, as if he'd just been dug out of an Egyptian tomb.

"You'll eat, Sir Richard!" she pronounced, and embarked on a culinary mission to restore his health. She also cleaned around him obsessively, as if the slightest speck of dust might cause his final ruination.

He put up with it stoically, too weak to resist, though there was one item he wouldn't allow her—or the maid, Elsie Carpenter—to touch, let alone dust: the rifle that leaned against the fireplace by his saddlebag armchair.

It was an anomaly, that weapon, and the image of it arose again and again in his Sufi meditations, though he couldn't fathom why.

A few days after his homecoming, a parakeet arrived at his study window. "Message from thick-witted Richard Monckton Milnes, otherwise know as Baron hairy-palmed Houghton. Message begins. I will call at three o'clock, bum slapper. Message ends."

The new 1st Baron Houghton arrived on time and found Burton wrapped in his *jubbah* and slumped in his armchair beside the fireplace, with a cheroot in his mouth, a glass of port in his hand, and Fidget the basset hound stretched out at his feet. Whatever greeting Monckton Milnes had planned died on his lips at the sight of the explorer. He stood in the doorway of the study, his mouth hanging open.

Burton removed his Manila, set down his glass, and gave a half grin. "What you see is the much-recovered model," he said, rising to his feet. He crossed to his friend and shook his hand. "You should have seen the state of me before! Hang up your coat, old man, and take a seat. Congratulations on your peerage. Would you prefer me to bow or pour you a drink?"

"Hell's bells, Richard! You look twenty years older!"

"I'm five years older. No, six, counting the year since you last saw me, the rest is down to the vicissitudes of Africa."

His visitor sat down and accepted a glass of port.

"By heavens, it's good to see you again. But five years? What are you talking about?"

"It will require a suspension of disbelief on your part."

"A little over a year ago you told me that Spring Heeled Jack was a man from the future and that history had been changed. Is what you have to tell me more incredible even that that?"

"As a matter of fact, yes, it is."

"Ouch! Very well, fire away. You talk and I'll drink."

Over the course of the next two hours, Burton told his friend everything that had happened in Africa, and he withheld nothing.

A long silence followed, as Monckton Milnes digested the tale, along with the copious amount of port he'd gulped.

Burton showed him the rifle and pointed out the inscription on its stock: *Lee-Enfield Mk III. Manufactured in Tabora, Africa, 1919.*

"You have to change history," his guest said softly.

"That's the problem," Burton replied. "To do so I have to outmanoeuvre myself, as well as Palmerston."

"And if you succeed," Monckton Milnes interjected, "if you create yet another branch of history, you'll just be adding to the chaos poor Algernon warned of."

Burton sucked at his cigar. "Not so much *poor* Algernon. He seemed very content with his new form. But, yes, you're correct. He told me to put an end to all the divergences, despite that doing so would wipe out the history in which he currently resides. How, though, am I to do that?"

He looked down at the rifle that lay across his legs. "How am I to do that?"

Quite without warning or obvious reason, the last words Burton had ever heard Detective Inspector Honesty speak leaped into his mind with such clarity they might have been muttered into his ear: *"Needs pruning, hard against the stem."*

§

Monckton Milnes, as Burton had requested, had spent the past year surreptitiously monitoring the prime minister. He reported that Palmerston had secretly quadrupled military spending, had reshuffled his cabinet so that it contained the most martial of his party's ministers, and was steadfastly refusing to make a decision regarding British America's slave population.

Burton thanked his friend, bid him goodbye, and spent the rest of the afternoon meditating.

That evening, he met Maneesh Krishnamurthy for dinner at the Athenaeum Club on Pall Mall. They grabbed each other by the elbows and shared a wordless greeting. Both grinned stupidly, both looked into the other's eyes, and both saw pain and loss.

They settled in the lounge and shared a bottle of wine.

"I've started on these foul tasting things," the police commander said, opening a platinum cigarette case and pulling forth one of the little tubes of Latakia tobacco. "Much worse than my old pipe, but I had to trade the damned thing to get out of a jam at Madege Madogo and I haven't the heart to replace it. It was a gift from my cousin, bless him."

"I miss him," Burton murmured. "I miss them all."

He raised his glass in a silent toast. Krishnamurthy followed suit. They drained them in a single swallow and poured over-generous refills.

"Sir Richard, I know I look like I've been starved, beaten and dragged backwards through a thorn bush, but if you don't mind me saying so, you look considerably worse. What in blue blazes happened to you?"

"Time, Maneesh. Time happened to me."

For the second time that day—and only the second time since he'd got back—Burton gave an account of what had occurred after he and Krishnamurthy parted company outside Kazeh.

"By James, it's unbelievable, Sir Richard, but looking at what's happening in the world today, I can easily see how it might develop into the hellish conflict you describe."

"Unfortunately not *might*, but *will*."

They drank more. Too much. Krishnamurthy described his journey from Kazeh back to Zanzibar. Burton's head began to swim.

A concierge approached. "Excuse me, sir," he said. "A message for you. It arrived by runner."

Burton took the proffered note. He looked at Krishnamurthy. "This will be from Palmerston."

"How can you tell?"

"Because the only way a runner would know I'm here is if it was sent by someone who's having me watched."

He opened the note and read:

This morning, a military court found Lieutenant John Hanning Speke guilty of treason. He will be executed by firing squad at dawn on Friday. His final request is to see you. This has been permitted. Please attend with due dispatch. Burke and Hare will escort.

Henry John Temple, 3rd Viscount Palmerston

Burton cursed and passed the note to his friend.

Krishnamurthy read it and said: "Because he aided the Prussians?"

"Yes. But he was never acting under his own volition. From the very inception of this whole affair, Speke has been manipulated and taken advantage of."

"Will you go?"

"Yes."

The two men continued drinking until past midnight, then bid each other farewell and made off—somewhat unsteadily—towards their respective homes.

On the city's main highways, electric lighting saturated the fog and made it glow a dirty orange. Black flakes drifted down and settled on Burton's shoulders and top hat. He wound a scarf around his face and, leaning heavily on his sword cane, walked a little way along Pall Mall then turned left onto Regent Street. Despite the late hour, the traffic hadn't cleared and the pavements were still crowded with bad tempered pedestrians, so he turned right and took to the backstreets, which, though dark and filthy, at least afforded a quicker passage.

He cursed himself for drinking so much. He wasn't recovered enough to cope with drunkenness; it made him feel ill and weak.

From alley to alley, he walked past huddled shapes and broken windows, lost his bearings, and drifted too far northwards.

He found himself in a network of narrow passages. A raggedly dressed man stepped out of the darkness and brandished a dagger. Burton drew his sword cane and smiled viciously. The man backed away, held up his hands, said, "No 'arm meant, guv'nor!" and ran away.

The explorer pushed on, turned left, stumbled over a discarded crate and kicked it angrily. Two rats emerged from beneath it and scurried away.

He leaned against a lamppost. He was shaking.

"Pull yourself together, you blockhead!" he growled. "Get home!"

He noticed a faded flier pasted to the post and read it:

Work disciplines your spirit
Work develops your character
Work strengthens your soul
Do not allow machines to do your work!

It was old Libertine propaganda. They'd been a force to be reckoned with a couple of years ago, but now the Technologists dominated and the Libertines were ridiculed in the newspapers. What, Burton wondered, would the world be like if the shoe had been on the other foot?

He resumed his journey.

What if Edward Oxford had never jumped back through time? The Libertines and Technologists owed their existence to him—would the world be so different if they'd never existed?

Edward Oxford.

It all went back to him. All the alternate histories had been made possible by his interference.

Burton turned another corner and stopped. He'd entered a long straight lane bordered by high brick walls, and despite the gloom and the fog, he recognised it—for he'd unconsciously drifted to the very spot where he'd had his first encounter with Oxford—with Spring Heeled Jack.

Richard Francis bloody Burton!

Your destiny lies elsewhere!

Do you understand?

Do what you're supposed to do!

The words echoed in his mind, and he said aloud now what he'd said then: "How can I possibly *know* what I'm supposed to do? How can I *know*?"

"What?" came a voice.

Burton turned. A vagrant had shuffled out of the fog.

"Was ye a-talkin' to me, mister?"

"No."

"I thought ye said sumfink."

"I did. I was—I was just thinking aloud."

"Ah, rightio. I do that. They say it's the first sign o' madness, don't they? Can ye spare a copper? I ain't 'ad nuffink to eat, not fer a couple o' days, leastways."

Burton fished in his pocket, pulled out a coin, and flipped it to the man. He turned to go, but paused, and said to the beggar: "How can I possibly know what I'm supposed to do?"

"Heh! Ye just carry on carryin' on, don'tcha mate! Fate'll do the rest!"

Burton sighed, nodded, and walked out of the alley.

S

Needs pruning, hard against the stem.
Do what you're supposed to do!
Lee-Enfield Mk III. Manufactured in Tabora, Africa, 1919.
The source of the Nile!
Edward Oxford.
The source!

Burton sat up, jolted out of his sleep.

Had that been Bertie Wells's voice or Algernon Swinburne's?

He looked at the four corners of his bedroom.

Nobody's voice. A dream.

He sat up, poured a glass of water from the jug on his bedside table, then opened a drawer and took out a small vial. Its label read *Saltzmann's Tincture.* He added three drops of its contents to the water, drank it, and stood up. After washing and wrapping his *jubbah* around himself, the king's agent went downstairs and was served a hearty breakfast by Mrs. Angell. He then went to his dressing room and outfitted himself in shabby workmen's clothing.

It was early on Thursday morning.

Burton caught a hansom to Limehouse. When it became ensnarled in traffic halfway there, he left it and walked the rest of the distance. He made his way along Limehouse Cut until he came to an abandoned factory, climbed one of its chimneys, and dropped three pebbles into its flue. The Beetle responded to the summons. The head of the League of Chimney Sweeps, who'd been safely transported from the Arabian desert back to his home, reported that, on Captain Lawless's recommendation, Willy Cornish had received a government grant to put him through private schooling, while Vincent Sneed had been released from the Cairo prison and was now working as a funnel scrubber at an airfield in south London.

Satisfied, the king's agent left the mysterious boy with a satchel of books and made his way homeward.

It was almost midday by the time he turned the corner of Montagu Place. He saw Mr. Grub, his local street vendor, standing in the fog with a forlorn expression on his face.

"Hallo, Mr. Grub. Where's your barrow?"

"It got knocked over by a bleedin' omnipede, Cap'n," the man replied. "Smashed to smithereens, it was."

"I'm sorry to hear that," Burton replied. "But you have your Dutch oven, still?"

"Nope. It was crushed by one o' them lumbering great mega dray horses."

"But, Mr. Grub, if you can't sell shellfish or hot chestnuts, what the dickens are you standing here for?"

The vendor shrugged helplessly. "It's me patch, Cap'n. Me pa stood on it, an' his pa afore him! It's where I belong, ain't it!"

Burton couldn't think how to reply to that, so he settled for a grunted response and made to move away.

"'Scusin' me askin', Cap'n—"

The explorer stopped and turned back.

"Did you ever find it?"

"Find what, Mr. Grub?"

"The source, sir. The source of the Nile."

"Ah. Yes. As a matter of fact I did."

"Good on you! That's bloomin' marvellous, that is! An' was it worth it?"

Burton swallowed. His heart suddenly hammered in his chest. He blinked the corrosive fog from his eyes.

"No, Mr. Grub. It wasn't worth it at all. Not in the slightest bit."

The vendor nodded, as if with deep understanding.

"Aye," he said. "I have it in mind that the source o' things ain't never what you expect 'em to be."

The king's agent bid him farewell and walked the rest of the short distance home.

Burke and Hare were waiting for him.

"A moment, if you please, gentlemen. I'd like to change into more suitable clothing, if you don't mind."

He left them waiting in the hallway, went upstairs, removed his patched trousers and threadbare jacket, and put on a suit. He was on his way back down when Mrs. Angell came up from the kitchen, all pinafore and indignation.

"You'll not be going out again, Sir Richard!" she protested, with a scowl at Burke and Hare. "You'll leave him be, sirs! He's not a well man! He's infected with Africa!"

Damien Burke bowed and said: "I assure you, ma'am, I have nothing but the good captain's wellbeing in mind, isn't that so, Mr. Hare?"

"It is absolutely the case, Mr. Burke. Ma'am, were it not the last request of a condemned man, we wouldn't dream of imposing on Captain Burton."

"It's all right, Mrs. Angell," Burton interrupted. "The restorative quality of your incomparable cooking has put new life into me. I'm fit as can be."

"What condemned man?" the housekeeper asked.

"Lieutenant John Speke," Burke answered.

"Oh," the old dame replied. "Him."

She threw up her chin disapprovingly and stamped back to the kitchen.

"She blames Speke for all my ills," Burton remarked as he put on his overcoat. He lifted his topper from its hook and suddenly remembered that more than a year ago—or, from his point of view, more than six—a bullet had been fired through it. He examined it closely and saw no sign of the two holes. In his absence, Mrs. Angell had obviously paid for its repair.

He smiled, pushed the hat onto his head, and took his silver handled sword cane from the elephant's foot holder by the door.

"Let's go."

Nearly two hours later, they arrived at the Tower of London after a difficult journey in a horse drawn growler.

"It would have been quicker to walk," the king's agent noted.

"Yes, Captain, my apologies," Burke replied. "The new underground railway system will solve many of the capital's ills, I hope, but I fear its opening is still some way off."

"Has Mr. Brunel encountered problems?"

"No sir, he's still drilling the tunnels. It's a project of immense proportions. These things take time, isn't that so, Mr. Hare?"

"It certainly is, Mr. Burke," Hare agreed.

They disembarked at the end of Tower Street and walked around the outer walls to the river-facing Bloody Tower Gate. The stench from the Thames was almost too much for Burton, and he snatched gratefully at the perfumed handkerchief proffered by Hare, pressing it to his nostrils. Palmerston's men seemed unaffected by the foul odour.

After a few whispered words with the Beefeater guards, the two odd-job men ushered the king's agent through the gate, across a courtyard, and into the Great Keep. They entered St. John's Chapel, and Hare opened a door in one of its more shadowy corners, indicating to Burton that he should descend the stairs beyond. The explorer did so.

Oil lamps lit the stone staircase, which went down much farther than he expected.

"You understand, Sir Richard, that the area we're about to enter is not generally known to exist and must remain a secret?" Damien Burke said.

"You can count on my discretion."

The stairs eventually ended at a heavy metal portal. Hare produced a key and unlocked it, and the three men stepped through into a wide hallway with doors along its sides. As they walked along, Burton observed small signs: *Conference Rooms 1 & 2; Offices A-F; Offices G-L; Administration Rooms; Laboratories 1-5; Clairvoyance Rooms 1-4; Vault; Weapon Shop; Monitoring Station; Canteen; Dormitories.*

At the end of the passage, they unlocked and entered through a door marked *Security.* The chamber beyond was rectangular and contained filing cabinets and a desk. There were six sturdy metal doors, each numbered.

A man at the desk rose and said: "Number four, gentlemen?"

Burke nodded. He turned to Burton. "You have thirty minutes, Captain. Mr. Hare and I will wait here."

"Very well."

Cell 4 was opened and Burton stepped into it. The door shut behind him. He heard a key turn in its lock.

The chamber looked more like a sitting room than a prison. There were shelves of books, a desk, a bureau, a settee and armchairs, ornaments on the mantelpiece, and pictures on the wall. A door stood open to Burton's right, and John Speke stepped out from what was evidently a bedchamber.

The lieutenant was barefoot, wearing trousers and a white cotton shirt, wrinkled and untucked.

"Dick!" he exclaimed. "I'm sorry old fellow, I had no idea it was that time already!"

"Hallo John. How are you feeling?"

"As healthy as a condemned man can expect." Speke waved towards the armchairs. "Come, sit down."

As they moved across the room, he leaned in close and quietly hissed: "They'll be listening."

Burton gave a slight nod of acknowledgement and sat down.

There was an occasional table beside Speke's chair. He took a decanter of brandy from it, poured two glasses, and handed one to his guest.

"Do you consider me guilty, Dick?"

"Absolutely not," Burton responded.

"Good. I don't care about anyone else. But I must ask your forgiveness. A weakness in my character caused me to take umbrage with you during our exploration of Berbera, and everything we've endured since stems from that act. I thought you considered me a coward. I was angry and resentful."

"And wrong, John. I never thought of you that way. But if it's forgiveness you need, then consider it granted."

"Thank you."

Hesitantly, Speke raised his glass. Burton leaned forward, clinked his own against it, and they drank.

"Do you remember all those dreadful days of illness in Ujiji?" Speke asked, referring to 1857, when they'd discovered Lake Tanganyika.

"How could I forget, John? I thought we were goners for sure."

"When I was at my lowest ebb, you used to sit beside my cot and read to me from Camoens. Would you do so again? I'd gain much comfort from it. They allowed me a volume of *The Lusiad.*"

"Certainly."

Speke stood, crossed to a bookshelf, and returned with a book in his hand. He passed it to Burton and sat down.

"I've marked a page."

Burton nodded, and opened the book where a loose leaf of paper poked out from the pages. He saw Speke's handwriting on the sheet and glanced up at his friend.

Speke met his eyes and held them a moment. His lens glinted.

Burton returned his attention to the book. He began to read aloud.

"'Ah, strike the notes of woe!' the siren cries;
'A dreary vision swims before my eyes.
To Tagus' shore triumphant as he bends,
Low in the dust the hero's glory ends—'"

Such was his familiarity with the Portuguese poet that he continued automatically, reciting the verse, expressively and faultlessly, though his eyes and mind were on Speke's note. He read:

Dick,

I have told no one of what occurred in the temple. Nor have we ever spoken to each other about it, for we were in no fit condition to converse in the days subsequent to those events, and, besides, I had little recollection of anything other than a bright flash and a deafening gunshot.

But in recent days, the veil of light that blinded me seems to have lifted. What I witnessed has gained clarity in my mind, and I feel instinctively that it might be of importance to you.

I shall try to describe what happened in its proper sequence, though, in truth, these are but facets of an instant.

Dick, this thing that Darwin and his cronies attached to my head, this babbage device, contains antennae of such extreme sensitivity that they detect the electrical operations of a human brain. At the moment the brass man fired his pistol, those sensors were hit by a transmission of subtle electrical force. It was the— I'm sorry, but I know of no other way to describe it—the final mental exhalation of Mr. Trounce. This same burst of energy seemed to activate the downward pointing pyramid above the altar. It suddenly blazed with light and lost its opacity. I was able, as if seeing through solid matter, to discern that its structure was comprised of alternating layers of material, one denser than the other.

Simultaneously, a pale blue lightning flashed from the diamond at the tip of the pyramid and jumped to the brass man's head, then from his to yours. In the slightest fraction of a second, your appearance altered—your hair became white, your clothes changed, and a rifle appeared beside you—and the energy then reversed direction, jumping from you back to the brass man, then to the diamond.

As I say, this all occurred in a single moment, and I don't know what to make of it, except—this may be nonsense, but it seemed to me that the clockwork man somehow channelled and directed the force.

I wish I could be of more help to you, but my time has run out.

I cannot forget that we were once as brothers. I hope, when you remember me, you will think of that time, and not of the wicked things I have done.

Your old friend,

John Hanning Speke

Burton continued to recite Camoens, but his eyes flicked up and signalled gratitude to the other man. Surreptitiously, he slipped the letter into his pocket.

The half hour ended and the door opened. Damien Burke leaned in and said: "Captain?"

Burton closed the book, put it down, stood, and shook Speke's hand.

"Goodbye, old fellow," he said.

Speke's mouth moved but he could find no words, and with his eye glistening, he turned away.

It was past three o'clock by the time the king's agent left the tower. He whistled for a hansom cab and ordered the driver to take him to Battersea.

"Bless me, sir! That's a relief!" the man said, climbing down from his seat. He took a couple of lumps of Formby coal from the scuttle at the back of the vehicle's steam horse and put them into the furnace.

"Why so?" Burton asked.

"South of the river, ain't it! A lot less traffic south of the river! Can't move for love nor money on the main roads north o' the Thames, but south—we'll have you on your merry way, no trouble at all, sir. In you go. There's a blanket under the seat if you feel the chill."

The driver climbed back up to his seat, waited for Burton to settle, then—with an unnecessary "Gee up!"—squeezed the velocity lever and got the hansom moving.

As the cab rattled along Lower Thames Street and turned left onto London Bridge, the king's agent sat back, tied Gregory Hare's perfumed handkerchief around the lower half of his face, and focused on his breathing. Keeping it slow and steady, he imagined each breath entering first his left lung, then his right. He matched his respiration to the rhythm of a Sufi chant:

Allāhu Allāhu Allāhu Haqq.
Allāhu Allāhu Allāhu Haqq.
Allāhu Allāhu Allāhu Haqq.

He started to complicate the exercise, altering the tempo, establishing a cycle of four breaths, visualising oxygen saturating different parts of his body.

At the same time, he listened only to the chugging of the hansom's steam horse, allowing it to block out all other noises.

By the time the vehicle reached the junction of Bankside and Blackfriars Road, Burton had slipped into a Sufi trance.

His mind drifted.

He saw formless light and colour; heard water and snatches of conversation:

"*—According to the evidence John Speke presented to the Society, the Nile runs uphill for ninety miles—*"

"—*The lake he discovered was, indeed, the source of the Nile*—"

The lights coalesced into a single bright ribbon, broad, snaking away through darkness, disappearing into the distance. He flew over it, following its course upstream.

"—*Captain Burton! Did you pull the trigger?*—"

"—*Is there shooting to be done?*—"

"—*I rather suppose there is!*—"

"—*The source!*—"

"—*Don't step back! They'll think that we're retiring!*—"

From far off to either side, he saw more ribbons of light. The farther upstream he flew, the closer they came.

"—*Don't step back!*—"

"—*Step back!*—"

"—*Pull the trigger!*—"

"—*Step back!*—"

"—*The source!*—"

Shining intensely, as if reflecting the sun, the ribbons began to converge around him.

"—*Step back!*—"

"—*The source!*—"

"—*Needs pruning, hard against the stem*—"

"—*How can I reverse the damage?*—"

"—*You'll find a way*—"

"—*Is there shooting to be done?*—"

"—*I rather suppose there is!*—"

"—*Pull the trigger!*—"

"—*The source!*—"

The bands of light joined into one blazing expanse. It shot upward in front of him. Burton gazed at it and became aware that it was falling water. He looked up and saw a rainbow.

The hansom cab jerked over a pothole, shaking his senses back into him.

He cried out: "Step back! The source needs pruning, hard against the stem! Pull the trigger!"

And, all of a sudden, he knew exactly what had to be done.

The hatch in the roof of the cab opened and the driver looked in.

"Did you say somethin', sir?"

"Yes. Make a detour to the nearest post office, would you?"

"Certainly, sir. We're just comin' up on Broad Street. There's one there."

A few minutes later, Burton paid for two parakeet messages. He sent the first bird to Commander Krishnamurthy: "Maneesh, hurry to my place and pick up the rifle next to the fireplace in my study. Bring it to Battersea Power Station. Utmost emergency. Great haste, please."

The second parakeet was sent to Mrs. Angell to alert her to the Commander's mission. It went on: "Mrs. Angell, I have an unusual job for you. You must do it at once, without hesitation or protest. Please remove from my study all my casebooks, journals, reports, and personal papers. Take them from the desks, from the drawers, and from the shelves nearest the window. Carry them into the back yard and make a bonfire of them. Do not leave a single one unburnt. This is of crucial importance. Destroy them all, and do it at once."

The king's agent returned to the cab and, thirty minutes later, it delivered him to his destination.

The glaring lights of the Technologist headquarters were turning the thick fog around it into a swirling soup of glowing particles, here a sickening yellow, there a putrid orange, in many places a deep hellish red. Burton picked his way through the murk to the front entrance, hailed a guard, and was escorted to the main hall.

Isambard Kingdom Brunel appeared from amid buzzing machinery and clanked over to greet him.

"An unexpected pleasure, Sir Richard. It's been more than a year."

"You've corrected your speech defect, Isambard."

"Some considerable time ago. I'm afraid young Swinburne will be disappointed."

"Swinburne is dead," Burton said, flatly.

"Dead?"

"Yes. Well, in a manner of speaking, anyway."

"I'm not sure what you mean, but I am truly sorry. What happened?"

Burton glanced at a nearby workbench around which a group of Technologists was gathered.

"May we speak in private?"

Brunel expelled a puff of vapour. The piston-like device on the shoulder of his barrel shaped body paused in its pumping, then continued. The bellows on the other side creaked up and down insistently.

"Follow," he piped.

Burton trailed after the Steam Man, across the vast floor, to where two of the huge Worm machines were parked. The explorer marvelled at the size of the burrowing vehicles—and, right there, the main area of difficulty in the scheme that had formed in the back of his mind found its solution.

Brunel reached out with a mechanical arm and opened a big hatch in the side of one of the Worms. He stepped in, gestured for Burton to follow, and pulled the doorway down behind the explorer. Lights came on automatically. The steam man hissed into a squat.

Burton pulled Speke's letter from his pocked and, wordlessly, handed it to the engineer. Brunel held it up with a metal pincer. It wasn't evident what part of his life-maintaining contraption functioned as eyes but something obviously did, and moments later he lowered the paper and said: "What does the alteration of your appearance signify? Does Algernon Swinburne's death relate to it?"

"I was sent through time to the year 1914, Isambard. What for John Speke was a split second, lasted five years for me. Algy was killed in Africa last year, but was present, albeit in a different form, in the future I visited."

"A different form?"

Burton sat on a leather-upholstered chair and, for the final time, told the full story.

When he finished, the Steam Man raised the letter again.

"Hmm," he said. "This pyramid construction appears to have the elements of a battery. You say there were other structures of alternating layers in the temple?"

"Yes."

"And a great deal of quartz?"

"Along with other crystals and gemstones, yes; an almost inconceivable amount."

"Intriguing. My hypothesis, then, is that the entire temple was constructed to generate and store piezoelectricity."

"Piezoelectricity?"

"A very recent discovery, Sir Richard. Or so I thought. I now learn that it was, in fact, employed in ancient times!"

"But what is it?"

"Put simply, it is electrical power generated by certain substances, crystals especially, when they are distorted by pressure."

"Ah. And the temple—"

"—has the weight of a fractured mountain on top of it. That, Sir Richard, is a lot of power. Having it hit you in the head should have been enough to burn you to a cinder in an instant. Yet, instead, it projected you through time."

"It passed through Herbert Spencer—or rather, through the priest K'k'thyima—first."

"It did. Or perhaps it would be more accurate to say that it passed through the seven stones of the Cambodian Eye. It seems to me that the intelligence in those stones was somehow able to control the force, and, I should think, set the coordinates for your destination in time."

"Good," Burton responded.

"Good, Sir Richard?"

"Yes."

"Why?"

"Because you've confirmed my own suspicions on the matter. If we are correct, my plan has, perhaps, some small chance of succeeding."

"You have a plan?"

"Of sorts."

"Then I think perhaps I had better hear it."

§

At four thirty in the morning, a strong vibration shook the floor of the rooms beneath the Tower of London. It rapidly increased in intensity and a loud rumbling shocked the secret institution's staff out of their beds.

People, wrapped in dressing gowns, ran into the main hallway.

"Earthquake!" someone shouted.

Damien Burke, in a long nightshirt, nightcap, and slippers, yelled: "Up the stairs! Now! Everybody out!"

A guard unlocked the entrance door and the staff quickly filed out.

The floor cracked. A siren started to wail.

Gregory Hare, also in his sleeping clothes, pointed to a lone figure at the other end of the hallway—a woman, white haired and fully dressed.

"Mr. Burke!" he called.

Burke followed his companion's pointing finger and saw the woman.

"Countess Sabina!" he shouted. "You must leave at once!"

The rumbling grew into a roar.

"I think not!" she mouthed, her voice lost in the din.

The floor in the middle of the hallway bulged and heaved. Dust erupted and filled the air. A spinning metal cone emerged from the ground and expanded upward. The deafening commotion caused Burke and Hare to press their hands to their ears. They blinked against the eddying dust and squinted through watering eyes at the massive drill as it thundered out of the floor and its tip bit into the ceiling. Shredded plaster and masonry exploded outward.

"Mr. Burke! Mr. Burke!" Hare bellowed, but the other man could hear nothing but the cacophonous machine.

The drill buried itself deeper and deeper into the roof, and, as it did so, the main body of the tunnelling machine rose into view. Steam belched out of holes in its sides until the atmosphere of the hallway was so thick that nothing could be seen, though electric wall lamps continued to glow.

Burke groped for Hare's arm, clutched it, put his mouth against the other man's ear, and yelled: "Find your way to the armoury. Bring weapons!"

He felt his colleague move away.

The noise suddenly died. There was a moment of absolute silence, then the rattle of debris as it continued to fall from the ceiling.

A clang and a creak.

Thumping footsteps.

A repetitive wheezing.

The hiss of escaping vapours.

Something moved in the murk—a shadow—then a man stepped out of the cloud. Though the bottom half of his face was concealed by a scarf and the eyes were behind leather-rimmed goggles, Burke recognised Sir Richard Francis Burton.

"Captain!" he exclaimed. "Thank goodness! What's happen—"

He was cut short as Burton's fist shot up and connected with his chin. Burke folded to the floor.

"My apologies, old thing," the king's agent murmured.

He moved back to the Worm. Two figures—Isambard Kingdom Brunel and Maneesh Krishnamurthy—were standing beside it.

"This way!" he snapped.

He led them towards the far end of the hall but stopped short when someone stepped into in his path. He drew back his arm, his fingers bunched into a fist.

"No!" came a female voice. "It's me!"

"Countess! What are you doing here?"

"They've been using me in their campaign against the Prussians, Sir Richard. I can stand it no longer. Besides, I foresaw that you would come. There is a role for me to play. I must accompany you."

Burton hesitated, then said: "Get into the vehicle, Countess. We'll join you in a minute."

As she moved away, the explorer strode forward and kicked open the door to the security section. He entered, Krishnamurthy followed, and Brunel squeezed through after them.

"This one," Burton said, indicating the entrance to Cell 4.

He moved aside as the Steam Man's multiple arms raised cutting tools and applied them to the metal portal. Moments later, Brunel pulled the door from its frame and threw it aside.

"John!" Burton called.

"Dick, what's happening?"

"We're breaking you out of here! Explanations later! Come!"

Speke, still in his shirt and trousers, groped his way forward.

"This way, Mr. Speke," Krishnamurthy said, grabbing the prisoner's arm.

They hurried back out into the main hall.

A pistol was pressed into the side of Krishnamurthy's head.

"May I ask what you think you're doing?" Gregory Hare asked.

Burton wheeled to face Palmerston's man and cried out: "Hare, it's me! Burton!"

"What's happening here, Captain?"

"I have to take Speke! Hare, trust me man! The future depends on this!"

"John Speke is a traitor. I can't allow you to remove him. Where is Mr. Burke?"

"Unconscious. I had to—" Burton suddenly shot forward and chopped at Hare's wrist with such force that the pistol went spinning away. He buried his fist in the man's stomach.

The breath whooshed out of Hare. He doubled over but clutched at Burton's clothing. As Krishnamurthy steered Speke out of the way, Palmerston's man yanked Burton backwards, threw his ape-like arms around him, and squeezed.

"No!" Burton objected. "You have to—" but suddenly he couldn't say another word; his breath was cut off; he couldn't move. Hare's arms were unbelievably powerful. They tightened around the king's agent like a vice. He felt his ribs creak. Two of them snapped. Agony cut through him. He couldn't scream. Darkness closed in from the edges of his vision.

Then he was free and on his knees, gulping lungfuls of dust-filled air. He coughed and keeled over. Pain stabbed into his side. He saw Hare's face just inches away. The odd-job man was unconscious on the floor. Blood was oozing from his scalp.

Metal hooked beneath Burton's armpits and he was hauled upright, lifted off his feet, and born to the door of the Worm.

"I rendered your attacker unconscious with a blow to the head," Isambard Kingdom Brunel explained.

"Wait! Stop!" Burton shouted. "Put me down."

The engineer complied. Burton clutched his left side and groaned. He pointed to a heavy door, barely visible through the steam and dust.

"The vault, Isambard! Get in there!"

The Steam Man clanged across the broken floor and started to work on the portal.

Burton stood, swaying, waiting. He turned his head to the side and spat. The taste of blood filled his mouth.

The siren was still wailing. He remembered the echoing "Ullah! Ullah!" of the wartime harvesters.

It happened, he reminded himself.

With a loud thunk, the vault door came loose. Brunel stepped aside, carrying it with him.

Burton limped forward and entered the chamber. He looked around and saw things he didn't understand: bizarre biological objects in bell jars; devices that looked like weapons; a necklace of shrunken non-human heads; a mirror that reflected a different room, and, when he looked into it, a different person.

"You were right, Algy," he muttered, for these things, he felt sure, had somehow slipped through from alternate versions of reality.

A flat jewel case caught his eye. He reached for it, opened it, and saw that it contained twenty-one black diamonds arranged in three rows of seven: the fragments of the Eyes of Nāga.

He snapped the case shut and was just about to leave with it when he noticed a particularly large leather portmanteau. He paced over to it, pulled it open, and saw white scaly material, a black helmet, a metal disk, and a pair of stilted boots inside. It was Edward Oxford's burnt and battered time suit; the weird costume that had earned him the name 'Spring Heeled Jack.'

Burton picked up the bag and left the vault.

Krishnamurthy's voice came out of the dust cloud: "Hurry! This is taking too long! They'll be back any minute!"

The king's agent found the door of the Worm and clambered into the vehicle. He sat and let loose a sob as his ribs grated together. Brunel's great bulk entered. The Steam Man pulled the hatch shut.

"Are you all right, Countess?" Burton asked.

"Yes," the clairvoyant answered. "But you're hurt, Captain!"

"It's nothing."

"Dick—" Speke began.

Burton cut him off: "Let's get out of here first, John. Explanations later."

They manoeuvred themselves around the cabin until Brunel was comfortably at the controls. He set the engine roaring and reversed the Worm back into the tunnel it had drilled.

With the short legs around its circumference racing, the machine hurtled along underground, passing far beneath the River Thames, following the burrow westwards until it angled upward and emerged from the wasteland at the front of Battersea Power station.

They all disembarked, striding and clanking and limping to the main doors, passing through them, crossing the courtyard, and entering the principal workshop.

Technologist personnel gathered around. Brunel ordered them to secure the building.

The group moved over to a workbench. Burton laid the diamond case and the portmanteau on it. Krishnamurthy walked away and returned with the Lee-Enfield rifle. "Here you are, Captain."

"Thank you, Maneesh. By the way, was Mrs. Angell organising a bonfire when you visited?"

"She was, sir, and she seemed rather distraught about it."

"If what I have in mind doesn't succeed," Burton said, addressing all of his friends, "then, at very least, I want the evidence of what has occurred destroyed. Thus I've instructed my housekeeper to burn of all my records."

"But why is that necessary?" Speke asked.

The Countess Sabina answered: "Different versions of history exist, Mr. Speke—I've seen them—and the boundaries between each are thin. If the wrong sort of person learned of this, they could make a Bedlam of all existence."

Burton thought of Aleister Crowley.

"We're almost ready," one of the technicians announced.

The king's agent turned to Speke. "Walk with me, John."

§

John Hanning Speke, lying flat on his back on a workbench, allowed Isambard Kingdom Brunel to remove the cover of the babbage in the left half of his skull.

The engineer used a pincer to indicate two hollows in the exposed mechanism.

"See, Sir Richard," he said. "These sockets were designed to receive two of the Cambodian stones."

Burton examined the cavities, then looked down at Speke. "You understand why we have to do this, John?" he asked.

"Yes," Speke replied. "Put them in."

The king's agent nodded to Brunel, and the engineer reached into the jewel case, retrieved a diamond, fitted it into one of the slots in Speke's babbage, and screwed down a delicate bracket to hold the stone in place. He repeated the process with a second gem, then replaced the cover of the device and stood back.

Speke sat up.

"Do you sense anything?" Burton asked.

"Nothing."

Countess Sabina stepped forward. "I do."

Burton looked at her. "What do you feel, Countess?"

"The Nāga intelligence has left the diamonds, Sir Richard, but the shape of it remains in them, like a mould, if you will. Mr. Speke has to allow his conscious mind to flow into it. That is the role I must play; I shall employ my mediumistic abilities to guide him."

The king's agent nodded, moved away with Isambard Kingdom Brunel, and asked him: "What of the rest of it, Isambard? Can you generate power enough?"

"Easily," Brunel replied. "My technicians are setting everything up now. But you realise that, if Mr. Speke cannot manage his part, you will be incinerated?"

"Believe me, I am very aware of that particular fact!"

They walked over to where Krishnamurthy stood by two workbenches. Technicians were positioning them beneath a hanging structure; a thing of multiple layers and looped cables. Brunel gestured toward it.

"This will feed power into Mr. Speke's device. If I have understood the process properly, he will be able to then channel it in the appropriate manner through the resonance that exists between the Cambodian stones and the diamond dust in your tattoo. The unique properties of the diamonds will then come into play and project you through time. Speke will guide you to the exact moment and location."

"But on previous occasions," Burton said, "a sacrifice—a death—has been required to activate the process."

Brunel pointed one of his clamp-ended arms at the workshop entrance. "We hope that will suffice."

Burton looked and saw a horse being led in.

Krishnamurthy addressed the king's agent: "Why are you aiming for 1840, Sir Richard? Didn't the first alternate history branch off three years earlier?"

"Edward Oxford's initial entry point into the past is the source of all the trouble," Burton replied. "If I kill him in 1837, he'll still arrive in 1840, and will still assassinate Queen Victoria, whereas, if I kill him in 1840, it will make it impossible for him to be thrown back to 1837."

"But that means you won't merely change 1840 onwards; you'll change the past of the history you are actually in. As far as I understand this whole business, no one has done that before."

"Cause and effect in reverse, Maneesh."

Krishnamurthy scratched his head. "Yes. But what will happen to you? To us?"

"I can't be sure—it's all theoretical—but I suspect that all the alternate histories will metamorphose from the Actual to the Potential, if you see what I mean. Whatever act caused each of them to come into being will be nullified, and they'll detach from what was meant to be, like branches being pruned from a bush."

"Will we remember anything?"

"That, Maneesh, is a question I can't answer. Perhaps each individual's subjective apprehension of the world will re-adjust, returning to the original version of history."

"And you, Sir Richard? Won't you exist twice in the same time? How old were you in 1840?"

"Nineteen. I don't know what will happen to me. I'll deal with it when I get there."

Burton watched as Speke was escorted to one of the benches and lay down on it. Two Technologists affixed cables from the contraption above to the lieutenant's babbage.

"They are ready for you," Brunel said.

Burton took a deep breath. Holding his arm pressed to his injured side, he paced over to the bench beside Speke and gingerly positioned himself on it. He put the Lee-Enfield rifle down with its barrel resting on his shoulder.

Krishnamurthy crossed to another worktop and returned from it with the portmanteau and the jewel case. He placed them on Burton's chest and stomach. The explorer wrapped his arms around them.

"Good luck, sir," the police commander said. He moved to the end of the benches where the horse had been tethered, took hold of the animal's reins, and drew his police issue Adams revolver.

Countess Sabina stepped closer to Speke.

The machine overhead began to hum.

"Is everyone in position and prepared?" Brunel piped loudly.

The gathered technicians answered in the affirmative.

Burton rolled his head to the side and said to Speke: "John. Thank you."

Speke looked back and gave a sad smile.

Brunel clanked over to a console and began to adjust levers and dials.

The apparatus hanging over the benches suddenly hummed—a deep, throbbing sound—and bolts of blue energy fizzed and spat across its surface.

"Now, please, Mr. Speke," Brunel said.

The lieutenant reached up to the key that poked out over his left ear, and began to wind the babbage.

"I just felt the booby trap arm itself," he muttered. "Maybe thirty minutes, then it'll explode."

Countess Sabina said: "Try to remain calm, please, Mr. Speke. I'm establishing a mediumistic connection with you now."

She flinched, gasped, and whimpered: "Oh, you poor thing!"

"I can feel your presence," Speke groaned. "It's—it's—"

"Intrusive? I know, sir. I'm sorry."

"I'm awaiting your word, Countess," Brunel said.

"Not yet!" The woman put her fingertips to her temples and squeezed her eyes shut. "I can sense the diamonds. I have to feel my way into them. Follow me, if you can, Mr. Speke. I'm trying to connect with your mind, too, Sir Richard."

Burton felt his scalp crawling, as if insects were running over it.

"Power's building!" Brunel called. "Hurry!"

From head to toe, Burton's muscles suddenly locked tight. Pain shot through his side. He cried out.

"Now!" the countess screamed.

A jagged line of blue lightning shot out of the overhead machine, hit Speke's babbage, and jumped across to Burton's head. The king's agent screeched and jerked, as his nerve endings seemed to catch fire.

"Krishnamurthy!" Brunel shouted.

The flying squad commander pushed his pistol against the horse's head and pulled the trigger. The animal collapsed.

Burton convulsed and began to lose consciousness.

"It hasn't worked!" Krishnamurthy shouted. "Turn off the power! You're killing them!"

"No!" the countess shrieked. She threw out her arms. Blood welled up in her eyes and ran down her cheeks. "It's me! I'm the sacrifice!"

"Countess!" Krishnamurthy yelled.

The cheiromantist flopped to the floor.

There was a flash of white light.

§

Sir Richard Francis Burton remembered his youth and his first independent visit to London. He'd been there before—he'd gone to school in Richmond when he was eight years old—but on this occasion he was nineteen, had come from Italy to enrol at Trinity College, Oxford, and was filled with grandiose ideas and a bottomless well of self-esteem.

As is so often the case with memories, they were conjured by his olfactory sense. His nostrils were filled with the gritty carbon smell of soot, the rotten stench of the Thames, the stale odours of unlaundered clothes and unwashed bodies, all lurking behind the powerful tang of grass.

Grass?

He opened his eyes. He was lying face down in long grass at the edge of a thicket of trees. A man had just emerged from them and, not noticing Burton, was walking away, down a slope. The explorer heard him mutter: "Steady, Edward! Hang on, hang on. Don't let it overwhelm you. This is neither a dream nor an illusion, so stay focused, get the job done, then get back to your suit!"

Bismillah! That's Edward Oxford!

He was too late! He hadn't counted on losing consciousness. He'd intended to shoot the visitor from the future among the trees before making a fast getaway. What now?

Burton pushed himself to his knees and almost cried out as his ribs scraped against each other. He reached for his rifle, the jewel case, and portmanteau—all on the grass beside him—picked them up and crawled into the thicket. He found a suitable spot, lay flat, and carefully—gritting his teeth against the pain—pulled himself forward until he was hidden beneath a bush. He looked out at Green Park.

Tick tick tick.

He could feel John Speke's babbage winding down. The black diamond dust in his scalp was somehow connected to it through the decades.

He leaned on his elbows, hefted the rifle in his hands, and glanced at the inscription on its stock.

1919!

He'd been fifty-six years into the future, now he was twenty-four years into the past.

He shook his head slightly, trying to dispel the odd sense of dislocation that lurked at the edges of his mind: the feeling that he possessed two separate identities. But, of course, it was the 10th of June, 1840, and he really was duplicated, for his much younger self was currently travelling through Europe.

If only that opinionated and arrogant youngster knew what life had in store for him!

Burton whispered: "Time changed me, thank goodness."

He peered through the rifle's telescopic sight.

"The question is, can I return the favour?"

The wooded area in which he was hidden covered the brow of a low hill overlooking the park. At its base, people had gathered along the sides of a path. It was a mild day. The men sported light coats, top hats, and carried canes. The women wore bonnets and dainty gloves and held parasols. They were all waiting to see Queen Victoria ride past in her carriage. Burton examined them, levelling the crosshairs at one person after another. Which of them was the man he'd seen moments ago? And where was that man's ancestor; the insane 18-year-old with two flintlock pistols under his frock coat?

"Damnation!" Burton groaned, softly. His hands were shaking.

He considered his options. He knew the assassin was going to fire two shots at the queen. The first would miss. The second should, too, but Edward Oxford was going to tackle his ancestor, and, in doing so, he would inadvertently cause that second bullet to hit Victoria in the head.

If Burton killed Oxford too soon, the crowd would start hunting for the killer, providing a distraction that might allow the assassin to strike with greater accuracy. So he must wait until after the first shot. If he could then put a bullet in Oxford during the panic, the man from the future would die before he could change history, and his antecedent would almost certainly be blamed for the murder.

The king's agent shifted cautiously, trying not to disturb the bush that arched over him.

He noticed a man in the crowd. It was Henry de La Poer Beresford, the "Mad Marquess," the founder of the Libertines.

"I'll be dealing with you," he murmured, "twenty-one years from now."

A cheer went up. Queen Victoria's carriage, drawn by four horses, had emerged from the gate of Buckingham Palace, off to his left.

Two outriders—the Queen's Guards—trotted ahead of the royal conveyance, which was steered by a postilion. Two more followed behind. They drew closer to the base of the slope.

Tick tick tick.

"Come on," Burton whispered. "Where are you?"

A man wearing a top hat, blue frock coat and white breeches stepped over the low fence onto the path. He paced along beside the slow-moving carriage, drew a flintlock from his coat, pointed it at the queen, and pulled the trigger.

The report echoed across the park.

Victoria, in a cream coloured dress and bonnet, stood up in her carriage.

Prince Albert leaned forward and reached for her.

People started to scream and shout.

The man drew a second pistol.

Burton held his breath and became entirely motionless.

The assassin raised his arm and took aim.

The queen reached up to her white lace collar.

Burton made a tiny movement, shifting the crosshairs of his sight slightly to the left of the monarch's head, their centre-point hovering over the young gunman's face.

The man from the future, Edward Oxford, suddenly jumped from the crowd.

"No, Edward!" he bellowed.

The two men struggled.

Burton took aim. His finger tightened on the trigger.

In 1864, John Speke's babbage exploded.

The shockwave crossed time and hit Burton like a punch between the eyes. In a moment of total disorientation, he thought he saw a blue flash far off to his left, and a faint voice yelling: "Stop, Edward!"

The assassin fired.

Burton fired.

Queen Victoria's head sprayed blood. She fell backwards out of the carriage.

Albert scrambled after her.

Edward Oxford, still alive, threw his ancestor to the ground, accidentally impaling the young man's head on the wrought-iron spikes atop the low fence.

"No!" Burton whispered.

A frantic police whistle sounded.

The crowd surged around the carriage. The outriders plunged into the mob, attempting to hold it back.

Oxford forced his way free and started to run up the slope.

"No!" Burton whispered again.

He snapped out of his shock and backed into the trees, pulling the jewel case and portmanteau with him, and found a place of concealment. He listened as Oxford reached the vegetation and pushed through it to where he'd left his suit, helmet and boots.

Burton lunged forward, hooked an arm around the time traveller's throat, squeezed hard, and crushed the windpipe. He put his mouth against the man's ear and hissed: "You don't deserve this, but I have to do it again. I'm sorry."

With his right hand, he twisted Oxford's head until the neck snapped, then released his hold and allowed the corpse to crumple to the ground.

He stepped back into hiding.

Almost immediately, he heard a voice calling: "Step out into the open, sir! I saw what happened. There's nothing to worry about. Come on; let's be having you!"

It sounded familiar.

Burton remained silent.

"Sir! I saw you trying to protect the queen. I just need you to accompany me to the station to make a statement!"

There was a pause, then someone began to push their way into the thicket. A policeman emerged from the leaves and looked down at Oxford.

"By Jove!" he exclaimed. "What in the Devil's name has happened here?"

Burton took up his rifle, raised it butt-forward over his shoulder, and stepped out of the undergrowth.

The policeman turned and looked him full in the face.

Burton hesitated. The young, square-jawed and wide-eyed features were those of William Trounce.

"Who the heck—?" the constable began.

Burton cracked the rifle butt into the youth's forehead. Trounce's cockscomb helmet went spinning away. He moaned and collapsed. The king's agent leaned over him and checked that he was breathing. He was.

Screams and whistles filled the air.

Burton straightened and returned to the portmanteau and jewel case. He took them over to where Oxford had hung his time suit, and, taking down the clean, unmarked material, pushed it into the bag with the older, scorched version of itself. With difficulty, he managed to squeeze the helmet and boots in, too.

He took off his jacket and wrapped it around the rifle, then, picking everything up, made his way through the trees towards the high wall at the back of the thicket. Horses' hooves and voices sounded from the street beyond. He followed the barrier around the border of the park until he came to a tree stump hard up against the brickwork. Stepping onto it, he reached up and placed the rifle and jewel case on top of the wall. He looped his arm through the handles of the bulging portmanteau and hauled himself up and over, dropping to the ground on the other side. His ribs creaked, and for a moment he thought he might pass out. He leaned back against the bricks.

"Sangappa," came a voice.

The explorer looked up and saw a street sweeper standing on the pavement nearby.

"What?"

"Sangappa," the man repeated. "It's the best leather softener money can buy. They send it over from India. Hard to find and a mite expensive but worth every penny. There's nothing to top it. Sangappa. It'd do that over-stuffed portmanteau of yours the world of good, take my word for it."

Burton used his sleeve to wipe beads of sweat from his forehead.

The street sweeper leaned on his broom and asked: "Are you quite all right, old bean?"

"Yes," Burton replied. "But I'm having a bad day."

"It looks like it. Don't you worry, you'll forget it by tomorrow!"

The man suddenly looked confused. He scratched his head.

"It's odd; I can't even remember this morning. I must be going loopy!" He lifted his broom and stepped from the pavement into the street. With a look of bemusement on his face, he began to sweep horse manure from it and into the gutter.

Burton swallowed and licked his lips. He needed a drink. He was feeling strange and disorientated. He wasn't sure where he was, what he was doing, why he was doing it.

He retrieved the rifle and jewels and started to move away.

"Hey!" the man called after him. "Don't forget! Sangappa! You can buy it at Jambory's Hardware Store on the corner of

Halfmoon Street." He pointed. "Thataway! Tell old Jambory that Carter the Street Sweeper sent you!"

Burton nodded and limped on. He tried to piece together what had just occurred, but his mind was a jumble.

He crossed the road, passed Jambory's Hardware Store, kept going, and entered Berkeley Street, where he saw an elderly man peering out of a ground floor window. He stopped and examined the white-bearded and scarred face, the sharp cheekbones and deep, dark, tormented eyes.

The man gazed back.

The man moved when he moved.

What? No! It can't be! That's me! My reflection! But how? How can I be old? I'm—I'm nineteen! Just nineteen!

He looked down at his hands. They were brown and wrinkled and weathered. They were not the hands of a young man.

What has happened? How is this possible?

He stumbled away, and passed through Berkeley Square into Davies Street, then on to Oxford Street, which was filled with horse-drawn traffic. Only horse-drawn. Nothing else. That surprised him. He had no idea why.

What am I expecting to see? Why does it all seem wrong?

Burton reached Portman Square, staggered into the patch of greenery at its centre, dropped his luggage, and collapsed onto a bench beneath a tree. He'd been walking towards Montagu Place, but it had just occurred to him that there was no reason to go there.

He laughed, and it hurt, and tears poured down his cheeks.

He cried, and thought he might die.

He was quiet, and suddenly hours had passed and a dense fog was rolling in with the night.

Muddled impressions untangled and emerged from behind a veil of shock. He tried to force them back but they kept coming. Around him, London vanished behind the murk. Inside him, the truth materialised with horrible clarity.

She had flinched to one side.

Just as he'd pulled the trigger, she'd moved.

The assassin's second bullet had clipped her ear.

Sir Richard Francis Burton's bullet had hit her in the head.

It was me. I did it.

He had killed Queen Victoria.

Here it begins.

Here it ends.

Not the source, but just another part of a circle.

He sat in Portman Square.

The thick fog embraced him.

It was silent.

It was mysterious.

It was timeless.

And, behind it, the world he had created was very, very real.

APPENDIX 1

A Lamentation
by Algernon Charles Swinburne,
from *Poems and Ballads*, 1866.

I.
Who hath known the ways of time
Or trodden behind his feet?
There is no such man among men.
For chance overcomes him, or crime
Changes; for all things sweet
In time wax bitter again.
Who shall give sorrow enough,
Or who the abundance of tears?
Mine eyes are heavy with love
And a sword gone thorough mine ears,
A sound like a sword and fire,
For pity, for great desire;
Who shall ensure me thereof,
Lest I die, being full of my fears?

Who hath known the ways and the wrath,
The sleepless spirit, the root

And blossom of evil will,
The divine device of a god?
Who shall behold it or hath?
The twice-tongued prophets are mute,
The many speakers are still;
No foot has travelled or trod,
No hand has meted, his path.
Man's fate is a blood-red fruit,
And the mighty gods have their fill
And relax not the rein, or the rod.

Ye were mighty in heart from of old,
Ye slew with the spear, and are slain.
Keen after heat is the cold,
Sore after summer is rain,
And melteth man to the bone.
As water he weareth away,
As a flower, as an hour in a day,
Fallen from laughter to moan.
But my spirit is shaken with fear
Lest an evil thing begin,
New-born, a spear for a spear,
And one for another sin.
Or ever our tears began,
It was known from of old and said;
One law for a living man,
And another law for the dead.
For these are fearful and sad,

Vain, and things without breath;
While he lives let a man be glad,
For none hath joy of his death.

II.
Who hath known the pain, the old pain of earth,
Or all the travail of the sea,
The many ways and waves, the birth
Fruitless, the labour nothing worth?
Who hath known, who knoweth, O gods? not we.
There is none shall say he hath seen,
There is none he hath known.
Though he saith, Lo, a lord have I been,
I have reaped and sown;
I have seen the desire of mine eyes,
The beginning of love,
The season of kisses and sighs
And the end thereof.
I have known the ways of the sea,
All the perilous ways,
Strange winds have spoken with me,
And the tongues of strange days.
I have hewn the pine for ships;
Where steeds run arow,
I have seen from their bridled lips
Foam blown as the snow.
With snapping of chariot-poles
And with straining of oars

I have grazed in the race the goals,
In the storm the shores;
As a greave is cleft with an arrow
At the joint of the knee,
I have cleft through the sea-straits narrow
To the heart of the sea.
When air was smitten in sunder
I have watched on high
The ways of the stars and the thunder
In the night of the sky;
Where the dark brings forth light as a flower,
As from lips that dissever;
One abideth the space of an hour,
One endureth for ever.
Lo, what hath he seen or known,
Of the way and the wave
Unbeholden, unsailed-on, unsown,
From the breast to the grave?

Or ever the stars were made, or skies,
Grief was born, and the kinless night,
Mother of gods without form or name.
And light is born out of heaven and dies,
And one day knows not another's light,
But night is one, and her shape the same.

But dumb the goddesses underground
Wait, and we hear not on earth if their feet

Rise, and the night wax loud with their wings;
Dumb, without word or shadow of sound;
And sift in scales and winnow as wheat
Men's souls, and sorrow of manifold things.

III.
Nor less of grief than ours
The gods wrought long ago
To bruise men one by one;
But with the incessant hours
Fresh grief and greener woe
Spring, as the sudden sun
Year after year makes flowers;
And these die down and grow,
And the next year lacks none.

As these men sleep, have slept
The old heroes in time fled,
No dream-divided sleep;
And holier eyes have wept
Than ours, when on her dead
Gods have seen Thetis weep,
With heavenly hair far-swept
Back, heavenly hands outspread
Round what she could not keep,

Could not one day withhold,
One night; and like as these

White ashes of no weight,
Held not his urn the cold
Ashes of Heracles?
For all things born one gate
Opens, no gate of gold;
Opens; and no man sees
Beyond the gods and fate.

APPENDIX II

Meanwhile, in the Victorian Age, and Beyond …

Sir Richard Francis Burton (1821-1890)

1863 started well for Burton—he was at last able to enjoy a honeymoon with Isabel, a full year after they were married. Unfortunately, he then had to return to his consulate duties on the disease-ridden West African island of Fernando Po. He made various forays onto the mainland but was not much impressed by the slavery-ravaged tribal kingdoms he found there.

In August of 1864, he returned to England. Fourteen months earlier, John Hanning Speke and James Grant had come back in triumph from their expedition to find the source of the Nile. Now Burton and his former partner engaged in an unpleasant duel, and much was done to besmirch Burton's reputation. The conflict reached its climax in September, when, the day before they were scheduled to confront each another at a debate in the city of Bath, Speke died. He had shot himself in the left side of his body while out hunting. There is no clear evidence whether this was suicide or a tragic accident. Biographers generally agree that, preoccupied with the forthcoming debate, Speke was uncharacteristically careless with his weapon and probably discharged it by accident while climbing over a wall.

Burton appears to have gone off the rails for a time after this incident. Given the consulship of Brazil, he went to South America and, unlike all his other excursions, did not keep a journal or account of his travels. Witnesses, such as Wilfred Scawen Blunt, recalled that he was drinking heavily for much of the time. While in Buenos Aires, Burton fell in with a rather unscrupulous character—a fat man named Arthur Orton, who was passing himself off as Sir Roger Tichborne.

"I ask myself 'Why?' and the only echo is 'damned fool! ... the Devil drives'."

—From a letter to Richard Monckton Milnes, 31st May, 1863

"And still the Weaver plies his loom, whose warp and woof is wretched Man. Weaving th' unpattern'd dark design, so dark we doubt it owns a plan."

—From The Kasîdah of Hâjî Abdû El-Yezdî, 1870

"Zanzibar city, to become picturesque or pleasing, must be viewed, like Stanbul, from afar."

—From Zanzibar, City, Island, and Coast, 1872

Algernon Charles Swinburne (1837-1909)

Swinburne travelled widely in 1863, visiting Paris, Genoa, and Florence, and enjoyed perhaps his most productive period, writing many of his most celebrated poems.

Here life has death for neighbour …
—From The Garden of Proserpine

The dense hard passage is blind and stifled …
—From A Forsaken Garden

One, who is not, we see; but one, whom we see not, is …
—The Higher Pantheism in a Nutshell (complete poem quoted)

A wider soul than the world was wide …
—From On the Death of Richard Burton

Herbert Spencer (1820-1903)

In 1863, Spencer, having published the year before his *First Principles of a New System of Philosophy*, was rapidly emerging as one of the greatest ever English philosophers.

An extreme hypochondriac, he also had little patience for the excesses of Victorian attire, and preferred to wear a one-piece brown suit of his own design. Apparently, it made him look like a bear.

He said:

Time is that which a man is always trying to kill, but which ends in killing him.

George Herbert Wells (1866-1946)

By 1914, H. G. Wells was an established and popular author; a pioneer of science fiction.

A time will come when a politician who has wilfully made war and promoted international dissension will be as sure of the dock and much surer of the noose than a private homicide. It is not reasonable that those who gamble with men's lives should not stake their own.

We were making the future, he said, and hardly any of us troubled to think what future we were making. And here it is!

Our true nationality is mankind.

I hope, or I could not live.

Richard Monckton Milnes (1809-1885)

In 1863, Monckton Milnes was raised to the peerage, becoming the 1st Baron Houghton.

Henry John Temple, 3rd Viscount Palmerston (1784-1865)

1863, for Palmerston, marked the middle of his final term as British prime minister. Nicknamed "Lord Cupid" on account of his youthful appearance and rumoured affairs, he was a popular and capable leader.

William Samuel Henson (1812-1888)

A very industrious inventor, Henson is best known as an early pioneer in aviation. He created a lightweight steam engine that he hoped would power a passenger-carrying monoplane, the "Henson Aerial Steam Carriage," but was never able to perfect the design. He also invented the modern safety razor.

Francis Herbert Wenham (1824-1908)

A British marine engineer, Wenham came to prominence in 1866 when he introduced the idea of superposed wings at the first meeting of the Royal Aeronautical Society in London. His concept became the basis for the design of the early biplanes, triplanes, and multiplanes that attempted flight, with varying degrees of success. Wenham is possibly the first man to have employed the term "aeroplane."

Oscar Wilde (1854-1900)

In 1863, aged nine, Wilde started his formal education at Portora Royal School in Enniskillen, County Fermanagh.

"Education is an admirable thing, but it is well to remember from time to time that nothing that is worth knowing can be taught."

"I can believe anything provided it is incredible."

"Experience is one thing you can't get for nothing."

"The tragedy of old age is not that one is old, but that one is young."

"To get back my youth I would do anything in the world, except take exercise, get up early, or be respectable."

"As long as war is regarded as wicked, it will always have its fascination. When it is looked upon as vulgar, it will cease to be popular."

"Popularity is the one insult I have never suffered."

"Whenever a man does a thoroughly stupid thing, it is always from the noblest motives."

"To live is the rarest thing in the world. Most people exist, that is all."

"Do not be afraid of the past. If people tell you that it is irrevocable, do not believe them. The past, the present and the future are but one moment in the sight of God, in whose sight we should try to live. Time and space, succession and extension, are merely accidental conditions of thought. The imagination can transcend them."

Isabella Mayson (1836-1865)

Married to Samuel Beeton in 1856, Isabella was made famous by her Book of Household Management, which had been published in 1861. 1863 was the last healthy year of her life. In 1864, she contracted puerperal fever, which caused her death on 6th February 1865.

"A place for everything and everything in its place."
—From The Book of Household Management

Ferdinand Graf von Zeppelin (1838-1917)

Count Zeppelin was a German General who later became an aircraft manufacturer. In 1863, he acted as an observer for the Union during the American Civil War, during which time he made his first ascent in a balloon. After serving in the Austrian and Franco-Prussian wars, he became increasingly fascinated by the prospect of steerable balloons and devoted himself to their development. By the turn of the century, his name was synonymous with rigid framed powered airships.

Aleister Crowley (1875-1947)

An influential occultist, Crowley challenged the moral and religious values of his time, promoting a libertine philosophy—"Do what thou wilt"—that earned him notoriety and the reputation for being "the wickedest man in the world."

He said:

"Ordinary morality is only for ordinary people."

Sidi Mubarak Bombay (1820-1885)

Captured by Arab slave traders when he was a young boy, Bombay was sold in exchange for some cloth, and was taken to India where he lived as a slave for many years. When his owner died, he was emancipated and returned to Africa, where he gained fame as a guide, working with Burton, Speke, Stanley and Livingstone. In 1873 he traversed the continent from its east coast to its west.

Mtyela Kasanda (aka Mirambo)

A Wanyamwezi warlord, he started out as a slave and ivory trader, travelling between Africa's great lakes and the coast, but later installed himself as king of the Urambo region. He was a sworn enemy of the Arabic traders at Kazeh. He died aged 44, after becoming too ill to rule.

Lieutenant-Colonel Paul Emil von Lettow-Vorbeck (1870-1964)

The commander of the German East Africa campaign during the First World War.

Major General Arthur Edward Aitken (1861-1924)

Commander of the Indian Expeditionary Force "B" in Africa during the First World War.

Jane Digby (Lady Ellenborough) (1807-1881)

An English aristocrat, Digby was involved in numerous romantic scandals. She had four husbands and countless lovers before eventually settling in Damascus, where she married Sheikh Medjuel el Mezrab, who was 20 years her junior.

Blut und Eisen

Otto von Bismarck made his famous speech in support of increased military spending on 29 September 1862. "Blood and iron" was, in fact, "eisen und blut." The words were reversed almost immediately by press reports and have remained that way in most accounts.

HMS Orpheus

The *Orpheus* was a Jason-class Royal Navy corvette, constructed in Chatham Dockyard, England, in 1861. She was commanded by Captain Robert Burton and served as the flagship of the Australian squadron. On 7th February, 1863, while navigating Manukau Harbour, New Zealand, the ship hit a sandbar and sank, with a loss of 189 men, including Captain Burton. Frederick Butler, a convicted deserter, served as Quartermaster aboard the vessel.

The Bombing of Dar es Salaam

Despite a number of prior skirmishes between British and German troops, the First World War didn't properly begin in East Africa until 8th August 1914, when the British launched an attack against Dar es Salaam. The naval vessels HMS *Astraea* and HMS *Pegasus* bombarded the city; the *Astraea* hitting and destroying the German radio station. The Germans responded by sabotaging the harbour so the British couldn't use it, which also had the effect of preventing their own ship, SMS *Königsberg*, from returning to port. Just over a month later, the *Pegasus* was docked at Zanzibar for repairs when the *Königsberg* launched a surprise attack and sank her. The *Königsberg* was herself eventually knocked out of action by British ships on 11th July, 1915.

The Battle of the Bees

Also known as The Battle of Tanga, this was an attempt by the British Indian Expeditionary Force to capture the German port, and became one of the worst defeats for the British in Africa during the First World War. The incident commenced when HMS *Fox* arrived at the port and gave the authorities an hour to surrender. The hour passed but no action was taken, which gave Lieutenant Colonel Paul Emil von Lettow-Vorbeck time to move German reinforcements into position. On the 4th November, 1914, street to street fighting began in the north, and jungle skirmishes in the south. The British found themselves hard pressed, and when swarms of bees, disturbed by the conflict, attacked both sides, the British were routed and took to their heels. In retreating, they left behind all their equipment, which the Germans appropriated. In later propaganda, the British suggested that the bees had somehow been a fiendish trap set by the enemy.

L.59 Zeppelin

A German dirigible used during the First World War, L.59 *Zeppelin* was known as Das Afrika-Schiff ("The Africa Ship"). In 1917, it was commissioned to resupply Generalmajor Paul Emil von Lettow-Vorbeck's troops. Its journey to Africa was intended to be a one-way voyage—upon delivering its 50 tons of supplies, the ship would be cannibalised; its outer envelope used for tents, its frame used to build radio towers, etc. Following the course of the Nile, L.59 *Zeppelin* was halfway along the river when she received an "abort" order transmitted by Lettow-Vorbeck, who, in his battle with British forces, had been unable to secure a safe landing place for her. She returned to Germany. The following year, the dirigible mysteriously exploded over the Strait of Otranto in the Mediterranean, with a loss of all 21 crew.

The Second Schleswig War

Beginning on the 1st of February 1864, this was a renewal of hostilities between Prussia, Austria and Denmark over control of the Duchies of Schleswig, Holstein, and Saxe-Lauenburg. The conflict continued until the end of October, when the Treaty of Vienna saw the territories ceded to Prussia and Austria. It confirmed Prussia's military might and thus advanced the cause of those who supported German unification.

The burning of Sir Richard Francis Burton's journals and papers

Of all the controversies concerning Burton during his lifetime, none compared with what happened after his death in 1890. His widow, Isabel, made a bonfire of his personal journals, the vast majority of his papers, and the unpublished book he regarded as his magnum opus, his new translation of *The Perfumed Garden*, which he'd retitled *The Scented Garden*. Her act incited such anger and condemnation from those who'd known Burton, including Swinburne, that she lost many friends and badly stained her own reputation.

About the Author

Mark Hodder was born in Southampton, England, but lived many years in London. He is an ex-commercial copywriter, BBC web producer, journalist, and editor. After too many years running the rat race, he threw in the towel and moved to Valencia in Spain, seeking quality of life rather than quantity of income. After a few months teaching English as a foreign language, he wrote his first novel, THE STRANGE AFFAIR OF SPRING HEELED JACK, which won the Philip K. Dick Award 2010. After that, there was no looking back, and Mark now works as a full-time novelist, thus fulfilling his wildest dreams, which he started having around the age of eleven after reading Michael Moorcock, Robert E. Howard, Edgar Rice Burroughs, Fritz Leiber, Jack Vance, Philip K. Dick, P. G. Wodehouse, and Sir Arthur Conan Doyle. In addition to speculative and detective fiction, he is interested in Buddhism, transcendentalism, all the ITC TV programmes of the 60s and 70s, and techie-gadgety things.